THE DRAGON IN WINTER

ALSO BY JONATHAN MABERRY

Cave 13

Son of the Poison Rose

Kagen the Damned

Relentless

Ink

Rage

Deep Silence

Dogs of War

Kill Switch

Predator One

Code Zero

Extinction Machine

Assassin's Code

The King of the Plagues

The Dragon Factory

Patient Zero

Joe Ledger: Special Ops

Still of Night

Dark of Night

Fall of Night

Dead of Night

The Wolfman

NecroTek

The Nightsiders: The Orphan Army

The Nightsiders: Vault of Shadows

The Sleepers War: Alpha Wave

The Unlearnable Truths

Ghostwalkers: A Deadlands Novel

Lost Roads

Broken Lands

Bits & Pieces

Fire & Ash

Flesh & Bone

Dust & Decay

Rot & Ruin

Bad Moon Rising

Dead Man's Song

Ghost Road Blues

Bewilderness

Glimpse

Mars One

ANTHOLOGIES (AS EDITOR)

Don't Turn Out the Lights: A Tribute to Alvin Schwartz's Scary Stories to Tell in the Dark

Joe Ledger: Unstoppable (with Bryan Thomas Schmidt)

Joe Ledger: Unbreakable (with Bryan Thomas Schmidt)

Nights of the Living Dead (with George A. Romero)

V-Wars

V-Wars: Blood and Fire

V-Wars: Night Terrors

V-Wars: Shockwaves

Out of Tune Vol. 1

Out of Tune Vol. 2

The X-Files: Trust No One

The X-Files: The Truth Is Out There

The X-Files: Secret Agendas

Hardboiled Horror

Aliens: Bug Hunt

Aliens vs Predator: Ultimate Prey (with Bryan Thomas Schmidt)

Baker Street Irregulars (with Michael A. Ventrella)

The Game Is Afoot: Baker Street Irregulars II (with Michael A. Ventrella)

Scary Out There

Weird Tales: 100 Years of Weird

Double Trouble (with Keith R.A. DeCandido)

The Good, the Bad, and the Uncanny: Tales of a Very Weird West

Weird Tales: Best of the Early Years 1923–25 (with Justin Criado)

Weird Tales: Best of the Early Years 1926–27 (with Kaye Lynne Booth)

THE DRAGON IN WINTER

JONATHAN MABERRY

ST. MARTIN'S GRIFFIN
NEW YORK

First published in the United States by St. Martin's Griffin, an imprint of St. Martin's Publishing Group

THE DRAGON IN WINTER. Copyright © 2024 by Jonathan Maberry. Map copyright © 2022 by Cat Scully. All rights reserved. Printed in the United States of America. For information, address St. Martin's Publishing Group, 120 Broadway, New York, NY 10271.

www.stmartins.com

The Library of Congress Cataloging-in-Publication Data is available upon request.

ISBN 978-1-250-89263-8 (trade paperback)
ISBN 978-1-250-89265-2 (ebook)

Our books may be purchased in bulk for promotional, educational, or business use. Please contact your local bookseller or the Macmillan Corporate and Premium Sales Department at 1-800-221-7945, extension 5442, or by email at MacmillanSpecialMarkets@macmillan.com.

First Edition: 2024

10 9 8 7 6 5 4 3 2 1

This one is for Weston Ochse (1965–2023), my brother from another mother and coauthor of *The Sleepers War: Alpha Wave*. A soldier, scholar, and superb writer. And for his wife, author Yvonne Navarro. You will both be family with me. Always.

And, as always, for Sara Jo.

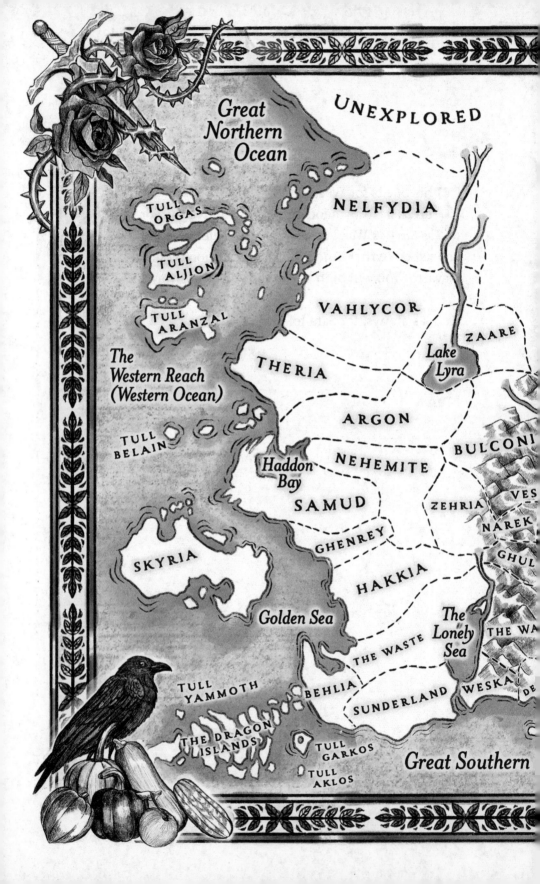

The Frozen Sea

THE WINTERWILDS

UNEXPLORED

OBA-WABAK

...AL MOUNTAINS

JAKATA

SKAYAN

PELLIA

THE SHADOWLANDS

AYU-MATHAN

PHAROS

TULL SOREN

...YA-TA

GEFHELM

CORZ-RAZAN

ASHGHULAN

KYRAN

THE JUNGLE BELT

KORTHA

YEHTEC

...eat ...and

SAUNDARYA

BERCLESS

THE EMPIRE ISLANDS

...KIEROD SUND

INAKI

TULL HELSYAROK

...AR

WYNDHOVEN

TULL MORGANROK

TULL MITHRAIN

TULL HEKLON (GOD'S FORGE ISLAND)

PART ONE
WARS AND RUMORS OF WAR

———

"How many times have I heard someone whisper the phrase, *'Magic has returned to the world'*? Ever since the Witch-king made his existence known on the Night of the Ravens, those words have been on everyone's tongues. Most, of course, have no real idea what that means. They think it refers only to the sorceries of the Witch-king and his court necromancer, Lady Kestral. They think it refers only to the magicks that allowed the Hakkians to conquer the Silver Empire all in a single night. But . . . ah, that is naive. That is like looking at the night without considering the day. Such people fear the bright eye of the full moon, but that is because they lack the knowledge to understand that the light of the moon is sunlight reflected. Dark magic is not all there is of magic; it is a shadowy reflection of magic's full strength. Consider this, for when we think of magic, it is shortsighted of us even to regard it as dark or light. Magic . . . *is*. It is chaos unchained. A sword is neither good nor evil; nor is an arrow. Intent is what matters in all things. In everything."

—KONREYD BLEMMEN, CHIEF LIBRARIAN OF THE LIBRARY
RESEARCH PROJECT OF SKYRIA

CHAPTER ONE

"By the splendorous balls of the god of beauty," growled Tuke Brakson.

He stood wide-legged in the middle of the road, a broken shield dangling in splinters from his left hand. The machete in his right dripped with blood, but the steel was notched and bent. His big body was crisscrossed with cuts, old and new, shallow and deep. He panted as he stood there, and he could feel every day of every year of his life. Sweat ran lines down his limbs, over the patterns of tattoos, along the gullies of wounds, mixing with the bright red blood to create paler streamers of pink.

Beside him, the smaller, slimmer figure of Filia alden-Bok leaned on the pommel of her sword, the point dug into the turf, shoulders hunched as she gasped for air. Horse, her brute of a dog, lay on his belly, tongue lolling, sides heaving. His armor was dented and splashed with blood, and too much of it was his own.

Fifty paces in front of them stood Captain Kagen Vale.

He stood alone, his daggers sheathed and no other weapon in his hands. Eighty yards in front of him, riding slowly forward, was the captain of the Hakkian Ravens, his yellow-and-black armor gleaming, golden cloak fluttering behind in the brisk easterly breeze. A bannerman rode beside him, a guidon seated into a leather bucket behind his right stirrup. Two flags flapped near the top of the pole—the Hakkian national flag and below it was a broad strip of unmarked white cloth.

The heavily forested Rinshaw Mountains provided a backdrop and at their foot was an army of two thousand soldiers. Earlier that morning there had been twice that number, but the rest lay dead on the field. A few crawled slowly, crying for their mothers now that prayers to the Shepherd God Hastur had failed them. Vultures circled above the field, and with each turn the hungry birds were closer to the cooling meat.

Tuke and Filia watched Kagen. He stood ramrod straight, his shoulders set, stance wide. They watched the enemy captain approach. He was a dignified-looking man with a precisely trimmed beard and no dents on his armor, no dirt or blood.

"Son of a bitch probably hasn't even drawn his blade today," grumped Tuke. "And now he comes prancing out on his horse like it's harvest fair day and he's the king of the parade."

"He'll ask for a pause in order for everyone to collect their wounded," suggested Filia. "Standard procedure."

Tuke grunted. Their own army had lost nearly seven hundred fighters, and what was left looked as tired as he felt.

"Wait," said Tuke, "let's see if we can hear what that Hakkian ass has to say."

"Have you ever seen Kagen negotiate before?" asked Filia.

"Not . . . as such. Why? He's noble born and has manners. I'm sure he'll do fine."

Filia merely smiled.

CHAPTER TWO

The captain of the Fifth Hakkian Army—the Firedrakes, as they were called—drew his horse to a stop ten feet from where Kagen stood.

"Greetings, Kagen Vale," he said, raising a hand to show that he held no weapon.

Kagen sucked at a dry inner cheek and spat on the ground between them.

"It's *Captain* Vale," he replied calmly. "Though Lord Vale will do."

The officer bowed in the saddle. "My apologies, *Lord* Vale. I am Captain Sheklyn of Hembria, deputy commander of the Firedrakes."

"Where's your general?" asked Kagen. "Too busy having his whores pop the pimples on his ass to be here with his troops?"

He said that loud enough so the breeze would blow his words to the waiting Hakkians. There was some laughter among their ranks and then the sharp growls of sergeants.

"My general is in Argon," said Sheklyn. "He is there at the pleasure of the Witch-king."

"Meaning he is afraid to be *here* because he's a fucking coward."

"My lord," said the captain, his tone still formal, "rather than trade insults, I come under a flag of truce to parley."

"To what end? If it's to surrender, then all you need to do is throw down your sword."

Sheklyn looked pained. "No, my lord. Nor am I asking for *your* sword."

"Don't much like swords. I've always preferred knives," said Kagen. "Feels more personal to be that much closer."

The Hakkian merely sniffed. "I've come to suggest that we each take an hour to see to our wounded."

Kagen smiled thinly. "Now why would we do that?"

"It's civil," suggested Sheklyn. "There are rules and honor even in war. Or, I daresay, *especially* in war."

"We both know that's a lie, captain. We both know that if I lose, you'll crucify any survivors from here to Argon."

"That's not true," insisted the captain, though he was a moment too long in offering that protest. "Besides, the wounded are no longer combatants. Surely you have not fallen so low as to have lost compassion."

"Say you so?" asked Kagen, smiling faintly. He took two paces forward and looked up at the officer. "It's my understanding that compassion died when your troops invaded the palace and butchered the empress. It died when your soldiers raped and murdered the Seedlings. It died when the Ravens burned every garden in the empire, sodomized the nuns, and crucified the Gardeners. You come here in your expensive armor on your prissy-ass horse and talk to me about compassion? About mercy? I piss on your compassion."

The captain's face went pale and then slowly turned red. He made a great and visible effort to rein in his anger and when he spoke, there was more of a pleading note in his voice.

"Surely, Lord Captain, you do realize that if you refuse this request now," said Sheklyn, "when you sue us for peace as this day unfolds—as you inevitably must—you will get none."

"Have I asked for peace?" asked Kagen, amused. "Or mercy? Have I asked for any rules of civilized combat? No, because I do not bargain with scum and bootlickers of a usurper who is devoid of honor."

He drew one of his daggers with his left hand and pointed the blade at Captain Sheklyn, smiling coldly as he did so. "It's time you crept back to the safety of your troops."

"Do you threaten me?" demanded the Hakkian officer.

Kagen grinned and pretended to notice that he held a knife. "So it would appear."

"This is a flag of truce," cried Sheklyn. "By the staff of Hastur the Shepherd God, have you no honor?"

"Honor? Well," laughed Kagen, "my own gods turned their back on me. I am damned, haven't you heard? The damned are soulless and therefore *have* no honor."

The captain licked his lips and tried a different tack. "Lord Vale, can't you hear the cries of the wounded? Surely even one who is *damned* has some trace of mercy left."

"Mercy? Aye, I'll show you mercy."

With a movement far too quick for the Hakkian to follow, Kagen's right hand whipped a throwing knife from its sheath and snapped his arm forward. The six-inch blade *thunked* into the socket of Captain Sheklyn's throat. The Hakkian's mouth went wide and for two seconds his trembling fingers clawed hysterically at the weapon. Then his eyes rolled high and he pitched sideways out of the saddle, falling to the bloody dirt with a heavy clang of armor.

The bannerman cried out in horror. Across the field, the enemy soldiers stared in shock for three full seconds, and then they leapt to their feet, shouting curses and oaths, their voices rising on the crest of their outrage and fury.

Kagen walked over to the dead officer, tore his knife free, wiped it clean on the man's cheek, slid it back into its sheath, and glanced at the bannerman with the white flag.

"Toss your weapons down," he said. "And then ride off. That is the only mercy I have left to offer."

The man hesitated, glancing from Kagen to the army in front of him—all of whom had also gotten to their feet. He saw hundreds of bowmen fitting arrows to their strings.

"All hail the Witch-king," he cried, dropped his guidon, drew a curved sword, and charged in for the kill.

Kagen made a noise of disgust, sidestepped the charge, and whipped the tip of his dagger lightly across the man's calf. The blade was soaked with *eitr*, the deadly poison known in legends as the God Killer. The *eitr* rippled like lightning through the aide's veins and he was dead before he knew he was cut, toppling sideways from his saddle. However, one foot snagged in the stirrup, and the bolting horse dragged him bumping and thumping across the corpse-littered field.

Kagen then walked over to the fallen captain. He sheathed his dagger, moved his leather codpiece, pulled out his cock, and pissed on the officer's dead face. He shook off, turned, and walked back to where Filia and Tuke stood with their entire army at their backs.

Filia shook her head, but she was grinning.

"By the cast-iron balls of the god of blacksmiths," growled Tuke. "That was a flag of truce. He came over to parley."

"I know," said Kagen, his voice as cold as winter ice. "But I came here to start a war."

He nodded to the captain of archers. Immediately there was a huge *thrum* and four hundred arrows darkened the skies as they flew toward the advancing Hakkians.

CHAPTER THREE

Kagen swung into Jinx's saddle, drew both daggers, roared a challenge to the Hakkians, and galloped forward. Tuke and Filia rode beside him, with Horse ranging ahead, filling the air with deep-chested barking.

The Bloody Bastards chased them, tearing the air with threatening howls in a dozen languages. And on their heels was the balance of Kagen's small army. Less than half of them had horses, and barely half that many had full sets of armor. But they moved with precision. The archers ran forward in squads, and then split off to the sides to act as skirmishers. The sergeants of each squad were Samudian Unbladed, and—as the old saying went—a Samudian archer was worth ten of any enemy. They proved it that day, firing even as they ran, their powerful yew longbows sending arrows that punched through plate and chain mail. As the distance dwindled, they used their superb accuracy to target the legs and hips of the riders, being careful to cripple the Hakkians without injuring the horses. It was an old Samudian tactic that had worked for seven hundred years. And it worked now.

The wounded soldiers fell screaming from their saddles as their horses panicked and broke the orderliness of the charge. The ranks behind them crashed into the frightened animals or tripped over the bodies of the thrashing wounded. Within seconds the bold Hakkian charge had become a bedlam of disorder, pain, confusion, and death.

Boys holding shields above their heads ran out onto the field between the armies and collected spent arrows, taking every shaft—theirs and Hakkian—plucking them from the dirt or pulling them from the bodies of the dead. Behind them came a wave of camp followers to drag the wounded away, with ambulatory injured holding shields to protect them. A few old women—widows and mothers of dead sons—slit the throats of every Hakkian they could reach.

It was not a civilized battle. This was mutual murder on a grand scale.

Other squads of Kagen's archers rode horses or ponies, racing along the flanks of the field of combat and shooting into the advancing horde. These squads targeted the Hakkian archers, outmatching their short bows with longer and more accurate ones. Each of Kagen's archers had oversized quivers of arrows slung from their saddles, and they proved why everyone in the west feared Samud's bowmen. While the Hakkians could fire ten arrows per minute with reasonable accuracy, the Samudians could fire thirty. Their hands were blurs, their eyes rarely even blinking. The yew bows bent and released so fast the arrows seemed to vanish only to appear in breast or throat or belly; and they had the next arrow nocked before the last had found flesh. An entire wall of Hakkians crumpled beneath the onslaught.

And then the Bloody Bastards hit the center of their main advance.

Jinx, Kagen's horse, was wrapped in lightweight chain mail, and he slammed through a narrow gap between two racing soldiers.

Kagen was a big man, but not huge; and all through his combat training, his mother—the dreaded Poison Rose—taught him to prize speed and accuracy above brute force. He twisted and ducked in the saddle, slap-parrying spears and swords, using deft flicks of his wrist to deliver tap-cuts with the poisoned blades, moving on without waiting to see the effect. Anyone he failed to kill with the *eitr* had to deal with Tuke, Filia, and the Bloody Bastards.

The substantial difference between the Hakkians and Kagen's army was that the enemy were ordinary soldiers with a few seasoned sergeants and knights to anchor them. The Unbladed were all professional fighters who had lived by their blades every day, and in situations more dire than a straight field of battle. The Unbladed were masters of every kind of weapon, from mace to morning-star, from spear to double-bladed axe. Some, in open defiance to their creed, carried swords and proved that they were masters of these as well.

Horse—Filia's war hound—had his own small army, a pack of hounds, many of which were half wolf or half coyote. They harried horses and riders both, leaping up to tear open legs and throats. The dogs were all clad in spiked armor, and then if they had no chance to bite, they slammed their bodies into legs and groins. Those spikes did awful damage. Those hounds that died did so with screaming meat between their teeth.

Kagen punched through the line and began hunting the officers, even as teams of archers did the same. The enemy's sergeants were also prime game. One of the first lessons of so-called civilized warfare was to target the officers and sergeants. Without a workable structure of command, whole sections of the Hakkian force began to fall apart. Even the toughest soldiers became terrified when there was no one left alive to tell them where to go and what to do.

"Kagen—ware!" yelled Tuke, and Kagen twisted in his saddle

to see a big soldier driving at him from his blind side. The man had clearly passed by him as the armies collided, then wheeled to try and take Kagen out. Probably hoping to do to Kagen's army what he had done to theirs—kill their leader.

The Hakkian had a small shield and a heavy cavalry saber. The blade was already falling as Kagen turned. There was no time to think, only to act. Kagen jerked Jinx's reins hard, sending his mount crashing into the side of the other mount with such force that the descending attack resulted in the Hakkian's forearm crunching down on Kagen's shoulder. It was painful, but it spoiled the intended blow.

Kagen leaned sharply forward, chopping downward and backward with a knife, drawing a red line across the horse's neck while, with the other hand, Kagen reached over and drove the point of the other dagger into the Hakkian's ear. It was a clumsy counterattack that might otherwise have resulted in a panicked horse and a rider with nothing but a minor wound. The *eitr* made the attack lethal, and Kagen grinned like a wolf as horse and rider collapsed and died.

An arrow slashed Kagen across the cheek as he turned to re-enter the fray. He spun to see a group of five archers clustered in a knot with their backs to a large boulder. Before he could snap out an order, Horse and his pack of hounds swarmed over them, savage teeth and bristling spikes doing terrible work.

"I love that gods-damned dog of yours," he yelled to Filia. Her response was a wild laugh.

Tuke was on his feet beside his mount, who had taken two arrows in the belly. The animal screamed in pain. Kagen knew that Tuke loved his horse, but the wounds were mortal, so the big Therian raised a machete and chopped down, ending its torment. Tuke whirled and vented his loss on every Hakkian within reach. And he had a very long reach.

Each national group within Kagen's army had its own scores to settle. The Hakkians, protected by the magic of the Witch-king, had conquered the entire Silver Empire in a single night. Since then, Hakkian soldiers and their mercenary hirelings had done unspeakable acts of cruelty. Two aspects of that horror were rallying calls.

One was the comprehensive slaughter of nearly every monk and nun and cleric of the Garden Faith, a clear attempt to exterminate the religion that was a central uniting element in the empire.

The other was the Red Plague, a terrible disease that both killed thousands and then raised them as mindless cannibals. Hakkia had used that weapon against some of their own remote villages and cast the blame on Samud—the nation where, centuries before, the plague first struck. But doubt had spread like wildfire that it was not King al-Huk who was behind the plague but a subtle bit of trickery by the Witch-king. The outrage was massive, and although the stain of doubt still lingered for many on Samud, the tide of belief had begun to turn. Even amongst the Hakkian people there was some open protest against the ruse.

The Samudian archers seemed to each feel that it was their personal responsibility to repay Hakkia for the outrage.

The battle raged, with advantage moving back and forth like a tide. Soon the horses and foot soldiers were tripping and trampling the fallen. The Samudian archers were relentless, and now many of them knelt behind rows of shields held by those too wounded to fight. They framed the battlefield on three sides, turning the interior space into a killing field.

Kagen saw Filia, still mounted on her horse—named Dog—and she was doing some combat tricks Kagen had seen only in jousting matches. Dog had sharpened steel hoof covers and as knights charged, Filia would jag her horse left or right and then the animal would rear up and kick either attacking mount or rider. The razor-sharp covers cut as easily through horseflesh as they did the knees and thighs of mounted soldiers. As the wounded fell, Dog would trample them. Filia laughed aloud like a demon in red glory all through the fierce battle.

A figure rushed past Kagen—Biter, a Weskan who was a member of the fierce Crocodile Clan—and he had what looked like the ornate sword Captain Sheklyn had worn. The Bloody Bastard yelled curses in a dialect Kagen barely understood as he bashed aside spears and gutted the spearmen. With him was the dour Ghulian, Borz, who fought in silence, his face set, eyes calm even as he filled the air with the screams and blood of the Hakkians.

Giffer, once an ordained Gardener from Zaare, moved like a festival fire-dancer, a pair of long-bladed butcher's cleavers in his hands. The moody Ghenreyan poet, Hoth, was at his back, fighting with a short close combat weapon that had a spearpoint at one end and a knobby iron ball at the other.

These—and a handful of men and women who fought with them—had been the first of the Unbladed Kagen had engaged when he began his formal opposition to the Witch-king. They'd gone with Kagen, Tuke, and Filia all the way into the nightmare forests of cannibal-infested Vespia and come out again. They were the core, the heart, of Kagen's army, and they fought with skill and fury, leaving silent or screaming enemies in their red wake.

"They're running!" someone roared, and Kagen stood up in his stirrups.

"By the Gods of the Pit," he bellowed.

"Kagen," called Biter, "shall we give chase?"

Many of the Hakkians had thrown down their shields and swords to make flight easier. Kagen called for the captain of his archers, the Samudian Gi-Elless. She came running over.

"Hunt them," he ordered. "Kill anyone who is still armed. Let the others go."

Gi-Elless grinned and ran off, calling to her sergeants.

And that fast, the tide of conflict ebbed and turned. The archers had great sport with the fleeing Hakkians. As soon as the enemy realized that the unarmed were being spared, swords and spears fell by the score to the turf. Then the remainder of Kagen's army stood and watched as the five or six hundred surviving Hakkians—unarmed and unprovisioned—fled for safety.

"They'll tell the tale," said Filia, riding up to stand next to Kagen.

"Aye," said Tuke, "and likely embellish it. Hm . . . I wonder how I'll be represented in tavern songs."

"You would think about that now, wouldn't you?"

"Why not?" laughed the Therian. "Today was definitely one for songs."

Kagen merely grunted. Then he turned and called his officers to see to their wounded.

"What about the wounded Hakkians?" asked Tuke, cleaning his blades with a dead Hakkian's yellow cloak.

Kagen's pale eyes were as cold as arctic ice. "What about them?"

The Therian glanced at Filia, but if he had hoped to see mercy there, he was looking in the wrong direction. He glanced up at the nightbirds. Their black beaks were stained red and there was no mercy in their eyes, either.

CHAPTER FOUR

Many hundreds of miles to the south, a lone figure stood at a high window of the grand palace of Argentium. For a thousand years it had been the home and the seat of power of the Silver Empresses.

Now it was the home of a usurper.

More than a year ago the Yellow Empire had nearly been born in that palace. The coronation of the Emperor in Yellow was unfolding, with the kings, queens, princes, and princesses from the member nations of the old empire all present and ready to ratify the change of government.

Had been.

The newly fashioned crown did not rest upon the head of the man who stood looking out of the window. It lay, mangled and bloodstained, on a table in a private room. Unused, unsanctified, unwearable.

The Witch-king of Hakkia—still king and perhaps never emperor—watched the clouds sail in fleets across the Argonian sky. The broad expanse of Haddon Bay was a lustrous and sparkling blue, and the furled sails of a thousand boats and ships seemed to argue innocence and purity.

But all the Witch-king saw was pollution, filth, and sadness. He leaned knotted fists on the stone sill, his jaw clenching and unclenching behind the lace veil he wore to disguise his features.

Below where he stood, on one of the many rows of spikes that lined the walls, was the skull of the woman who had betrayed him. The ravens had long since devoured every inch of flesh, though some of her long, dark hair still clung stubbornly to the bone. When he had ordered her head placed there, his heart had turned black with rage. Now, months later, the Witch-king felt different emotions.

Grief.

Loss.

Hurt.

Sadness.

"Lady Kestral," he murmured, giving his words to the breeze from the bay. "Why, my lady? Why?"

Questions he had asked a thousand times since that dreadful night.

"Why?"

The skull could not answer, and the sea breeze held its tongue.

His favorite hound, a great female brute with a scarred face and hungry eyes, looked at him and whined.

In the slow process of rage becoming hurt, the mind of the Witch-king had turned like a miller's wheel, grinding pain and fury into something colder, finer. Into something more useful.

He stood there as the day wore on and twilight began to paint the sky in shades of purple and black. No one dared interrupt him.

No one.

CHAPTER FIVE

Her name was Frey, and she was every bit as old as she looked.

The mirror, always truthful and treacherous, showed every line and seam on her face, and every mile she had traveled. In her long career as a senior investigator for the Garden's Office of Miracles, she had lived what felt to her like a dozen lifetimes.

As morning light fell over her features, she studied them, looking for shadows of the bookish girl and the ambitious and idealistic young woman she had been. Those shadows were there, but faded now. Instead she saw a crone who, despite a sharp and active mind, was nearing the end of her years. Bent, with a dowager's hump, withered limbs, liver spots, and the scars of hard use. Neither intellect nor ambition were proofs against entropy.

"A silver dime for your thoughts," said a voice, breaking into her sour reverie.

Frey turned to see Helleda Frost standing in the doorway to her apartments. The younger noblewoman wore a gown of dark blue velvet adorned with pearls and sapphires. Frost, though occasionally as cold as her name, was a good and trusted friend, and one of the patrons whose vast personal fortune funded the army Kagen Vale was building.

"You would get sour thoughts and change back from your dime," she said, waving her friend in. "I was wondering who this old woman in the mirror is."

"She is old, to be sure, but with many years ahead of her still."

Frey did not bother fending off the compliment. It was the

kind of well-intentioned thing people say when they can't bear to speak the truth.

"Has word come from the west, yet?" asked Frey. "I expect that Kagen and his troops will not outrun the Firedrakes."

"No word yet," said Frost. "But I am optimistic."

"Are you?"

"I am. I admit that I was a hard sell on Captain Vale," said Frost, coming over and sitting on the edge of Frey's bed. "But he continues to impress. Lord Clementius and Lord Gowry both think the world of him. Others of the cabal do, too."

"Yes," said Frey simply.

She sat in a chair that had a cushioned footstool, sighing as she settled in. "I've sent word for him to meet me."

"Oh? Can he afford to get away right now? What with the Firedrakes hunting him."

"I do not expect the Firedrakes to succeed against young Lord Vale. Besides, there are important matters for us to discuss."

Frost nodded. "By that I assume you mean the Hsan manuscripts and our complete inability to have them translated."

"Well, that, yes. But other things as well. I need to reassure him that the cabal will continue to fund his operations. And no, I don't mean just you. Generous as you are, Helleda, I have asked every member of the cabal to dig a little deeper. We cannot wage this kind of war on a budget."

Frost nodded. "Tell me, though, about those scrolls. Kagen went to incredible lengths to obtain them and it seems as if that journey was for naught."

"Perhaps not, my dear. My guess is that when I return them to Kagen he'll immediately ride to Arras."

"To give them to the witch?"

There was bitterness and fear in Frost's tone. Frey shook her head.

"Lady Maralina is a faerie princess and a sorceress of great age and learning. She is also Kagen's lover. I believe she is our last, best hope of translating the Hsan scrolls."

"It is a shame we failed."

"Not completely. The preamble," said Frey, "was written in a newer language than the rest, and that we *could* translate. It spoke of a ceremony called *the ascension*. I've heard rumors of that elsewhere over the years. It has something to do with a process in which a great sorcerer can be elevated to the status of demigod. How that will happen is unclear, which is why we need Lady Maralina. However, there was also a vague reference to a god being made flesh."

"And you think this prophecy—or whatever it is—means that the Witch-king becomes a demigod and *his* god, Hastur, becomes—what? How is a god made flesh? Doesn't that limit the god's power?"

"Apparently it does not," said Frey. "With Hastur and the other Great Old Ones, he exists in a dream state. That means he is not entirely on our plane of existence, and therefore his power is necessarily reduced. Greatly so. Once manifested on earth—and I think the phrase 'made flesh' doesn't mean that he'll be a flesh-and-blood mortal—his power will be very much greater. With a demigod as his avatar and chief priest, the Shepherd God would be unstoppable."

"Gods of the Harvest," breathed Helleda as she made a warding sign in the air.

"So," said Frey, "as you see, that meeting with Kagen is imperative."

CHAPTER SIX

Kagen walked the battlefield, pausing now and then when he saw the face of someone he recognized. There was even one soldier, a blond-haired woman, he had known from his days at the Imperial

Palace in Argentium. He paused and knelt beside her body. She held an axe handle in one hand and on her arm was a splintered shield.

"Ullyria," he murmured. "Damn."

A shadow fell across her and he glanced up to see Filia standing there with the big hound, Horse, beside her.

"Did you know her?" asked Filia. "Before she joined us, I mean? Her armor is Argonian."

"Aye. I knew her," said Kagen. "She was a sergeant of scouts. Her husband died during the Night of the Ravens. Her daughter, too."

Filia knelt across from him and reached out to brush hair away from Ullyria's face. Then she glanced around. There was a half circle of Hakkian corpses, each bearing the marks of a war axe.

"She accounted herself well."

"She did," agreed Kagen. "Damn it, she deserved better than this. She joined us to avenge her family, but . . . also to follow me. It's unfair."

Filia opened her mouth as if to comment on fairness in battle, but closed it, leaving those words—both obvious and unkind—unsaid. Horse leaned forward and sniffed the fallen soldier's hair. Then he gave her cheek a single lick. He sat down and whined very softly.

Another shadow made Kagen and Filia look up. Tuke towered above them.

"I wish we had that big flame-eyed son of a bitch with us," he said. "He'd have kept more of our friends' names from the list of the dead."

Kagen merely nodded. Tuke often said he wished that the razor-knight they encountered while on an expedition into the wilds of Vespia had joined their ranks. Although conjured by dark magic—as was the other of its kind who had killed the Poison Rose, Kagen's warrior mother—the one that attacked them in the ancient city turned on its creators. It roared aloud that it was going to find and kill the Witch-king. None of them knew how or why that change occurred, but if the monster really *was* fighting their enemy, then its presence in battles like this would be invaluable. It could not easily be killed and even fighting alone it was a literal engine of destruction—created from blood and steel and hellfire.

"We did well enough," said Filia.

Kagen glanced past Tuke to where camp followers were stacking looted Hakkian gear. "Where are we?" he asked.

Tuke shrugged. "All of the enemy dead have been stripped of armor, weapons, food, and money. We recovered seven dozen horses and thirty pack animals. Actually, we took their entire baggage train. A lot of our lads who didn't have top quality armor before have it now."

"Good," said Kagen. "What about the heavier armor that the Firedrake knights were wearing? We don't need it right now but I don't want the Hakkians to come along and take it."

"We should grab it," said Filia. "This was a battle but real war is coming, and once that's in motion we'll get more fighters. Some of them will know how to act in a line of heavy cavalry. That stuff is expensive as hell and we need whatever gold we have to pay the lads."

"Good idea," said Kagen. "As for the yellow Hakkian cloaks, if there's dye available use it. Or—"

Filia tapped him and pointed. Kagen looked to where a group of camp followers—old men and women and young children—were laying the yellow cloaks on the ground, the corners weighted by rocks, and were using a mixture of water and mineral pigments to paint a sigil on the material. He got up and walked over to see what it was. The image was of crossed daggers very much like his own, and behind them, standing straight, was a short sword with a matching hilt. Curled around the apex of the three blades was a twisted figure in gold and inside its coil was a splash of red.

The artwork was crude but he understood it. His blades, a blade representing the Unbladed as a whole, with a dragon curled protectively around a rose.

"What is this?" he asked in wonder.

"Something Tuke and I cooked up," said Filia. "Every army needs a standard. Why? Don't you like it?"

Kagen slowly shook his head. "No . . . it's . . . it's beautiful."

She patted his shoulder. "Don't start crying, you'll embarrass yourself."

"Oh, shut up."

She laughed and led him over to where their expanded baggage train was being organized.

"The wagons look full," said Kagen.

"The Firedrakes were prepared for a campaign," said Filia. "Nice of them to bring us so many presents."

"Very kind," agreed Kagen. "Have each set of armor tied in bundles and those can be slung on the archers' horses. They never carry much weight and the armor shouldn't slow their mounts down." He paused and glowered at Filia. "What are you smiling about?"

She shrugged. "You're even starting to sound like a field commander. Maybe you should promote yourself to *General* Vale."

"Not a gods-damned chance," Kagen said sternly. "I earned my captaincy and that's what I'll be until the end of this. Besides, generals are political and I'm not."

"You're not ambitious either," she said. "And there's a damn short list of young noblemen of that stripe."

"I don't care," said Kagen. "You of all people—you and Tuke—know why I'm doing this."

She touched his chest for a moment. "I do."

"So do I," said Tuke, "but if you two are done kissing each other's asses, can we get back to the matters at hand?"

Filia laughed at him and lowered her hand. Kagen merely scowled.

Tuke gestured to where a group of the Bloody Bastards were busy with shovels and pickaxes. "The lads are digging a pit for our people." He nodded to the fallen Ullyria. "This woman's the last."

Kagen hated the thought of her burning instead of being buried on Argonian soil, but he was too practical to argue. He touched Ullyria's chest over her heart, just as Filia had done to him.

"Sleep and dream of the garden, my sister," Kagen said. "May your harvest be plentiful and your days filled with joy. And may your family be there to greet you in the green valley."

Although he had been rejected by the Gods of the Harvest, the dead woman had been a faithful believer. The prayer came easily to him because of her.

Then he rose and nodded to Tuke.

"Be gentle with her," he said.

Tuke nodded. There were other soldiers within earshot and four came over, placed Ullyria on a Hakkian cloak that was tied around broken lances. They lifted her with silent reverence and bore her to the pit.

It had taken a full day after the battle to tend to the wounded and handle the hundred tasks that war requires. The sun was a high, hard light in the west. When Ullyria was laid with care among her brothers and sisters in arms, Redharn and Gi-Elless poured oil on the bodies and in a ring around the pit. Then Filia handed a torch to Kagen.

"All of them are here because I put out the call," said Kagen, his tone soft and morose.

"They're here because the fucking Witch-king started a war," countered Tuke. "By the squelchy balls of the god of jellyfish, this is not *your* burden."

"Yes," said Kagen. "It is."

He raised the torch high as he walked over to the pit's edge. There he stopped and stood, head bowed in silent contemplation.

Then he nodded to Giffer, the former Gardener, who said a short prayer. When it was done, Kagen touched the torch to the ring of oil. Flames leapt up, bright and hot. There was a purity to it, Kagen mused. He laid the brand down and walked backward as the flames shot up, partially obscuring the many bodies. Filia and Tuke came and stood with him.

The pyre of their dead comrades blazed high, reaching with arms of flames toward the heavens. Smoke was caught by a capricious wind and coiled upward in columns, twisting together like titanic serpents. Or, like the coils of a burning dragon, he thought.

Ten thousand nightbirds launched themselves from the trees and flew toward the smoke, then began circling it high above the fire. They uttered strange, mournful cries that drove the vultures from the field.

The soldiers stared at this spectacle in awe, even those who had seen the nightbirds join Kagen's battles before. Redharn unslung his axe, stood it on end with the two curves of the blade biting into the soil. He knelt, one leathery palm on the handle, and bowed his head. Gi-Elliss, standing near him, did the same with her bow. Then—first in ones and twos and then by the score—the other soldiers knelt. Filia and Tuke studied each other for a moment, with much said though unspoken.

They knelt.

Kagen was the last one standing. He bowed his head and prayed for the souls of the brave men and women inside that conflagration. He did not care that the Harvest Gods had abandoned him— these people were of that faith and had lived and died to defend freedom and to avenge the slaughter of the Gardeners, monks, and nuns.

When the prayer was done, Kagen raised his head and looked out across the pit. When he spoke again, his voice was a deep bellow of rage.

"There is blood on the ground between us," he growled, "and

by all that is holy and unholy I shall see that justice is done. So swear I, Kagen Vale, son of the Poison Rose, captain of the Bloody Bastards. I swear this by blood and bone, by hate and by love."

He looked at the kneeling soldiers.

"Stand with me," he said, and they got to their feet.

Then Kagen beat his fist against his chest seven times.

"For the empress and her family—her Seedlings—I so swear," he said, his voice ringing out clear in the smoky air. "For the innocents slaughtered throughout the Silver Empire since the Ravens came, I so swear. On the blood of my brothers and sisters who stood with us and fought beside us, I so swear. I swear this to any god who will listen. I swear this to the heavens and the earth and to every citizen of the Silver Empire. And I swear on my life that I will kill the Witch-king and tear his dreams of conquest to blood and ruin. This I, Captain Kagen Vale of the Unbladed, so swear."

His words echoed across the field and rose above the trees and swirled with the smoke. Tears coursed down Kagen's face.

A moment later the air was split with thunder as every fighter on that field swore the same oath. Adding their names to the oath. Accepting the blood obligation to the fallen. As they shouted this, they, too, beat their chests.

Over and over again until the thunder of it drowned out the crackles and hisses of their burning friends. In the air above them the thousands of nightbirds cried out with their own curses and prayers and promises.

CHAPTER SEVEN

The Witch-king of Hakkia lay face down on the floor.

He was naked, without veil or jewelry or any decoration to offer even the slightest illusion of protection. He was covered in rare oils that had been prayed over for weeks, and his body gleamed in the light of one thousand candles. Even with all that light, the room held onto its darkness, with cold shadows that refused to yield ground to warm light.

"My lord and god, great Hastur of the fields," he intoned. "Shepherd God who leads his flock of the faithful to glory, I abase myself before you."

Above the prostrate Witch-king stood a statue that loomed fifteen feet high and was painted in a hundred subtle shades of yellow. It was of a tall figure whose face was entirely hidden by the hood of a heavy cloak. It leaned upon a shepherd's stave and looked down at the supplicant, giving the impression of doing so from a very great height.

"Hastur," continued the Witch-king, "everything I have is yours. Everything I *am* is yours."

The sculptor had been in a trance when he carved it according to the Witch-king's very precise instructions. Upon completion of his work, his eyes had been put out and he was now in one of the lowest dungeons beneath the palace. No one was allowed to speak with him or even look at him. His food was pushed in through a slot and there were no windows in the one locked door.

"God of the celestial realm, use me as your vessel. Guide me through the steps of ascension so I may be in truth your servant and son here on earth. Let me, in turn, bring you back into this world—not as a dream but as a living god, that you may regain what is rightfully yours. Whatever is required—whatever sacrifice of others or of self, I will make, even unto the death of my immortal soul."

The statue seemed to regard the naked man, and the flickering candlelight made the shadows of his cowl shift, suggesting movement. Or, perhaps, in that sacred and solitary place, the statue *did* move. Who can say?

"All that I do, I do in your name and for your glory."

Even the rats in the walls fell silent as they moved past this room. The bones of those who lingered warned their kind of the dangers of tarrying.

"All that you have asked of me is being done," whispered the Witch-king. "The spells have been cast. I will empty Hakkia of every adept and user of magic and when they are here, we will begin the spells that will tear open the gates of dream and all the faithful will rejoice."

As he chanted his prayers, the Witch-king wept. As his tears struck the stone, they turned to chips of ice.

CHAPTER EIGHT

ONE WEEK AFTER THE NIGHT OF THE RAVENS
His name was Alibaxter and he was a wizard.

Sort of.

Wizard was his *official* title, as it was for his father and grandfather, and on and on back through eleven hundred and eighty-two years. His mother's side of the family were high priestesses whose lineage was over thirteen hundred years. A grand tradition.

Except that it was in name only.

Alibaxter, who was far more effective and successful as a historian, wrote many books on the subject of magic's demise. He collected diaries, journals, ships' logs, and other accounts from all across the continent. The lands east of the Cathedral Mountains were unaligned and did not follow the precepts of the Silver Empress or the Faith of the Garden and did not recognize either institution's prohibition against magic. And yet over the years, magic failed there, too. No one knew why. There were hundreds of theories, many quite reasonable. But a theory was not an answer.

Only Hakkia retained a strong connection to magic and used it in their own ceremonies and religious rites. Until, that is, this practice was discovered. For centuries the Hakkian Witch-kings practiced their dark magicks in secret, hiding even the simplest spells from the Office of Miracles. When imperial spies discovered the truth, the great warrior Lady Bellapher the Silver Thorn was dispatched with a massive army and, after months of bloody combat, crushed the Hakkians, slew their priests, executed the Witch-king, and left behind an occupying force whose punishments for even *mentioning* magic were severe.

Magic left the world, as far as Alibaxter and the other scholars knew.

And yet the tradition of magic lingered.

On the island of Tull Ithria, deep inside the sprawl of the Dragon Islands, the School of Nature was established. It was made up of clerics who were ostensibly Gardeners but whose actual job was to keep alive the rituals and practices of white magic—natural magic—should the empire ever allow magic to return.

The sorcerers, wizards, witches, and warlocks were all descendants of actual magic users, though none of the descendants could levitate a fluff of goose down let alone guarantee an abundant harvest or stave off a destructive hurricane. The spells were performed on given days in a calendar of sacred days. All of the various steps and incantations, potions and prayers were said in their correct forms. The right kind of candles were lit, the right sacrifices made—mostly of livestock bred for that purpose and later used as centerpieces for feasts—and everything was done to perfection.

Except that none of the spells ever worked. Not one. Not in Alibaxter's lifetime, or the lifetimes of his ancestors going back a thousand years.

Which was why Alibaxter and his group of novices stood in total shock, eyes wide, mouths open, bodies trembling as rain fell on Tull Ithria.

Not that rain in and of itself was unknown. It was, after all, an island in a tropical sea. Rain was common.

But rain that began at the precise moment in the ritual known as the Sky's Blessing where it was *called* to begin . . . that was something else. Precise to the moment, to the exact word spoken aloud by Alibaxter.

The young wizard stood there, arms still held wide, his robes sodden and clinging to his body, his arms and legs encircled with the green ribbons the novices had wrapped so carefully around him. The *Book of Sacred Remembrance* opened to the page of that spell.

Alibaxter stared at the falling rain.

At how it gleamed like silver in the sunlight.

He looked up at the sky.

At the completely cloudless sky.

As the rain fell on his upturned face.

His very first thought, once thought was even possible, was, *I need to tell Mother Frey.*

CHAPTER NINE

DREAMS OF THE DAMNED

That night, when Kagen wrapped himself in furs and drifted off, he sank into dreams. Since boyhood he had always had two different kinds of dreams. There were the common ones that everyone had, composed of a mélange of memories, fragments of recent incidents, stray thoughts, and the unfettered imagination of the sleeper.

The others, though, were far different.

In the second kind of dream, Kagen seemed to be two people at once—his current adult self and a younger version from when he was a lad. Sometimes he was a boy, other times a stripling or young man, but always younger than he actually was.

At times, when awake and contemplating those dreams, he wondered if the younger version represented his innocence and also the power youth possess for believing in the impossible. That made sense, since the young were like vessels only partly filled with life's experiences—not yet glutted on ecstasy and pain, accomplishment and failure, glory and bitterness. Somewhere inside his scarred heart, Kagen knew that that feckless boy still lived.

Or, he sometimes thought, the younger aspect might represent the Kagen Vale who had not failed to protect the Seedlings, the imperial children; the version of him who had not failed in his oath-sworn duty to protect the empire. The version of him that had not been damned and abandoned by the gods.

Two aspects of him—young and older, possessing an immortal soul and being soulless—witnessing the same things in the world of dreams.

But why, though? That puzzled him. Those dreams were strange, surreal, unnatural, and untrustworthy. There were contradictions in some of them, with conversations being shaped differently in different dreams. What did that mean? Was it the imprecision of a dreaming mind? Or was it evidence of something else? Did it suggest that the past, like the future, was somehow in motion—subject to change through unknown ways?

Or did it mean that his *memory* of the past, whether real events or from dreams, might not be or might not mean what he thought?

He had been dwelling on this as he swirled around the whirlpool of sleep . . .

. . . *Kagen stood once more in a vast cave of ice that he knew was deep in the heart of a glacier in the far north of the Winterwilds.*

His body was fourteen, but his thoughts were twice that age. His current age.

The cavern was dark, with patches of cold blue-white light that seemed to have no source. The air smelled bad, like meat thawing slowly in ice. He remembered the first time he smelled this precise scent. He, Jheklan, and Faulker had accompanied their older brother, Gardener Herepath, to a glacier on an expedition to find ancient secrets. The frigid air seemed to hold memories of all of the death it had witnessed. And there, in the frozen north, ice trapped whatever died upon it, storing it imperfectly and releasing its smell like a threat of death.

That sweet, ugly, heavy stink of slowly rotting meat permeated this glacier now. What unnerved Kagen was that there was a wrongness to the stench of death. Because it did not feel truly dead. There was an awful vitality to it, as if somehow death itself lived.

Kagen began walking. He had no purpose, no direction, and merely moved toward whichever patch of light was brightest. The child in him feared the cold darkness; the man in him accepted that fear as rational. There were things here that refused to die. Or, perhaps, were not governed by death in the way anything natural should.

"Find me," whispered a voice. Deep, throaty, ancient, and painful, that voice filled his thoughts. He was not sure if he actually heard it or whether the words were spoken through some eldritch means that let him hear it regardless. "Save me."

Kagen paused and looked around. "Where are you?"

"I am dying," said the voice. "Save me before all is lost."

"I don't know where to look."

"Yes, you do," said the voice. "You have always known."

He licked his chapped lips and decided to take a terrible risk. "Are you Fabeldyr?"

Suddenly the ice walls around him shuddered. Deep cracks appeared and chunks of broken ice crashed down to the ground, forcing him to dodge out of the way.

Kagen reeled and clapped his hands over his ears as a scream of impossible volume blasted through the frozen corridors of the ice mountain. He staggered, eyes shut, until his knees buckled and he fell . . .

. . . Kagen woke with the echo of that scream in his ears.

He found that he was not wrapped in furs in his tent near the field where the Firedrakes had been butchered. Instead, he was in the middle of the field itself, his knees sinking inches into the muddy, blood-soaked dirt. He gasped and raised his head, looking wildly around.

The tents—more than three hundred of them—were burning.

Screams of a different kind filled the air. Men and women shrieking as they roasted. Children running, their bodies blazing like torches as they beat frantically at their burning hair. Horses, Jinx among them, straining to break free from where they were tied as their tails and manes burst into bright fire.

"*Filia!*" cried Kagen, staggering to his feet. "*Tuke!*"

He saw them. Both of them.

They lay on the ground near the pyre in which their fallen comrades had been turned to dust and ash. Filia's body was torn to pieces. Tuke was mangled nearly beyond recognition. Close by, Redharn sat slumped over with the corpse of Gi-Elless in his arms.

"No . . ." said Kagen, his voice cracking from the heat and the horror.

Above him—far above—there was a massive sound. At first, he thought it was thunder, but it was too loud even for that. It came again, and again, and Kagen strained to see through the pillars of smoke.

He caught a glimpse as something impossibly vast moved across the sky, blotting out the moon and stars. Kagen could not make out anything except its outline, those details picked out by starlight above and firelight below.

Huge wings stretched across the whole of the field. Not merely big, but incredibly vast. The thing was so massive that surely its wings—even those titanic ones—must surely snap. Yet they did not. They flapped slowly, and each beat was like the world cracking asunder.

It was a dragon.

He knew it was a dragon.

He spoke the name he had said in his dream.

"Fabeldyr . . ."

But even as he said that name, he knew that this thing was not the trapped and tortured dragon he had glimpsed in the glaciers in so many dreams. It was not the last dragon Lady Maralina had embroidered on a tapestry in her lonely tower.

It was not anything as small and fragile as that.

What he beheld was far greater. And he knew, without knowing *how* he knew, that this was what had come in answer to the desperate, dying cries of earth's last dragon.

Earth's last.

Not *the* last. With a profound and existential horror, Kagen understood that now.

This was something greater and it had come across the gulfs of space because one of its own had called it. To free Fabeldyr, perhaps, or avenge her inevitable death.

Kagen, on his knees, could only stare at the thing that had come to punish all of humanity for the cruelties of a few.

"I'm sorry," he said, weeping as the understanding dawned. "I'm so sorry . . ."

. . . and then he woke in his tent.

The night was silent.

The world was unbroken.

When he pushed back the flap of his tent, he could see that the sky above was filled only with stars and the last full moon of autumn. The heat that had lingered so long into the season was gone, and an unexpected and bitter wind from the north seemed to proclaim winter's advent with icy malice.

"Gods of the . . ." he began, but his words faltered.

In his mind, the echo of those monstrous wings battered his mind with cruel promise.

CHAPTER TEN

Lord Jakob Ravensmere was historian to the Hakkian king and—in title only—imperial historian for the Yellow Empire. That such an empire effectively died at birth was troubling to many, but less so to a historian who understood that much of his professional charter was propaganda. He told the version of the truth that suited his master. If that was sometimes hard to stomach, he had but to walk through the richly appointed rooms of his luxurious palace to placate himself. It worked every time.

Now, though, he sat in a room in the palace in Argentium, sweating his way through an unusually hot late autumn afternoon that sweltered despite open windows.

"Gods of the Pit," he muttered. "Someone left hell's furnace door open. And there's not a fart of a damned breeze."

Across from him, apparently melting inside his brocade robes of office, sat the wizened old chamberlain, Lord Nespar. He looked gray and corpselike, his eyes were bloodshot, and his hand trembled as he lifted his wine cup to take a sip.

"Last winter was so bitter I prayed for warmth," muttered Nespar. "Now I wish I had sewed my own lips shut."

Jakob sighed. "I'd have threaded your needle for you."

"For what it's worth," said Nespar after a long pause, "our weather witches say that we will have an early winter."

They watched the blue of Haddon Bay, whose surface was as flat as a mirror. The sails on the many fishing and patrol boats hung slack, requiring slaves or crewmen to pull on oars to move the vessels to or from a dock. Sailors carried buckets to the crosstrees in order to douse the sails in hopes of making them dense enough to catch a whisper of a breeze. Heat shimmered upward in the humid air, untroubled by even a rumor of sea wind.

"Tell me, Nespar," said Jakob, "have you noticed anything peculiar about the king?"

Nespar smiled faintly. "He is a sorcerer. What is the specific *flavor* of peculiarity to which you refer?"

"Oh very amusing," said the historian. "Very droll. No, what I mean is that does he seem ill or out of sorts to you?"

Nespar considered. "Sometimes, yes. At times during court proceedings he tends to look away as if lost in thought or—dare I say—fretting about something. Which is understandable, given the state of the world and the real likelihood of war. But unwell? No. Not in particular. Why do you ask?"

Jakob shrugged. "Perhaps it's nothing. It's just that I have heard him gasp a few times when he moved suddenly, as if he had an injury. And one of the sergeants of his personal detail reported to me that the king sometimes seems dizzy and out of breath."

"Perhaps he has a summer cold and some body aches. Even Witch-kings are mortal."

"And likely you are correct."

"Besides," said Nespar, "and perhaps more to the point, he has begun preparations for his great ascension."

"Which is *what,* exactly? Not being Hakkian I am somewhat confused. Is he trying to become a god, or is it a matter of bringing Hastur to physical life on this plane? Every reference I read seems to be deliberately vague."

"Oh, it's confusing even to those of us who grew up in the religion of Hastur," admitted Nespar with a laugh. "But as I understand it, the ascension will fill the Witch-king with some of Hastur's limitless energy, making him immortal and elevating him to the status of demi-godhood. While at the same time Hastur, who—like his half brother Cthulhu—exists in the Dreamlands and not on this actual plane of existence, will manifest here."

Jakob considered this for a moment. "Tell me, is this literally what will happen or is this somehow a symbolic ascension?"

Again the chamberlain laughed. "Oh, hell, my friend, even I don't have the answer to that. Hakkian theologians have wrangled over that for three thousand years. Personally, I do not know what I believe except that I believe in the Witch-king. And I will leave it there."

"Fair enough," said the historian. "Changing the subject, I have been reading some of the writings of our beloved Witch-king."

"And how do you find them?"

"Slow going, if I'm to be honest," said Jakob. "Scholarly to be sure, but dry, with a style that will never make for casual or entertaining reading. And also dense, requiring a great deal of additional knowledge going in which I do not always have. I need a half dozen or more supporting volumes on hand just to grasp the context and meaning. Sorcery, at the level we're talking, is not for amateurs."

Nespar nodded. "Are there any that you find particularly interesting?"

"One stands out, yes. 'On the Nature of Consciousness, with Additional Notes on Thought Transference and Psychic Theriomorphy.' I find that one quite fascinating."

"Why so?"

"Have you read it?"

"I . . . have," said Nespar. "But, as you say, it is dense stuff."

Jakob mopped his face with a handkerchief. "Our lord wrote it before he visited the Winterwilds, back when he was part of the Hakkian chapter of the Garden research team on Skyria. It was dismissed by the High Gardener as—and I quote a memo— *minutely well-documented fluff of no interest to an enlightened scholar.*"

"And your personal assessment?"

"I think the High Gardener did not grasp the importance of what he was reading."

◄──────────────────────────► **CHAPTER ELEVEN**

"Sire," asked the captain of the palace guards, "are you unwell? Should I fetch a doctor?"

The Witch-king leaned against a wall a few dozen steps from the chamber in which he said his most private prayers. His breath was rapid and shallow, and everything about his posture suggested exhaustion and pain. The bitch hound danced around, whining with concern.

Yet the king shook his head.

"It is nothing, captain," he gasped. "I am performing rituals to prepare for the ascension. Some are . . . necessary but unpleasant."

"Should I have a chair and bearers brought?"

The eyes behind the lace veil turned to him for a moment, then he shook his head again. He straightened and smoothed his robes. "It is already passing. Your concern is noted. You may leave me now."

The captain clearly wanted to say more, but he bowed and retreated.

Alone, the Witch-king touched himself—his stomach and chest, the muscles of his arms, his face beneath the lace. He could feel the changes already. Some were subtle while others were extreme. Had it not been for the voluminous yellow robes, his cowl, and the veil, those changes would be seen by all.

The process of his ascension had begun.

The king waited until his heart was beating with a more comforting regularity, and then he walked slowly away.

Behind the wall near where he had been, in a secret passage that only a handful of people knew of, two sets of young eyes watched him.

The small bodies of the brother and sister the Witch-king swore were his own, held hands in the dark and tried to understand what they had just seen.

CHAPTER TWELVE

Kagen, Filia, and Tuke sat at a small table in the Spear & Fang, a tavern in northern Vahlycor owned by a retired member of the Unbladed. It was late and the place was mostly empty except for Kagen's other two lieutenants, Redharn and Gi-Elless, who were huddled suspiciously close to one another and who shared looks that Kagen reckoned would likely lead to their sharing a bed. The thought pleased him. They were both good people and very fierce fighters.

Filia caught his eye and glanced in their direction, then looked back at Kagen.

"Flowers bloom in the strangest places," she said, quoting a line from an old Garden psalm.

Tuke snorted. "Love or lust, take your pick."

"Either way," said Kagen taking a wine bottle and filling his friends' cups, "I'll drink to something happy. The gods know there are few pleasant things happening these days."

"Only you could make a toast to lovers sound gloomy."

"Kiss my ass."

"Thanks, but no," said Tuke.

They drank.

Tuke set down his cup and studied Kagen. "What's wrong with you anyway? We won a major battle a couple of days ago and you look like someone pissed in your wine cup."

Two or three biting returns occurred to him, but instead Kagen merely shrugged. "It's nothing. Haven't been sleeping well."

"You shock me. Just because we're fighting an unwinnable war against monsters and sorcerers, you let that disturb your rest?"

Kagen ignored that. "I saw you talking with a rider earlier. Let me guess—sending your weekly report to Mother Frey?"

"Actually, no," said Tuke, unabashed. "Receiving a note."

He reached into his loose shirt and retrieved a folded slip of parchment from an inner pocket and placed it on the table next to Kagen's cup.

"She's asking for a meeting," said Tuke.

Kagen picked up the note and read aloud. "'At the Plover's Nest.'" He tossed the note down. "That's a long way from here. She expects me to drop everything just on her say-so?"

"Maybe she's finally found someone who can translate those damned scrolls—the Seven Cryptical Books of Hsan."

Kagen snorted. "She's been trying to do that for months. We went all the way into Vespia for those scrolls and they might as well have been blank for all the good she's made of them."

"Even so," said Tuke. "Will you go?"

Kagen shrugged. "Maybe. She's worried about something new with the Witch-king. Rumors about some ceremony called the ascension."

Tuke looked amused. "She didn't explain what that was. Do you know?"

"Not really. So, I suppose I'd better go and find out."

Filia said, "She may have news of your brothers."

That made Kagen brighten a little. Months ago, shortly before he first met the old woman, Frey had engaged the services of Jheklan and Faulker, who—despite being a year apart in age—were known in the Vale family as the Twins. They looked alike, talked alike, and had the same penchant for going on wild adventures in hopes of becoming fabulously wealthy but were also magnets for trouble in all of its many forms.

"There's that," grudged Kagen. He loved Jheklan and Faulker and had gone on hunting trips and adventures with them, including one to the Winterwilds, led by Herepath. Now the Twins were in that frozen wasteland again, and no word had come south since they crossed the Cathedral Mountains.

The three of them sat, each of them staring into different parts of the darkened tavern. Not *at* anything, but in truth looking inward. Although it was less than a year since the Hakkians conquered the empire, it felt to them as if they each had lived lifetimes on the run. There were bounties on all three, with Kagen's being the greatest. Anyone bringing him alive—or bringing his heart and head—to the Witch-king would receive a wagonload of gold coins, an estate, and other riches. Every time fresh news reached them, the amount of that bounty had increased.

"If I go," said Kagen after a very long pause, during which Gi-Elless and Redharn vanished upstairs, "I think I want to get those magic books back from her."

Filia cut him a look. "Why? No, let me guess. You want to take them to your faerie princess, don't you?"

Kagen said nothing. But Filia saw the corners of his mouth turn upward in the faintest of smiles.

CHAPTER THIRTEEN

Lady Maralina came out of her tower and stood watching the waves rise and break upon the rocks a few hundred yards away. Gulls floated on the hot wind, their bellies blindingly white against the hard blue of the sky. The wind played with her long hair, making it dance.

She mostly saw the world only as shadows passing through the enchanted mirror that hung above her loom. It was rare for her to come out and stand at her tower's apex, looking at the world for real. It had been more centuries than she cared to count since she had been truly free of those walls. When her mother, the queen of the faeries, had condemned her to that prison, the world was a much different place. Even the oldest books of history did not describe the world she had once known—the gulf of time was far too vast to allow those kinds of insights. But she remembered. Athens and Camulodunum, Tikal and Carthage, Çatalhöyük and Heraklion . . .

All lost to time.

Many hours passed as she stood there, her eyes looking west but glazed and without focus. Several times her lips moved, and each time they formed a single word. Though in each instance that word was weighted differently, carrying so many meanings.

"Kagen . . ."

All along the stone battlements were birds. Crows and starlings, grackles and cormorants, red-winged blackbirds and black vultures, cowbirds and blackbirds. They huddled close, but they did not shiver from the wind. They trembled in perfect harmony with the thoughts that raced through Maralina's mind. Through their eyes—and the eyes of hundreds of thousands of their kind—she looked far and looked wide.

And looked very, very deep.

Something indefinable made her turn her face to the northeast where, thousands of miles away, the miles-high glaciers waited out eternity in frozen silence. Yet there was something that had tugged at her awareness. It was like hearing the very last echo of thunder before its warning faded out completely. Something was coming. The air was filled with the promise of it and that energy sent ripples of fear deep into her heart. That sound had been less like thunder and more like the beat of monstrous wings.

"Kagen, my love," she whispered. "The storm of war is coming. Were I not trapped here, I would be at your side and bring with me the armies of the damned."

The birds heard those words.

No one else.

No one living.

Far below, in the swampy grounds, in pools and puddles nearly hidden by the riot of brightly colored flowers, other ears heard her. Buried in the mud or beneath mossy stones, in shallow graves and ancient barrows, lay the many champions and heroes, princes and kings, who had in ages past attempted to find the lost faerie princess. Some had come to steal the secrets of magic from her; others had fallen in love with her from dream visions. Each had scaled her tower, and each had, indeed, found Maralina. Now they slept and dreamed unquiet dreams, still longing for her, forever in love with her. Every one of them heard her words, and in their troubled sleep they moaned, skeletal hands scrabbling at rusted blades.

The day wore on and when night wrapped its soft arms around the stone pillar, the battlements and the platform were empty. And yet the pale kings and princes moaned. Softly, to be sure, but more loudly than ever before.

CHAPTER FOURTEEN

"It's suicide," said the Samudian deputy marshal. "It's like they came here to be slaughtered."

Ul-Fen, second in command of the 5th Royal Infantry, sat atop horse on a knoll. Beside him was Captain yr-Tulan, the commandant of the training halls on the small island of Tull Athris.

"I cannot understand it either," said yr-Tulan. "Sentries spotted them before dawn. Fifty Hakkian regulars. They're not even Ravens, and there's too few of them. The gods only know what they hope to accomplish."

Below them, on the westernmost of a dozen large fields that covered nearly half of the island, were fifty soldiers wearing the yellow and black of Hakkia. More than a score of others lay in pools of their own blood as Samudian soldiers beat them back, step-by-step.

The fields were separated by thick stands of trees, brooks, and the ruins of an ancient fort, and for the last eighty years it had served as one of Samud's training centers. There were nearly a thousand foot soldiers and archers on the island to perfect new combat strategies in preparation for the coming war. The deputy marshal was on an extended tour of such places, bringing fresh news and orders, and sending reports back to the king.

"If I were to guess, sir," said the captain, "I think they followed poor intelligence and thought there was only a modest garrison here."

The deputy marshal nodded.

"Sir, look, they flee the field," cried yr-Tulan, pointing with his riding crop.

It was true, the Hakkians fled toward a line of trees. From where the officers sat it was easy to see beyond those trees to another field beyond which was a slope that ran down to the sea.

"They're going to try and ambush them," said the marshal. "They think the trees will confuse your troops, captain. They think that will impede your archers."

"Then they are even less wise than I thought," said the captain with a smile. "My archers are country lads. Hunters to a man. The woods are their home. If they can fill a game pouch with rabbits and grouse in half a day, then they can take down their full count of men hiding behind slim trees."

The deputy marshal smiled, caught up in the dark amusement of seeing an enemy demonstrate strategic weakness. That boded well for the coming war.

As the Hakkians entered the woods they fanned out, running in apparent panic, fleeing laterally through the stretch of trees instead of making for the field beyond. The sergeants in charge of the Samudian troops sent their platoons in pursuit, and the wind carried their wild laughter and taunts to the two officers. Arrows flew and there were screams as Hakkians fell.

"What is that over there?" asked the marshal, stiffening in his saddle.

The captain rose in his stirrups, shading his eyes with a hand. Beyond the wall of trees, at the edge of the far field, a dozen Hakkians were lighting torches.

"What in the burning hells are they doing?"

"Are their men so dense that they need torches to show them the way to their ships? See? They're entering the woods, waving the blazing brands overhead." Immediately the Hakkians wheeled around and ran toward the torch men.

Deputy Marshal ul-Fen's lips were parted, what he had been about to say fading to dust on his lips. The Hakkians were forming very specific lines, falling into single file as they ran, each racing toward the torches.

"I was right," said the captain, laughing. "They are really that stupid that they need to be shown the way through a copse of trees."

"No," breathed the marshal. "Gods of the Pit, *no.* Captain, sound recall. Get your men out of those woods. Do it now. *Now, damn your eyes.*"

Confused, the captain turned toward a sergeant a dozen yards away. "Sound recall," he said, almost with emphasis.

The sergeant signaled a pair of trumpeters, and they raised their horns to their lips. They blew a series of six notes, the clear call rising into the humid air.

But it was one second too late. The last man in each fleeing line dove past the torch men, rolling onto the grass, rising and turning to watch as every soldier carrying a torch threw them into the woods as the Samudians charged. Not one Samudian had yet reached the field. All of them were in the woods when the entire stretch of forest erupted in a towering sheet of furious orange. It all went up at once. There was no slow process of grass setting bushes alight and sparks igniting leaves. Everything caught fire at the same time.

The screams of all those soldiers rose as the trumpet calls died away into a ghastly silence. The two officers stared in utter horror as they saw blackened figures dance and twist and writhe in an inferno none of them could escape. The trees caught fire, too, as did the field from which the Hakkians had fled. It was only when the breeze blew smoke to the knoll that the officers smelled the oil that had been used to douse everything.

The flames raced over the field, burning the fallen Hakkians and the few dead Samudians, and tearing upland toward the knoll. With cries of horror, the officers wheeled and fled.

A woman climbed nimbly to the top of a cracked volcanic rock. Her aides climbed with her but none dared offer a hand. Once she gained the top, Lieutenant-General Mari Heklan—known as Mad Mari to everyone who hated or loved her—watched the Samudians burn. She was tall, broad-shouldered, with a face long since marked by blade and arrow. Her armor was plain except for a Hakkian eclipse bordered in gold between her armored breasts.

Mad Mari looked out on the destruction and was well-pleased.

Just as she knew her cousin, Gethon, would be pleased.

CHAPTER FIFTEEN

Lord Nespar, chamberlain of Hakkia, and the royal historian, Jakob Ravensmere, met in a private sitting room in a high tower. The weather was still hot but now, at least, there was a wind from the west. A warm wind, but it was better than sitting in an oven.

"What you said yesterday," began Nespar as he poured a light-bodied wine for each of them, "it kept me up all night. Haven't had more than a wink of sleep."

"Which particular parts?" asked Jakob as he accepted his cup with a nod of thanks.

They sat in their usual chairs. A third, one that had been so often used by Lady Kestral, stood empty. They were aware of it, and her conspicuous absence, but they chose not to speak of that shared loss.

"The two papers written by the younger Gethon Heklan," said

the chamberlain. "One in particular." He cut a look at the historian. "Care to guess which?"

"It's not 'Impermanence, Transition, and Displacement in Ancient Religions,'" said Jakob with a wry smile. "The content is as obvious as the title, and we have seen that play out all around us. At best it's a manifesto for what Hakkia has done to the Harvest Faith. At worst it's trite and repetitive."

"Agreed."

"Then that leaves the much more interesting 'On the Nature of Consciousness, with Additional Notes on Thought Transference and Psychic Theriomorphy.'"

"Quite," agreed Nespar. "I had to go and look up 'theriomorphy.' Shape-shifting. Disturbing but not extremely so. There is a clan of lycanthropes in the service of the Witch-king. The van Keltons of northeastern Hakkia."

"Just so," said Jakob. "I believe two of them—the twins, Lord Amarok and Lady Tikaani—were dispatched to hunt and kill Kagen Vale. A patrol of Ravens found what was left of them in the woods."

"No doubt Captain Kagen had help when attacked," said Nespar. "Otherwise those Ravens would have brought back *his* remains."

"Perhaps," said Jakob in a tone that conveyed some doubt. "So, what about theriomorphy kept you awake all night?"

"It wasn't that, exactly," said the chamberlain. "It was the whole phrase—*thought transference and psychic theriomorphy.*"

"Perhaps it plays into this ascension thing," suggested Jakob.

"Perhaps."

Jakob sipped the wine and stared over the cup's rim to the sunlight twinkling on small wave caps in the bay. "And yet . . . thought transference is a theoretical ability acquired through magic of some kind, and I admit that my knowledge of the mystic arts is lacking in many areas."

"I have some small understanding of those arts," said Nespar, "though it's been learned from association with Lady Kestral and in service to the Witch-king. Even so, it is something of a spectator's understanding and not that of a practitioner. That said, I was able to grope my way through various books in the library. Thought transference is the ability to either switch minds with another person or, in some rare cases, with animals. The twelfth Witch-king was reputed to be able to shift his mind into that of his favorite raven."

"Yes, I read that," said Jakob. "If true, it suggests that the actual size of the brain of the—shall we say—*target* of the transference does not need to match that of the spellcaster. However, of much more interest to me is the concept of theriomorphy. The various books I read do not seem to agree on the rules of that. Some say that a person needs to be born with the ability, as with the van Keltons, each of whom were born as werewolves. Others say that it is a skill that can be acquired."

"Yes," said Jakob, nodding.

"None of the books have much that deals with the duration of that transference."

"Do they not?" mused the historian. "I will have to consult my own library back at my estate. I have some volumes that are not yet copied for the palace library."

He got up and walked to the window and looked out, then turned and leaned a shoulder against the frame. "Where are you going with this, my friend? What is the specific thing you fear?"

Nespar studied him as he rolled his wine cup back and forth between his palms. "Surely you've heard the rumors that Kagen Vale claimed to have seen the king's face and that he claims it was that of his older brother, Herepath. My fear is that Herepath may have somehow transplanted his consciousness into the body of Gethon Heklan in order to steal his spiritual *and* political power."

"And you think he hides his face because that transformation was also physical, and that Herepath Vale is pretending to be the king?"

"I am not sure I believe it. Not yet, at least," said Nespar. "But haven't you noticed that the king has been acting strangely lately? More aloof? Distant?"

Jakob nodded. "But, that may be part of his process of ascension."

"In either case," said the chamberlain, "I am feeling . . . unsettled."

"And now so am I," said Jakob.

CHAPTER SIXTEEN

Kagen made his decision to go visit Mother Frey. But he was loath to do it because he felt he was needed there at the camp.

"Oh, for the love of Dagon," complained Tuke one morning. "You do realize that Filia and I have five times the experience you have in recruiting troops? Or is hubris your preferred state of mind?"

That stung and Kagen had no real riposte.

"Just give me the current numbers," he said. "I should share that with Frey anyway. We need her cabal to cough up enough gold to feed the troops and buy some proper armor."

Gi-Elless, who—along with Redharn—had been deputized as lieutenants of the army, said, "We have six thousand mounted fighters, thirteen thousand foot, and three thousand archers."

"More than I thought," grunted Kagen, nodding approval.

"But not nearly enough," said Filia, her face dour. "Mother Frey's network of spies says that the Hakkians have sixty-one thousand cavalry, with twenty thousand of those being heavy and the rest light. They have three hundred thousand foot and forty-four thousand archers. A fair number are mercenaries, and there are rumors of more marching from the east across the Cathedral Mountains. Who knows how many they can put in the field."

"Aye," agreed Tuke. "The Hakkians spent years preparing for a war they didn't actually have to fight, the pricks. The Witch-king won without taking very many losses. And they've been recruiting ever since."

"Gods of the Pit," breathed Kagen.

"The good news," said Redharn, who was far more of an optimist than Gi-Elless, "is that they are spread across the entire empire. We're spread a bit thin, too, but being smaller, our people can react and respond more quickly. Being Unbladed, they're also used to traveling light."

"Not sure how *good* the news is that we are outnumbered fifty to one."

"By the . . . balls of . . ." began Tuke but it trailed off because he had nowhere to go with it.

"Before we all nip out and slit our own throats," said Filia dryly, "let's not forget that we are talking about Unbladed, Argonian resistance, and volunteers. We do not yet know how many swords, bows, and spears we may get from the nations of the former empire."

Gi-Elless looked at her. "Nor do we know how many soldiers from those countries will go to war alongside the Hakkians. Don't forget," she said, "the fear of the Witch-king is still potent. It can't be dismissed."

"True enough," said Tuke. "And a lot of those soldiers may be ordered to stand down as their monarchs watch to see which way the wind blows."

"I bet there are six times as many soldiers join us as fight against us," insisted Redharn. "And if it looks like we're winning, more of them will find their backbones and remember what their swords are there to do."

"I love your optimism," said Kagen, only partly meaning it.

CHAPTER SEVENTEEN

Hannibus Greel sweated in the furnace heat of the audience hall in the capital of Samud. His green robes clung to his bulky frame, and the extra pounds the Therian diplomat carried were impossible to ignore. Were he anywhere else, Greel would allow himself to collapse.

Here, though, he merely endured.

Twenty feet in front of him, and seated on a beautiful throne, was King Hariq al-Huk. He was broad, short, and heavily muscled. His olive skin was smooth except for many old battle scars. He reclined on the throne, ringed fingers slowly stroking the three spiked points of his black beard.

Across the room, seated at a desk and busy copying classics in five languages, was a lad of fifteen who was a younger, leaner version of the king. Prince el-Kep was a studious young man, well-versed in literature and mathematics, and adored by a veritable horde of girls of the very best families. But his interest in politics was virtually nil. His father encouraged him to do his lessons in private rooms like this in the hope that he could catch the fever of statesmanship because he was al-Huk's only child—his only heir. But he barely glanced up as the king and the envoy talked about the coming war.

"You have become a more faithful visitor at my court than half the official courtiers," he said, smiling thinly.

"I am honored that I have been welcomed so often and so graciously," said Greel.

"Tolerated is possibly a more accurate word."

"As Your Majesty wishes."

"Are you here again to inquire about the Red Plague?"

"No, Majesty. Like all open-minded people I am convinced that the plague was a Hakkian plot to discredit Samud in the eyes of the world. And it seems that the Witch-king has abandoned the plan now that it has done all the damage it could."

"Then what is the purpose of your visit?"

"I have come to talk about rebellion, sire," said Greel. "I have come to talk about the overthrow of the Witch-king."

The king studied him for a long moment. "Speak then," he said.

CHAPTER EIGHTEEN

Kagen rode out at first light on the following day.

Tuke and Filia were the only ones to see him off. The rest were asleep, and the world was so quiet it was as if nature herself held her breath. There were nightbirds in all the trees outside of the Spear and Fang, but they watched with the silent patience of their kind.

Filia handed him a bundle of papers tied with string. "For Mother Frey," she said, then stood on tiptoe and kissed his cheek. "Be safe, you stupid city boy."

He returned the kiss. "I promise not to do anything foolish or dangerous."

"Liar," she said, stepping back.

Tuke wrapped his massive arms around Kagen and nearly crushed the life out of him with a hug. When he released him, Kagen staggered back, gasping. "May Father Dagon watch over you."

With a simple nod as his answer, Kagen mounted Jinx, then turned and rode in the direction of the dawn.

CHAPTER NINETEEN

"That's him, I tell you," said the shorter of the two men.

He and a taller companion huddled together in the dense shadows beneath a canopy of oak leaves a hundred yards down the road from the tavern.

"How can you be sure?" asked the taller man.

"The daggers. See them? I've seen a hundred likenesses of them on handbills from here to the coast," said the short man. "That's Kagen Vale. Kagen the Damned, as some call him, the son of the Poison Rose. That's the one those Ravens are always looking for. The one that has that bounty on his head."

They faded back as Kagen cantered past. When he was well out of earshot, the taller man said, "We don't actually have to capture him, do we? He looks like he could turn mean as a snake."

"He *is* mean," agreed the other. "And, no . . . Gods of the Pit, I wouldn't step on his shadow for ten times my weight in gold."

"Then so much for the bounty," said the tall one.

"Ah, maybe and maybe not. There's gold for anyone who can sic the Ravens on him. Might not be a king's ransom, but it would set us up for life. No more gravedigging for me and no more goat herding for you. We'd be country gentlemen with servants of our own, and a couple of nice houses. One for you and mine next door, with an acre or two of land for vineyards between."

"Just for telling on him?"

"Aye," said the short man.

They watched the lone rider until he reached a crossroads and angled more directly east.

"Listen," said the short man, "you have longer legs. I'll watch where he goes while you cut across the fields to the town hall. That Hakkian sergeant is there. You tell him and make sure he writes down our names."

The tall man hesitated. "Enough for houses and vineyards and servants? You're sure?"

"Hand to the gods."

The tall man chewed his lip for a few seconds, then gave a sharp nod, turned, and ran off as fast as a jackrabbit.

The Witch-king looked up from a very ancient text as an inconspicuous door opened in a corner of the large room used for strategic meetings and planning. The man who entered bowed low but without the mockery or irony he had often used in the past for courtly gestures. Not that the Prince of Games looked in any way contrite, but at least restraint was not unknown to him.

He padded silently over to the worktable and stood by an empty chair, clearly waiting for an invitation to sit. However, the Witch-king made no such offer. Instead he placed the pad of one forefinger to mark the place where he had stopped reading and studied the man.

The hound got up from where she had been sprawled in front of the fire and sat down facing the prince. Where once she seemed amenable to his touch, now she looked at him with animosity and a fair amount of hunger. The prince kept his distance.

"Do you have news of any value?"

The prince smiled. "Still angry with me?"

"The word you are searching for is 'disappointed,'" said the Witch-king coldly. "Why ask? Have you done anything to ameliorate that?"

"Majesty," said the prince, "you can blame me for what happened in this room and in far Vespia as much as you wish. I do not need or require your forgiveness. Although . . . it is inconvenient because it digs a moat between you and my counsel."

"What value do you think I should place on your counsel?" asked the king, leaning back in his chair. "You advised me to use the Red Plague against Hakkian towns in order to cast blame on Samud. And to what end? I have murdered a few thousand of my own people and the sub-monarchs have not risen up against King al-Huk."

"Nor have they aligned themselves with him," replied the

prince. "Are there armies in the field marching under the banners of a united empire?"

"A delay in open rebellion is hardly the comfort you think it is. War *is* coming, and my generals tell me that we will face at least half of those nations, with the others watching to pounce once we are on the retreat."

The prince, a slim knife-blade of a man with a saturnine face, sensuous lips, and merry eyes, raised his eyebrows. "And have you already accepted defeat as inevitable?"

"Of course not," snapped the king. "But my position is less secure than it was. Far less than it should be. And weakened further by the deaths of so many of my court magicians."

"Ah," said the prince. "Well, that was unfortunate, I will admit."

"Unfortunate," echoed the Witch-king sourly. "I have been made to look weak, and that alone has done more to endanger Hakkia's future than anything else. Yes, I will be able to turn this catastrophe to my advantage—for we do want this war—but it will be harder to prosecute than it should have been. However, war may happen before I have completed my ascension, and during that process I will not be able to use my powers to help our armies. Therefore, I will need to call in mercenaries from the east. That will be expensive, for mercenary generals such as the WarBride and Unka the Spider will want much for their troubles. And I will likely have to bring in *other* help. They, too, will have their fees. So, my prince, I am not happy at the current state of events. More to the point, Lord Hastur is not pleased."

That wiped away much of the prince's smirk. "You know this?"

The Witch-king glared at him. "I do. He has visited me in dreams, and I have felt the heat of his displeasure. If you think that is only words . . ." He pushed up his sleeve to reveal dreadful burns on his arm. They glistened with ointments. "These are five weeks old and have still not healed. They have not *begun* to heal."

"I . . . do not know what to say," admitted the prince. He looked genuinely aghast. Although he was not really a man but a chaos trickster spirit in human form, his mockery and open defiance did not extend to the gods.

The Witch-king watched the prince's face, enjoying the fear he saw. He wondered how many centuries had passed since the last time this creature felt true fear.

"The Shepherd God is watching," he said, twisting the knife. "I promised him conquest, and that I have accomplished. Now he wants dominion, but your clumsiness and the treachery of Kestral have endangered that."

The prince had no comment to make and even bowed slightly as if acknowledging his part in the catastrophe.

"So," said the Witch-king, smoothing his sleeve, "what *news* do you have?"

The prince cleared his throat. One of the most human acts the king had seen him do. No drama or showmanship.

"The razor-knight has been spotted in Zehria."

The Witch-king grunted. "So far away? It has had months to travel, I expected it to be in Argon by now."

"We have ambushed it a dozen times, so maybe that has slowed it," suggested the prince. "But there is no need to worry. We have a few canisters of banefire here in the palace to burn that creature to ash."

"That is to be used only in the defense of this palace," snapped the king. "We have very little of it left."

"Oh? I was under the impression there was quite a lot of it handy."

"You are wrong, prince. More is being made but it will take a great deal of time to bring it here from where it is being manufactured."

The prince seemed interested. "I know many secrets, my king, but I don't actually know where—or even *how*, for that matter—

banefire is made. All I hear are rumors that it is made somewhere in the far north and the ingredients are of limited quantity."

"That is all you need to know," replied the king. "Is there anything else you need to share? Because I am quite busy with my preparations for the ascension."

"There is one thing," said the prince. "I am reliably informed that Duke Sárkány has crossed the border and is riding toward Argentium."

The Witch-king said, "Ah. Finally. Does he ride alone?"

"He does not, Majesty. He has a hundred knights with him."

"Knights belonging to which country?"

"To no country populated by the living," said the Prince of Games. "He rides with an army of his own kind. Vampires of the oldest clans. They will be here within a week."

"That is excellent news," said the king, who felt a real thrill of excitement in his chest. "Nespar did not believe that Sárkány would come in on this."

A familiar slyness crept onto the prince's mouth. "I may have enticed him."

"With what?" asked the king sharply.

"I told him that Lady Maralina had taken Kagen's side."

The king nodded slowly, smiling behind his veil. "Yes . . . that was well done. And it goes a long way into repairing the damage you've done, my friend."

The Prince of Games bowed again. "To serve you well and help bring the Yellow Empire into being is my greatest wish," he said.

The bitch hound eased her tension a little and lay down instead of sitting up and alert.

"Is there anything else I can do for you, sire?" asked the prince.

"No. You may go," ordered the king. Then he added, "Tell Nespar I will be in the grand hall in an hour. Until then, no one is to disturb me."

The prince bowed once more and left.

CHAPTER TWENTY-ONE

It was a very old crow that saved Kagen Vale's life.

Kagen was half dozing in the saddle, nodding beneath a relentless sun that persisted in its indifference to the time of year. Flies buzzed around him and, as the miles passed, their droning became a kind of lullaby, soft and soothing in its way. Jinx clopped along the road that led from the southeast turnpike that slanted down through Vahlycor to the place where that country touched borders with eastern Theria, northeastern Argon, and western Zaare. The road was long and he was saddle weary, and so he drifted.

He had been vaguely aware that the crows that seemed to wait for him on tree limbs and farm fences were familiar. One in particular was a disreputable-looking example of the species—ancient, with a scarred beak, and threadbare feathers. Kagen could not be certain but he believed it was the same crow who showed up whenever there was danger, and who led the armies of nightbirds into battle on his behalf. As his mind slowed toward sleep, the bird flapped lazily through his thoughts, and for some reason it reminded him of the Tower of Sarsis and the sad, beautiful lady who lived therein.

When the crow cawed, his fading mind added that to the fabric of his dream.

When the crow screamed a second time, Kagen roused himself, becoming aware that it was not a dream sound at all.

He looked around and then ducked as the crow launched itself from a gatepost and flew straight at his head. Kagen lost his balance and fell from the saddle, landing hard as he heard Jinx suddenly scream in pain.

Then the world crystalized around him and he became aware of several things all happening at once. He saw Jinx staggering sideways, an arrow standing out from one of the saddlebags, and blood running fast down the horse's thigh. He saw the crow rise into the air and wheel before diving, this time at a figure who had sprung up from behind a shrub, bow in one hand and the other reaching for a fresh arrow. He saw three other men rushing out from behind stacked bales of hay, glittering blades in their hands.

Kagen threw himself across the narrow road, tucked into a tight roll, and came up in a fighter's crouch, his matched daggers in his hands. He was acutely aware that the blades were not seasoned with *eitr,* and in his mind he wondered if that error was going to be the one that killed him.

The archer fired a second arrow and Kagen twisted to one side, whipping a blade over and down, chopping the shaft in two. Then the first of the other men was on him, swinging a sword at his head. They were dressed like yeomen, but the weapons were military. Ravens, Hakkian regulars, or mercenaries. They had to be—no one else would dare to carry a long blade.

The swordsman was fast, trying to end this while Kagen was still off-balance. But Kagen had been taught by a master of the art of close combat—his mother, the Poison Rose. He ducked and lunged into the rush, checking the man's mass with a shoulder to the solar plexus while thrusting his right-hand dagger low and forward. The wickedly sharp blade sliced through trousers and groin, and he danced away to his left before the swordsman could even utter his scream. And what a scream it was—a rising, keening wail of torment and horrified awareness.

The second killer thrust at him with a spear, but he was aiming at a moving, turning target. Kagen took the shaft of the spear on the left shoulder and spun inward along its length, moving very fast. In less than a full turn he was chest to chest with the man, checking the man's handling of the spear because the turn had pinned the spearman's own arm against his stomach. Kagen headbutted him, using his forehead to smash the man's nose and, as the fellow staggered back in a spray of blood, Kagen whipped him across the throat with the tip of his left knife.

An arrow slashed past him close enough to open a burning cut on Kagen's cheek. He spun and used the force of his turn to put real power and speed into a snap of his arm. His right dagger appeared as if by magic in the man's belly, dropping him.

That left the fourth man. He was more cautious than his comrades and held a pair of fighting hatchets in meaty hands. Big, rough, swarthy, with important teeth missing from his killer's grin.

Kagen moved in a circle, drawing it out long enough for him to verify that there were no others lurking in wait. The man with the broken nose had lost his spear and was pawing blood from his eyes. The one with the slashed groin was on the ground, cupping his crotch, crying out for his mother. And the archer was dead.

It was just him and the hatchet man.

"I will cut your balls off and make you eat them," said the fourth man, his voice heavily accented. A foreign accent. Ashghulan, Kagen guessed. Which meant that he was a mercenary from east of the Cathedral Mountains. A Hakkian lackey.

He did not bother replying to the threat. Banter was not his style, that being more Tuke's game. Particularly the comment about balls.

Instead Kagen hooked the toe of his boot under the fallen spear and kicked it at the man's face. The mercenary laughed and chopped it down with one hatchet. Which was a mistake.

As the man did that, Kagen leapt into the air, twisted and slashed the Ashghulanian from above his right eyebrow, through his nose, and down to the right side of his chin. As he landed, Kagen spun again, this time very low, like a dancer doing a crouching turn; and as he completed the rotation he cut again, this time severing the tendon in the back of the mercenary's knee.

The man cried out and fell. Kagen rose and stamped his heel down on the back of the man's neck. Once, twice, and on the third stamp he heard the brittle crack of vertebral bones.

He looked around, saw that the man with the broken nose had

drawn a short, curved sword. Kagen once again hooked a toe under the spear, kicked it to chest level, caught it with his left hand, pivoted, and threw it. The spear's steel point bit deep into the killer's chest.

That left only the man with the slashed groin.

Kagen walked over to him, kicking his fallen weapon away. Then he squatted down, took a handful of greasy black hair, jerked the screaming man's head back, and looked into terrified eyes.

"How many more?" he asked.

The man did not want to answer. Kagen could see him trying to figure out the best lie that might spare his life. It exhausted Kagen, and so he just cut his throat.

He recovered his other blade and jogged fifty yards up the road, looking behind trees and shrubs. He saw four horses tethered in the shadows of a copse of pines, nodded, and returned to Jinx.

The arrow had lodged in the saddlebag and an inch of the point had pierced the horse's flanks. Kagen removed it and used strips of the dead men's cloaks to bandage and bind the wound. Then something occurred to him and he tore open the saddlebag to see what damage was done.

And his heart sank.

The small crystal bottle of *eitr* lay in shards, the poison seeping into a bag of dried beans. For a wild moment he was afraid that the god-killer had infected Jinx, but the animal—though in pain and jittery—was fine.

Even so, the loss of that poison was a powerful blow.

The bottle had been given to him by Maralina and no matter how often he used it, the quantity always restored itself. Now that enchanted bottle was destroyed.

Being very careful, and cursing under his breath as he worked, he tilted the leather saddlebag and poured what was left into the scabbards of his two daggers.

"Gods damn it," he said, dumping the rest of the contents

out. It was too dangerous to keep the bag now, and the slightest scratch from the broken crystal would kill him.

He glanced at the old crow, who now perched on the fence.

"Thanks, my friend," he said.

The crow answered with a caw so soft that it was barely a sound.

Furious and frustrated, he fetched the other four horses, transferred Jinx's saddle to the freshest-looking one, tied the other three to Jinx, and rode off with the horses behind.

Thereafter he did not allow himself the luxury of dozing as he rode.

CHAPTER TWENTY-TWO

Captain Beké of the Therian ship, *Odakon*, waited as the castaway was ushered up the side by his sailors. They had spotted her standing alone on the beach of a small island and Beké sent a boat to rescue her.

"Thank you," said the castaway. She was young, with Argonian features, and dressed all in black.

"What is your name?"

"Ryssa," said the castaway.

Beké waited for more, got none, and asked, "Were you shipwrecked with the Hakkians?"

"With them? No," said Ryssa with some bitterness in her tone. "I came here on a ship from Tull Yammoth."

"They left you there?" asked the captain.

"By my choice," said Ryssa, "for they were not going back to the mainland, which is where I desire to go."

"And the Hakkians?"

Ryssa merely shrugged.

The captain studied her for a few moments. "What is your business on the mainland?"

"A war is coming," she said.

"What if it is? You are a child."

"I'm sixteen."

Beké smiled. "My youngest daughter is older than you. And it's clear you're no fighter. You don't even carry a blade or a bow."

"I am able to protect myself."

"Say you so?" laughed the captain. But then Ryssa gave him such a cold, strange, dangerous look that it made Beké take a half step back. He sketched a warding sign in the air.

"Who *are* you?" he breathed.

She did not answer, but instead looked away into the heart of the vast ocean.

Captain Beké signaled to two sailors to stand watch over her as he vanished below. He returned in a few moments.

"There is someone below who wishes to speak with you," he said. "Come with me."

He led her aft to what would normally have been his own luxurious cabin in the ship's stern but was clearly reserved for some special guest. Two soldiers in richly appointed armor barred their way with scowling faces and drawn swords laid across their chests. The guards looked at her and then at Beké, who nodded. They lowered their swords and stepped aside.

"Now, ma'am," said Beké, "you mind your manners and do not speak unless spoken to, do you hear?"

"Yes," said Ryssa. And when the door was opened, she walked inside.

The cabin was gorgeously appointed, with a writing table to one side and a longer dining table across from it. Between these, with huge gallery windows showing a great expanse of the bright blue sea, was a chair. But the Widow saw at once that it was no ordinary chair, but a kind of throne of the kind called a "traveling siege" in old books.

The woman who sat upon the chair was slender and beautiful,

but also cold and aloof. She wore a sleeveless gown of sea green silk set with pearls. Her skin was the rich brown of polished walnut, and her black hair hung in bejeweled braids down to her shoulders. Four muscular guards were positioned in the corners of the great cabin, their dark eyes locked on the guest.

Ryssa curtsied low but did not drop her eyes with either deference or modesty. Instead, she met this highborn Therian's gaze with her own.

"Do you know who I am?" asked the woman on the throne.

"No, my lady," said the Widow. "I do not."

"I am Theka, queen of Theria."

The words hung in the air, and it was clear the woman and the guards were waiting for some kind of reaction.

Ryssa curtsied again, a bit more formally this time. "I am honored, Majesty," she said. Her tone, though, was leaden and the words nearly without inflection. She glanced past the queen at the empty sea visible through the stern windows.

The queen—though only a few years older than Ryssa—wore a knowing smile. "If you're looking for the rest of my fleet, girl, we are quite alone out here. This is not my official state ship, nor even the flagship of my fleet."

"You are traveling incognito?" suggested Ryssa.

"Clearly."

The truth was that Theka *had* been with a small but powerful squadron of ships on a visit to various Therian holdings down in the Dragon Islands—the pearl beds of Tull Quinta and the emerald mines on Tull Restovel. All of that was a cover because her real purpose was to take a long voyage in order to reach her true destination on the return voyage. King al-Huk had invited her to a special private meeting of several monarchs of the former empire. The main part of the squadron would continue their tour of the islands, with one of Theka's stand-ins waving convincingly from the larger, grander flagship. However, after *Odakon* left the others and set to sea, a series of unexpected and intense squalls delayed them, compelling Captain Beké to seek shelter in a protected cove of an uninhabited island. Once there, the squalls dwindled. The *Odakon* was about to set sail and resume the covert mission when a lookout spotted Ryssa standing alone and apparently helpless on the beach.

"My captain tells me your name is Ryssa," said the queen. "What is your family name?"

"I have no surname or title, Majesty."

"An orphan without patronage," remarked the queen.

"As you say."

"How came you to be stranded on that island?"

"It is where the last ship left me."

"Intentionally left?"

"Yes."

"Why?"

"They did not feel it necessary to tell me, Majesty."

"Did they molest you?"

"They did not," said Ryssa.

Theka studied her. "Ryssa," she mused. "I have heard that name spoken. But always in conjunction with another name. A title. The Widow."

Ryssa just looked at the queen.

"The stories I have heard are strange," continued Theka, but then she smiled. "Of course, much is strange in these times."

"Yes, it is, Majesty."

"Are you this *Widow* spoken of in stories?"

Ryssa's smile was faint and sad. "I am sometimes called the Widow."

"Why are you called that?" asked the queen. "You're barely of marriageable age."

"And yet I am a widow."

"The widow of . . . ?"

"Her name was Miri, Majesty, and she died," said Ryssa. "My heart died, too."

Queen Theka began to speak, stopped, considered. Then she said, "You're a girl. And girls are prone to drama. All loves are the greatest loves, all losses tear the fabric of the world asunder." She held up a hand. "No, I do not mock you. I will admit that I did not believe the stories I heard. They are fantastical and easy to dismiss."

Ryssa said nothing.

"But there is nothing immature or prankish about you," said the queen. "A blind man could see that much."

"I don't know what stories have been told about me," said Ryssa. "Moreover, Majesty, I don't care. If my presence aboard your ship is in any way upsetting to you, I make no apology, for it is not of my doing. If you wish it, I can be dropped off at any port or beach."

Theka raised an eyebrow. "*Any* port or beach? Even Hakkia . . . for I perceive you are Argonian."

"It doesn't matter where you drop me, Majesty."

"Does it not?"

The Widow stared at her for a long, unblinking time. "No, Majesty, it does not."

"Confidence like this in a young woman in *these* times is unusual," said Theka. "Or is it the fatalism of the victim I hear? Pray, tell me what makes you so—"

She never finished her question because a lookout's cry cut right through.

"*Deck there! Sail ho!*"

The captain's voice bellowed back. "Where away?"

"Two points off the larboard beam," came the reply. "It's hull up. A sloop-of-war under Hakkian colors."

And then the air was filled with the sound of drums and the slap-slap of running feet.

Queen Theka did not rise immediately but instead gave Ryssa a reappraising look. "I wonder," she said, "if they are coming for me or for you."

The Widow stood there, enduring the scrutiny, and said nothing.

CHAPTER TWENTY-THREE

The creature stood looking at the burning fort.

The stout gates were splintered wrecks. Bodies lay everywhere, each of them still gripping the swords and spears that had not saved them. Vultures circled patiently while crows—always bolder—were already plucking at the tenderest bits of the corpses.

One old crow stood on a hitching post and looked at the monster who had attacked the fort. It turned to look at him.

The crow cawed softly. A subtle note of approval for the slaughter of the Hakkian soldiers.

The razor-knight nodded its head but said nothing.

Instead, it turned and continued its long march from Vespia to the palace in Argon.

CHAPTER TWENTY-FOUR

"Attend to your lessons," snapped Madame Lucibel, her tone slicing neatly through the children's whispered conversations.

They looked up to see a figure that inspired both loathing and dread. Lucibel was a thickset woman with heavy, muscular arms, legs like tree stumps, an enormous bosom from which no kindly warmth could ever be kindled, and a smile that would frighten an alligator. She had her fists jammed indignantly against her hips, and through the ribbon of her frilly apron was a short yard-long whip with a leather-wrapped handle.

In a move that had become familiar to them, she opened her

right hand like the petals of a dark flower and let the pads of her fingers trail slowly across her waist until they encountered the leather handle.

"Or do you require a kind touch . . . ?"

She called her whip the "wand of kindness," and Madame Lucibel had long since established with no trace of uncertainty that she knew where to hit and how to hit to coax different kinds of screams from them. And it was a science that both children knew she enjoyed exploring—the way a flick across the right part of the back of their thighs or the soles of their feet was uniquely and horribly different. Those, and dozens of other places, each teased and punished just so. She rarely drew blood and never left a mark that would not heal completely. She was an artist and loved her work.

The twins, Gavran and Foscor, were supposed to be writing out the names of the lineage of Witch-kings going back two thousand years. Many names, with few commonalities to inspire memory. Errors were costly. Already they had been made to stand barefoot in buckets of ice water or kneel for an hour on grains of uncooked rice, and it was not even noon yet.

As summer turned to autumn and autumn began finally to yield to winter, the lessons had become more difficult, the pauses for *kindness* more frequent, and the punishments more precise.

"I asked a question," said Lucibel in her sickly sweet singsong voice. She curled her fingers around the whip handle. "Or does my question require punctuation?"

"No, Madame," said Gavran contritely.

"No, Madame," said Foscor, looking down at his folded hands.

Madame Lucibel stood her ground, her bulk seeming to oppress and abuse the marble floor. What warmth there had been in the twins' study room had faded, as if the governess brought a chill with her.

"Then be about your work," she said. "You know what will

happen if I come back in here and find that you have been gossiping instead of learning your history as your father—bless his name to Hastur—requires."

"We will," said the twins.

She turned to go, but it was her habit to let her body turn but not her head—not immediately, for she was ever watchful of a sneaky smile, a mocking expression, or a rude gesture. Satisfied, Lucibel turned and lumbered out of the room.

The children lowered their heads, dipped their quills into the inkwell, and began to write. Or at least they pretended to do that, aware that the governess was likely watching through a peephole.

"Do you think she knows?" asked Gavran in a tiny whisper.

"No," Foscor assured him. "She thinks we're still Gavran and Foscor. If she knew, she would tell on us."

"And beat us."

Foscor nodded. "Better a beating than *him* knowing."

They cut very quick glances at one another.

They began writing, careful—so very careful—to make sure the penmanship matched the less elegant script of the imperial twins. Careful that there was nothing to reveal the truth that there was not even the slightest hint that those two scratching quills were in the hands of Alleyn and Desalyn.

They were very, very careful about that.

CHAPTER TWENTY-FIVE

Everyone bowed low as the Witch-king left the grand hall. His feet made no sound on the marble floors, and there was but a faint whisper as his yellow robes swirled around him. Behind him, the hound followed, her nails click-clicking. Two guards trailed along behind, each of them a decorated warrior whose loyalty was beyond question.

The strange procession approached an ironwood door guarded

by more soldiers, who snapped immediately to attention. The King in Yellow produced a peculiar-looking key, fitted it into a complex lock, opened the door, and stepped through.

The yellow king climbed a long winding staircase to a landing with another door, though this had a bronze façade in which were protection symbols in a dozen languages. Words of power were written there, and not even a cockroach or fly would crawl on its surface. The Witch-king unlocked this and stepped inside. Untouched and unbidden, the door shut and locked itself behind him. His hound went over to a wicker bed near the fireplace, climbed onto the wool blankets, and went to sleep.

The room was his private place, and dark potential seemed to writhe unseen in the air. Even the motes of dust disturbed by his entrance swirled and formed unsavory patterns before finally settling back onto the furniture and floors.

The chamber was very large and crowded with tall bookcases that reached all the way to the lofty ceiling. There were fat volumes bound in reptile skin and human flesh. There were ancient tomes with titles written in gold leaf and some with no title at all. Some shelves were crammed with the rarest codices and scrolls, while others were stacked with clay tablets.

Bizarre and improbable creatures hung from the rafters, each carefully preserved by taxidermists used to working with unsavory specimens. Dragons, a dwarf rhinoceros with a single eye, a mermaid with the body of a goddess and the wicked face of a hagfish, the skeleton of a wyvern, and gigantic snakes that, though long dead, seemed to wriggle and twist. Below them were rows of glass tanks filled with triple-distilled spirits of wine in which floated creatures that had no name in any modern human tongue.

There were many tables on which were tools and devices of the alchemist's trade—flasks and vials, retorts and ampules, beakers and tubes. There were very many jars and pots of chemicals in liquid, gel, powder, and paste states, while nearby were stills to condense liquids, and burners on which tiny cauldrons bubbled and smoked.

And in one corner, set in the precise center of a circle of protection, was a block of ice ten feet tall and four feet per side. It radiated a bitter cold and yet, despite the heat of that strange autumn, did not melt. The sides were mostly opaque but as the Witch-king came and stood before it, they seemed to clear. Soon they were as transparent as glass.

Inside the ice was a shape. Man size and man shaped. Silent and immobile. His pale skin was barely visible, showing the shape of his face, the musculature of his limbs, and a slender scar over his heart as if he had long ago been pierced by a thin and delicate blade.

The Witch-king raised his hands and removed his yellow lace veil. He folded it very neatly and placed it on a nearby table. Then he stood looking at the face of the man trapped inside the ice.

He looked and looked.

He smiled and smiled.

And never said a word.

CHAPTER TWENTY-SIX

Greel spoke for a good while and the king of Samud listened with no interruption.

A chair had been brought in and Greel invited to sit during his presentation. When Greel was done and had drunk two more cups of cool water, he waited patiently for a reply. Al-Huk sat brooding on the diplomat's words, idly toying with a golden pendant fashioned to look like an arrow.

"The Witch-king is a usurper," concluded Greel. "He is not the legal ruler of anything beyond the borders of Hakkia. He has not been crowned as emperor."

"True, though his coronation was approved by all of the sub-monarchs, myself included," said al-Huk. "The ceremony was interrupted by an attempted assassination."

"While that is true, it is important to remember that the coronation process includes an opportunity for someone holding a legitimate objection to forward it. That was, in fact, done. Captain Vale objected on the grounds that the entire coronation was illegal because there is another and more verifiable legitimate claim of succession."

"You mean those children," said the king sourly.

"I do."

"That claim was refuted by those very children."

"And they are minors, Majesty, and although their claim is legitimate as the surviving children of the empress, they cannot prosecute this claim themselves. Not until they are fifteen. Kagen Vale, as captain of the palace guard and bound by oath to the protection of the Seedlings, was within legal rights to make a claim on their behalf."

"That does not change the fact that the Witch-king claimed them as his own children, and that the children refuted Kagen's words. They spat in his face, in point of fact."

Greel spread his hands. "Majesty, those children suffered tremendous trauma seeing their mother and siblings butchered. And they are prisoners of the most powerful wizard alive. Is it not reasonable to assume that they are under the Witch-king's sorcerous control?"

"Reasonable, perhaps, but difficult to prove."

"There were people in that hall that night who knew those children, Majesty," said Greel. "I was one of them. Mother Frey was another. There were nobles in the audience—Lord Gowry and Lord Clementius, among others—who also knew Alleyn and Desalyn."

"And where are these others? Mother Frey sits in the center of her web, spinning far-fetched stories and running her network of spies. As for the Argonian nobles in attendance, they participated in the rebellion and are now outlaws wanted by the state."

Greel shook his head. "Majesty, we both know that they are not wanted by any official state. They are not in rebellion against a lawful ruler but have chosen to oppose a false king's claim on both the imperial throne and the throne of Argon. They are patriots, Highness, not insurrectionists."

"That does not change the situation," said al-Huk. "The children refuted Kagen's claim. That calls any claim to legitimacy through bloodline into question."

"A claim that could be settled one way or the other by interviewing those children."

The king looked amused. "Do you see that ever being approved by the Witch-king?"

"Alas, Majesty, I do not," said Greel.

The king grunted and looked at the air above Greel's head for nearly half a minute.

"Tell me, Lord Greel," he said at length, "have you heard the rumors about the identity of the Witch-king? That he is actually Gardener Herepath Vale?"

"I am aware of several rumors," he replied.

"What is your opinion?"

"I know that Kagen himself believes it," said Greel. "He claims to have seen his brother's face that night in the palace."

"Indeed. What sense can you make of that?"

"The Witch-king is a sorcerer," said Greel. "It is my understanding that a glamour is a simple spell that would offer no challenge to someone of the Witch-king's abilities."

King al-Huk nodded but did not comment on that. Instead he said, "You want to talk of rebellion. That is a discussion best had in rather more privacy. As it happens, Lord Greel, your timing is propitious. Come with me."

With that he rose and bade Greel follow him. Prince el-Kep hurried to join his father. The guards fell into formation in front and behind as they left the hall and walked through a series of corridors that led to a heavy iron door set in the stone walls. One guard opened the door, but then the soldiers took up stations outside once the king and the diplomat entered.

Greel saw that there were several people in what turned out to be a well-appointed chamber. The Therian jerked to a halt when he saw who those people were. Each person was well-known throughout the empire. Each was a powerful player in the catastrophic drama that had rocked the west since the invasion.

He saw the tall, cold-eyed Queen Weska of Behlia on a divan, and seated near to her was Ifduril, the crown prince of Ghenrey. On the other side of the room, paused in a half turn away from the window was the wiry King Thespo of Sunderland, once known as the Pirate Prince. The battle-scarred King Horogillin of Nelfydia was at a table with Prince Regent Mondas Huvan of Zaare. And in a corner, holding a dusty old book, was Vulpion the Gray, king of Zehria.

"I believe," said al-Huk, still wearing that sly smile, "you know most of my brother and sister rulers. I know they know you."

CHAPTER TWENTY-SEVEN

"You are a fool," said Gavran, "and I will have my father skin you alive."

The boy was six. He was slim and tall for his age, but only a child. His voice was young and the threat sounded like it belonged to some kind of game. A child pretending to be someone of importance.

And yet the soldier paused, his words faltering. "I . . . I am sorry, young master," he stammered. "I m-meant no disrespect."

"Then apologize to my sister," demanded the boy.

The guard turned to a girl of the same age. She was much like the boy, and they were still young enough for fraternal twins to look identical. The same rounded face, the same length of dark curling hair, the same haughty posture and arrogant sneer.

"Apologize . . . my lord?" asked the guard, confused. "How have I offended Lady Foscor?"

"You offend me by existing," said the girl. "Now, on your knees."

The guard, who in truth had done nothing offensive, had been stationed outside of a door that led to a suite of rooms set aside for the Witch-king's personal use—a sitting room, a library, and a kind of museum where unusual artifacts were kept. The children had demanded entry and the guard had explained that no one was allowed to enter that suite.

"My lady," he protested, "I was ordered to guard this door and admit no one, not even the lord chamberlain or the Prince of Games."

"Do we look like either of them?" demanded Foscor, her words dripping with acid. "Am I a wizened old man? Is my brother a mere courtier?"

"I . . . I apologize, my lady," cried the guard. "His Royal Highness charged me personally with this task, and it is more than my life is worth to betray his trust."

Gavran took a step closer and the guard recoiled as much as he could while on his knees.

"Do you know who we are?"

"Yes, my lord."

"Who are we, then?"

"You are the royal twins. You are the son and daughter of his Highness the Witch-king of Hakkia."

The girl stood next to her brother. "And did our father say that we—we—were to be barred from entering his rooms?"

"I—"

"Be careful, fool," snapped Gavran, laying his small hand on the hilt of a dirk that hung from his belt. "Be very careful how you answer."

"My lord," whispered the guard, nearly in tears, "my lady . . . I am forbidden to allow *anyone* to enter. The Witch-king, who is my sacred liege, said that no one may enter. His orders were clear and he made no exceptions."

Quick as cats both children drew their dirks and touched the tips to his face, his below the man's left eye and hers below his right. The needle points pricked the guard's flesh and two beads of red trickled down his face.

"Look," said Foscor. "He's weeping."

"What a baby," said Gavran.

And they began laughing as they withdrew their blades.

"Silly baby crying red tears," they said, singing it over and over.

Then, without a further word, they turned and walked away, leaving the guard to slump against the locked door.

He rested there for a moment, panting as if he had climbed a mountain or outrun a jungle cat. Then, he got heavily to his feet, still trembling inside his leather and steel armor. The man pawed the blood from his cheeks, looked at the red smears. His fear was still with him and he hated himself for having been cowed by those two little brats.

Yet he would also never speak of what happened. Not to his sergeant or captain, and not even to his closest friends.

He plucked a sweat rag from inside his cuirass, spat on it, then used it to wipe his face and hands. His hands shook and it took him longer than it should have to remove all signs of red.

Then he took his station once more, eating his anger and shame in the quiet solitude of that lonely hallway.

Gavran and Foscor peered at him from around the far corner of that stone hallway. Then they hurried to a closet in which brooms and other cleaning items were stored. They entered and closed the door behind them and were plunged into utter darkness.

Foscor felt along the rear wall, low near the floor, until she found the one brick that protruded ever so slightly from the others. She pressed the lower left corner and there was a faint *click*. Part of the closet wall shifted inward on silent hinges and they went through, closing the secret door behind them.

There was a candle burning—one they had lit before going to confront the guard. In its glow they looked at each other, both still wearing their evil scowls. But those expressions melted away within a single heartbeat, replaced by faces unmarked by spite.

"Did you see?" asked the boy. "He was so scared."

"I know," said the girl. "I felt bad for him."

The boy nodded. "He's a Hakkian, though."

"But he's not one of the bad ones," countered the girl.

"No, Desalyn, they're *all* bad," insisted Alleyn. "We can't trust any of them. We can't *like* any of them, either."

Desalyn walked over to a little bench near the wall sconce in which the candle burned. She sat and hugged her arms to herself.

"I hate having to play that . . . that . . ."

"I know," said Alleyn. "I hate being Gavran, too. But we have to. When we're around anyone else, we *have* to. Or they'll know."

Desalyn looked both alarmed and sad. "They'll kill us if they know."

"No," said Alleyn. "They won't kill us."

"They'll do worse, then," said the girl. "They'll do something to make us into Foscor and Gavran again. For real and for always, maybe."

He sat on the bench next to her and took her hand.

"We won't let them," he said. "We'll be careful and they won't know."

They held hands and sat in the badly lit secret passage, and in that hidden place, they wept.

CHAPTER TWENTY-EIGHT

Alleyn and Desalyn spent a lot of time in the palace walls.

Before the Hakkians had come, their older siblings had taken them on adventures through hidden doors, up and down secret stairs, along passages the Hakkians did not know about.

Once, even Captain Kagen had taken all of them through what he called the *unseen ways,* instructing them on how and where to hide if something bad ever happened. It was a secret that only Kagen and his own siblings shared with the imperial Seedlings. There were places where Kagen's sister, Lady Zora, had come to write poetry—and there were dozens of her notebooks filled with verse.

Their other sister, Belissa, had used colored chalk to draw strange pictures on the walls—mostly of dragons. Each of these impossible mythical monsters was different and each was given a name. There was one that looked like a gigantic pink snake, with one set of arms ending in claws and very long, narrow wings. Belissa had named this one Vorth the Worm of Nightmares. Another was black and bulky, with eyes filled with flame and two sets of muscular legs ending in feet with monstrous claws, and Belissa had named him Scriosta the Destroyer. That was Alleyn's favorite. Desalyn preferred Uktena the Horned Terror, who had a massive head crowned with pointy horns of all colors and lengths. And then there was grim Yamraaj, the splendorous Winged God of the Underworld, who was dark blue and whose scales were set with colored stones.

A fifth dragon, ten times bigger than all the others combined, was drawn in silhouette only, and his wings stretched all the way down one of the hidden passages from end to end. The name Vathnya was written, but no other description was provided.

Alleyn and Desalyn loved those drawings and, in the days of living the false public lives of Gavran and Foscor, they often came and sat near the wall of dragons. The fantasy monsters—not at all real, they knew—provided comfort for them.

CHAPTER TWENTY-NINE

Queen Theka and the Widow stood together on the deck. The sailors had swarmed up into the rigging to trim the sails, and there was frantic activity everywhere as the crew ran to their action stations.

Captain Beké hurried over. "Majesty, it's not safe up here."

"Tell me what is happening, captain," ordered Theka.

He nodded, casting nervous looks at the enemy ship. "They're flying the Hakkian flag, but see that smaller dark gray flag just above it? That's a privateer's flag. The sloop is ship-rigged in the way the pirates do who sail out of one of those northern islands. If I'm right, Majesty, they'll be crammed full of fighters."

"Can we get away?" asked the queen.

"Not on this tack, Majesty, no. They have the weather gauge—meaning the wind is behind them, fine on their quarter. It pushes them toward us and allows their captain to decide where and when to engage. We're on a tack because we're heading to windward. We can't sail past them. Our only options are to stand and fight or wear ship, pack on all the canvas she'll bear, and try to lose them in the islands."

"If you did that, can we outrun them?"

Beké looked dubious. "We can try, but ours has a broader beam. Even with this wind I doubt we can make much above nine knots. Ten if we want to risk some sails carrying away. My guess is they're doing eleven or twelve knots. We can't outrun them but with any luck at all we can reach the northernmost of the Dragon Islands and perhaps lose them there."

"What are our odds if they catch us?"

The captain tried not to let his feelings show on his face, but the doubt was there.

"They're faster and almost certainly have twice as many men aboard, Majesty, though we do have your retinue of soldiers. That will help. And, if they catch us, I'll have my best archers in the tops and along the rail. Depending on how the wind lies *when* they come alongside, we could risk fire arrows. If they try to board us, we'll do our best to set her sails ablaze."

"And if they *do* board us?"

The captain looked away. "I, ah . . . won't lie, Majesty, but that would be bad for all concerned."

"What about those clouds?" asked Ryssa, and the captain frowned at her, unsure as to whether it was proper for her to speak and him to answer. However, Theka gave him a nod.

"There's another storm brewing in the southwest. If we're lucky—and if Father Dagon gives his blessing—that storm might hit around the time the Hakkians catch us. I like our odds out-sailing *any* other ship in a blow. The *Odakon* is a fine sea boat—dry and weatherly." He looked straight into Queen Theka's eyes. "My family has served the crown for more than three hundred years. I swear on my soul and the souls of my children that if there is anything we can do, then I will see it done."

The queen touched the tentacle tattoo on his cheek. "You have my trust, captain. I will pray to Father Dagon and Mother Hydra for protection."

He bowed to her and, almost as an afterthought, to Ryssa, then turned and hurried away.

When the two women looked at the approaching ship it seemed far too close, as if in the few seconds of conversation it had leapt forward. Now Ryssa could see that the deck was packed with men, all of them armed with throwing spears and bows.

"They are going to catch us," she said.

Queen Theka shook her head. "Captain Beké is a wise old sea dog."

"They will catch and board us," said the Widow.

And in less than three hours, that is exactly what the privateers did.

During the chase, Theka had changed from her traveling clothes into Therian war armor. Elegant but practical. She also strapped on a sword belt, adjusting it the way a seasoned fighter would.

"What about you, Ryssa of Argon?" asked the queen as she loosened her sword in its scabbard. "Perhaps you should hide in the cable tier. I can give you one man as guard, but the rest will need to be on deck."

Ryssa shook her head. "I will not hide. I would prefer to be on deck as well."

"Can you shoot a bow?"

"No. If I may have a knife, though . . ."

Theka snapped her fingers. A servant took several knives from a chest and offered them to Ryssa. She chose one with a plain wooden handle and simple steel crosspiece. No jewels, no fancy filigree. Ryssa drew the blade and studied its edge, nodded, slid it back into the sheath, and thrust it through her belt.

The queen waved her servants away and when they were alone, she stepped close and spoke quietly. Not queen to peasant, but woman to woman.

"If they capture me, girl, they won't hurt me. I am too valuable as a hostage, and even pirates will know that. I do not think that it is mere chance that they are chasing us. But you, Ryssa, you know what they will do to you. I tell you now, that if it looks like we are losing, take that knife and plunge it into your own heart. A moment's courage will save you from unbearable torment. Do you understand me?"

"I do," said Ryssa. "They will not take me alive."

Theka placed her palm against Ryssa's cheek as she had with the captain's. "I am a queen and a warrior, but apart from all of that I am a woman, and this world both hates and fears women. Greater strength is used as a weapon against us, to teach us our place, to allow weak-minded men to pretend superiority. Were I not the ruler of Theria, I would also fall on my sword."

"Men should fear women," said Ryssa, but she said it softly as if talking to herself.

Through the decks she could hear sailors yelling in anger and barely controlled panic.

"They are here," said the queen. "May Dagon bless and keep you."

Ryssa did not respond. As they both turned toward the door, Ryssa mouthed a small prayer to her own god. It was a soundless prayer because she knew how people tended to react when she said that name. And, in truth, it was more the Widow who prayed and not the orphan girl from Argon. The difference was monumental.

CHAPTER THIRTY

"Your Majesties," said Hannibus Greel, bowing low, mindful of his manners despite his astonishment. "I am pleased to see that you are well and I am humbled to be in your presence."

That earned him a few nods, but mostly the monarchs stood or sat in silence.

Into the silence, al-Huk said, "The Honorable Hannibus Greel of Theria has come to my court to talk of rebellion and to share news of the world."

"I hope it's good news," snorted Crown Prince Ifduril of Ghenrey. "I've had about all of the doom and gloom that I can stomach."

Queen Weska of Behlia peered at Greel. "I remember you. That old witch Frey sent you to see me after the coronation."

"Coronation *attempt*," corrected Thespo, King of Sunderland, most southern of the nations formerly belonging to the Silver Empire. "He visited me as well. Clearly he is making the rounds."

Prince el-Kep walked over to a sideboard and poured two glasses of wine. He handed one to his father and the other to Greel, then went and sat quietly in a corner, silent but attentive.

"Greel," said al-Huk, "tell my cousins what you told me."

Greel accepted the wine with a bow, took a small sip to lubricate a throat gone dry, and launched into his comments about the overall political situation, the legal status of the Witch-king's claim on the throne, the royal twins, Kagen Vale and the army he was building. As he spoke, he watched the faces of the royals. At the outset they mostly wore expressions of elaborate indifference, hauteur, or skepticism; by the time he finished they were all focused like a pack of hawks. Greel finished and drained the rest of his wine.

"By the harrow of Father Ar and the scythe of Mother Sah," said the Zaarean prince regent, Mondas Huvan. He looked around at his peers. "Can this be true about the imperial twins?"

"It is a lot to swallow," murmured King Horogillin of Nelfydia. His scarred face was pinched with doubt.

"What if it's *all* true?" wondered Ifduril. "What then?"

"Then it's war," said Horogillin. "What else can it be?"

"Says the king of the largest nation with the smallest population," said Weska.

"Second largest," Huvan said quietly. "Vahlycor is bigger."

No one took notice of his remark.

King al-Huk leaned his buttocks against the sideboard and rolled his cup slowly back and forth between his palms. "Horogillin isn't wrong, though. But let's not get ahead of ourselves. If Herepath Vale is the Witch-king and those twins are his children, then he *has* a claim. If they are the legitimate children of the empress, that claim is solid no matter who the father is. The imperial consort was a nobody. A pretty face. Yes, there is a wrinkle if the empress engaged in criminal conversation with Herepath, but what of it? That still leaves a claim on the throne stronger than anything a natural-born Hakkian can make."

"*If* Herepath is the father of the twins, then he has certainly taken the wrong route to prosecute his claim for the throne," said Thespo. "Besides, at best, his own role would be that of steward until the children come of age."

"That is not entirely correct," countered Weska. "There are very old laws on the books—written into law but never used—that allow for a violent takeover of the nation if the empress is proven to be corrupt and if there is a competing claim for the throne. If Herepath was Gessalyn's lover and she sent him away to die while claiming his bastard children were sired by her consort, then there are several laws broken right there."

"Except that Herepath did not make a claim under his own name," said Thespo. "I read that in the old laws, too."

It was clear to Greel that all of them had taken time to either read the long, densely written charter of the Silver Empire, or at very least had it cogently summarized for them. He found that particularly interesting, and it likely explained why they were here, meeting in obvious secrecy.

"If I may ask, Your Majesties," he said, taking a great risk, "is it your desire and intention to resurrect the Silver Empire?"

The royals exchanged looks. When it was clear no one else was willing to be first in response, al-Huk said, "No, friend Greel, we do not want to resurrect the Silver Empire."

"If I have offended by presumption," said Greel quickly, "let me offer my—"

"Peace," said Weska, raising her hand. "No, you are not wrong in substance. We here are all committed to the downfall of the

Witch-king. But, as a scholar, I believe you will agree that precision matters. Your choice of words is not a precise fit with our intentions."

"My cousin is quite right," said Thespo. "At first, we thought it was our mission—nay, our great purpose in this troubled age—to bring back the Silver Empire. But now we have come to a different understanding."

Greel tensed. "Majesty, may I know the nature of this new understanding? What will take the place of the Silver Empire? A new empire with one of you on the throne?"

Weska laughed. "You misunderstand me, my friend. It is time for the age of empires to end here in the west. Just as it is time for the rise of an alliance of free states."

"Well past time," muttered Horogillin.

"Aye," agreed Ifduril.

"Would that not invite a new age of warfare?" asked Greel. "Would such a dissolution of unity not invite conquest and confusion?"

King al-Huk shook his head. "Only if we let it. The Silver Empire let us down. Among the pieces of its destruction we can see the rot at the heart. Prejudice and oppression were hidden beneath the empire's cloak of benevolence. And while we will not condemn Empress Gessalyn—for she was but the last in a long line of rulers who lived by rules and laws created a thousand years ago—we will also choose not to follow in her footsteps. That time has passed. We allowed ourselves to become weaker than we should have been. We borrowed power from the empire rather than cultivating our own."

"My cousin speaks truth," said Vulpion the Gray, king of Zehria. "Had we chosen other courses, each nation would have had its own court magician and seers. Who knows what tragedy might have been thwarted or even averted had we embraced the truth of magic's existence rather than live in forced ignorance of its power? That will now change. Each of us here are hungry for freedom—*true* freedom—just as we hunger for individual sovereignty."

Greel felt a spark of hope flicker in his chest. "I hear you all, Majesties, but I must ask . . . will you fight the Witch-king or merely cede Argon to him and otherwise endure his presence?"

Queen Weska drew her ancient and much-storied sword, Espalian, and laid it across her thighs. She traced the razor-sharp edge with her thumb and then licked off a drop of blood. "To be free," she said with utter coldness, "we would march on hell itself."

CHAPTER THIRTY-ONE

The Hakkian privateer seemed to fly across the water, and although Captain Beké tried every trick in his considerable collection to avoid the attack, the wind and tide were against him. The ships ground together with a scream of wood and the *chunk-chunk-chunk* of grappling hooks. The Therian ship had steeper, higher sides, but the invaders hurled grappling irons and swarmed up the ropes.

Therian archers fired volleys into them, killing and wounding many, but the attackers boiled out of their ship in incredible numbers. They screamed with wild delight, knowing that this fight was theirs.

The Therian soldiers in Theka's retinue met the invaders as they clambered over the rails. Many in the first wave of Hakkians fell maimed and screaming down onto their climbing comrades. Those on the ropes did not try to save anyone but merely let them fall and continued up to join the fray.

The Widow stood near the binnacle, studying the battle. The pirates threw hatchets and spears at the *Odakon*'s archers. Above them, more of their comrades swung spiked balls on thin chains, smashing heads and chests and breaking limbs of the defenders.

Others stabbed with boarding pikes and hooked gaffs. Already the sides of both ships streamed with gore and in the narrow gap between the vessels, sharks thrashed and bit, frenzied by the smell and taste of blood.

Captain Beké led the counterattack, a boarding pike in one huge fist and a heavy cutlass in the other. For all his size, he moved with incredible speed and delivered murderous blows with considerable power. Queen Theka had drawn her sword from her belt and held it with professional competence, but her guards pulled her back, daring to lay hands on her royal person and ignoring protests. It was their job to protect her, and they were willing to suffer royal punishment rather than let harm befall her. They bundled her back to the hatch that led down into the ship, but Theka would go no farther. She shook them off and stood wide-legged, her sword clutched in two very strong brown hands.

Everyone seemed to have forgotten about Ryssa. She was not yet a person of any importance to them. She felt the clenching, crushing weight of terror. This was probably her end. Ryssa already felt dead inside—but not entirely. If this was to be her last hour, then Miri would be waiting for her beneath those waves.

Miri.

Just the thought of her lost love made Ryssa angry. She could *feel* her, hear her voice. Miri had a sweet laugh and a knowing smile and the brightest eyes. It made Ryssa so furious to think that Miri was down in the ocean's depths, rotting away or being consumed by ten thousand fish and crustaceans and other creatures.

"Oh, my sweet love," she whispered even as men fought and screamed and died all around her.

The privateers were driven to a wildness that was horrifying. They flung themselves at the Therians, taking terrible wounds, losing limbs, and all the while uttering their war shrieks. They seemed maddened, beyond their minds, willing to accept being maimed or killed as long as they ultimately overwhelmed their prey.

The Therians were equally filled with battle madness, and Ryssa saw some of them step into the path of arrows or hurled spears so that their flesh accepted the mortal wound rather than let anything reach where the queen stood. It was the same kind of sacrifice that the privateers were doing, but its value changed in the meaning. Fighting to protect the life of their queen was matched against the lustful desire to conquer. At first, Ryssa could not see how this difference mattered in the fight, and then she did.

Captain Beké, streaming blood from half a dozen wounds, waded into a crowd of the enemy who were trying to rush toward the queen. Beké, already a big man, seemed to swell with a righteous inner power. His blows landed with impossible speed and force, crushing men all around him. Within seconds there was a half circle of corpses and men so badly wounded that all they could do was utter inarticulate screams. Beké's eyes were bright with holy purpose as he fought, and Ryssa lost count of the privateers who fell before him.

The Therian soldiers in Theka's retinue were much the same. They knew the full value of winning and the terrible consequences of losing. This was no simple battle on a field in a forgotten corner of the empire. This was them doing what every solider in their nation's long history trained to do—to defend their sacred monarch.

For a long time, Ryssa thought this was going to be enough. If the battle had been even odds, the Therians would have won. Had it been two-to-one they would like to have carried the day. But there seemed to be an endless stream of privateers pouring out of their ship. The Therian soldiers stood like a wall between their queen and the killers, and though they fell one by one, they levied a terrible toll on the attackers.

Ryssa saw the boatswain die, his body seeming to lose its shape as silver blades flashed and chopped. She saw a foremast sailor, standing with her back to a rail, lay about her with a heavy axe. The woman killed two enemies and sent four others staggering back with dreadful wounds; but each time one of the Hakkians fell, two others rushed in to take their places. The last Ryssa saw of the sailor was when a privateer, laughing with mad glee, held up her severed head and then hurled it to the hungry sharks.

Above, on the fighting tops, archers rained down hell, but none of them used flaming arrows. That strategy had gone by the board when the freshening breeze drove the two ships together. Now it was just archery, and they did their best; but the Hakkians were archers, too, and from their spars and ratlines they fired continuously, and one by one the Therians fell.

A sound made her turn and Ryssa saw that the storm was closer now. *Much* closer, with clouds that had turned from a threatening gray to a furious purple-black filling the entire southern sky from horizon to horizon. Lightning forked within it, the glare pulsing like the beating heart of the god of all dragons. Thunder crashed so loud that it made her cry out and press her palms to her ears. The lightning came faster and faster, hurting her eyes, freezing moments into images that lingered on her retinas—a man falling, another stabbing an opponent through the heart, a woman on her knees as she fumbled to stuff her intestines back into a gaping stomach. Glimpses of hell.

Then she saw the wall of heavy rain come sweeping across the sea like a veil of lead so dense it blotted out the ocean behind it.

The sailing master grabbed Ryssa's shoulder and shoved her toward the closest hatchway.

"Get below, girl!" he roared and then screamed as a hatchet spun through the air and buried itself between his shoulder blades. The master pitched forward, his fingernails raking Ryssa's arm. He collapsed and died with his head on her left foot, eyes open and staring at whatever was beyond this world.

Ryssa looked at her arm. The master's nails had scratched her and there were drops of blood that seemed oddly dark in the strange light of the coming storm. Almost black. Ryssa felt a sudden and powerful shift in her consciousness, and it was as if she was no longer completely in her body, but instead standing a few feet away, watching herself. Seeing herself from hair to shoes. Feeling a mournful sadness for this young woman. Feeling . . .

Then she was moving.

Without conscious thought, without meaning to or wanting to, she walked across the heaving deck toward the rail. She felt a flash of fear that this was her end, that her mind had snapped, and she was going to climb the rail and step off. Out of this tormented life, down into the hungry sharks, ending the failure of being Ryssa. Stepping out of this world forever.

She drew the knife Queen Theka had given her. She felt her hand do it and *saw* her hand do it. The double perspective was so strange. The lightning flashes made the blade look as if it was made of fire, and yet the handle was so very cold. Ryssa placed the knife edge against her palm.

"*Y' gokln'gha gn'th llll ya gn'th'bthnk,*" she said, but the voice was not entirely her own, and the language that of the people of that strange island of Tull Yammoth.

With a slow stroke she pulled the blade across her palm. Blood welled up, running hot and quick, for the cut was very deep. The knife tumbled to the deck as she leaned forward to let her blood fall into the troubled waters between the ships.

"*Ymg' fhalgof'n llll stell'bsna ymg' nnn'drn, throdog gnaiih.*"

Tears were hot on her cheeks. Her prayers rose into the wind and also fell into the sea.

"*Llll ya mgleth gn'bthnknyth Y' ymg' stell'bsna.*"

Then she crumpled to her knees, clutching the bleeding hand to her breast. All around her the storm rose up, huge and black and horrifying. The dueling fighters did not care. They were trapped too deeply inside the envelope of their mutual hate. They did not care about the lightning. They did not heed the thunder. They barely felt the rain.

And none of them—not one person aboard either ship except Ryssa herself—saw the things that came in answer to her prayer.

Then, a moment later, *everyone* saw.

Everyone knew.

And everyone screamed.

Two massive gray shapes rose from the depths and drove straight at the Hakkian ship. Sperm whales, each forty-five tons of muscle and blubber, their eyes blazing with a hatred that looked strangely human. They struck the ship fore and aft, crushing the flat stern and turning the bow into matchwood. The ship had been designed to punch through waves and take heavy cross seas on their quarters without damage, but the whales crushed it between them. Then the animals dropped down into the inky depths as two more came up behind them—monstrous bulls, giants of the ocean—and hit the ship again. And again.

The Hakkians suddenly screamed in terror. Whalers told of the big sperm whales fighting when attacked, but not like this. Never like this.

The crippled privateer leaned away from the Therian ship, its weight causing grappling ropes to stretch and snap, widening the gap. Then new shapes hurled themselves out of the water. Black and white shapes that moved with incredible speed. Killer whales—at least half a dozen of them—leapt up and snatched Hakkians from the sides of the ships or plucked them from newly severed ropes. The orcas dragged their prey down into the water, which had turned a furious red.

The captain of the privateer fought to control his men despite the utter madness of this attack. "Take the ship," he roared, waving his bloody sword at the *Odakon*. "Take the ship, for the love of Hastur!"

This rallied the men for it was some kind of reprieve, some measure of possible escape, and those that were not already on deck scurried up the ropes, ignoring the cries of the men still aboard the privateer. With a fury born more of madness than anything, they redoubled their attack.

Ryssa was sitting now with her back to the rail, a pool of blood spreading around her from the deep wound in her hand. She saw Queen Theka forty feet away, blade in hand, staring at her. At her, as if she understood what was happening. There was horror in that look, and revulsion, but also something else that Ryssa could not define.

The sperm whales had continued to batter the enemy ship and it was sinking quickly. The killer whales still leaped to snatch men from the rigging, but the Hakkians were pushing away from the side of the ship out of reach.

Then something new rose from the sea on the larboard side. Slender and tall, like the trunk of an island palm—gray and mottled. It rose and rose, and as it did, it turned, exposing its other side, which was a paler gray tinged with pink. All along that side were countless rows of round, fleshy suckers, and inside each of these was a ring of teeth as sharp and large as the teeth of a great white shark. This monstrous thing—this tentacle from the stormy deep—bent down and curled around three men. Three *Hakkians*. Then with a kind of snap like the flick of a whip, it snatched them from the deck and bore them down beneath the surface.

Sailors screamed—all of them, on both sides. Then all at once the sea exploded with jets of spray as twenty more of the tentacles burst upward, some smaller than the first and others vastly larger. Some slapped down, smashed privateers to crimson jelly on the deck; but most wrapped like constrictors around the pirates and ripped them off the deck and into the sea.

The Therians fell back, screaming prayers to Father Dagon and Mother Hydra because they had not yet realized that these monsters were only attacking the Hakkians. As the whales had attacked the enemy ship.

Each tentacle returned over and over again for more prey. The Therians fled from them, forming a defensive knot around Queen Theka. Less than half the crew could still fight, and all of them were bloodied, but they held their ground, blades forming a thornbush around Theka.

And then . . . a stunning silence fell. The Hakkians were gone.

Every.

Single.

One.

The last of the tentacles wavered in the air sixty feet above the deck, then it slipped down, straight and fast, into the water, which closed over it completely.

The lightning continued to flash and the thunder boomed, but even the tossing sea seemed unwilling to attack the *Odakon*.

Slowly . . . so slowly . . . the wind and the sea grew calm and a watery yellow sun peered out from between streamers of torn clouds.

The whales and orcas and tentacles were gone.

The *Odakon* rocked gently on slow rollers.

Ryssa looked down at her hand.

There was blood, but there was no trace at all of the deep cut.

CHAPTER THIRTY-TWO

Summer had long overstayed its welcome, lingering like a usurper to the very last day of autumn, but then winter rose up with armies of ice and snow.

By sundown on the first day of winter, the campaign was fully entrenched. The grasses, lush only days before, grew rigid with a terminal stiffness and above them the leaves screamed with their dry voices and fell in their millions to the hardening ground.

In farm fields from Ghenrey to Nelfydia the late autumn crops died on the vines, shedding leaves and inedible fruits to the iron-hard ground.

The change from blistering heat to bitter cold happened so quickly that Kagen nearly froze to death in his sleep. He woke in the blackest hour of night, shivering, teeth chattering, limbs heavy with pain.

The small cooking fire he had built the night before had dwindled down to coals and he scrambled to gather anything that would burn, then huddled over it, blowing on the embers until they caught. Then he built it high and moved the horses closer to it, for they were crying out from the cold.

Huddled there in a thin blanket, Kagen tried to recall the dream he'd been deep inside of before he woke. The details were slippery and elusive, and all he could recall were disjointed images of his brothers, Jheklan and Faulker. They ran through endless caves of ice . . . then they were engaged in a fierce battle with Hakkians. And one last image tore at him—it was of Faulker holding Jheklan's limp and lifeless body as the great dragon reached for them both with a massive, deadly claw.

He did not fall asleep again that night.

And the night was very long.

CHAPTER THIRTY-THREE

Lieutenant-General Mari Heklan knelt before the throne, her head bowed nearly to the floor.

"Rise, cousin," said the king.

She did and stood there—squat, ugly, powerful, and clad in battle-scarred armor.

"How may I serve my lord and king?" she asked. There was no trace of the unctuous tone common to so many courtiers and even her fellow senior officers.

"I read the reports of your recent victories. Give me your opinion of the armies that you've met on the field?"

"They are earnest, I'll give them that," said the general. "The Samudians are arrogant, and that made it easy to fool them into bad tactics. As for the Ghenreyans . . . they fought well until their own officers told them to yield and lay down their weapons. I credit them with heart."

"Is that why none of them have been tortured?" asked the king.

"It is. And it's why I've extended a forgiving hand to those who fought to the end," said Mari. "Once these ceremonies were done, I gave each surviving soldier a chance to join us or die."

"You did not do so on Tull Athris."

Mari shrugged. "It was an island and there was limited space in our boats."

"Ah," said the king. "As to the Ghenreyans, did any accept your offer?"

"Many did, Highness."

The king nodded. "Excellent. Continue with that policy."

"As you command, sire."

"Listen to me, Mari, for I have two things to tell you," said the Witch-king. "First, the night of my ascension draws near, and I will be briefly vulnerable. I tell you this in confidence, but know that once the ceremony is completed there will be no military power on earth that will stand before us."

"And I pray every night that this may come to pass," said Mari.

"The second thing is that I am appointing you as lord high marshal of my armies. You will answer to me and to no one else, is that understood?"

Mari Heklan stared in total shock. "My . . . lord . . . I do not know what to say? I am nothing but a humble soldier."

"You are more than that, Mari Heklan. You are my strong right fist. You are smart and you have faith in your own policies. This pleases me, and I believe you will lead our forces to a complete and total victory over our enemies."

Mari bowed again as tears streamed down her face.

"You do me more honor than I deserve, Majesty," she said. "My life, my heart, my blood, and my honor are yours."

"And I accept these things with gratitude. Now, rise, Lord Marshal, for I have a special mission for you."

She stood and beat her fist against her breast. "How best may I serve the will of the Witch-king?"

"There is a threat in the east," said the king. "It is not an army of which I speak but something every bit as dangerous. Something which none of my generals have been so far able to impede."

She licked her lips. "Does my king speak of the razor-knight, sire?"

"I do," said the Witch-king, and behind his lace veil he smiled.

CHAPTER THIRTY-FOUR

The sea was empty. Except for some drifting wreckage, there was no sign of the Hakkian privateer. The only bodies that floated in the bloody salt water were Therians. The only bodies on the deck were Therian.

Not one Hakkian was left anywhere.

Finally, Captain Beké found his voice. "See to the wounded," he croaked. And then gave orders to tend to the sails and man the wheel. The crew looked at him for a moment as if he were speaking some unknown tongue, and then they gradually began to shamble toward their stations. All of it happened with a dream-like quality, and even the sounds of wind and breeze and the wooden ship were muted and distant.

Queen Theka stood looking at Ryssa the whole time. Her face was drawn and pale, and her eyes were filled with strange lights.

Then the spell seemed to break, and she looked down at the sword she held. There was blood on it, but the queen frowned as if uncertain how it could have gotten there. She let the blade fall and even its landing was muffled.

Then she took a step toward Ryssa. Two of her aides tried to check her, but she spoke sharply and they stepped back, looking fearful and worried. Theka walked very slowly across the red-washed deck until her shadow fell across Ryssa. The queen abruptly shifted to one side so that her shadow did not touch the young stranger at all. Her mouth moved, forming words but failing to speak. She stopped, blinked, and tried once more.

"How . . . ?"

Ryssa looked at her but did not reply.

Theka nodded, accepting no answer as answer. "I . . . am indebted to you, Ryssa of Argon. More than I can ever express or repay. I did not know that you were so powerful an . . ." And here she had to fish for the right word, finally saying, ". . . ally."

Ryssa stood there on the bloody deck, trembling, weary, sick to her stomach. "I am not your ally, Majesty," she said in a strange little whisper.

"What . . . *are* . . . you, then?" asked the queen.

Ryssa turned and stared out to sea. "I am the enemy of Hastur and his priests."

The queen licked her lips and nodded. "That will do."

Ryssa did not respond. She leaned on the rail and watched the ocean and did not say another word. The *Odakon* turned, finding the wind now on her quarter and blowing toward the northeast. Toward Samud, where kings and queens were meeting to decide on how to fight a war against the most powerful sorcerer the world had ever known.

Ryssa did not know that.

All she knew was that something inside her had changed.

Something had been done to her that could not be undone. She was terrified of that knowledge. But when she wept, her tears were tears of joy.

A very dark and quite terrible joy.

The queen went below, her eyes filled with fear and wonder.

No one disturbed Ryssa. The captain was busy with repairs. The sailors kept cutting looks her way, but they did not dare make actual eye contact. Anytime they saw her glance in their general direction, they would touch a wooden belaying pin or scratch a backstay for luck; or touch a sacred tattoo of Father Dagon or Mother Hydra and whisper a prayer. A few cast warding signs at her when the Widow's back was turned.

She was aware of all of this. She knew she should be upset that fear, more so than gratitude, was what the sailors felt, but she could not conjure any emotion but sadness.

And rage.

The ship moved on through the dark blue sea. As the daylight began to fail and twilight painted the sky in shades of bruised purple and bloodred, she left the deck and descended the companion ladder. Belowdecks everything creaked and lanterns swayed and rats ran along the floor close to the walls.

The Widow found her cabin, entered, closed and locked the door, and sat down on the bench that, apart from her slung cot and a vanity made from a sea chest, was her only furniture. There was a small mirror hung from a beam, and she looked into it.

Miles melted away beneath the keel of the Therian ship. For all that she cared, it might have been sailing through the stars. Or drifting through shadows.

The Widow—Ryssa—sat for a very long time staring into that mirror.

And all the time it was Miri who stared back.

CHAPTER THIRTY-FIVE

The Witch-king and the Prince of Games sat in one of the many formal gardens within the complex of courtyards in the palace. Although it was cold, braziers had been lit around them.

"Have you received any word from the latest expedition you sent north to the Winterwilds?" asked the prince. He was not wearing jester's clothes today but wore buff-colored leather trousers under a tunic marked with the Hakkian sign of the eclipse picked out in yellow and black.

"Not very much, alas," replied the king. "But I expect to hear soon. I sent word to close down the operation up there and bring everything of value to me as soon as possible."

"If I may ask, what is the main purpose for closing things down up there? Is it because of the Vale brothers?"

"You know about that?"

"Nespar and Jakob Ravensmere have spies, and so do I."

"No doubt." The Witch-king watched a winter waxwing bird peck at the frozen ground. "Mother Frey sent the Vale brothers there for reasons as yet unclear. Some believe that they are meant to slay Fabeldyr and thus end all magic."

"You sound skeptical."

"I am not among those who believe that Frey wants magic eradicated. Even if it would mean defeating me—should this occur before my ascension. No, my dear prince, I think the Vales are hoping to *free* the dragon in hopes that she will take their side."

"Mm," said the prince, "I've heard that case made. I rather agree that it's closer to the truth. After all, Kagen Vale has at least one ally on his side who is from the larger world."

"Yes. Lady Maralina, the disgraced daughter of Queen Titania à-Mab and Lord Oberon Erlking."

"Disgraced because she was seduced and infected by our own Duke Sárkány, my king. Imprisoned by her mother for her foolishness and impurity. It makes a great story and is mostly true, but Maralina is trapped in the Tower of Sarsis, and no earthly power can free her. Nor can she free herself."

The Witch-king nodded. "Even trapped she is ally to Kagen Vale. It is possible, even likely, that the Seven Cryptical Books of Hsan were taken to her for translation."

"With your ascension so close," said the prince, "I doubt Maralina's translation will do them any good. Luckily they don't know that. But . . . tell me, sire, about Fabeldyr. Once you have gotten what you need from her, will you let her live?"

"She is a danger while she lives," said the king. "Her death would serve me better."

"There are many in the larger world who will not take kindly to that."

The Witch-king shook his head. "They do not yet possess enough power in this *material* world for their displeasure to matter. If the dragon dies, those who fled through the veils to other realms will never be able to return. Those who are here but who do not bend their knee to me, will be hunted down and made examples of. All of this, my friend, is in hand."

"Unless she, in her immolation, casts her essence to the winds," said the prince. "Surely you know the old legend about the Dragon's Gift. Technically, I suppose, it is the *Last* Dragon's Gift."

"It is a story told to children," said the king, dismissing it. "And I do not fear stories."

"Not if the ascension is accomplished," agreed the prince. "If Hastur is made flesh in this reality, then he will be able to grant you unlimited power."

"He will grant me such power as he chooses," corrected the king. "And I will use it for his glory."

"Of course, of course." After a quiet moment, he said, "Your pet propagandist, Jakob Ravensmere, has been busy gathering books of ancient lore. At the risk of incurring your royal rebuke, I am compelled to wonder why Hastur has not merely *imparted* this wisdom to you."

"The Shepherd God has his reasons; I have no doubt."

"Ah," said the prince, smiling. "I daresay I have known of Hastur longer than you. I do not claim to be his favorite—far from it—but I believe I understand him and his place in this complex cosmology that includes *our* world as part of the larger one. And yet there are questions—key questions—about him that remain mysteries even to me. His apparent nature and his actions are not always in clear alignment."

"Explain what you mean."

"He is the Shepherd God," said the Prince of Games. "That does not mean he actually tends to sheep. *You* are his flock. You and everyone who bows down to his power and glory. *You*, my dear Witch-king, are the chosen avatar of Hastur on earth, and with his patronage you are working to bring about a new age of the world. I wonder how you stoke your confidence in the outcome."

"You are dangerously close to heresy."

The prince smiled. "No, no, my king, I do not mock. I am merely exploring the cosmology and theology that you embrace. Hastur is eternal—or as close to it as makes no difference—and that means he has been part of every fall of mankind. He has *allowed* it. Understand, chaos—which is my path—is not a *lack* of order but a lack of stagnation. Mankind has proven over and over again that all gods are, in their way, poor stewards of this earth, and often indifferent to the suffering, the successes, the failures, even the mass slaughter of their followers."

The Witch-king said nothing, but his hands had balled into fists.

"I am not blaspheming against Hastur," said the prince quickly. "I am, however, questioning his motives, as I do of all who set themselves up as gods. Or as kings or queens of the larger world.

The faerie folk are just as bad. Queen Titania of the *Baobhan sith* let her people grow wild and, as such, it forced them into violent collision with men. These faerie folk may be powerful and each might be worth a hundred humans in battle, yet the ratio is not a hundred to one but a hundred thousand to one. Mankind has won in every protracted battle against the larger world."

"Get to your point," said the king in a dangerous tone of voice.

"My point is this," said the Prince of Games. "War is coming. You need men and magic to fight. Men you have, between Hakkians and mercenaries from the east. But they are not enough. You have used magic to allow the older races to return. The vampires come to mind, as well as werewolves and the Hollow Monks, but without an army of human and inhuman—something which has never once existed in this world—you cannot win. Hear me, o' king, you cannot. Hastur will not manifest in whatever passes for *the flesh* when it comes to gods, and he will not be general to your troops. Don't swell up about this for we both know it to be true. I remember crusades many thousands of years ago where two religions went to war over pieces of empty desert land, and neither version of their god appeared to prove one side right or smite the enemy."

The Witch-king's fists slowly relaxed. "Although you say it in ways intended to be provocative, my friend, you are not wrong. Hastur will not appear in that way."

"Which makes me wonder how you will prevail," insisted the prince. "Your forces and those that will ultimately align against you are—by any metric—evenly matched. And if Lady Maralina *does* translate those Hsan books, then the balance may well swing in favor of your enemies. And I do not believe you are mad enough to release the Red Plague in its fullness because then, in your certain victory, you would rule over a world populated by the mindless dead."

"That plague had it uses," admitted the Witch-king, "but no,

I never intended it to be used without a measure of control. It was intended to weaken King al-Huk and delay an alliance of my enemies, and in that it was successful."

"Indeed, sire," said the prince, "but what now? What other trick do you have to play? Sárkány and his vampire knights? Their nature is known as are their vulnerabilities. How long before Mother Frey suggests to Kagen to arm his archers with arrows tipped with hawthorn and dipped in garlic? No, what I ask is whether you have enough actual *magic* to fight and win this war."

"Ah," said the Witch-king, "perhaps it is time to show you what I have been doing. My magicks are not useful merely for transporting my armies."

The prince looked surprised. "Are you saying that your powers are restored?"

"That," said the king, "and more. Come, let me show you."

With that he led the prince into another courtyard. A larger one. The air was filled with growls and shrieks and snarls and cries that even the Prince of Games had never heard before.

CHAPTER THIRTY-SIX

They met, as they so often did, in secret, in a room that only a handful of people in Samud knew existed. Hidden as surely as the one in which King al-Huk had recently entertained his cousin monarchs.

The king sat on a divan, leaning wearily against pillows and staring moodily into the dancing flames in the fireplace. Incense burned in beaten-copper bowls, and there was good wine on a table near at hand.

When the hidden door opened, al-Huk did not bother to look up. He knew who it was. Only one person had permission to come and go without ceremony or summons.

Major-General Culanna yl-Sik, deputy field marshal of Samud, closed the panel behind her and, seeing the king, removed her cloak and hung it on a peg. She went and poured a tall flagon with plain water and sat down across from her liege.

"And . . . ?" asked the king.

"And the parties are all away safely," said the general. "I had guides with them to our border and sent observers on fast gallopers to make sure they are each heading home without incident."

Al-Huk nodded.

A log shifted loose from the burning stack and fell onto the hearth tiles. The general began to rise, but the king waved her back.

"Let it burn where it is," he said.

Nearly a quarter hour passed while they watched that lone log burn itself out, each drawing their own inferences from its implied symbology. One of many, burning alone.

"There is no road back from this," said al-Huk.

"I fear not, sire," said the general. "May the gods stand between us and evil."

That drew a sour grunt from the king. "Aye, for they have done such good works to that end already."

Neither spoke again after that.

And they sat there long into the cold first night of winter.

CHAPTER THIRTY-SEVEN

The sorcerer and the trickster strolled side by side along a board-walk laid between huge cages made of iron bars. Iron, not steel, for the base metal's qualities were best left undiluted.

The Witch-king walked slowly, hands clasped behind his back, looking without haste from one cage to another. The Prince of Games was a slight half pace behind, dutifully playing the role of lesser being because he found that wonderfully amusing.

The air was redolent with the mingled smells of unwashed skin, wet fur, offal, and pain. That also amused the prince.

"You've been busy, I see," he said. "Is this a hobby or something else?"

The Witch-king nodded. "Something else entirely."

They stopped before one cage in which a creature very much like a stunted dragon was screeching as it pulled with savage force against the chains that bound it. Hakkian priests, naked to the waist and many bleeding from scratches, used long rods tipped with jagged and glowing pieces of sacred crystals on the beast. They poked at it, slashed at it, and the monster also bled. The thing had a reptilian body and stood upon two bent and scaly legs, with a thrashing tail behind, and winged arms ending in terrible claws. The tips of each claw were bound with wads of jeweler's cotton tied in place with yellow string that had been dipped in sanctified water and dried in the smoke of special incense. The confines of the cage and the chains on legs, tail, and wings kept it more or less contained, but it thrashed wildly and with bursts of shocking speed. One priest had already been taken away on a litter, his guts ripped open before the pads were tied in place.

"A wyvern," said the prince. "I have never seen a live one."

"It is not a true wyvern," said the king. "Nor is anything here true to nature."

"Oh?" mused the prince. "It's rather beautiful. Is this one fully grown?"

"In truth I don't know. My handlers tell me it grows at an enormous rate. By any normal standards it is still little more than an infant."

The prince turned to look at him. "Normal standards," he echoed. "That's intriguing. May I ask what you mean?"

The king spread his arms to embrace all of the zoo. "Everything here is specially bred. Nothing is a true child of nature, though parts of each are. They are modified to suit very particular needs."

"Ah," said the prince. "You are warping things from the natural world?"

"As you see." The king looked at him. "Is that disapproval I hear in your voice?"

"Not as such," the prince said slowly. "But I am surprised. Magic relies on the structure of the natural world. Even what we call the 'larger world'—those interlocking realms of reality in which creatures such as I, the faerie folk, elvinkind, and others exist—is balanced on the firmament of the natural world. Manipulation through, say, animal husbandry is one thing, but changing the nature of an animal—dare I say *forcing* it to become something other than nature intended—is a risky endeavor. There is a very long history of such practices playing out badly for the magic users who have attempted them."

"There is," admitted the king. "But I am not averse to risk."

"So I gather."

"And I'm surprised to find you timid. You who are a spirit of chaos itself."

The Prince of Games stood looking at the false wyvern for several quiet moments. "As I said, magic rests upon a foundation of reality. There are some I have known through the years who regard magic as a form of science as yet unquantified. Although that spoils some of the fun of magic, I tend to hew pretty close to that viewpoint."

"Then what I am doing is a new form of husbandry, is it not?" asked the Witch-king. "How is this different or more dangerous than grafting different vines together to produce richer berries for new wines?"

"That is done *with* nature, my lord," said the prince. "This is a different matter because sorcery has been used to change nature. That is a much, *much* rarer thing than people believe. Else vampires and werewolves would have used magic to change the poisonous nature of hawthorn, rose, and wolfsbane."

"Perhaps they should."

"And perhaps the larger world might push back against such a thing." He shook his head. "When the Great Old Ones came to earth—Hastur, Cthulhu, and the rest—they did not change the fabric of reality. People think they did, but it was never the case. They introduced elements of reality from the natural worlds of other planets. Like the flowers whose colors drive men mad. That is organic warfare that merely *looks* like magic, for those flowers are part of another world's nature. And the impossible sights used to attack the minds of unbelievers and convert them to mad followers are not perversions of the natural world, but exposure to overlapping *other* worlds. What is a monster to seekers after magical truths but merely another animal? Surely you know this."

The Witch-king began walking again and the prince hurried to catch up.

"Have you no answer, sire?"

"I have no fears, my dear prince. I have delved deep into sorceries that do not rely on the natural world. I have gained much knowledge and power by refusing to bend to any rules except those I make."

"And what if, in your quest for ultimate power, you crack the foundation of the natural world? Will that not send ripples through all of the realms of the larger world? Would that not threaten the realms of faerie, the abode of dragons out there among the stars, or any of the countless precariously balanced dimensions?"

The king turned sharply. "And if it does?"

"Then you could crack the universe itself apart like an egg."

Behind his veil, the Witch-king smiled. "And what is an egg but a vessel from which something new is born."

For once the Prince of Games was speechless.

The Witch-king again gestured to the hundreds of cages, large and small, that filled the large space in which they stood.

"See what I have wrought? Things out of legend. Things hunted to extinction because they lacked the power to survive. I have found their bones, their eggs, and I have labored over them with spells both old and new, and I have remade them in the image of what I want and need."

The prince walked a few steps on, looking around. There were a pair of basilisks, each the size of adult weasels; a sinister-looking colocolo with feathers instead of fur; and a birdlike reptile called a snallygaster; a dour belled buzzard who watched with eerily human eyes as the two men passed; a very tall manlike beast with reddish fur covering every inch of its enormous body and who crouched weeping in the back of its cage; a glawackus—an animal that was a haphazard mix of bear, boar, and lion—and dozens of others. Some cages held other examples of previously seen specimens though changed in dreadful ways; and more that even the prince could not name. While some cages were empty and waiting.

He stopped, turned and looked at the Witch-king. There was no playful mockery or twisted joy on the prince's face. Now he looked old and strange and inhuman. His eyes swirled with many colors—sickly greens and browns, harsh yellows and reds—and all of it moving, moving.

"You play a dangerous game," he said in a voice that was not at all human.

"Say you so?" laughed the king.

"Even for one who aspires to ascension, sire, you take great risks in what you do here."

"What I am creating is something new, even to a world as old as this. I have sent very many of my new children out in covered wagons. Even now they are positioned in places where they will aid my war in ways the enemy cannot ever predict. Let them throw their armies of men and swords and spears against me, and my children will rend them down to spoiled meat and splintered bone, and on this they will feast."

The prince gaped at him. "You have done this already?"

"I have done this and more," said the king. "Are you surprised that my plans are so bold and so far-reaching? Do you shrink from the truth that I care *nothing* for the laws of men or the traditions of the larger world? My patron is a *god,* and I am answerable to no laws but those of Hastur the Shepherd."

"But this is so risky. This is not the way to build a stable empire . . ."

"Ah, my dear prince . . . how can one be as old as you and as subtle as you pretend to be and yet think my goal is to conquer the Silver Empire and merely repaint it in Hakkian yellow? How little you think of me. I have small interest in the west alone. The Cathedral Mountains to the east and the Western Reach are not barriers to my ambition. I will remake the *world*. This world. And beyond that . . . we shall see."

He took a few steps closer to the prince.

"You came to my court to offer your advice and support, Prince of Games," he said. "Where stands that offer now? Does my truth frighten you? Will you retreat from the path of glory? How is what I am doing *not* the epitome of the chaos that defines you?"

The prince said nothing. His eyes swirled and swirled. And then, very slowly and very carefully, he bowed his head and lowered himself to one knee.

"I stand in the presence of greatness," he said softly. "Your will be done."

CHAPTER THIRTY-EIGHT

Tuke and Filia were weary of the administrative part of raising an army. In Kagen's absence they were in charge, and it seemed that everyone from the recruiting sergeants to the latrine diggers needed to report this or that to them.

"I don't suppose you want to run away with me," said Tuke during a rare lull.

"Where to?" sighed Filia.

"I hear winter is lovely in Bercless." That was a country on the far side of the continent, many thousands of miles to the east.

"I'll pack a lunch," she said.

They smiled at one another and then called for the next person to come and ask their question. However, it was a stranger who entered, escorted by a sentry.

"This woman says she knows Captain Kagen," said the guard. "Name of Selvath. She asks for an audience."

Filia raised her eyebrows. "Selvath, is it? Thank you, Veers, you can go."

The woman was around forty, and those looked to have been hard years. There were lines etched deeply around her mouth and between her brows. Her face was dark and weather-worn, and it was surrounded by lots of wild black hair. Her eyes were a smoky gray nearly as pale as Kagen's icy blue ones. She wore a simple frock belted with leather, and a threadbare cloak of walnut brown.

"You are Selvath?" asked Filia.

"I am," said the woman.

"Tell me how you know Kagen Vale."

"I met him a few weeks after the empire fell," Selvath said. "He saved me from a bunch of louts from the village where I'd been staying." She paused. "They accused me of being a witch and were going to hang me but wanted to *use* me first."

"What did Kagen do?" asked Tuke.

"Do, sir? Why he killed them all like the vermin they were. He was drunk at the time, but even so he served them up a treat and left them for the flies."

Filia studied her. "Kagen told a similar tale. And he said that the Selvath he saved actually *was* a witch."

"That's not what I call myself."

"Then, pray, what *do* you call yourself?" asked Tuke.

"A woman," replied Selvath with fierce defiance.

The big Therian glanced at Filia. "I like this one quite a lot."

"If you have the *old gift*," said Filia, using the phrase Kagen said the woman used when he'd met her, "then tell me the three prophecies you made for Kagen."

"That is a lot to ask," said Selvath.

"These are troubled times," Filia observed. "There are spies and traitors around every corner, and we have been lied to more than once by people claiming to know Kagen Vale."

"Yes, I know," said Selvath. She cut a look toward the flaps of the interview tent, and by doing that indicated the camp beyond. "There are indeed spies everywhere. However, I am not one of them. Kagen Vale saved my life. He could have taken me had he wanted to, but he is not that kind of man. He is a good man, and fate has laid his hand on him."

"Then tell us the prophecies you shared with him," Tuke said quietly.

"The first thing I told Kagen," said Selvath, "was that he had many long and dark roads ahead of him and that he thought he knew what was ahead but did not."

Filia nodded. "Go on."

"The second thing I told him was that things are not at all what they seem."

"That's pretty much always been true," said Tuke.

"And that is exactly what Kagen said to me. But it does not change the truth. To him, I mean. There are secrets waiting to be unlocked, and they will change the world as Kagen knows it."

"And the third thing?" asked Filia.

"You know the third thing," said Selvath, "for that prophecy involved the two of you. I told Kagen that he would be brought in chains before the Witch-king. I said that it was his destiny. The Witch-king of Hakkia would see his heart and his blood. This happened on the night of the coronation, when you both— and your friends among the Unbladed and the royal houses of Argon—brought Kagen Vale before the throne of the usurper."

Tuke and Filia exchanged a glance but said nothing.

"There was more to that prophecy than this," Selvath said. "I told him that he and the Witch-king were locked together in a wheel of fire. And that this wheel would turn and turn, and I said that this world will catch fire before it stops turning."

"That's cheery," said Tuke with a sigh.

"Very well," said Filia. "We believe you are who you say you are. Kagen has spoken of those prophecies to only three people. The two of us and—"

"—and an old woman," interrupted Selvath. "A Gardener, or one who had been such. You are both tied to her, and together the fates of all three of you are bound to Kagen Vale."

After digesting this for a moment, Tuke said, "But why come here? Forgive me for saying so, my lady, but you are no fighter. Do you come to share more prophecies? I ask, because the prophecy about being brought in chains to the Witch-king gave Kagen an idea that nearly got us all killed. And which did not have a happy outcome."

The woman cocked her head appraisingly. "Did it not? Is the Hakkian usurper now emperor? Has the Yellow Empire of Hastur risen?"

Tuke said, "Well . . ."

"Besides," said Selvath, running thin fingers through her wild hair, "the future is not carved in stone. It is always in motion. Prophets can only say what is clear to them, on the deepest level, in that moment."

"Is this what you offer to Kagen?" asked Tuke.

"In part, though I have no control over when such visions will speak to me."

Filia frowned. "What, then . . . ?"

"I have other powers," said Selvath. "Powers that have grown and grown ever since I met Kagen. Powers that define me now."

"What powers? Can you conjure an army for us?"

Selvath almost smiled. "No. But I can tell you who in your current army is true of heart and who is a Hakkian spy. Let me walk among the people here. Give me a few days and nights, and I may reveal the vipers in your nest."

"You are so sure they are there?"

Selvath's eyes glittered like sharpened steel.

CHAPTER THIRTY-NINE

The young man walked to the edge of the sea, paused, considered, then dug a rock out of the icy beach and tossed it underhand. It struck the surface of the water, bounced, and skittered a dozen yards.

"It's completely frozen," said Jheklan Vale.

His brother, Faulker, walked down the slope and gave him a long, pitying look. "It is literally called the *Frozen* Sea, dumbass."

Jheklan sniffed and rubbed at his nose, which was bright pink from the cold. "I *know* that. I was merely stating that it is still frozen despite it still being autumn."

"Well, it's not called the *Occasionally* Frozen Sea, is it? What were you expecting? Palm trees and leaping dolphins?"

"Would be nice," grumped Jheklan.

They climbed up to where their horses stood blowing steam into the frigid air. Behind them was an endless stretch of snowy nothingness. Before them was the pale blue-white ice of the sea. They stood in identical postures of frozen discomfort. They looked like twins even though they were a year apart, with the only obvious difference being that one was blond and the other ginger. They had the same lean build, high-cheekboned faces, and clear eyes.

"So help me Father Ar," said Faulker, "if you say that it looks cold, I will cut you and leave you for the wolves."

"Wasn't going to," said Jheklan in a tone of voice that sounded like he had planned to do exactly that. He pretended to cough but only to say, "Officious jackass."

Their team—eight men and two women, plus a string of hardy northern horses—were fanned out on either side of them. They glanced at one another, but no one dared intrude on the conversation between the Vale brothers. Reprisal tended to come in the form of rapier-sharp sarcasm and extra watches on the long arctic nights.

When the long journey from Vahlycor to the Winterwilds began, the brothers were jovial, lighthearted, and agreeable. It made a frightening and difficult mission enjoyable. However, the endless miles tested that attitude. Bitter cold, incessant storms, packs of wolves, attacks by polar bears, and the other hardships had chipped away at their bond.

The journey, according to Mother Frey, should have taken them two months to reach this far, but the obstacles had doubled that, and now winter was upon them. Its bitter assault had turned the Twins waspish and snippy, and no one else seemed to be having much fun.

With one exception.

The lieutenant of the twelve-person team was a Therian woman with intensely dark skin and intensely green eyes. Because of those eyes, everyone—even her own family—called her Cat. She was tall, lean, powerfully built and, uncommon for her Therian countrymen, very comfortable in the frozen lands. Prior to the war, she had served as a caravan guard that ran between Theria and northern Nelfydia. When unemployed, Cat often took extended hunting trips well up into the unexplored lands above the borders of the old empire. Although she never came as far north and east as they were now, one snowfield was enough like another to make her feel at home. The Frozen Sea was new to her, but there were plenty of frozen lakes and rivers across the thousands upon thousands of miles of snowy wastelands.

In hopes of preventing another argument between the Twins, she steered her horse over to stand between theirs.

"We're so far north that the ice here should be thick and safe," she said.

"How sure are you?" asked Faulker.

"Sure enough to risk my own life," Cat said. "And I prize that more than yours, my lord."

"Please don't call me that."

She ignored him. "The Winterwilds are basically a large island in the sea. It's huge, though. About the size of Vahlycor." She pulled out a map that had been carefully copied onto sealskin. It showed that part of the world. The northernmost foothills of the Cathedral Mountains were a hundred miles due south, with the strange region known as the Shadowlands on the eastern side and an unclaimed stretch of snowy nothing to the west before the upper orders of Zaare, Vahlycor, and Nelfydia were stacked one atop each other.

Unlike the rest of the old Silver Empire, there was very little detail provided about the arctic. There were some scattered settlements, small trading towns, hunting lodges, and semi-permanent camps established by nameless nomadic peoples who refused to interact with anyone from the south. All across this map were additional marks made by Cat herself based on things she knew firsthand or learned from people she trusted. She tapped a place on the map with a gloved index finger.

"See here?" she said. "That's where we are. And the southwest spur of the Winterwilds presses into the sea so far that the gap between that and the mainland is at its narrowest."

"Doesn't look all that narrow," said Faulker.

"Narrow-*est*," corrected Jheklan. "Try listening."

"It's half as wide as any spot I know of without traveling five hundred miles east," said Cat. "Unless, of course, you want to add another ten days to our journey . . ."

"I'm fine with here," said Jheklan.

"Here looks pretty great," said Faulker.

Cat turned in her saddle and studied the sky to the southwest. "There's a storm coming. It's dry enough, though. The snow will be powder. We should camp over there, in the shelter of those rocks. The lads will need rest because tomorrow we'll have to build the ice-riggers. That will let the horses restore themselves, too, because if we don't get a good wind the day we need to cross the ice, then we'll have to wrap their hooves in burlap and have them pull us across the ice."

Faulker shook his head. "I still have a hard time believing we can *sail* across the Frozen Sea in boats."

Cat smiled. "Oh, it'll be fun."

"You've done it?" asked Jheklan.

"Many times. Mostly on the winter lakes in Nelfydia. Raced a few times, too, but only came in third."

"Who came in first?" asked Faulker, interested.

"Giril One-hand."

"What happened to his other hand?" asked Jheklan.

"He fell overboard during another race that same season. The rear ski cut through his forearm neat as you please."

"Gods of the Harvest," said the Twins at the same time.

Cat laughed. "Don't worry, my lords. That kind of thing almost never happens."

"'Almost' is not as comforting a word as you might think," said Faulker.

"Oh, don't worry, my lords. I'll keep you safe."

With that she turned away and began shouting orders to the others.

Jheklan and Faulker sat on their horses a while longer and watched.

"I think she was laughing at us," said Faulker.

"Yeah."

"Kind of can't blame her."

"Yeah," said Jheklan.

They looked at the white and icy sea.

"Shit," said Faulker.

"Shit," agreed Jheklan.

CHAPTER FORTY

"I have to leave," said Tuke.

Filia peered up at him from a nest of furs. She was naked but she sat up sharply.

"Leave? Why?"

"I just had a conversation with Selvath," he said. "She told me something of great importance. Something that may help us in this war. I've already sent a galloper ahead to try and overtake Kagen, or at least reach him while he is with Mother Frey."

"What are you talking about?" demanded Filia.

Tuke told her.

Filia pushed aside the furs and, shivering with the cold, came and hugged Tuke. Then she pulled on some clothes and helped him pack.

CHAPTER FORTY-ONE

The monster stepped out of the shadows of the forest in central Vahlycor and stood in a bright fall of golden sunlight.

It stood in man shape, but only barely so. It was far taller and more heavily built than any human had ever been. The thing was dressed all in black, with a helmet that hid the face entirely, showing only a pair of fiery red eyes. It had voluminous sleeves that formed part of a vast cloak made from long blades of steel painted a flat and featureless black. Steam rose from its burning eyes, and across its shoulders there were snapping and hissing arcs of red electricity.

The field before him was gray and brown, with a dusting of withered leaves obscuring the dead grass. It was a slanted field, rising from the forest wall to a crest on which some large and lonely trees brooded in solitary isolation.

Between two of the largest trees sat a group of figures on horseback, and beyond them a large army of Ravens. There were several Hakkian officers and courtier-knights atop the hill along with clerics in yellow hooded cloaks, a flag-bearer, and Lord Jakob Ravensmere. Three others sat on their horses on the very crest of that hill slightly ahead of the others. One was Lord High Marshal Mari Heklan, wearing her understated armor and smiling faintly the way she so often did, as if she understood the punch line of a joke others were still trying to suss out.

The razor-knight lifted its armored head and sniffed the breeze as it blew past him. A growl broke from deep in its massive chest and it was full of red pleasure and dark promise. It spread its arms wide so that the many black blades set into the fabric of its voluminous sleeves looked like the wings of some great dark bird. In many Hakkian songs, that fell creature was often called the God of Ravens.

But not now.

"*Bring me the Witch-king of ancient Hakkia,*" it roared. "*I am come for him and I will feast on his heart and bathe in his tainted blood.*"

"Well," said Mad Mari, "he seems like a charming lad."

"That thing has killed more than eight score of our soldiers," said Jakob nervously. "He has been pierced with a hundred arrows, struck with boulders hurled by trebuchets, and doused with burning oil. Yet he lives on."

"The day is young," said Mad Mari.

Jakob almost made a comment but chose silence instead. This venture was strange and dangerous enough.

"If you want the Witch-king," shouted the lord high marshal, "you will have to get past us first. And I don't think even you can do that."

"If you stand between me and the king of evil, then you stand in death's way," cried the razor-knight. *"Even your god, Hastur, cannot save you from me, for I am thy doom."*

With that, the monster began moving up the hill. Slow, at first, its heavy boots landing like the deep booming notes of kettle drums. Then it drew its own blade, which was also black as midnight. It was six feet in length—a cleaver, a man-splitter, and no mortal could have hefted it, let alone raised it with such ease. It spoke to the immense power of the thing that was born of necromancy and infused with the soul of a demon from the deepest hell.

The creature broke into a run, tearing uphill with increasing speed and ferocity, growling like a savage tiger. The very air crackled around it, with arcs of electricity dancing across its shoulders. Sparks fell to the dried leaves and set them alight, so that as the monster ran it left behind it a trail of fire.

Jakob, watching, saw the yellow fire on his master's sword and the deeper orange fire in the wake of the oncoming razor-knight. "Gods help us," he whimpered. "Surely we are going to die."

Mad Mari merely laughed.

The razor-knight, seeing that no knight or soldier dared charge, cried out in ugly joy. As the distance shrank from two hundred yards to a hundred, to fifty, and closer still, the razor-knight's laughter filled the sky.

He was no more than a dozen paces and yet Mad Mari did not move her horse. Her officers and flag bearer trembled. Jakob was making small mewling sounds.

Then the razor-knight uttered a sharp cry of surprise and alarm as the very ground beneath his boots collapsed and the monster *fell*. It plunged downward through a thin lattice of brittle branches and false ground made of dun-colored cloaks and heaped leaves.

It plunged into a deep pit whose bottom was a forest of spear-points. The war cry of the razor-knight changed to a piercing shriek of unnatural pain as its body was pierced through and through.

Atop the hill, Jakob Ravensmere stood up in his saddle and cried out in shocked surprise.

"A trap?" he cried. "This was all a trap?"

Mad Mari threw back her head and laughed like a hyena.

CHAPTER FORTY-TWO

Kagen was glad to be alone. He could have taken Tuke or Filia, or both, but the truth was that the larger the army grew the less he wanted to be there.

I'm no goddamn general.

He said that to his friends so often lately that when he began that declaration one or the other would finish it. And he told it to himself over and over.

It was the truth, too. Some officers aspire to the ultimate command rank, but Kagen felt he was born to be a captain. Small groups that were mobile and quicker to pivot—like the Bloody Bastards who followed him to Vespia—were his favorite. He wanted to be in the thick of things, reacting to the situation as it evolved. Last thing he wanted was to be the grand man who sent others to do the blood work. But no matter how much he argued and protested it, the army was being built around *him*.

And so an escape of a few weeks was a relief. To be alone and out in nature appealed greatly. No one out there asked anything of him or looked to him for answers.

It also gave him time to think things through.

The Seven Cryptical Books of Hsan, though *potentially* valuable in the war effort, so far had been a profound disappointment. Good fighters had died to help him obtain them, and for what? Frey's so-called experts had accomplished nothing of real value except a warning about some magical nonsense called the ascension.

It also gave him the time he needed to understand and accept all that had happened to his family. His parents and Hugh had died on the Night of the Ravens. Then Degas, the eldest of the family, had been crucified to the door of the family manor house.

Grief hit him in waves about that.

He knew he had not yet truly accepted that Herepath was the monster behind all of this.

"How could you be a monster?" he asked aloud.

The cold wind took his question and whipped it away, tearing it apart and leaving nothing but regret.

He camped alone and tried not to brood, but there seemed to be no other path for his thoughts to take. And so he wrapped himself in furs and drifted off to a troubled sleep.

CHAPTER FORTY-THREE

DREAMS OF THE DAMNED

. . . In dreams Kagen ran through endless corridors of ice looking for Herepath.

He shouted his brother's name and flinched as the echoes—twisted and amplified by that strange place—came back in mocking and malicious tones. He pressed on, frightened but undaunted.

The air was oddly humid for a place so thoroughly frozen, and Kagen realized that the walls glistened differently than they had before. He slowed to a stop and touched one, drawing his fingers across it. When he looked at his fingers, he was surprised to see that they were slick with wetness.

With melting ice.

It was then that he realized his breaths no longer plumed out the way they always had in this frozen place.

"What the hell . . . ?" he said aloud, and for once his voice was not a blend of his younger and current selves but was purely the voice of who he was now. That disturbed him in ways he could not identify.

He walked slowly along one corridor, trailing his fingers along the walls of melting ice. Within a few score steps he heard soft splashes and looked down to see that there was a half inch of water here. Kagen squatted and dipped his fingertips in it, but winced when he sniffed it. It smelled of rot and age and badness. There was a faint fish stink to it.

He'd smelled that before, though at the moment he could not remember where. Was it here? Or—

A sound snapped that thought apart and he whirled, his hands flashing for his knives.

It was so loud a sound that the sheer volume of it made it hard to understand. Only as it faded to echoes did he realize that it was something he had heard long ago, in dreams he'd had as a lad. A mingling of three distinct emotions woven together into one roar.

Great pain.

Terrible despair.

And massive anger.

Kagen took a few hesitant steps toward the source of the sound.

When the last echo faded, he raised his own voice and said a name.

"Fabeldyr . . . ?"

He painted the name on the damp and clammy air.

The roar came again. Louder this time, and it lasted so long that Kagen feared it would burst his eardrums. Or his heart.

Even so, he walked more quickly, wincing in pain but unable to retreat from it. He broke into a trot and from a trot to a full run, feet splashing in water that was now up to his ankles. The closer he got to that dreadful roar, the deeper the meltwater became.

That should have terrified him.

Had he been able to read the implications of it in the moment, it most assuredly would have.

CHAPTER FORTY-FOUR

Jheklan and Faulker entered one of the tents, drawn by the promise of hot soup and shelter from the freshening wind. One person was already there, the young scholar Alibaxter, formerly a ceremonial wizard from the Garden on Skyria. He looked up with a hopeful smile.

"How are things progressing?" he asked. Alibaxter was a dumpy, unfit-looking young man with a hopeful attempt at a proper wizard's beard, though it remained somewhat threadbare despite ointments and a touch of dye. He was dressed in heavy wool trousers and a fur-lined coat. The cap he wore was—he insisted—a sorcerer's pointed hat, but as the cap was soft and floppy, with a pompom on its point, the effect inspired no awe. On the whole, though, he was an earnest fellow who was eager to please. His mood waffled between two distinct points—cheerful optimism and self-doubt—with few pauses in between.

"Cat is getting ready to start building the ice-riggers," said Faulker as he sat down heavily on a bundle of furs.

"And a storm's coming in," said Jheklan, sitting next to his brother.

Alibaxter ladled soup into tin mugs and handed one to each. "Well, it is the *Frozen* Sea after all," he said brightly. To which Faulker cleared his throat suspiciously loud.

Jheklan, resisting the urge to knife the both of them, glowered into his soup.

"I'm rather looking forward to the ice-riggers," said Alibaxter, who clearly did not pick up on the ambient mood. "I read an account of one of the early expeditions here, and they had quite a few adventures."

Jheklan glared over the rim of his cup. "What *kind* of adventures? And, if snow apes or winter eagles factor into it I will do extreme physical harm to you."

Unperturbed, Alibaxter said, "Oh no. Nothing like that. A bit of frostbite, but really . . . who needs *ten* toes?"

"I might," said Faulker.

"But what excited me then, as now," continued the young wizard, "was the anticipation. There are thousands upon thousands of years of history trapped in that glacial ice. Gardeners have been digging things out for centuries."

Jheklan asked, "What kinds of *things?*"

"Oh, many items," said Alibaxter brightly. "They range from ancient books that were, for reasons entirely unknown, hidden there, and artifacts whose nature defies understanding. For example, the expedition two hundred and sixteen years ago led by Gardener Thessalan Goflen of Ghenrey found a number of metal contraptions in which there were preserved corpses of people. Four of them, plus a dog, seated on leather benches within a box made of metal and glass, and some bendable material no one has since identified. It had four wheels and inside the front of the contraption was some kind of device made from metal, but its purpose has never been deciphered. I've seen drawings and it all looked like a kind of carriage, but there was nothing to attach horses."

"What about weapons?" asked Faulker. "Please tell me they've found something we can use against the Bitch-king."

"'Bitch-king,'" repeated Alibaxter and chuckled. "That's quite funny."

"Tell me," said Jheklan, "what do you think we'll actually find up here?"

"Yes," agreed Faulker. "Curiosities are all well and good, but it would be comforting to know that there will be a horde of magic swords—"

"—or bows," cut in Jheklan. "Magic bows and arrows would not come amiss."

"—or some barrels of banefire."

Alibaxter's smile faltered but a little. "Oh, nothing like that, I'm afraid. But don't despair—Mother Frey believes that there are great books of magic here. Books, by the way, that were mentioned in your brother's correspondence." He sighed. "Ah, it would be the luck of the world to find that Gardener Herepath was still here and alive. That is Mother Frey's dearest hope."

"Herepath isn't a sorcerer," said Faulker. "I mean, sure, he's weird as weird gets, but he can't do magic."

Alibaxter said, "We cannot be sure of that."

"Meaning?" asked Jheklan.

"Well, it's well-known he was an alchemist of some note. And rumors that he had a great interest in learning the secrets of magic. I believe it's one of the reasons he came here. To learn how to do magic."

The Twins exchanged a look.

"Herepath the Sorcerer?" suggested Jheklan.

They both burst out laughing.

"Well, it's what I heard," said Alibaxter defensively. "Besides . . . a lot of people are discovering magical abilities. I've even been able to perform a few simple spells. I made it rain a few months ago."

"Can you forestall winter storms?" asked Faulker between large gulps of the excellent soup.

"Not . . . as such," Alibaxter admitted, "though I have been giving it some thought. Perhaps there are modifications of the other weather spells."

He did not sound very hopeful, though, and the conversation stalled.

The Vale twins ate their soup, treasuring the warmth it restored to their muscles.

"If nothing else," said Jheklan, "you make one hell of a soup. Gods above, I feel like a new man."

Faulker leaned back to drain the last drop. "Damn. Me, too. Makes me even want to go back out and help Cat with those ice-riggers."

Laughing, they got up, clapped him on the back, and headed outside.

Left alone, Alibaxter smiled down at the cauldron of soup. He chanted something in an ancient language and waved his hands in complex patterns over the pot.

<hr>

CHAPTER FORTY-FIVE

"He's not coming," said Hop Garkain as he and his partner stood shivering in the darkness outside of the Plover's Nest in eastern Vahlycor.

Once upon a time he had been a huntsman from the dense forests of Behlia in the deep south, but that was not for him, and Hop had gone adventuring. Many of the jobs he took were on the disreputable side of questionable, and he had plenty of scars as souvenirs of battles won and lost. He joined the Unbladed, mostly for the travel and the chance to fight, drink, and whore his way through the Silver Empire.

"He's coming," insisted his companion, Bracenghan ah-Fahr—a Samudian known as "Brace." He had been a minor noble from a good family but was cast out because of gambling and dueling.

The pair made a strange combination. Hop was very short, broad, pale-skinned, heavily muscled, and sported a fierce black beard. Brace was tall, lean, dark-skinned, and graceful as a dancer, and his black hair was dyed a golden blond. Hop had a heavy double-bladed axe slung down his back, while Brace wore a slender weapon that he called a knife but was really a cut-down dueling saber. And not cut down far enough, which constantly put him in danger of arrest for breaking the old laws that forbade anyone who was not a nobleman or a knight in service to a lord to carry long steel. Brace looked, spoke, and acted highborn, which kept most town beadles from demanding papers or bringing out their measuring cords to certify the length.

They stood in the shadows beneath an elm tree that looked so twisted and old that the world might have grown up around it. An owl sat in a high branch and occasionally shat on Brace, though the Samudian did not notice. Nor did Hop point it out.

"He was due here two days ago," complained Brace, stamping his feet in the cold, trying to promote warm circulation. Being a man of small imagination he failed utterly except in making his feet even more sore.

"And . . . ?" prompted Hop.

"And maybe that means the Ravens caught him and his head and heart are on their way to the Witch-king in spirits of wine."

"Or," said Hop, "maybe they did catch him and he chopped them into dogmeat and has been hiding out until things cooled down."

Brace grunted. "You think the sun shines out of his ass, don't you? It's been all hero worship ever since we met him."

"You can kiss my hairy ass," said Hop without rancor. "And while you're down there you can polish my balls."

"That's the other thing. Ever since we met Kagen's goon, Tuke, you've been making a lot of comments about balls."

"Balls are funny," said Hop. "What's your point?"

"My point is," huffed Brace, "that—"

"You two are a couple of complete fucking idiots," said a voice behind them.

Hop cried out, leaped sideways, twisted in mid-air as he grabbed for his axe, and landed with the weapon in both hands. Brace made a *yeep* sound, spun, and drew his blade.

Six feet behind him, a shadowy figure leaned against the wall of the tavern. Several horses stood behind him placidly eating night flowers that grew alongside the road.

"Kagen!" gasped Brace. "We were . . . we were waiting for you."

Kagen plucked a stem of withered sweetgrass from between his teeth, looked at it, and let the breeze whisk it away. "Which makes me wonder how long you fools would be waiting out here looking the wrong way if I hadn't said anything."

"We, um, were just playing, is all," said Hop. "Pretending that we didn't hear you come up behind us."

"Right," said Brace, lunging at that. "We knew all the time. You and your horses."

Kagen studied them for a moment. "You two remind me of my brothers. Jheklan and Faulker."

Brace brightened. "Why, thank you."

Hop elbowed him. "I don't think he meant that as a compliment."

"Well," said Kagen, "at least one of you has a spoonful of brains."

Brace turned away to hide his glare.

Kagen held out the leads to Jinx and the other animals. "Stable them and give them a good brushing. Is the old woman inside?"

Hop took them, looking mildly confused. "We're not stable lads . . ."

"Well, it's something to aspire to," said Kagen. He turned and walked away without waiting for an answer.

Brace looked down at the reins he now held.

"I knew he was there all the time," he said.

"Of course," agreed Hop.

The hoot owl shat on both of them this time.

CHAPTER FORTY-SIX

The Witch-king sat cross-legged on the paving stones of a private courtyard, his yellow robes gathered and tucked, his hood pushed back, and his lace veil folded neatly and set to one side. There were no guards present, and the doors to this place were locked, and he was entirely alone.

He sat inside a circle of mingled salt, black sand, and hawthorn ground to a powder. Small pieces of clear and smoky quartz, black tourmaline, obsidian, peridot, shungite, and amethyst, with each adding its own special qualities to the overall spells of protection he had carefully set in place.

Outside the circle and attached to a flagstone by a chain clamped around its neck and attached to a spike driven deep into the stone, was a young mountain lion. From where it crouched it was unable to reach the Witch-king, but it tried nonetheless—lunging forward to take random swipes with its claws. Those attacks struck an invisible barrier that shimmered and coughed sparks onto the ground.

The Witch-king was aware of it but did not look at it. His eyes had rolled up white and the whites slowly transformed into orbs of deepest red veined with black. Except for his lips, the rest of his body was utterly slack. His chest barely moved as he breathed.

Those lips moved, though, speaking in a language that was forgotten even before the volcanoes tore the old world apart and darkened the skies with uncountable tons of ash. It was not a language created by men, nor one ever intended for their use. It hurt him to speak it, and blood bubbled to his lips from his lacerated tongue and gums. Lines of crimson rolled down his chin and splashed onto his robes. Even if the Witch-king was aware of it he would not have cared.

He spoke in that awful, transgressive, forbidden tongue for hour upon hour. Time was as meaningless as discomfort or pain.

The lion lunged and lunged and swiped the air with claws. Its eyes were filled with terror. *It* felt pain. It was aware—on a primal level—that the words the man spoke were connected to the agony it felt. Its roars became piteous cries as, within its body, organs shifted into new shapes, blood flowed along new and strange pathways, and its very bones creaked and ground as they took on new shapes. If it could have wept, its tears would be as red as the blood on the sorcerer's mouth.

"*Ah nafl ahf' ymg' ah mgng ahf' Y' gotha,*" intoned the Witch-king.

Be not what you are but what I desire.

The lion changed slowly and with terrible pain. It changed and changed until it was no longer anything that the eyes of nature would recognize as a lion. Or even as a cat.

All around that courtyard, behind stout bars, other creatures felt the pain of this animal and they, too, cried out in outrage and horror.

CHAPTER FORTY-SEVEN

When Kagen entered the Plover's Nest and spotted Mother Frey, he was shocked at how much older she looked. Although it had been a few months since they last met, the network of lines in her face were deeper and more comprehensive, and her gray hair thinner and duller. She also looked less physically substantial, and he wondered if it was stress or illness. Or both.

Kagen crossed to the alcove where Frey sat. She began to rise but he waved her down and bent over to kiss her cheek, which was dry and papery. He sat across from her and signaled to the barman for beer and steak.

"Well met, Kagen Vale," said the old woman. She reached for his hands and squeezed his fingers. Her hands were small and cold but there was still strength there. "It is good to see you."

"It is good to see you as well, Mother."

"You don't have to call me that," said Frey. "That title belonged to the Garden Faith and it is gone now."

"Is it actually gone?" he asked, gently taking his hands back. "The Hakkians burned down the Gardens but surely they have not killed faith itself."

She studied him with her piercing eyes. They were curious eyes—filled with the wisdom of her years but yet looked like a young woman's eyes in an old face. "Are you saying you retain some faith of your own?"

"Understand me," said Kagen, "*I* did not leave the Harvest Faith. It left me. I was cast out by its gods. Literally. I saw them, so it's pretty hard for me to become a disbeliever after that. I'm just not *of* the faith anymore."

She nodded in a way as if his comments confirmed a thought. "If I may ask, to whom do you pray these days?"

"That depends on how drunk or pissed off I am. The Gods of the Pit are useful for that. Dagon has his moments, too."

"But you don't worship them."

"I don't *worship* any gods," he said with asperity. Then he softened and in a lower tone added, "Though I would not step on their shadows. I'm damned but I'm not a damned fool."

"That is useful to know," she said.

"Is it? Why?"

"Because faith, in times like these, matters more than doctrine. Faith can be a secular thing, and the stronger for it. We will all need that kind of faith in the coming days."

The barman delivered his food and drink then slipped away.

"Faith is tricky," Kagen said after a deep swallow of beer to wash the road dust from his mouth.

"I spent most of my life investigating false miracles," said Frey. "I am aware of the tricks and traps of faith."

"Fair enough, but I didn't come all this way for a discussion of theology," he said. "Have you brought what I asked?"

He felt something press against his calf and did not have to look beneath the table to know that Frey had pushed a parcel to him.

"The Seven Cryptical Books of Hsan have been studied and faithfully copied," she said. "I take it you are still committed to bringing them to Lady Maralina."

"Have your people managed to learn *anything* from them?"

"Some. The preamble was written in a more modern dialect and my scholars were able to translate it," she said. "It speaks of a complex series of spells that will guide a chosen one through the steps of ascension. We can infer that this is why the Witch-king wanted these scrolls so desperately, or wanted to keep them out of our hands. In either case, it seems likely that he will attempt this ascension in order to achieve demi-godhood. If he succeeds, then his powers will increase many, *many* times. Increase beyond our ability to even fight him."

"Gods below . . ."

"And that same preamble talks of a companion ceremony to bring one of the Great Old Ones out of the realms of dreams and make him manifest as a living being on this material plane."

"You're talking about bringing Hastur to life," said Kagen, appalled.

"That seems like the likely intent."

"I should have burned these damned things," he said, kicking the bag under the table.

"No," said Frey quickly. "It is far more likely the Witch-king wants them so we do not. If the full details of these spells are included, then a sorcerer of some other kind might be able to create a counter spell, or at least some way to thwart this ascension."

"Yet we don't know this for sure?"

"We don't, so I support your decision to take them west to Arras and give them to the lady."

Kagen cut a piece of steak. "And if even she is unable to read them? What then?"

"Then we will continue to hope that your brothers, Jheklan and Faulker, are more successful in their mission to the Winterwilds."

"Ah. That. I don't suppose there has been word from them?"

"Not since they left, no."

"Which means you haven't been able to tell them that our brother, Herepath, is the evil prick pretending to be a Hakkian sorcerer."

"Word was sent," she said. "But I do not think it reached them in time. They said they would take less-traveled roads and none of my people have seen or even heard of them with one exception. I had arranged for a guide for their expedition. Cat Dolthis. She knows the Winterwilds as well as anyone and better than most."

"I've heard of her," said Kagen. "Smart and tough."

"Yes. Oh, and I arranged for your brothers to take a young Gardener with them. His name is Alibaxter."

"Why? Is he a fighter? A tracker?"

"No," said Frey, "he is a wizard."

CHAPTER FORTY-EIGHT

"So, to understand this," said a scowling Kagen, "you sent a snot-nosed lad who aspires to be a wizard with my brothers in the hopes that proximity to the dragon, Fabeldyr, will somehow enhance his magical powers? Do I have that right?"

"It is hardly how I'd phrase it," said Frey. "But it is essentially correct."

"Gods of the smoldering Pit, woman, I've seen children's puppet shows that made more sense."

Frey's eyes turned cold. "Would you rather I sent no one with them who understands the nature and history of magic? Would you prefer no scholar accompanied them who could identify important books and writings? Or do you think Jheklan and Faulker, as clever as they are, could tell the difference between a book of magic and an herbalist's codex?"

"Ah, well . . . there you have me," conceded Kagen. He sighed. "Did you at least send some Unbladed with them?"

"Sixteen Unbladed, actually. Men and women whose names were suggested by Filia alden-Bok."

Kagen nodded. "That's something."

"If I may change the subject?" asked the old woman. "Tuke has sent me detailed reports of your recruitment and training. And just this morning I got his message about the battle with the Firedrakes."

"That was fast," said Kagen with a mouthful of food. "And . . . ?"

"The defeat of the Firedrakes is going to wound Hakkian credibility. They were a well-known and much revered battalion."

"They fought well enough," conceded Kagen.

"I will have broadsheets prepared and sent to every town in the empire," said Frey. "Within a fortnight everyone will know that General Kagen and his army defeated the Firedrakes easily."

"I wouldn't call it easy," he said, still chewing. "Also, I'm not a general."

"It is politically useful that we call you that," said Frey. "As for the battle, the broadsheets will call it a rout."

"It was hardly that."

Frey shook her head. "Understand, Kagen, that this was the first open, formal battle in this war. Even though no nation has openly declared for or against the Witch-king, all of the nations are arming. A full-blown war is inevitable at this point. A resounding victory such as yours is worth a legion of rabble-rousers buying beers to bribe people to listen to a recruitment speech."

"You exaggerate."

"Do I? I've already seen the effect your victories have had. The fight you had with Branks at Ghuraka's camp in Nelfydia has brought thousands to us already. The people are rallying around you, whether you call yourself a general or not. You are becoming a hero to the people."

"Yes, I'm wonderful," said Kagen dryly. "Crowds cheer as I pass."

Frey smiled at that. "They will."

"Gods save me." He slopped down a mouthful of ale, then gave her a hard, frank stare. "So, what have *you* been doing while we're out fighting and dying?"

"Me?" she asked, her eyes twinkling. "Knitting and taking in stray cats. What else would a useless old woman be doing?"

Kagen laughed. "Okay, okay . . . we each fight in our own way. I apologize for the implication."

She waved it away. "And I apologize for the sarcasm. It's a bad habit of the old who are too used to being judged by the number of lines on our faces rather than the functions of our brains." Frey sighed. "Even in my youth I was not a fighter. Not like your mother or Filia. I have always been a manipulator, a scholar, a seeker of truths."

"From what Filia tells me, your whispers here and there have drawn at least as much blood as my Bloody Bastards have."

She merely smiled and sipped her wine. He ate in silence for a few minutes. Once his plates had been cleared and a board of cheese and dried fruits placed on the table, he said, "I am concerned about my brothers."

"They are tough lads," said Frey.

"They are going to the Winterwilds to find a dragon."

"Ah," she said. "There is that."

"What do you expect will happen if they find Fabeldyr? Will they free her? Kill her? Collect tears and blood to help your pet wizard, Alibaxter, become the next great sorcerer?"

"Actually, Kagen," said the old nun. "I left that decision up to them."

"Gods below! You left something that important to those buffoons? The world is truly mad."

"If it was sane, my friend," said Frey, "you would still be a captain of the palace guards and—the gods bless her—your mother would still be alive."

Kagen accepted that and they drank to the Poison Rose.

Something occurred to Kagen, and he said, "You've mentioned the tears and blood of the dragon, and I've heard that same reference elsewhere, that those two things are the source of magic. But how? In what way? Do the tears do one thing and the blood something else? Or are they combined in some way?"

"Oh, I've wondered about that myself, and have asked various scholars. I even asked Herepath once. Shall I tell you what he said?"

"If you please."

"This was before his last trip to the glacier," said the nun. "He mentioned that he had read a paper by a learned colleague about—how was it phrased?—*the practical and spiritual uses of dragon magic.* He did not go deeply into the specifics, but it was his understanding that the tears of a dragon were tied to the presence and function of magic in the physical world, while the blood of dragons served the same purpose in the larger world."

Kagen grunted. "I'm not sure that makes it clearer."

"Oh, and there was something I read in an old case file by one of my predecessors in the Office of Miracles. He wrote that it was believed that dragons were somehow tied to the making of banefire. Alas, he did not include any specifics."

"That's a shame. If we knew how to make banefire, this war would be a hell of a lot easier to fight."

"Without a doubt," said Frey. "But that effectiveness is why the secrets of how to make it were always kept secret. So secret that there was a gap in the process of handing down this knowledge and eventually it was lost."

"Until Herepath rediscovered it," said Kagen bitterly.

"If he did. It may also be that he found where a large cache of it was stored. In either case, we can wish for some but should not count on having any."

Kagen sighed and nodded.

Setting her cup down, Frey asked, "When will you ride to Arras?"

"I'll get a good night's sleep, then set out at dawn."

"Good," said Frey. She dug into a sleeve pocket and produced a small scroll, considered it for a thoughtful moment, then handed it over.

"What's this?"

"A list of friends who have estates more or less on your way to Arras. Nobles, mostly. They will provide food and shelter for you." She leaned closer. "Listen, now. These men and women are part of my cabal. They have been so since the start. They are very wealthy and important, and they have access to great resources. More than enough to hire and equip an army of the size we'll need. They are also very quietly but effectively raising troops. I think you will be encouraged by the numbers."

He laughed. "You are a devious old witch, aren't you?"

"Devious and old? Yes. Witch . . . ? I wish I had those powers."

"You get by," observed Kagen.

"Listen, Kagen," she said, "about Jheklan and Faulker. Please don't be overly concerned for them. I'm sure they're fine. But just in case, I'm equipping a rescue party to go searching for them and, if needed, to complete the mission they were attempting to undertake."

"Send them if you want, but I may have a better plan," said Kagen. "Or, at least, the chance of one."

She studied him. "Surely you're not going to tell me that you will go look for them yourself."

"I might."

"But that is madness," she cried. "And it's strategically unsound. Despite this heat, winter is coming, and even if you set out at this moment, you could not hope to reach the Winterwilds before it is at its worst. Not to mention the time spent in doing that. Six months there and back at the very least."

"That," said Kagen, giving her a small, sly smile, "depends on the route taken."

Frey's eyes narrowed. "May I ask what you mean by that?"

But Kagen did not answer. He finished his share of the cheese and bread and shifted the conversation to matters related to the war.

"We're going to need a flag," he said. "And I've been debating what kind. Frankly, I'm not sure that it should be the flag of the Silver Empire, but what it *should* be is uncertain."

Frey smiled. "I had that conversation with Lord Clementius. He's on that list. He has been working on a banner of war for us and may even have it ready by the time you reach him. A rebel flag for a rebel army."

"That's something."

"It's important. People don't follow a piece of cloth, but they will march into hell behind a banner that symbolizes all of the things worth fighting for."

"I agree." After a moment, he said, "Have your spies heard anything about the Seedlings?"

"Foscor and Gavran, you mean?" she asked, her eyes twinkling.

"Alleyn and Desalyn, damn it."

She bowed to concede the point. "They are alive and well, but beyond that I have no news."

"If this war turns as ugly as we all think," said Kagen, "I want assurances that none of the soldiers recruited by your noble friends will do them harm. Hear me on this, Frey, and tell your people. Anyone who harms those children makes an enemy of me. That is no idle threat."

"I hear you, Kagen. But what if, should we retake Argon and liberate the palace, those children act as they did on the night of the coronation. They denied being Gessalyn's children. They openly declared that the Witch-king was their father."

Kagen was silent for a very long time.

"What is it?" asked Frey.

"There . . . is something I have not told you," he said slowly. "Something I haven't told anyone."

"Tell me, then."

"When I was in Vespia, when I was going down into the crypt to retrieve those damned scrolls, I had visions. I know it was the shoggoth creature I then fought in the dark. It tried to distract me and unsettle me with fragments of difficult truths. It thought that such truths could weaken me and so leave me vulnerable to its attack. And, I tell you truly, that it nearly worked."

There was great apprehension in Frey's eyes. "What truths?"

"I had clear visions of Herepath back in Argentium. You know he lived in the palace for months before he left for the Winterwilds. In my visions I saw him talking with the Empress Gessalyn. I *heard* their conversations. It was not empress and vassal. Hear me when I say this. They spoke as lovers."

Frey closed her eyes for a moment, and he saw her wince as if in physical pain.

"It is as I feared," she whispered.

"Tell me what you feared," said Kagen gently.

"One of my spies who worked in the palace tending the flower gardens said that she thought the empress had a lover."

"She did."

"And her friend, another of my agents, who was an assistant body servant of the empress said that it was odd that Gessalyn got with child and had stopped menstruating a month before the imperial consort returned from a diplomatic mission. That timing is right for when the twins were born. The consort, never the brightest of men, did not notice. Even when the children had paler eyes than is common in either imperial family line, and fairer skin. Gods of the Harvest," she murmured, "at first she thought the children's father might have been you. No one ever suspected Herepath, and your brother was gone from Argentium long before those children were born."

"Yes," said Kagen bitterly. "Gessalyn sent him to the Winter-wilds and, I think, hoped he would die there, as so many who traveled that far north did. Had he planned to return, I believe she might have sent assassins to make sure he never reached Argon."

Frey's eyes were wet, but she did not weep.

"And then," she said in a shakier voice, "when Herepath did return, he took on the mantle of the Witch-king—how, we may never know—and sought revenge on Empress Gessalyn."

Kagen nodded. "What was the upshot? The only two children to escape that revenge—that slaughter—were Herepath's own. He wanted the throne for them perhaps more so than himself."

If Frey had looked older when he first saw her that night, she now looked deathly.

Kagen took her hands and held them. He wanted to say something that would give comfort to her, but try as he might there was nothing in his own soul but pain.

CHAPTER FORTY-NINE

The man who crouched outside the window looked like a child. He often dressed like one to fool people, and he played his role very well. With the right clothing and time to prepare he could also be a young woman or an old one, an ancient man with a stooped back, a mendicant tinker, a vagabond looking for a handout, or any of a dozen roles.

In none of his aspects, not even when he was dressed as himself, did he look like a spy.

He was in boys' clothing now, though covered entirely by a thick wool cloak with the hood pulled forward. The clothing was not for warmth, for this man heeded not the cold. His thin body was always cold, though only to the touch. He felt no cold. Only the living care about such things, and he had been dead for nearly three hundred years. He wore garments that blended him—and his pale skin—with the shadows and the night.

The mullioned window where he squatted was small, with thick panes of opaque leaded glass. One of them had a crack in it—something he had done himself with a deft application of a cold chisel, and through that crack he could hear every word spoken by Mother Frey and Kagen the Damned.

His memory for the things he heard was every bit as subtle and effective as his many disguises. In his sheltered darkness, the spy paid close attention and smiled a small and secret smile.

That smile was filled with many very sharp white teeth, as his smile was as red as sin.

CHAPTER FIFTY

The Twins walked with Cat to the frozen edge of the Frozen Sea and looked out across a vast white wasteland.

"Can't even see the Winterwilds from here," said Jheklan. "Somehow I imagined that we could."

"I imagine being at home, in bed with Karley," said Faulker. "You know, that redhead who owns the Hound and Horse. Both of us half-drunk, naked, with a warm fire blazing."

"Pig," said Cat, but without rancor.

"Ah," said Jheklan. "Karley. Yes." His eyes had a dreamy, lascivious glaze to them.

"If you two are quite done," said the Therian. She pointed to the horizon behind them. "We have two choices. We can stay here and be buried under three feet of snow—maybe thoughts of Karley's red hair and pink loins will keep you from freezing to death. Or we could get moving and let the advance winds of that storm push us away from it. It's your call, lads."

She picked up a leather bag of tools and headed over to where the team were finishing unpacking the pieces of the ice-riggers.

"She makes a compelling argument," said Jheklan.

"Articulate and cogent," agreed Faulker.

They ran back to see what help they could provide.

As it turned out, Cat had made sure that the ice-riggers could be assembled quickly, and they were bigger than the Twins thought. More like small schooners. The pieces of the hull needed to be bolted together snugly, but because there would be no immersion in liquid water, the extra weight of copper hull sheathing was eliminated. That also reduced the overall weight. Bamboo from the southern islands was used for the outrigger structures, and the sails were heavy storm canvas, oiled to prevent freezing.

The construction was completed despite several blinding snow squalls. Oddly, Cat seemed to grow more cheerful as the storm loomed, and her ebullience had a good effect on the others. Faulker and Jheklan noticed that their team began to make rough jokes and even laughed aloud whenever the strange winter thunder boomed.

Tugging on his sleeve and leaning close, Jheklan said to Faulker, "Is it me or has everyone gone mad?"

"Oh, I think we left 'mad' a few thousand miles back. 'Stark raving' is the rule of the day."

Jheklan considered. "I can actually live with that."

They gathered their gear, loaded it onto one of the ice-riggers, and within half an hour they were on the ice, moving at incredible speed as the storm hurried to try and catch up.

The storm tried very, very hard.

CHAPTER FIFTY-ONE

The door to the Witch-king's study opened and a Raven captain stepped in, bowed low, and said, "The Prince has requested an audience, sire."

The monarch in yellow nodded and the slender trickster entered the room, bowing courteously.

"Sire," he said in a plain tone that lacked his normal unctuous quality, "I need only a moment. I pray I do not disturb anything of importance."

"As it happens, I'm relaxing." The Witch-king waved the prince to a chair. "Pour your own wine."

"Thank you, Majesty," said the Prince of Games. He went to the sideboard and made a thoughtful selection, then filled a goblet with a dry red from Tull Aranzal. He swirled it in the glass, then leaned in to inhale its aroma, which smelled of mulberry and plum. Then sipped it and noted hints of coriander seed, oregano, fennel seed, mushroom, and cinnamon. "This is excellent. Shall I pour you some?"

"Just sit."

The big hound looked at the prince and sniffed, taking his scent as he had taken the wine's, and with the same connoisseur's attention to detail. Though for her it was meat and bone in their many varieties of taste.

"What do you want?"

"Majesty, I have spent much time of late in the conjuring chamber of our poor, lamented Lady Kestrel."

"To what end?" said the yellow king. "Have you managed to uncover how she turned the razor-knight against me?"

The prince sipped the wine. "Alas, no. That secret died with her. We may never discover the truth."

"That is unfortunate. Is that all you came to say?"

"No, sire. The truth is that I have been contemplating dragons."

"To what end?"

"Your plan about storing up enough of Fabeldyr's essence to give you power well beyond your ascension is interesting. What if the dragon does not die and becomes free?"

"Then I will put her in chains again. It was done by others of less power, and I know the restraining spells."

The prince did not comment on that but instead asked, "And what if what your men are doing up in the Winterwilds actually *causes* her death?"

"Then she dies," retorted the king. "And what of it? She has been dying for years."

"Death—as a concept—does not apply as easily to dragons as it does for other creatures. They were born *with* the universe. At least the Eldest, the god of fire and tears and his four consorts. The succeeding generations of dragons may not share their level of power, but death comes to them differently."

"Many dragons were slaughtered over the last thousand years."

"Many younger dragons, sire," said the prince. "Those who were born here on earth are subject to death in a more material way. Fabeldyr may not be part of the first family, but she is old. The oldest dragon to ever live on earth, but she was born out among the stars. Great-granddaughter to Vathnya. Yes, she can die, and after all these years of imprisonment and torture she is near death now. But it will not be a natural death. And woe to us all if Vathnya and his consorts believe Fabeldyr died at our hands."

"Vathnya is a myth."

"Say you so? Even one as you can believe that the god-king of all dragons who have ever lived is a myth."

"Hastur has told me as much."

The prince turned away for a moment, then he looked again at the Witch-king. "I say this to you, my king, my brother—let no Hakkian still her heart. You think you have seen real power? I tell you that you have seen its shadow only."

The Witch-king shook his head. "You underestimate me, my prince. I will soon ascend and become something this world has never seen. And in doing so, I will call into reality Hastur the Shepherd God in his true form and as a living god. Together we will reshape the infinite worlds. Already I have made magic more powerful than it has been in many lifetimes of men."

"My awakening is proof of that, Majesty," said the prince. "But hear me. Despite what many believe—and *have* believed of me—I am not a creature of darkness. I am not evil. I am an agent of chaos. It is my preference to align myself with humans such as yourself because you are waging a war, which is a forced change. In the past, I have stood behind thrones and tables of the war-like, the greedy, the conquerors, and the users because they—like you—want to reshape the world. I thrive on this."

The Witch-king nodded. "Ah. So this is proof. For if my spells awakened only dark magic . . ."

". . . I would still slumber in my tomb."

They sat in silence. After a while the prince got up, refilled his glass, and brought another for the king. They drank and watched the fire.

"Tell me, Majesty," said the prince, "how well-guarded is your prisoner?"

Beneath his veil the Witch-king smiled. "There are troops stationed in the glacier."

"That is comforting. For we want Fabeldyr in chains. We want her tears and her blood, as you have so often said. But again I say woe to us if she is free, and woe to all if she dies by a human hand."

CHAPTER FIFTY-TWO

"We meet again," said Jakob Ravensmere, eyebrows arched in comical menace.

Nespar looked past him, up and down the hall, then took him by the arm and pulled him inside. "Hush and come in. Quickly now. There are eyes and ears everywhere."

Jakob entered, amused. "You worry too much, my friend. We have both checked every inch of the hall beyond and here in your chambers. We are safe here."

"Safety is a concept in which I am losing faith," complained Nespar.

They sat in their usual seats. A bottle of very old port stood open with two glasses filled and waiting.

The sudden onset of winter was something of a relief to each of them, as they were required to wear heavy and complex robes of office. Now, at least, those garments were comfortable and even comforting as drafts wandered like pernicious ghosts through the stone corridors of the huge old palace.

"Tell me, Jakob," said Nespar, "what have you heard lately?"

"I've heard many things," said Jakob, sipping the Zaarean wine. It was rich and full-bodied, and he found it quite the thing after a long day. "Pick a topic."

"War, what else?"

"Oh, please be specific, Nespar. *Everything* is about the war we all know is coming."

"Invasion, of course," said Nespar. "You've read the reports from my spies. Samud has been building ships faster than I've ever heard of. At last count, they have fourteen hundred troop transports, one hundred and twenty warships, and countless support craft, tenders, and livestock transports. King al-Huk has conscripted every man, woman, and child old enough to lift a sword or shoot an arrow. The report I had a fortnight ago puts the numbers at one hundred and twenty-six thousand soldiers, and thirty-eight thousand warhorses. They have whole tenders crammed with bundles of arrows, and fletchers are working in dockside warehouses around the clock to make more. The same with spears, shields, and light armor."

"Yes," said Jakob, looking uneasy. "Theria has closed all of its ports to foreign shipping, and they have littered the sea off their coasts with ships. My people tell me that some of those ships sail at night to carry weapons and troops to many of the small islands off the coasts of Theria and Samud."

"Yes. Yet Vahlycor is going the other way," said Nespar. "They are moving troops and arms across country to where Argon touches their southeastern border, hard by Zaare. There are many trade routes they can use to bring armies down here."

"What I don't yet know," said the historian, "is whether these preparations are done individually by those three nations, or if it's being done in concert. I can make a hypothetical case either way, but I can't prove it."

Nespar sighed and nodded. "They have surprised—and, I admit, impressed—me with their subtlety and policies of obfuscation. They are all using thief-takers to hunt our spies, and doing so cleverly, because none have been formally arrested or put on trial. No letters of outrage have been sent here to the Witchking."

"Of course not," said Jakob. He sipped his wine and pinched stray drops from the corners of his mouth. "To do so would be to open conversations that they don't want to have. Nor, for that matter, do we. Not yet anyway."

They sat and drank and brooded.

"Will they invade?" growled Nespar, flapping a hand. "And, more to the point, why haven't they yet done so? What are they waiting for? Beyond mere field position, I mean?"

"Oh, come now, Nespar, you know what stays their hands."

"Magic," Nespar said with a long sigh.

"The *fear* of it," corrected Jakob. "It may be nearly a year since the Night of the Ravens, but the memory of it has not faded, and is hardly likely to do so."

"And yet that fear is not as potent as it was."

"No. It has taken some real damage," agreed Jakob. "The Yellow Empire remains hypothetical following the assassination attempt and the failed coronation. There are lawyers turning themselves inside out to determine the status of right to rule. Technically we are without an empire or emperor, and so are in a strange place of waiting with every nation arming."

"It is a bit like living in a house beside a battlefield," said the chamberlain.

"Oh," said Jakob with a smile more fragile than he intended, "we *are* living in such a place. Neither of us are fighters but both of us must stay until the very last drop of blood falls."

CHAPTER FIFTY-THREE

DREAMS OF THE DAMNED

Kagen slept deeply that night and drifted from worries about his brothers, and of the coming war, and down into a darker, colder place . . .

. . . He stood on a tall spike of rock that overlooked the Frozen Sea.

Far below him he watched as a pair of ice-riggers shot across the ice. Although it was too far to make any details, Kagen yet knew that his brothers, Jheklan and Faulker, were down there.

"Still alive," he said aloud. "Thank the gods."

Beyond the ice-riggers, Kagen could see a great and jagged hole in the ice. The surface waters were still churning as if some huge mass had dropped into it mere seconds ago. Kagen felt a pang of an emotion he could not define but which was sharp. He wished he could have seen what made that hole.

"When this war is done, the world will not be what it was," said Kagen. "Not even what it was before the rise of the Witch-king."

The boats bearing his brothers vanished into a bank of dense mist that covered much of the sea. The skies above were filled with clouds that cast strange shapes over the frozen water. Those shapes drew his eye and he saw some that looked like ordinary animals—wolves and huge bats and rats—but they seemed to be following the Twins. Chasing or, perhaps, hunting them.

But then another shadow, very much larger than all the others, blotted them out. At first Kagen thought it was some great bird, for it had titanic wings. But it was no bird, and on his deepest level he knew it.

Just as he knew what it *was.*

Fear took hold of Kagen, blinding him to what happened next in the dream.

He woke in the middle of the night, shivering from a cold that was deeper than the air around him. Without knowing he was doing it, he sketched a warding sign on the wall beside his bed.

Then a gentler sleep took him, and he drifted away into dreams of summer fields and lazy afternoons.

CHAPTER FIFTY-FOUR

The ice-riggers shot across the sea of ice, chased by snow squalls. As Cat predicted, the wind pushed them straight as an arrow in the direction they wanted to go.

Unlike many frozen rivers the Twins had known, this was not a body of water that ever thawed, and centuries of winds had smoothed the ice to the flatness of glass. The only danger in terms of obstacles were snowdrifts. Closer to shore these were mostly of powder and there were some joyful, nearly childlike shouts as the riggers punched through them. It was like sledding on Argon's gentle hills back home.

But after a while the storm grew damp and the snow began to fall in heavy wet flakes that clumped into mounds like sand dunes.

Hitting those drifts was no pleasure at all, and Cat—steering the lead boat—had much work to do. Skirting them presented separate challenges, because it meant balancing tiller work with sail trimming. A few hours into their run the squall veered, and they had to tack in long zigzags in order to sail closer to the wind than the ice-riggers could sail directly. With a kinder wind they could have jibed, but the wind was now well forward.

Both Faulker and Jheklan had done a fair bit of sailing and understood the basics of navigation, though they had rarely seen winds as capricious and changeable as these. It seemed that every time Cat had their boat and the following one on a good course, the breeze came at them from a different direction. Cat was deft, though, and kept as close to the direction of the breeze as was possible, avoiding the deadly no-sail zones where the wind would become entirely treacherous.

"Ware!" cried a voice from the second craft. *"Ware ahead!"*

The brothers turned to see the man in the bow pointing wildly and they followed his gesticulations to see something ahead of them, half-hidden by the swirling snow. At first glance it seemed like another wet snowbank, and Cat began to angle away, even though the only path of avoidance put the rigger in danger of taking the main force of the gale amidships. The whole boat rocked dangerously.

"Wait," gasped Alibaxter, his voice filled with dread, "what *is* that?"

The great lump ahead was not snow. That much became immediately apparent. It was the surface of the frozen sea *bulging* upward. In a lull in the screaming wind they could hear a series of sharp cracking sounds. Deep sounds, speaking to a great depth of ice that was being split apart under an unknown but tremendous force. Shards of it shot into the air only to be swept aside by the wind to fall clattering and smashing down.

The heaving mound rose as something unseen but massive

pushed from below. Jets of blue water shot upward, the curling spray freezing immediately into sleet. Whole sections of ice, some two or three times the size of the ice-riggers, stood up like menhirs and then leaned outward like the pillars of some great temple falling to ruins in an earthquake. Lightning flashed and flashed overhead, and—defying what any of them knew about storms—struck the icy sea with bolt after bolt of heavenly fire. The thunder challenged the howling wind and together they rose to a din so grotesque that any sailor with a free hand pressed it to their head in a hopeless attempt to block it out.

"Gods of the Harvest!" yelled Faulker in a near-shriek, making a warding sign with one hand while clutching a manrope with the other.

Beside him, Jheklan was staring in wide-eyed astonishment and horror. "What *is* that?"

The ice mound was fifty feet high now and the shattered slopes of it blocked their way forward. Massive cracks split through the ice and seemed to lunge in the direction of the ice-riggers. Cat wore the ship—turning in its own length—in the hope that the wind might push them at least as far as safety, even if that meant heading back to shore. There was still room to maneuver, but at the rate the frigid sea was cracking apart there would be no safety anywhere.

"Faulker, *Faulker—do you see it?*"

Jheklan's cried was so loud as to pierce the howl of the storm.

Faulker did not answer. He could not.

No one could.

As the pillars of ice reached the apex of their rise and began to fall back, the thing in the center of the mound was revealed. It was not a storm surge or the shockwaves of a subterranean cataclysm. No, this was a living thing. For one hopeful moment the Twins thought it was a whale, one of the big gray ones, but there was never a whale born in the earth's seas as massive as this. The surface of frozen water on the sea was a hundred yards thick and it had crumbled and shattered as this creature rose to the world above. Great geysers of water a thousand feet high rose with it, obscuring the thing for a moment, but the winds whipped the spray and foam away to reveal it.

It.

The main body was like that of a man, with a gigantic torso covered in a strange mix of pale feathers and glittering translucent scales. From its shoulders stretched arms heavy with a denser snowy fur, and which ended in hands with webbing between three taloned fingers. The claws alone of each finger were longer than the ice-riggers. Arctic barnacles and mollusks fell from the limbs and vanished into the churning waters. The head was not at all human but more like a nightmare vision of a deep-forest moose, with soft antlers that uncurled as it rose until they stretched across the visible sky. The snout was mooselike, but the eyes were not, the sockets round and more like those of some monstrous infant child. Those eyes were closed yet, but the Twins could see the eyeballs moving behind the lids as if it still dreamed. It threw its head back and uttered a cry that was disturbingly human but so loud that it overmatched all other noise in the world. As that cry rose, even the storm held its breath in awe or fear.

Then the monster hunched forward and, as the ice-riggers tacked again to catch the savior wind, they saw its back bulge and swell and then tear open as wings burst out in sprays of blue-white blood. The wings spread wide like those of the god of all eagles.

The wind died suddenly and completely and the ice-riggers skidded and slid and stopped at the very edge of the creature's vast shadow.

Everything seemed to freeze into stillness—the boats, the watching crews, the storm, breath, reality. Everything. The monster was still submerged to the waist in the seawater, but what stood above the shattered surface was five hundred feet above the watching humans. It was impossible for so massive a thing to live or to stand, speaking to vitality capable of lifting uncountable tons without shattering its own bones.

Faulker and Jheklan were absolutely still, forgetting to breathe, staring at something neither was prepared to accept as real. Each knew they witnessed a thing beyond them in every possible way. If any man or woman in those boats held lingering doubt that magic had indeed returned to the world, such a belief could not endure this moment of witness.

The creature stood there, its chest moving with slow, deep breaths that sent new gusts of wind across the sea, tossing the ice-riggers, spinning and turning them. Cat and the other pilot had to fight to keep the vessels from overturning.

The Twins and Alibaxter stared up at that hideous face, at the eyes that were no longer twitching like a dreamer's but were blinking faintly. Like something waking up. When the lids opened, they saw eyes of crystal blue—an exquisite blue richer than any sapphire. The blue at the heart of the oldest glacier.

For a moment those eyes were completely vacant, betraying no thought, nothing inward or outward, and focusing on nothing. The eyelids blinked and blinked again, and suddenly awareness *blossomed*. Then awareness of light became awareness of self. They could see it—literally see the thing become sensitive to itself. The blue sharpened and deepened, and as the humans cowered those eyes swept across the world into which it had awakened.

It was a terrifying and yet beautiful thing to behold. Was this something magical returning to life after a long banishment? Or was it something entirely new being born into the world? Either way, it was a sight they all knew that no other living person had ever witnessed. In his breast, on a level deeper than terror or even the knowledge that death was likely at hand, Faulker felt true awe for the first time in his life.

Beside him, Jheklan was weeping. Not in fear, but as his own understanding of the nature of the world and the universe was cracked apart—as the frozen sea had cracked—and was being reassembled into a vessel capable of containing awareness of wonder.

Of magic's true power. Of its natural correctness and its limitless scope.

The creature threw back its head and uttered a cry. Perhaps the first it had ever made. That strange mouth funneled a howl of awakening, of power to the heavens, declaring its existence. Insisting upon it. Imprinting on the unending sky in the eternal winter there at the top of the world.

Those titanic wings trembled . . . shivered, then stretched wide, angling to catch the wind. The giant's body rippled with muscular tension as it crouched and then lunged upward, ripping through the last of the cracked ice. The wings beat with a noise a thousand times more powerful than thunder's greatest aspiration. And it rose.

Rose.

Impossibly, it rose.

Uncountable tons of mass lifted beneath the pounding of those wings, pulling legs from the thrashing water that were reptilian in form and ended in clawed and many-toed flippers. The creature fought its way into the air, winning greater lift with each beat of those wings. Water fell from it as it rose, drenching the crews of the ice-riggers. The sailors were smashed down and half-drowned, and yet they fought to lift their heads and watch as the creature flew higher and higher and higher still.

Far above them, nearly lost in the blizzard's clouds, it uttered that cry once more, and echoes returned in a litany that buffeted the ice-riggers and sent them moving once more.

Then it was gone.

The storm, abashed and humbled, dwindled until only a light snow fell on a cold breeze.

Cat was the first to move, though she did so as if in a dream. She took the tiller in her right hand and turned the craft around the massive hole in the ice. Her other hand was laid flat over her heart.

Behind her, the pilot of the second boat followed suit, and the ice-rigger moved across the Frozen Sea in utter silence.

CHAPTER FIFTY-FIVE

Kagen was up before first light. He roused the innkeeper and bribed him with a silver dime to have hot breakfast on the table in a quarter of an hour, and his horses ready shortly after.

He ate alone in the quiet of the tavern, the bag with the Seven Cryptical Books of Hsan resting on the floor beside his leg. While he ate, he studied a map Frey had given him that marked the estates of her allies in the cabal. Kagen did not like the thought of wasting time making house calls—not with the pressing need to get the Hsan books to Lady Maralina—but they were necessary. Whether the lady could read them or not, the war was coming and those nobles had the money, the supplies, and the soldiers Kagen would need.

He finished, left a handful of extra coins on the table and went outside, the satchel with the scrolls slung across his body under his cloak.

As he prepared to mount, Hop Garkain came out of the tavern at a quick run.

"What is it now?" growled Kagen irritably.

The bodyguard held out a piece of crisp parchment. "Her ladyship told me to give you this."

Kagen took it with some apprehension, unfolded it, and read:

My dear Kagen,

A messenger arrived in the middle of the night with word from Tuke Brakson. He visited with Lord Gowry on a recruiting errand and Gowry told him that there was something of great potential value in a cave in the Forest of Elgin, which is on your way west. He said he would meet you there.

He will explain.

Safe travels and may all the gods watch over you.

-Frey

"What does this mean?" he demanded.

Hop shrugged. "Hell if I know."

Kagen sighed, tucked the note into his pocket, mounted, and rode off.

CHAPTER FIFTY-SIX

His name was Duke Leofellka du Belloq vell Sárkány and he was dead.

He had been one of the dead for a very long time, and now it was the only life he could remember. In vague shadows of the old days, he recalled only faces and faint fragments of incidents. His mother's face was dear to him, even now, and he had paid a Nehemitian sculptor a great deal of gold to cast her likeness in onyx, which he wore around his neck. The duke did not really know if the likeness was accurate, for there was a gulf of many thousands—uncountable thousands—of years between her death and even the rise of the Silver Empire.

Even his dukedom—the true, original one—had faded from the memory of all but three or four living beings on this tired and battered old world. The *new* dukedom was itself eight hundred years old, and it was not the second or fifth or even twentieth version of that estate. He had long since forgotten the names and faces of his siblings and could not with any certainty remember the name of the country into which he was born. In dreams he heard *Rome* and *Italy*, but those words had no meaning at all to his waking mind. Nor did they matter.

Not that he was awake and aware all those tens of thousands of years. For long, *long* stretches he slept. Either by choice, taking his rest in carefully constructed crypts he ordered built, each locked away from human eyes by complex spells and each unlocking when certain stars aligned. Or, he slept a deeper, dreamless sleep in chained coffins with stakes of holly or iron through his heart and with the added indignity of his mouth stuffed with garlic and his lips sewn shut. Those punishments held power only as long as the faiths endured whose priests had hunted him. Now, there was no one alive who kindled the fires of belief in those forgotten gods.

Each time he rose.

Each time he reclaimed his buried wealth—or obtained new and vast fortunes—and each time he became more powerful. Others of his kind were less fortunate and far less able to withstand the various rituals of exorcism that had been used on him. Once, in ages past, he had feasted on the blood of a true immortal—a daughter of the faerie folk—and the power of her blood transformed him and sustained him.

He was, he knew, a plague upon the earth, and that was a delight to him.

Recently, in the days following the Night of the Ravens and the Witch-king's spell that had brought magic back into the world, he had risen again. It took time and effort to locate the descendants of his brethren and gather them to his standard. Vampires who had fallen so low as to skulk in sewers and feed on vermin. Or ghostly and mostly insubstantial creatures who haunted graveyards and the ruins of old churches.

Those times were done.

Now he rode into Argentium under a winter moon, with sixty of the undead. They rode horses of midnight black or bone white, and the bard for each horse was beautiful in the most dreadful way, with chanfron plating over each animal's long face that was sculpted from steel to look like equine skulls. The crinets along their necks were fashioned of segmented sections that were distinctly insectoid in appearance, as was the crupper and tail guard. The peytral chest pieces bristled with spikes, and on each hoof covering there were more spikes that called to mind the barbs on the ends of scorpion tails.

The knights themselves wore heavy plate, for their unnatural strength could support it even on long rides, and they suffered not at all from either heat or cold. Like their mounts, their gorgets were spiked, as well as their steel-shod shoes.

All of these fell knights had huge and ancient double-handed swords strapped to their sides, each of which were storied and had drunk oceans of blood in wars across the face of the continent. Part of the process of acceptance into Duke Sárkány's army was to find such a sword and obtain it at any cost and by any means, from bargaining to outright murder.

Only Sárkány himself did not bear such a weapon. He preferred the elegant and ancient narrow-bladed longsword, God's Thorn, which hung at his side. He had been buried with it more than a dozen times, and with each resurrection he read more spells into the steel. When he fought, it was so light and quick that it might as well have been an extension of his hand. His armor was lighter, too, tending toward elephant leather stained dark and traced in crimson.

They rode through the gates of Argentium, capital of both the nation of Argon and what had been the Silver Empire. The guards opened the massive iron doors as the procession approached, their sergeants told to be ready. Each soldier bowed low, placing a hand over their hearts, which was the appropriate salute for the lord of all vampires on earth and his army of the undead.

High above, the entrance was watched by two figures—one in yellow and one dressed in jester's colors.

"Oh, what a war this will be," said the Prince of Games.

The Witch-king said nothing. He gripped the windowsill and stared long until Duke Sárkány became aware of his gaze, and the ancient monster placed his own hand over his heart in both salute and pledge.

Once the procession had passed into the palace, the King in Yellow turned to his advisor.

"More will come," he said.

They smiled at one another and withdrew into the warmth of the candle-lit room.

CHAPTER FIFTY-SEVEN

There were many trees along the avenue from gate to palace there in Argentium. For months now legions of ravens stood there, watching, waiting to be called.

There were fewer of them now, though. Many—very many—of their brothers and sisters had died in battles fought in the air above the bloodshed of Ravens and rebels. Even so, there were thousands of them. And more were coming from the south, from old campaigners to strong young hatchlings. Coming to join this war.

In a grove of oaks that once marked the entrance to the Imperial Garden of Argentium—which was now a brothel by decree of the Witch-king—other birds waited beneath the dying leaves on that winter's night. None were ravens. Most were coastal cormorants or grackles from the nearer farms. But there were crows among them.

One such crow looked to be a hundred years old, though in

truth he was older. An ancient bird who had watched the world fall and rise, fall and rise. Its feathers were tattered and streaked with gray; there were scars on its beak older than the palace across the plaza.

Old Grandfather Crow watched the procession of vampire knights, but throughout the parade his focus was on the lord who rode first. The crow's eyes were black beads as dark as shadows and filled with specks of light that looked like the endless stars in the sky above.

The crow made a single sound, a caw so soft that even someone passing below the tree could never have heard it. Yet all the other birds in those oaks heard it. The ravens in all the other trees felt more than heard it, and it made them uneasy, for there was a deep and bottomless hatred in that sound. An old hatred whose scope could never be calculated.

Then, once the knights were all inside and the gates closed, the crow leapt from the limb and flew high into the night sky. It turned north, flying on the wings of the wind. Toward Vahlycor. Toward a lonely tower on a cliff above the churning sea.

CHAPTER FIFTY-EIGHT

"And now we have a regiment of bloodsuckers," said Jakob as he flung himself down into an armchair and glared at the fire. "Gods of all the burning hells. How is it that a pair of educated and scholarly pragmatists like us live in such times?"

"We serve a sorcerer," said Nespar slowly. "And our lord has brought magic back. I am afraid that all of the things we heard about in songs and old tales and—gods help us—bedtime stories are now proved to be real."

The historian's lips were twisted into a sour knot. "The only people who will be delighted with all of this . . . this . . . *drama* . . . will be whoever reads my histories in centuries hence."

"And may it give them nightmares."

Despite everything, they smiled at one another. Sad and weary smiles, cynically amused.

"To that point," said Jakob, "I think the Red Plague has not been as overwhelmingly successful as *some* advisors led us to believe." He never openly mentioned the Prince of Games, the enigmatic stranger who had come out of nowhere and now stood beside the throne.

"No," said Nespar slowly, "but on the whole the Vespian debacle has done us more damage."

But Jakob shook his head. "With respect, brother, I disagree. At least in terms of public perception. What the people know is what they've heard in tavern songs and campfire whispers, and only the very stupid place much stock in that. They know the stories that Kagen Vale and his people have begun to spread—that they defeated the magicks of the Witch-king in Vespia while succeeding in discovering ancient books of sorcery that might bring down the Witch-king for good."

"All of which is true, though."

"So what if it is?" laughed Jakob. "When has the literal truth ever been allowed to shine so brightly that it changes all hearts and minds? Never, in my experience. The reality is that our lord still sits on his throne, and the Ravens still patrol the empire." He raised his eyebrows conspiratorially. "Besides, there are twice as many songs and stories out there telling other versions of the tale, and they do not put Kagen Vale in any kind of heroic light."

"You mean you have *your* people spreading lies," said Nespar.

"I prefer to think of it as competing truths. Who can prove one or the other right or wrong?"

They sipped their port and smiled.

CHAPTER FIFTY-NINE

"Are you certain this is where you want to be?" asked Queen Theka.

They stood by the rail, watching as sailors lowered a boat into the calm waters where Ghenrey and Samud met. The shoreline beyond the easy waves was deserted except for a pair of wild camels grazing on grass.

"Yes, Your Majesty," said Ryssa. "This is where I *need* to be."

There was a slight emphasis on *need,* but the queen did not pursue it. Ever since that horrific day when sea and storm came seemingly at the Widow's call, there had been few real conversations. Ryssa had either stood in the bow watching the water as the ship sailed north, or she sat alone in her tiny cabin. She politely declined all invitations to dine with the queen and in those rare times she did speak, it was in short answers filled with basic information but no depth. No explanations.

Captain Beké came over, bowed, and said that the boat was ready.

"Very well, my sister," said Queen Theka, taking Ryssa by both hands. "I wish you the blessings of *all* the Gods of the Deep. Father Dagon and Mother Hydra, and your great dreaming god, Cthulhu. May the road you walk be clear and may no new thing arise."

Ryssa studied her face. Theka was only a few years older than herself, but she seemed at once older and younger. Older, because the weight of queenship, especially in such times, seemed to have settled on her shoulders with ease but the strain was evident in the young Therian's eyes. They were not the eyes of a girl. But younger, too, because Ryssa herself felt very old, as if she had lived many lifetimes in the last year.

She squeezed those strong hands and offered a small smile, which was all that she could manage.

"May you sail untroubled seas, Majesty," she said. Then she echoed the old Therian saying. "May no new thing arise."

In the history of the west, "new" things were seldom happy. There was a corollary in the Therian curse, *May you live in eventful times.*

On impulse, she stood on tiptoes and kissed Theka's cheek.

Then Ryssa turned and went down the ladder to the boat.

She did not look back at the *Odakon,* but instead studied the empty beach and the forest beyond. Once the sound of the oars faded and she was alone, Ryssa heard a sound from deep inside those dense woods. A growl of sorts. Low but very deep, suggesting size and mass. It was not a pleasant growl. Not at all.

But that was fine with her.

She knew what it was that waited for her.

CHAPTER SIXTY

"Steady on, lads," said Cat.

Those were the first words spoken by anyone since that creature rose through the ice many miles behind them.

Jheklan stood in the stern, staring back the way they'd come. With one hand he held onto a waxed line. His other hand pressed into his chest over his heart. He had wept openly for a while, moved to a place beyond words by the event. Now, his face was dry but pale beneath his lingering summer tan. His lips parted as if he was about to say something, perhaps a prayer, but he remained as silent as all the others.

Amidships, Faulker rose from where he'd been sitting, pulling the bearskin more tightly around his shoulders. Following the disappearance of the creature into the winter sky, he had felt a chill bite deep, all the way to the bone and could not get warm. Even the herbal tea prepared by Alibaxter and handed around had not raised his inner temperature by one degree.

Faulker made his way forward and stood beside Cat, who was using a long line back to the tiller and a shorter one to control the mainsail. Ahead, shrouded in a fog that hung low and stretched across the horizon, he could see a mass of paleness rising high.

"How long until we make landfall?" he asked in a voice gone dry from disuse.

"Four hours," said Cat. "If this wind holds."

That was all the conversation. When Faulker turned to look aft, he saw Jheklan still maintaining his vigil. He caught Alibaxter watching him watch his brother, and the young wizard offered a small nod. It was not an attempt at a conversation. They didn't know each other well enough for that kind of telepathy. In truth it was merely an ac-knowledgment. They had all been through an event. Each man and woman on the two boats had to process it, understand it, find a way to adjust to the enormous reality of it, and all of the implications for what the world was now. What it was becoming.

Jheklan, Faulker knew, was deeper than he was, and a bit more religious. That creature—its majesty and beauty and, most importantly, its innocence—represented a world beyond their understanding. And it was at odds with the teachings of the Garden, which preached that magic was inherently evil.

There was nothing evil in that creature.

Jheklan had to be wrestling with faith and personal under-standing. It was hurting him.

For Faulker's part, he felt incredibly humbled to have been a witness to it. His connection to the Garden had been the most tenuous of any of the Vale children, with the possible exception of Belissa, their eldest sister. Although as much a scholar as Here-path, she had strayed from orthodox teachings in order to pursue studies in alchemy. Often scolded by her teachers and the senior Gardeners, she had confided to the Twins once that she wanted to be a witch. Had she said as much openly she would have been ar-rested and put on trial for both blasphemy and heresy. At the time she said it with a laugh, as if joking, but Faulker always thought Belissa was telling a secret truth.

What would Belissa make of what they witnessed? What would Herepath have to say on the subject? Faulker wanted to lean into their wisdom for direction so he could understand it himself.

The ice-riggers raced across the Frozen Sea and the likelihood of even greater mysteries.

CHAPTER SIXTY-ONE

Kagen rode west, going as fast as Jinx could manage. He occasionally switched mounts to keep his pace. But even then, it was a grueling pace for all of the horses. He avoided the main highways and turnpikes, opting instead for more of the less traveled byways and even game trails if they were well-worn.

Summer seemed to be finally fading and the days were growing colder. Kagen pulled his wool cloak around him and the warmth, plus the steady rhythm of the horse's progress, made him sleepy, and he dozed as the miles melted away behind him. Often it was Jinx taking an uncertain step to avoid a gopher hole that woke him. Sometimes it was a cold wind from the newborn winter. Or the sudden caw of a crow.

Not now, though.

In his half doze he heard a sound that did not fit into the orchestra of woodland noises—birdsong and insect buzz and the soft crashing wave noise of wind through the leaves.

This time, it was the *music* that made Kagen come completely awake.

He sat up straight in the saddle and strained to hear. But as he opened his eyes, he saw something that made him wonder if he still dreamt.

While all along his path summer had begun to collapse beneath the weight of the oncoming cold weather, here, in the purple-shadowed bottom of a densely wooded valley, it was as if he had ridden back in time. Summer lingered down there with a strange persistence. The forest around him was dark green and lush with ten thousand shades of new life. Flowers of incredible richness rose up from the thick grass, declaring themselves in shouts of color.

The music had come from the woods ahead and off to his left. He was sure of it. Notes from an instrument he could not identify, and lyrics in a language he did not know. Who was singing? And . . . why would they be all the way out here?

"What in the countless hells . . . ?" he murmured.

Kagen slid from the saddle and took a few steps off the trail, pulled by the strange music. Jinx nickered and tossed his head, so Kagen tied his lead to a sturdy sapling near fresh grass.

"I'll be but a minute," he told the horse. Jinx stamped a hoof in equine disapproval, but Kagen ignored him.

The music was so beautiful. Subtle yet . . . compelling.

And the forest was the most beautiful he had ever seen. It was so green and alive that it soothed him more and more with each step. His brooding mind softened, his nerves eased. Even his memory of the fall of his beloved Argon, the death of his parents, the murder of the Silver Empress, and his own gods turning their backs on him seemed to fade as he made his way into the woods.

Then—minutes, hours, days later—the music changed.

It was no longer a lilting tune. In the space of a single heartbeat, it became a woman's cry of pain. It broke the spell, but only a little. Even so, he drew his matched daggers from his belt and quickened his pace. Rabbits scampered away from him, birds fluttered up to higher branches or flew away. Far, far behind him he could hear Jinx snorting, but it had a dreamlike quality.

He broke from the foliage into a small clearing through which a brook gurgled. And there, on the far side of the crystal water, was a tableau that jolted him to a halt. A hill rose from that side and cut into its face was a shallow cave, in the mouth of which was a flat rock that served as an altar. Upon it, held fast by flowering vines around wrists and ankles and waist, was a woman of such surpassing beauty that it punched Kagen in the heart. She wore a dress of some old-fashioned kind, like something seen in tapestries of the age before the rise of the Silver Empire.

Figures clustered around her, and Kagen found it hard to understand what he saw. They were slender and small, hardly larger than children, with eyes that slanted downward, sharp noses, full-lipped mouths, and sharp little white teeth. They wore clothing that seemed to be woven from living flowers, moss, and leaves. One of them held a small knife.

They all froze and looked across to where Kagen stood. The little folk and the woman. With a thrill of atavistic terror, Kagen realized what they were.

Elvinkind.

He had seen the paintings, had the stories read to him by his mother, saw plays and read poems. Before the coming of the Witch-king and his Hakkian armies, such things dwelled somewhere in the shadowy cleft between ancient history and tales made up to frighten children.

But the world was different now. Magic was real again. Potent again. And these creatures—banished so long ago—were there before him.

The elvinkind stared at him with shock as evident as his own.

"It is a man," whispered one in a voice that was, itself, more like music than human speech. "It is a human man."

"He can *see* us," gasped another.

One of the creatures pointed at him with a bloody knife. "The queen was right," she said. "The veils are tearing. The doors are opening."

"See him," said an older elf. "He is the one. He has been touched by the eternal. Destiny sings of him in my dreams."

"Quick!" cried another. "Complete the ritual. There must be blood if the veil is to be torn entirely."

In a flash, the elf with the knife raised it above the woman's chest. The woman cried out again as sunlight danced along the edge of the blade.

"Leave her be!" bellowed Kagen. "Spill her blood and I will drown you in your own."

The elvinkind stared at him.

As did the woman.

Her face was lovely beyond words and it called to mind Lady Maralina. She was one of the faerie folk, cousins of a sort to the elvinkind. Her beauty was ancient and magnificent in its power. This elf woman's was far more childlike, with an innocence that exuded its own limitless power. Her eyes locked on his. Pleading. Entreating.

Kagen charged forward, brandishing his daggers, teeth bared with ferocity.

And the woman spoke a single word.

"No," she said.

Then she raised her hands and Kagen saw that although there were vines around her wrists, they were not tied to anything. Nor, he now saw, were her legs. The vines, fashioned with flowers, were nothing more than decoration.

It stopped him.

The woman reached up and her slender fingers touched the wrist of the elf with the knife. With the other hand she tugged at the loose neckline of her simple frock, pulling it down until her upper chest was bared. The skin was pale as milk, graced with soft shadows where the small breasts curved down and out of sight beneath the dress. Then, with the gentlest of effort she pulled the knife down until the blade touched the flesh of her breast directly over her heart.

The eyes of every elf were upon Kagen, and there was a complex mix of emotions to be read there. Fear and curiosity, pleading and hope. And joy. A species of it, at any rate, and one he could not interpret or define.

With her fingers still lightly touching the wrist of the older female elf, the woman on the altar guided the wickedly sharp tip so that it pierced her flesh and moved in a slow arc. Blood, rich and red and dark, welled from the wound and flowed down her side.

Kagen stood and watched all of this as if in a trance. He felt like he was in one of his own dreams, and yet knew he was not.

The elf priestess—if that was what she was—lifted the knife away from the wound. Blood dripped from the steel and Kagen's heart spasmed in his chest as he saw what happened as each drop landed on the ground. The dirt drank it greedily and then seemed to split apart as tiny green stalks rose to greet the sun. All around the elvinkind, and all through the woods around Kagen, every plant and shrub and wildflower began to sway as the creatures began once more to sing.

Kagen looked slowly down at the deadly weapons in his hands. Those weapons were made for battle, for mayhem and destruction, for death. Yet he stood in a place where everything around him seemed to cry out in exultation of life.

The elves studied him, watching his eyes, his face, his panting chest, and the knives he held. They were many but they were small, and except for the priestess none of them had weapons. He could rush them and kill every one of them. They were unnatural. They did not belong to his world.

But, he realized with a thunderous shock, nor did he.

He was damned. He was abandoned by his gods and likely had no immortal soul living in his breast. He was a monster, a killer, a destroyer of things.

As these inhuman creatures watched—all of them aware of the dreadful power he possessed—Kagen slowly slid his daggers back into their sheaths. He placed one hand over his own heart.

"I . . . I'm sorry," he said. Though for what he was never there-after able to understand.

The woman on the altar sat up. Blood ran freely down her body, soaking her dress, but she did not appear to be in any pain. Two younger elves helped her to stand. Then she turned to the priest-ess and spoke quickly in a language like birdsong, of which Kagen understood nothing. The priestess frowned, casting an uncertain eye at him, but then she nodded and handed the sacrificial knife to the young woman.

"I'm sorry," Kagen said again, this time for lack of something else to say. He did not understand what was happening. Had he ruined their ritual? Was he to pay in some way? Was this elf woman going to attack him?

The woman raised the knife above her head. She spoke again, this time to him. Her words were not birdsong, nor was it the common tongue of the Silver Empire. It was some other language entirely and it amazed Kagen that he could somehow understand her.

"You are human," she said, "and not human. You stand with a foot in this world and the next. The gods have seen you and so have we. So have I."

"Wh-what . . . ?" he stammered.

"She who is ageless holds you in her heart. I feel this," said the woman. "She, too, stands in two worlds. In many worlds."

"Maralina . . . ?" he whispered.

The woman's eyes darkened, and two vertical lines of concern formed between her brows.

"There is more," she said, and as she did this, she used her other hand to touch the cut on her breast. "*He* is coming."

"Who? The Witch-king? My brother?"

The elf shook her head. "*He* comes from the stars. He has heard the call of his own and he comes on wings that blot out the sun."

"Of whom do you speak?" he demanded, but the woman did not answer.

Instead, she said, "Woe to those who harm his children, for he will burn the skies and drown the worlds of men."

"I . . . don't understand. Do you speak of Hastur? Will the Witch-king raise his god in flesh rather than as a dream? Is that what your warning tells?"

The elf stepped forward, pointing the knife at his heart.

"He is coming in all his rage, man of two worlds," she said. "He does not bring mercy but retribution."

Kagen took a step toward her.

The world—all color and sound and meaning—vanished and he fell into a lightless forever.

CHAPTER SIXTY-TWO

As the ice-riggers closed on the icy banks of the Winterwilds, Faulker gestured for Jheklan and Alibaxter to join him behind the baggage amidships.

"Look, lads," said Faulker, "after what we saw, it's pretty clear that things are changing. The world that we're in isn't the one into which we were born."

"Behold the lord of understatement," said Jheklan with something like his former humor.

"Magic is not only returning," said Alibaxter, "but it is taking on new forms. I have studied the old books and that thing we saw in the ice was never mentioned once. And why? Because I do not believe it ever existed before. It is *new*. Do you understand?" Before they could reply he answered his own question. "Yes, silly question. It would not have affected us all so deeply if it was merely a monster from old myths or old histories."

"Are you going somewhere with this?" asked Faulker.

"I am," said the young wizard. "Mother Frey's network of spies has brought many stories to her. More than just the movement of Hakkian troops. All manner of creatures and beings. Hollow Monks and redcaps, mermaids and vampires, and all that lot. We've all seen flowers of a color that does not exist on earth—a color that cannot even be described because it has no corollary in nature or the prism of the rainbow. Tuke Brakson said that Captain Kagen fought werewolves and goblins. And now we have seen something absolutely new."

"Again I ask . . . what's your point?"

"That monster did not attack us. It *saw* us, but there was no animus in its eyes, no threat in its actions."

"So?" said Jheklan. "That's a good thing, isn't it?"

"I believe it is a very good thing," said Alibaxter. "I think it's very hopeful."

"How so?" asked Jheklan.

"It means that magic is not our enemy any more than, say, a sword is. Neither has its own intent. The danger lies in how it is used, and by whom. I believe magic has no bias but is true chaos. It can be shaped and directed and—as with Fabeldyr—suborned. The Witch-king has demonstrated this. Mother Frey said she planned to ask Kagen, Tuke, Filia, and their followers to venture to Vespia to find books of magic. We are on a quest to find your brother Herepath."

Faulker turned to Jheklan. "He's rattling on like Gardener Murto used to do after harvest break. Reminding of us stuff we already know."

"Please, please," entreated Alibaxter, "let me finish."

"Oh, by all means," said Jheklan, "because it's not like we're on an urgent mission or anything. Take all the time you want."

"I can fetch you a cushion to make you more comfortable," suggested Faulker.

The wizard sighed with barely controlled impatience. "We are going to try and find a dragon. Something few people have ever seen these last thousand years. I think we need to decide right now how we should go about that. The Silver Empire hunted her kind to the edge of extinction, and someone—perhaps the Hakkians or perhaps our very own Gardeners—chained her and have been torturing her. We *believe* it's the Witch-king and that is how he gained his powers."

The brothers nodded.

"What if that is a consequence of someone else's actions, though? What if the dragon was trapped by someone else who wanted to see magic return, but wanted to try and control that return?"

"Control?"

"Oh yes. To limit its spread so that magic served one agenda."

Faulker made a face. "Right, like the—what's his name again? Oh yes, the Witch-king."

"Perhaps, perhaps," said Alibaxter, "but if the dragon was completely enthralled by the Witch-king, then why was that sea monster born?"

"Because he chooses to enslave it . . . ?" suggested Faulker.

"You think so? For my part, I do not. I think we saw an example of what the ancients called wild magic," said Alibaxter. "Magic that is raw and new and belongs to no one but itself. The innocence, the total lack of guile in its eyes spoke of absolute freedom for it to be itself. There was none of the inherent maliciousness you could reasonably expect of something conjured for fell use."

"Tiger cubs are adorable and innocent and grow up to eat people," observed Jheklan.

"And while that is true in nature, consider the razor-knight. It was born of *dark* magic and as soon as it draws breath it wants to draw blood. That is how dark magic works. It manifests according to the will of whomever brings it forth into this world." He pointed to the empty ice sea behind them. "Did that thing look like it was born for murder and to serve the will of a dark sorcerer?"

The Twins exchanged a look.

"Not . . . as such . . ." said Faulker diffidently.

"Not as you would say *murderous* from birth," said Jheklan.

"By extension of that hypothesis," continued the young wizard, "we know that dragons came to earth, bringing magic with them. They were not summoned by sorcery, dark or light."

The Vale brothers said nothing, but they both leaned forward, their faces alight with keen interest.

"When we reach the Winterwilds and enter the glacier," said Alibaxter, "and if we find the dragon Fabeldyr, much may hinge on what we say to it and what we do. *To* it and *for* it. What will its first impression of us be? As enemies who fear the magic it embodies? As self-serving people who want to force it to share its power with us? Or is there some *other* path we might take in that encounter? I ask you, my lords Vale, when meeting such a creature, who do we want to be?"

They all looked forward to the fog-shrouded coastline of the Winterwilds.

None of them spoke as the ice-riggers sailed on.

CHAPTER SIXTY-THREE

"They are all assembled in the map room, your Highness," said Lord Nespar.

The Witch-king looked up from a book he was discussing with the Prince of Games.

"I will be along directly," he said.

Nespar bowed and left and the king returned to his conversation of a very ancient and exceedingly rare tome, the *Book of Azathoth*.

"I had thought all copies of this had vanished in the great cataclysm," murmured the prince. "Even then, the only copy I knew of was in the private library of a rather charmingly insane scholar who had the great misfortune of building a fortress of a house on lands below which was a slumbering caldera. It was vaporized—or at least I thought so—when that super volcano erupted and triggered the end of the so-called Greatest Age of Man. Ha!"

"This copy was discovered in the glacier up in the Winterwilds," said the Witch-king. "It was a great find. Not the greatest . . . but that is a different conversation."

"Found by the research team led by Herepath Vale," said the prince with a playful smirk.

"Even so."

"A great find."

"It has been the work of years to complete its translation," said the king.

"Had I known," said the prince, "I could have done it in a matter of months."

The Witch-king did not comment on that. Instead he turned a page and tapped a passage. "Read that and tell me your mind."

The prince bent low and studied the text. "Some of this is a variation of the thirty-ninth passage of the *Dhol Chants* from the people of Leng."

"Yes. I thought that was interesting."

"And there is phrasing particular to the *Parchments of Pnom* and the earliest translations of the *Testaments of Carnamagos*. Yet I thought this book predated those."

"As did I," said the king, his excitement matching the prince's. "But now it's clear that the *Book of Azathoth* came first."

The prince straightened and walked a few paces away from the dais, hands clasped behind his back. Then he stopped and, without consulting the book, recited the passage.

"Five hundred centuries after the world catches fire, the mask behind the mask behind the mask will rise to power and the world will tremble. And in the days of his rule, all veils will be torn, all doors flung wide, and the numberless hells will vomit forth their horrors and they will raise a cry that will shake the heavens. Then woe to all men and beasts and beastly things should that call be answered. For the answer will change the face of the world and men will drown in floods and fire."

He turned and studied the king.

"That prophecy seems to speak of you, my lord," he said.

"And, I think," said the Witch-king, "of Hastur's return. Not as a dream but as a living god, returning with all of his power to this earth."

"Yes," said the prince slowly, his eyes not meeting the king's, "it could mean that."

"You doubt it?"

"I am uncertain, Majesty," said the prince. "These old texts are trickier even than I. The scholars and mystics who wrote them were all mad in one way or another. Surely you've read other prophecies that could be interpreted any number of ways. This one *seems* to lean toward your interpretation, but how can we be sure?"

"I am sure," said the Witch-king. Then he added, "I have sent a strong party of Ravens to the Winterwilds to bring down the rest of what was discovered there. There are hundreds of scrolls and books of commentaries on ancient books. Perhaps they will allow us to be more precise in our interpretations."

"Oh, I think that is a very wise course," said the Prince of Games. Though he still did not meet the king's eyes.

CHAPTER SIXTY-FOUR

When Kagen woke, every part of him that he could feel, hurt.

He rolled over and vomited, then cowered on hands and knees, trembling like a sick dog. Somewhere nearby he heard Jinx blow softly and stamp on the grassy path.

It took forever for Kagen to climb to his feet. He shivered and then realized that the green forest had changed. The trees overhead were nearly bare of leaves and what remained was brown and dry. There were no flowers, no green shrubs except for some pines and holly. Brittle grass crunched beneath his feet. The air was very cold and there was a breeze blowing along the valley floor.

He rubbed his head, feeling for a lump, certain that he had fallen off his horse and knocked himself out. That must be the case, for the images lingering in his mind were bizarre and had to have been born in dreams. Strange music, elvinkind, and . . .

Kagen found no bump, no torn scalp. Even so, he realized that he was in pain. More than his aching limbs. He stumbled forward a few paces but stopped as pain flared in his chest.

"What in the burning hells?" he grumbled and pulled off his jerkin and shirt.

There, over his heart, was a wound. It was small and nearly healed, but it was there. A slender scar as if a narrow blade had stabbed him.

A crescent, like a waning moon.

Kagen touched the wound and as he did, he thought he heard strange music from far away.

"Too far to travel," he said aloud, then stood there wondering what he meant.

The forest around him held no promise of magical things. It was merely a forest.

The wound, though . . . that persisted.

The pain was fading quickly and by the time he pulled himself into the saddle, it was gone. The scar, however, remained.

Kagen sat on Jinx's back and stared at nothing. He did not even know how to think about what had happened to him. If it wasn't for the scar, then all of it would be easy to dismiss. He had, after all, been dozing in the saddle.

And yet.

The scar was there, and with it fragments of memory.

"Gods above and below," he breathed.

Jinx, unbidden, began to walk along the valley floor. Soon, he began to run. Heading west toward Arras and the Tower of Sarsis.

CHAPTER SIXTY-FIVE

Although the forest paths he took were silent and seemingly empty, eyes nonetheless watched Kagen. When he stopped for food and rest, he felt that unseen scrutiny, though he could find nothing and no one.

"You're a foolish and paranoid dolt," he told himself one evening as he settled down with his back to a stout oak.

The oak was tall but twisted, with one side withered by blight that caused its bark to bulge in ugly lumps. Hairy vines strangled the tree, or tried to, but it had outlived generations of those parasites. Like the forest itself, the tree *endured*.

Within its heart, in a hole begun centuries past by woodpeckers and then widened by squirrels, something huddled in its own darkness and studied Kagen Vale. Small and strange. Sharp-eyed and sleepless. It watched.

All through the woods, eyes watched with the patience of things immortal. Sprites, cat-sìths, gnomes, ogres, fauns, sprites, balayangs, vetalas, pamolas, alkonosts, griffins, strixes, gaunts, grims, sigbins, and many, many others.

They all watched him. Curious about the man with a broken heart with strange energy about him. They watched and watched.

As did the dryad in the oak tree and the small knot of elvinkind who were impossible to see among the flowers and weeds. They were a different species of elves than those Kagen had encountered, though. Older, stranger, harder for mortal eyes to discern, even in a forest going bare and stark with winter.

"He is but a mortal man," said one of them in a whisper that sounded like rattling leaves. She was young, barely older than the millennium oaks that rose on either side of the path.

"Mortal, aye," said her uncle, who was half as old as the mountains. "But he is marked."

"Marked by *her*," said another even older creature.

The young one looked at the elder. "Her? Do you mean . . . ?"

"He has been given the mark by our cousins to the east," said another. "I can feel the crescent on his skin beneath his clothes. He has done some kindness to our kind."

"No," said the eldest firmly, "that is not the mark of which I speak. The faerie lady has touched this one."

"The lady? She of the tower?" gasped the youngest. "Surely not. She feeds on such as he."

"And feed she has," said the eldest. "Though it was not blood taken but offered. *Given*. That human man saved the lady's life with his own blood. Aye, there is deep faerie magic all around him and in him. Mortal he may be, but he has traveled much and walked between the worlds."

The eldest sniffed the wind, taking every subtle scent and reading each for the story it wanted to tell. Then he stiffened.

"Ware, *ware*," he cried. "There is *dragon* magic about him."

The others stared in mingled horror and wonder.

"Dragon magic," cried the youngest, casting her eyes around as if expecting a scaly and winged monstrosity to appear in the woods, conjured by fear. "What can that mean? Are these the end times?"

The eldest and his cousins stood and looked at the dozing man. Dappled sunlight painted him in patterns of yellow and gray. When the eldest finally spoke, his voice was hushed and filled with a complexity of emotions.

"There is a north wind coming, children," he said. "Chaos follows this man."

He bowed his head and let his tears fall onto the soil. Immediately the frozen ground sucked the moisture down and within seconds the dirt parted and something pushed upward. A stem uncurled from the soil, straightening as it rose, with new leaves and a single flower blossoming from bud to full vigor in moments. They all bent low to study it, divining great truths from it. The shape of the leaves was as slender and sharp as dagger blades, and the flower was like unto a rose. Yet the color of that rose was strange, even to the eyes of elvinkind. Only the eldest and one or two others understood something of what they were seeing, while the others chattered among themselves. None of the younger ones could agree as to the shade of that rose, for it was no color that existed in any part of any forest on the earth. It was a hue born beyond the skies, out where the stars burned in their cold loneliness. A color out of space itself.

"What do you see, eldest of the woods?" begged one of them.

"I see storms of fire that will burn the fields of the earth," intoned the eldest. "I see a wall of water higher than the trees. I see the sky torn as gods make war." He looked up at the faultless blue of the sky far above. "There are voices raised in plaintive cries. Great and terrible voices who speak in tongues older than the mountains. They call. Oh, they call."

"They call to whom? This man?" asked one of his children.

The eldest shook his head. "No. *Him.* They call the god of fire and tears. Woe to the earth if he hears that call. Woe if any should call loud enough, for the beat of his wings is the drumbeat of doom."

"And what of us?" begged the youngest. "Is this our salvation or our end?"

The eldest did not answer. Instead he touched the scar—ancient and nearly invisible—that had been cut into his breast uncountable years ago.

He rubbed it slowly as the weary man slipped into deep sleep, down where dreams were waiting.

CHAPTER SIXTY-SIX

They filled the whole front of the grand hall, standing not in a mass, but like a sea of small islands of power and strangeness.

There were witches from a score of covens, each with its own goals and spiritual biases. There were druids of five different kinds, belonging to sects that normally would not deign to so much as spit on one another in any circumstance other than this. There were conjurers and magicians who were still only discovering their powers; mages and archmages who, in this age of returning magic, were drawing on ancient texts to relearn the precision of spell-casting that had grown rusty and uncertain during the violently enforced prohibitions of the Silver Empire.

The alchemists were a scholarly and somewhat stuffy lot, and it seemed to Nespar that their chief concern was competing to see who could grow the longest beard and wear the most absurd hats. Yet, the Witch-king himself was an alchemist, and so they were treated with a great show of respect.

There were warlocks—a smaller, shifty lot—who huddled together, casting hateful looks at the witches, who had always been more highly respected. An ages-old suspicion of those warlocks yet lingered, for they were believed to prosper by making particularly unsavory pacts with the less appealing creatures of darkness.

Three enchantresses stood apart from the main group, looking elegant and serene, though this demeanor was largely affected. Their arts—only recently restored—were based on charismatic influence, though they had little power in such a court as this.

Then there were the wizards with their staves and sorcerers with their bejeweled pendants. For most—even to Lord Nespar—there was little to distinguish one from the other, but to *them* the difference was as drastic as noon and midnight. The enchanters held themselves above both groups, though in historical perspective their feats, though grand in the moment, had little impact on the flow of politics.

In the middle of the group were a loose scattering of conjurers, street magicians, shamans, and village compounders of potions. None of these appeared confident in any way, notably in their inclusion among the truly powerful.

In the rear of the group stood a handful of silent, dour figures belonging to the very ancient Family of the Dead, the league of necromancers. Once the foundation of much of Hakkia's magical power, and recently buoyed by the rise of Lady Kestral to a place of great honor in the court of the Witch-king, but now fallen. Kestral's betrayal was known, and they were not at all sure how they stood in the yellow king's favor.

One of the largest groups there were those adept in the various forms of divination—clairvoyants, geomancers who understood the energetic powers in the substance of the earth, and topomancers who chose a more specific path to finding secrets in the shape of the surface and the profile of mountains; abacomancers who sought truth in dust, zygomancers whose truths were told in weights and measures, water dowsers; uranomancers who looked to the sky for answers and umbromancers who sought their knowledge in shadows and shades; ailuromancers who learned from cats and alectoromancers who believed the behavior of chickens held the answers; stigonomancers who found understanding by burning writing onto tree bark and libanomancers who poked around in wood and incense ash; pedomancers who were convinced the soles of feet held critical clues; and sola romancers who stared into the sun with the same intensity as crystallomancers peered into crystal balls; there were oryctomancers with their crystals in hand, and ovomancers with their pockets filled with the right kind of eggs; there were mathemancers and hydatomancers and hundreds more.

No field of arcane study had been omitted when, on behalf of the Witch-king, Lord Nespar and the Prince of Games had sent out the call. Everyone answered. Everyone came. More than two thousand of Hakkia's wisest and subtlest minds were there, and a great many charlatans and well-intended frauds. Most were aware that some of the most powerful and revered of their nation's magic users had died already in the service of the King in Yellow.

Lord Nespar was exhausted from introducing each group in what had become a day without apparent end. But in truth, he reached the last entry on his list, and here he paused for a moment, cutting a look at his aide who nodded in answer to the silent query. Then Nespar read out the last visitor.

"Archmage Drell Phendaar of the Sacred Family of Fire, court advisor to His Majesty, Pethryan the Great, king of Bulconia."

All heads turned toward a figure who stood by the east wall. He was a man of middle years, with a short and precisely trimmed goatee and a band of nearly transparent black gauze around his eyes. A flickering flame was tattooed on the center of his forehead, and small blue tears inked onto his cheeks. His clothes—a long doublet over cotton shirt and trousers—were neither rich nor decorated. He sported no jewel and leaned upon no staff, and around his waist was belted a sword with a handle wrapped in plain and much-worn leather.

Archmage Phendaar bowed low and held the bow for a long moment, reinforcing the message of humility and deference. When he straightened, he looked past his peers to make eye contact with the Prince of Games and then the Witch-king.

"You are an unexpected guest," said the Witch-king. "But welcome."

"Majesty," said Phendaar, "my king sends greetings to his cousin here in the southwest and offers his hand in fellowship."

"And what is in that hand, I wonder?" mused the Prince of Games.

The archmage took no visible offense. "Friendship," he said. "And possibilities."

The Witch-king studied him and then looked slowly around the room. Some small murmurings had begun when Phendaar spoke, but that melted into an expectant silence.

"You are all welcome to my hall," he said. "We have great work ahead of us as we prepare for my ascension and for the great glory of Hastur's awakening. I bid you all follow my chamberlain and his aides to find places of rest, for your journeys have been long. Refresh yourselves, my brothers and sisters, for tomorrow we begin an undertaking that will usher in a new age in which tyranny is cast aside and magic exulted. In the name of our great god, Hastur of the Shepherd's Crook, be welcome here."

With that, he rose, gathered his robes about him and—with the prince in tow—exited the great hall. There was an important event to be held that night. A veil would be removed.

The Witch-king said nothing as he hurried to his room, with the Prince of Games having to run to keep up with him.

CHAPTER SIXTY-SEVEN

The Twins and their team made an easy landfall, and everyone scrambled out to pull the ice-riggers onto the beach. And immediately set about dismantling the boats and rebuilding them as sleds.

The work was completed within an hour. Ropes of light weight but great strength and padded with wood were used to create yokes so that teams could pull each sled across the snowy fields. They hurried off and Cat kept looking at the movement of the sun and then back at the shoreline. Each time she told them to hurry.

They hurried, and soon the Frozen Sea had vanished behind them.

Once more the wind was behind them, and Cat rigged short masts on each sled with reefed sails to help push the sleds, making the labor of the team much less arduous. The Twins approved of this, because they did not want their team to arrive exhausted. Especially since Frey warned them that there might be Hakkians up here on a similar mission.

The two sleds reached the top of a ridge, and from that vantage point they could see that there was barely a mile to the foot of the glacier. It had been a misty, snowy day but now it was clearing, and they stared in wonder at the wall of ice rising so high and sheer that none of them could see the top.

"Please tell me we don't have to climb that," said Jheklan. A few of the others laughed more heartily than a small joke of complaint necessitated. Relief, stress, anticipation, and a shared awareness of the strangeness of everything fueled that laughter.

"I thought you boys had been here before," said Alibaxter.

"We were lads," said Jheklan. "And it was a different part of the glacier. There was a big crevasse in the ice that led us to a chamber. But we've never been exactly here before."

"And where *is* here?" asked Faulker, bending over to study the complex lines.

Cat spread a map out atop a crate and touched the line that marked the face of the glacier. "There are dozens of cracks and clefts all along this part, but our destination is a bit over six miles. Frey says that there should be a crevasse that was used by the Garden expedition."

They all looked at the darkening sky.

"If it wasn't so late, I'd say push on, but there's no moon tonight and I don't want to walk past it in the dark," said Cat. "Let's all get some hot food and a full night's sleep and head out at first light."

"Good," said Jheklan.

They made camp and Alibaxter once more earned his passage by cooking a stew of salt beef, dried peas, and the last of their fresh vegetables, into which he added a bewildering mix of herbs and spices. While it cooked, he murmured some words over it. When Faulker asked what he was doing, the wizard looked sheepish.

"It's not a prayer," he said. "It's a very old spell."

"A spell to do what, exactly?" asked Jheklan.

"Protection for body and soul," said Alibaxter.

Jheklan studied his face, leaned in to smell the stew, then nodded.

Perhaps it was the abundant hot food after the privations of crossing the ice sea and pushing the sleds this far. Perhaps it was the mix of herbs. Perhaps it was the spell. Or perhaps all three, but they all fell into a soothing, restorative sleep.

Even the sentries drowsed a bit.

And none of them were aware that death hunted them on the ice.

PART TWO
THE HOUNDS OF WINTER

———

"Complacency is a wretched thing. For a thousand years, the people of the west were complacent. They allowed themselves to accept the peace of the Silver Empire as something that would naturally last. There was no thought, not even a discussion, that this peace was fragile. They prayed to the Harvest Gods for good crops rather than safety; they allowed storied swords to rust on their pegs above fireplaces. They embraced hubris as if it was irrefutable truth. And what happened? When the Hakkians invaded, they lost in a single night."

— SEPTOL HEDRON OF HATH, SENIOR TEACHER OF POLITICS AND RHETORIC AT THE UNIVERSITY OF LLYFIA IN SUNDERLAND, FROM *THE WEST: A HISTORY WITH COMMENTARY*

CHAPTER SIXTY-EIGHT

They came in the night.

Silent feet in silent snow of the Winterwilds.

Steel dull in the shadows cast by the glacier.

Eyes used to those shadows because they had been there for weeks.

Twenty figures moving like ghosts, skirting the places where drowsy sentries stood. Coming at those pickets in the deep of night. Using arrows and then knives to keep the silence intact. Rolling the bodies out of sight and then changing into their furs and taking up the stations vacated by murder. If any eye looked, they would see guards standing where they should be. The fiction of all being well was accomplished with great subtlety and skill.

They waited until a palpable calm settled over the camp. And then a ring of killers stalked through the frozen shadows toward the clusters of sleeping forms.

CHAPTER SIXTY-NINE

Faulker woke from a dream of swimming in deep oceans, able to breathe down there, with strange fish all around him. Creatures with the faces of seals and sea lions, but human eyes. It was a beautiful dream, though also deeply disconcerting because in that dream *he* was as unnatural and alien as the animals who swam and swirled around him.

One of them, a bull sea elephant, came slowly toward him, eyes both curious and knowing.

"Do you love your brother?" it asked.

"Jheklan? Of course. He's my best friend."

"No," said the sea elephant, "the other one."

"Kagen? Sure. He's a bit stiff but a good lad."

Once more the sea elephant said, "No. The *other* one. The cold one whose heart is frozen."

"Herepath . . . ?" ventured Faulker.

"Yes."

"I guess so. He's kin. A bit of a pain in my ass at times. Stuffy, snobbish, but also the smartest person I ever met. Maybe smarter than Mother Frey."

"Will his heart ever thaw?" asked the animal.

"I don't even know how to answer that."

The expression on the sea elephant's face changed to one of sudden alarm.

"They are here to kill your brother," it said. "They are here to kill you all."

"Who?"

"The Ravens."

"What?"

And then the screams woke him.

Faulker went from being deeply asleep to being fully awake in the space of a single heartbeat. He kicked free of his furs and shot to his feet, reaching for his sword. There was movement all around him. The light from the campfire threw wild shadows everywhere and also glimmered on raised steel.

"Wake!" he roared. "We are beset! Wake! Wake!"

A dark form rushed at him with a raised spear. Had he thrown it, Faulker might have died right then, but the Hakkian took one additional step in hopes of driving the point into his chest.

Faulker stepped forward, bashing the spear aside with his forearm, feeling the shock rip painfully up his arm, and then a nearly simultaneous jolt as he drove his sword into the man's side. It punched through fur, leather, stomach, and liver. Faulker kicked the screaming man away, letting him fall and die as he whirled to try and assess the situation.

There were many figures moving with swift and deadly precision, stabbing down into sleeping forms, slashing at others who were trying to rise. An arrow shot past his head and he ducked and pivoted, ready to charge the archer, but it was Jheklan. Both of the Twins were superb archers, but even Faulker would admit that Jheklan was better. Not that he would admit it *to* Jheklan, though. Now he delighted in his brother's skill as Jheklan drew and fired, drew and fired, filling the night with a new chorus of agonized screams.

Faulker turned fast, shifting to intercept another of the enemy, who wore black cloaks over their leather armor. The closest of them grinned with white teeth and cruel eyes as he swung an axe at Faulker's chest.

Faulker threw himself forward and to his knees, drawing a curved knife while sliding under the swing. He drove his sword up under the man's chin and slashed the knife downward into the Raven's crotch. Then he rolled backward, tearing both blades free amid a spray of red and a piercing shriek.

Then he was on his feet, moving at an angle, yelling to attract attention so that the enemy came at him rather than attack those who were still tangled in their furs. A trio of Ravens tried to catch him between them, but that was an old game Mother had taught them—never let the enemy set the rules. So he danced to one side of the converging attackers, slashing down and back with his sword as he did so, slicing through the tendons of one man's knee. Not a killing blow, but the leg buckled and Faulker rammed him with his shoulder, sending him crashing into the others. Faulker followed this, using the curved knife—his *talon*—to slice across the eyes of one and the throat of another. They fell and he moved on.

Jheklan was circling the camp at a galloping run, firing as fast as lightning, his arrows sure and deadly, and the range well-suited to mayhem. Like Faulker, he was less concerned with outright murder than crippling wounds. This allowed him to do far more damage in a short time than would be possible if he was going for kill shots.

Between the brothers, the members of their party were trying to organize themselves while also using the four sleds for cover. This worked well enough at first, but as the Ravens closed in, the sleds became obstacles barring flight. Cat and three of the team were trapped in a three-walled kill floor as Ravens pressed their attack.

Faulker saw that Alibaxter had climbed atop one of the sleds and was doing some mummery with his hands. No flashes of fire appeared; nor did he conjure an army.

Bloody fool, thought Faulker, though he hoped the well-intentioned young wizard would not pay too heavy a price for his faith in his nascent magic.

The battle was lopsided, with the Ravens heavily outnumbering the members of the expedition. However, Faulker and Jheklan were fighting the way their mother, the Poison Rose, had taught them on countless afternoons of their childhood. Jheklan filled the air with pain and death; Faulker moved like a dancer inside his own net of flashing steel.

It took the Ravens—as a body—to realize that they were no longer engaged in a slaughter but were instead inside a pitched battle. The balance of advantage was teetering.

"Kill those two," roared a leathery voice, likely a Hakkian sergeant.

Faulker saw him in the distance—a compact and powerful-looking man holding a heavy two-handed sword. Four Ravens peeled off from the main attack and ran where the sergeant was pointing. Straight at Faulker.

Faulker grinned.

He was afraid, but all real fighters are afraid. Fear was useful. Fear was not panic and it was not cowardice. Fear made Faulker move fast, as his mother taught him.

Use what the enemy gives you.

Another of the Poison Rose's aphorisms. It and a companion lesson—*Fear will make you fight or flee, but it can also make you freeze. Choose the action that gives you the greatest chance to win. Do something because doing nothing is certain death.*

And so Faulker ran at the four men, just as he had the trio a few moments before.

The distance between them was twenty paces and he shortened it by running rather than walking. When he was fifteen feet away, he threw the talon, which tumbled so fast in the air it looked like a disk of steel rather than a knife. And between that throw and his next step he snatched a brand from the campfire and a half step later threw that.

The talon struck a man in the chest, but the curved blade was not built for deep penetration. The force of the throw, though, stalled the Raven and tore a cough from him. That made the others outpace him. Two men dodged left and right to avoid the brand and the third used his spear to parry it away. All of this within the space of a full second.

Then Faulker was among them, angling fast to engage the left-most soldier, timing a long step to bring him chest to elbow as the Raven tried a huge backhand cut. The Raven's elbow was a cruel, hard blow, but Faulker used it as a lever to turn his own body so that there was extra force behind his own sword thrust.

He slapped the dying man across the jaw, turning him just as the second Raven swung an axe. The big woodsman's blade bit deep into his companion's shoulder, half severing head and arm. Faulker kicked past the dying man and caught the second man on the inside of the knee, buckling it.

Then he abandoned those two, spun to gain power, and dropped low to cut the third man across the shins right above the ankle joints. His sword passed completely through one leg but jammed hard into the shinbone of the other. Rather than wrestle with it, Faulker rose up fast, shoved the screaming soldier in the chest, and drove him onto the point of the fourth man's spear.

He slapped one hand down on the impaled Raven's shoulder as he jumped up and forward, bringing his fist down on the top of an iron helmet. The force drove the nose piece down so sharply that it cut through the bridge of the man's nose.

Only then did Faulker retrieve his sword. The spearman had a mangled face but was otherwise unhurt, but Faulker's sword licked out and drew a red line beneath his chin.

Then he ran to where Cat and her people were losing their fight.

Arrows whipped past him, proof that Jheklan had the same idea. Faulker took one Raven in the kidneys and sliced another above the wrist, sending axe and hand flying. The sergeant of the Ravens was there—wiser, more experienced, and less prone to fall for battlefield tricks. He had a sword in one hand and a hatchet in the other and he met Faulker with a very fast attack, swinging the sword to force Faulker into a defensive retreat and the hatchet to try and cut something important.

Suddenly the man's entire head caught fire.

Just like that.

There was no spark, nothing thrown, no collision with a torch. One moment the sergeant was growling as he fought with murderous efficiency, and the next he was screaming the most awful screams Faulker had ever heard. The flames were pale yellow-green and they enveloped the man's entire head, burning as fiercely on flesh as hair.

When the sergeant dragged in a breath to scream louder, he sucked fire into his lungs. Faulker stepped aside as he fell.

The other Ravens froze, staring at the impossible thing that had just happened.

Cat—bleeding from a dozen wounds—took that moment to rally her people. They were a pitiful few, and none uninjured, but they rushed the Ravens, dragging them to the ground, stabbing and beating and biting. Now it was revenge and terror come home to roost.

Jheklan's arrows struck with more precision now, and wounded soldiers still able to fight, died. Those who tried to retreat, died.

Every single one of the Ravens died.

And the whole fight, from first blow to last, was over in three minutes.

Gasping, Faulker staggered back from the last dead Raven and looked around, still completely confused by what happened to the sergeant. Movement caught his eye and he looked up to see Alibaxter, still atop the sled, swatting at yellow-green fire that burned in spots on his sleeves. His fingers looked badly burned.

The wizard stared down at Faulker.

"I . . . I . . . Gods of the Harvest . . . did you see what I . . . what I did?"

Then Alibaxter's eyes rolled up in their sockets and he fell unconscious to the ground.

Jheklan and Faulker looked around the camp. There had been twenty of them, including the Twins.

Now there were nine.

"Gods of the . . ." began Jheklan, but he did not finish.

All Faulker could do was nod.

CHAPTER SEVENTY

No one slept for the rest of that cold night in the Winterwilds.

No new Hakkians appeared.

Faulker and two others—il-Vul, a Samudian master archer and hunter, and an Argonian caravan guard named Jace, who was an excellent tracker—headed out into the night. They found the tracks left by the Hakkians, for the enemy had made no attempt to hide their trail.

"Arrogant gits," muttered Faulker, though he was pleased enough that such arrogance made their back trail easy to follow. It took a couple of hours, but they found the Hakkian camp. Four men guarded it, but two were seated by a fire, with the others walking on the opposite side of a pair of heavy sleds. The marks of the sleds trailed northward and vanished out of sight.

Faulker drew his men to a safe distance to discuss their plan.

"These lads are coming *from* the glacier," he said quietly. "Taking something back the way we just came. I think they saw our campfire and made some likely guesses as to who we were."

"Or maybe they're just killing anyone who's not wearing yellow cloaks," said il-Vul.

"Or that," Faulker conceded. "In any case, their camp is far enough from the glacier that if we get up to some mischief it shouldn't bring more of them."

"What should we do?" asked Jace. "And if the answer is murder the bastards, I'm all for it."

"We need to ask questions of one of them," said Faulker. "The two at the fire are probably senior in rank to the poor sons of bitches walking the perimeter. You two lads take the sentries. Are either of you too badly injured to shoot straight?"

The Samudian grinned as he bent his bow and looped the string over the end. "If I can't take them both in under five seconds then feel free to skin me alive."

"I can shoot, too," protested Jace.

"You're better with a knife, brother," said il-Vul. "Why don't you go with Faulker? You can kill one of the two by the fire and then the two of you can wrangle the last man."

Faulker gave him a wink. "Five seconds," he said. "I'll be counting."

They crept back and il-Vul took up a position behind a snow-drift, one arrow on the string and the other dangling from a loop formed by the little finger of his draw-hand. A Samudian trick used in horseback archery. Faulker said nothing. He and Jheklan—both excellent archers—had tried that trick a number of times and neither bragged about their results.

Jace patted his pockets as he made a choice among the many knives he carried. He picked a throwing blade that had a crossbar nearly at the halfway mark, the kind of weapon designed to make a single turn during flight and then sink deep. Faulker nodded his approval. Kagen carried some like that.

He and Jace moved like ghosts through the snowy night, the white powder absorbing all sound. They could not see il-Vul, but knew he was watching. The cue would be when the second sentry fell.

As if by magic a shaft appeared to materialize in the eye socket of one of the sentries and before his body could even collapse a second shaft struck the other guard in the throat. As Faulker lunged forward, Jace threw his knife and it buried itself between and slightly left of the shoulder blades of one of the two men at the fire. He grunted, leaned forward, and fell face-down into the flames. The fourth man cried out and shot to his feet—then froze as a line of cold steel pressed into the softness of his throat.

"Shhhhh, laddie," whispered Faulker, who held a double-edged dirk below the Hakkian's windpipe.

"All clear," called il-Vul, and then he and Jace materialized out of the night.

Faulker gave the Samudian a mock stern look. "You said you could do it in five seconds."

"But I—"

"It was two." Faulker grinned. Then he pushed the prisoner down to his knees and held the knife in place while Jace lashed his wrists. "Somebody drag that prick out of the fire. He's stinking up the place."

Il-Vul stuck his bow upright in a snowbank, grabbed the burning man by the ankles, and dragged him away. He doused the lingering flames by kicking snow over him.

"Go scout," ordered Faulker. "Make sure we're alone."

The other two melted away.

Faulker rolled the prisoner onto his back, then hauled him up to sit with his back to the sled. He squatted on his heels, letting the dagger dangle between his knees.

"Hello, my friend," he said, and offered a very large, very happy smile.

It did not make the Hakkian very happy at all.

CHAPTER SEVENTY-ONE

Kagen met Tuke at the house of Lord Gowry, a rich merchant who belonged to Frey's cabal.

There were pleasantries, congratulations on the victory over the Firedrakes, and promises of soldiers and funds; then Gowry left Tuke and Kagen alone. Kagen produced Frey's note and handed it to Tuke.

"What's all this about? I have had a very strange and deeply unpleasant trip so far and I'm in something of a hurry."

"A hurry?" said Tuke, eyes wide. "No kidding. Really? Gods above, you'd think there was a war brewing."

"Very funny. Tell me."

"Your seer friend, Selvath, has joined our campaign."

Kagen grunted. "Has she, by the gods. That's unexpected. And by 'joined,' in what capacity?"

"Mainly she is ferreting out Hakkian spies in our midst."

"What?"

"She's found seven so far," said Tuke. "When I left the camp, Filia was interrogating them. Admittedly, I fled because I rather dislike that side of my lover."

"I'd call you a coward, but I feel the same," said Kagen. "She is fierce."

"Strong women are often stronger than we are, brother," laughed Tuke. "You saw the old women on the battlefield using their knives to kill the Hakkian wounded. None of them so much as blinked."

"Can you blame them?"

"Oh, hell no. But I don't like to watch, either." They both nodded. Then Tuke said, "Selvath had a vision of a weapon of great power hidden in a cave near here."

"A weapon? If you tell me that we're looking for some kind of gods-damned magic sword, Tuke, so help me I will skin you alive."

Tuke grinned but said nothing. Which said everything.

"Seriously," said Kagen. "Skinned, roasted. Fed to hogs."

"You can always mount up and ride on and never know if you bypassed something that could help win this war."

That sat heavily on Kagen and he took it to bed with him. At breakfast he was not at all surprised to see Tuke dressed and through the window the horses stood saddled and ready.

"I hate you," said Kagen.

Tuke merely laughed. They ate and rode out.

CHAPTER SEVENTY-TWO

"Come, children," called Madame Lucibel. "It is time for your lessons."

Alleyn and Desalyn looked into each other's eyes as they put on the aspects of Gavran and Foscor. It did not require magic. Merely effort. They straightened their postures in imitation of the rigid bearing of the Witch-king. They narrowed their eyes and forced secretive smirks onto their faces. And they made sure to never touch hands. Not when anyone was watching.

The governess stood with the Wand of Kindness in her plump hand, studying them like a hawk looking into a nest of newborn mice.

"Look at you," she said in her sickly sweet singsong of a voice. "Your clothes are disreputable. Foscor, you have stains on your skirt, and Gavran, there is meat grease on your tunic. What have I told you about table manners?"

She did not wait for an answer but told them both to turn around and bend over the low back of a divan. With each whistling blow of the wand, first on one and then the other, they had to apologize and thank her for her kindness. If they did not say it loud enough, the next blow was much harder and across their thighs rather than buttocks. If they did not sound truly grateful, the following hit was to their ankles or the palms of their hands. Even if they did everything perfectly there were extra swipes.

When it was over, they dared not cry or else they would spend an hour kneeling on grains of dried rice while holding heavy books from which they had to read the rules of deportment for young ladies and gentlemen.

Even at six years old, Alleyn and Desalyn had learned to lie. They praised her and thanked her and apologized with theatrical perfection. They did not complain when those dried rice pieces dug into the soft and tender flesh of their knees. They held back the tears with more personal power than many grown adults could manage.

And they never stopped smiling.

That was their weapon, their shelter, their knife. If Lucibel saw those sneaky smiles vanish, then she would accuse them of treachery, or deception, of being their *wrong* selves. The twins had learned long ago not to make that mistake.

Today was not one of Lucibel's more intense days. Harsh, nasty, and vicious, but not brutal. Nothing that would keep them in bed moaning into their pillows. Nothing that would keep them from sneaking into the walls again.

The twins knew why she was lighter that day. It was not from any kindness or compassion. The governess was merely exhausted, worn-out, pale and drawn. That was the result of spending most of the night in the privy after Desalyn and Alleyn slipped one of Kestral's potions into her teacup. They'd had to look up what an *enemata* was, but once they understood it, sneaking into the woman's room and dosing the tea was a true joy.

They had enough of the potion to do it again that night, and maybe the next.

When it was gone, they would figure something else out.

And so they endured and plotted their revenge. Neither had yet gotten to the point where they would slip poison into that strong tea.

Not yet.

━━━━━━━━━━━━━━▶ **CHAPTER SEVENTY-THREE**

Back at the camp on the snow, Jheklan and Lehrman—an Unbladed fighter from Zehria—who were among the least injured, labored with ice-axes to gouge shallow graves for their companions.

Alibaxter and the others dragged the bodies from where they lay and arranged them in the graves, then covered them with chunks of ice and mounds of snow. It was sad work and they undertook it in silence. The other survivors, wounded as they were, tended to each other's wounds as they kept watch.

The ice fields between them and the glacier were empty except for drifting cloud shadows and morning mist. When the burials were done, and after Alibaxter had spoken old prayers over the dead, they gathered for a meal. It was good food, and the warmth of it helped, but grief was in every averted or shared look, every giving and receiving of bowls of stew, every grunt of pain stifled out of respect for those beyond pain.

Fear was there, too.

When Faulker, il-Vul, and Jace appeared out of the night, everyone began to rise, but Faulker waved them back down. He looked old and grainy and accepted hot food gratefully.

"We found the rest of the Hakkians," he said. "They were pushing a sled filled with bottles of liquid. The one I talked to said that they were filled with the blood and tears of a dragon."

That statement shocked them all.

"Oh," added Faulker, "he said they collected dragon spit, too."

"Was he joking?" asked Alibaxter.

"Neither of us was in a jocose frame of mind."

Jheklan said, "At least we can settle the question as to whether dragons are real."

"Did you doubt that?" asked Alibaxter, genuinely surprised.

"Of course I did. We all did."

Everyone nodded.

The wizard looked around at them, astonished. "But why? You know that's why Mother Frey sent us."

"She sent us to find books of magic—and those are easy to believe in," said Jheklan. "Dragons, less so."

"A lot less so," agreed Faulker. "I mean . . . *dragons*, after all. This is the real world."

"So where did you all think magic comes from, if not the tears and blood of dragons?"

No one had a ready answer.

"So, if I'm interpreting this correctly," said Alibaxter, "it's more a matter of none of you *wanting* to believe in dragons."

"That says it," Jheklan admitted. "The world is strange enough without that."

"And now you want to believe it?"

"'Want to' is not how I'd phrase it," said Cat. "More like have to."

"Aye," said Faulker. "The Hakkians sure as hell do. That fellow back there said the Witch-king sent an expedition up here more than a year ago. They attacked the Gardeners, killing many."

Jheklan shot him a look. "What about Herepath?"

"He said that Herepath left before they arrived. There was a Hakkian expedition already here, working with the Gardeners. Well . . . technically they *were* Gardeners. I sometimes have to re-member that the Hakkians either were of the Green Religion or faked it."

"Probably a bit of both," said Alibaxter. "Some may even have been devout. I suspect there were dedicated Hakkian Gardeners in that earlier expedition. Most of us were apolitical and some, I am almost ashamed to say, more focused on archaeology and history than matters of faith. In any case, they were invited up by Herepath because he was investigating—among other things—the legitimacy of dragon magic, and who knows more about such things as Hakkians? After all, their state religion was based on a belief in magic."

"A religion that was forbidden by the Silver Empire," said Cat. "Or that's what I thought."

"Forbidden in practice," corrected the wizard. "Not forbidden to scholars for study. So, yes, some of the Hakkians who came up here were likely in earnest. But like all things with a political bent, there were probably others who pretended to be objective researchers but who were preparing the way for the Witch-king."

"That seems to square with what the Hakkian told me," said Faulker. "He said Herepath left with them, leaving a fair-sized team here to continue the research. But *his* group, the newest Hakkians, were all military. It was their job to collect as much blood and tears from the dragon as possible and then begin shipping it down to Hakkia once the Witch-king was in control of the empire." He shook his head. "They thought that by now the Witch-king would be the emperor of a new empire. The Yellow Empire, dedicated to Hastur."

"And it almost was," said Jheklan. "Kagen put a stop to that, but—who knows—he might have been crowned since we left."

That was a sobering and deeply unpleasant thought.

Cat asked, "What else did he say?"

"Oh, he was quite chatty. He said that there were sixty Hakkians working up here. Not counting the ones who attacked us."

"Does that mean they know about us?" cried Alibaxter, alarmed.

"I don't think so. The ones who hit us tonight were on their way south with the first load of the dragon stuff. They saw our fire, sent a spy to see who we were, did not see anyone who looked Hakkian, and decided to kill us so that we didn't interfere with what was going on back at the glacier."

Jheklan looked past him into the night. "Did he tell you a good way into the glacier?"

"He told me that his lot had a way in, but it was heavily guarded. Sentries and an iron door set into the side of the ice mountain. He did not have a key, and from the way he described it, we couldn't get in that way. Even before we lost so many. No, brother, we'll need to find another way in."

"There are many crevasses," said Cat. "We'll manage."

"Crevasses are all well and good," said Jheklan, "but the glacier is thousands of miles long and we don't know that any open up in the right place to let us into where the scholars worked *or* where that dragon is kept."

That was a problem none of them had a ready answer for.

"Do you think that man you interrogated might know another way?" asked Alibaxter hopefully.

Faulker shook his head. "If he knew, he would have told me."

"He could have been holding it back."

Jheklan snorted. "If Faulker says he would have said, then he would have said."

Alibaxter studied Faulker's eyes and understanding dawned. He said no more.

"There's no one out on the ice," said Faulker. "We can get some sleep."

"Tell me," said Alibaxter, "what did you do with the sledful of dragon blood and tears?"

"We smashed every last gods-damned jar. Why? Do you think we should have kept it?"

"No," said the wizard. "I think you did exactly the right thing."

That was the end of the conversation for that night.

Before bed they had been a strong party of twenty. Now there were nine and none of them uninjured. It did not matter that they had killed a greater number of Hakkians. The truth was that in the span of that bad night their expedition had dwindled to a force that might well be inadequate to the daunting task ahead. And everyone was aware of this without it being said.

They set two of the fittest of their team to stand watch and everyone else huddled into their furs to try and sleep.

No one succeeded at this.

In the morning, weary, heartsick, and with no visible optimism, they set out again.

CHAPTER SEVENTY-FOUR

Tuke and Kagen sat on their horses at the top of a low rise. Behind them, the Forest of Elgin was darkened to a purple nothingness. Ahead, the road sloped down and snaked through a maze of ancient trees. The sun was a fading rumor and the moon a growing promise.

"How in the burning hells did I get tricked into joining another of your stupid fucking quests?" asked Kagen.

"Another . . . ?"

"Chest of Algion, remember that? Turned out to be a myth that nearly got us both killed?"

"And yet you met your great love, Maralina, while looking for it."

"That's not the point."

From Tuke's expression, though, he rather thought it was. The big Therian was huddled into furs, and his eyes had the merry lights of someone whose well-attended waterskin was filled with wine—and there wasn't much left of it.

"Two things," said Tuke. "No, make it three. First . . . you're a sour pain in the ass, you know that?"

"Fuck you."

"Second, we are making war against the most powerful sorcerer alive. We have plenty of men and even a nicely filled war chest, but we have nothing to counter his magic. This ancient sword may be exactly what we need."

Kagen glowered but could pick no holes in that. "And the third thing?"

"Third . . . fuck you."

Kagen sighed. "Yeah," he said. "Fair enough."

They rode on.

A mile later, just as the eye of the moon began peering over the edge of the world, Kagen said, "What kind of magic sword are we talking?"

Tuke, who'd nodded off in the saddle, snapped awake. "Goat balls."

"What?" asked Kagen.

"What?" said Tuke, blinking away the sleep. "Um . . . what was it you said?"

"I asked what kind of magic sword?"

Tuke avoided Kagen's eyes. "Oh, a legendary one, to be sure. Storied. There are tavern songs about it. Some ballads, too."

"Really? Sing one."

"What?"

"Sing me one of those songs," said Kagen. "I want to hear about the glories and powers of this mystical sword."

"I . . . don't know any by heart . . ."

"Give me a title, then."

Tuke looked everywhere but at him. "'The,' um, 'Legend of the,' ah, 'Magic Sword' . . . ?"

Kagen stared at him. "You are a terrible liar."

"I'm not lying."

"'The Legend of the Magic Sword.'"

"Yes."

"That's a real song?"

"Yes."

"Swear it."

"What?"

"Swear to it on Dagon," suggested Kagen. "Take that little icon you always carry, hold it in your hand, and swear by the king of your people's gods that there *is* such a song, that there *is* a sword, and that this isn't just another of your tricks to try and sober me up and get me to straighten myself out."

The horses walked a fair way along the road before Tuke answered.

"Okay," he admitted, "that's not the name of the song."

"I'm shocked."

"But there *is* a sword."

"Uh-huh."

"A legend of one."

"There's a legend that there are women on Orgas Tull with four breasts, two of which flow with wine."

Tuke's dark skin turned a shade darker still. "There *is* a legend about the sword," he grumbled.

"What does the legend *actually* say?"

Tuke had to fumble around in his memory for the exact words, but then he nodded to himself and said, "*In the Forest of Elgin, beneath the demon tower, is a cave carved by an underground river now dried to dust. There, hidden forever from the eyes of men, is a city of goblins that fell to the hand and blade of Prince Vorlon of Old Shimele. Vorlon brought his army there and did engage in bloody battle with the Goblin King, and slew him upon his own throne of skulls, cleaving the fell beast with a mighty blow of the enchanted sword,* Caladbolg. *Then, having vanquished the lord of the goblins, did Vorlon sit himself upon the throne of skulls to wait until the needs of his people did call him forth once more. Disturb not the rest of the Prince of Dust and Shadows.*"

Kagen studied his friend.

"Now . . . let me see if I grasp this . . ." he said slowly. "You've tricked me into looking for a magic sword used to fight and kill the king of the goblins, yes?"

"Yes. It was a great victory."

"Have you ever read about the goblins? In history books, I mean, from before the first Silver Empress outlawed magic across the whole of the world."

"Not . . . as such . . ."

"Goblins are not particularly hard to kill."

"There were a lot of them."

"That's not the point. *Killing* them is not much of an act of heroism. But do you remember what happens in every single story about someone killing a goblin?"

"I . . ."

"Killing a goblin under the best of circumstances incurs bad luck for seven times seven years. Even if you die, the bad luck follows your family until those forty-nine years have passed."

"Well, sure, there's that, but—"

"That's in self-defense," said Kagen sharply. "Attacking them in their own lands incurs bad luck that lasts—and I quote—until the sun and the years have turned the mountains themselves to dust and shadows."

"Poetic license," said Tuke, dismissing it with an airy wave of his hand.

"Or a dire warning."

"It's a metaphor."

"For *what*?"

Tuke waffled. "I mean . . . it's probably meant to scare off tomb raiders and such."

The road curved again, and soon they were plodding along between the shattered stones of a small city that had clearly fallen many centuries ago.

Kagen took a piece of goat jerky from his pack and chewed thoughtfully, eyeing Tuke all the time. "Are you not seeing how your tale of ancient valor is really a warning for us to stay the hell away?"

"I see it differently."

"Gods of the Pit . . ."

"Besides, Kagen," said Tuke, bristling, "what's it matter? You cannot even *be* cursed. You do know that, right?"

"How the hell do you figure that?"

"Well," said Tuke, "not to put too fine a point on it, but you're actually damned."

Kagen's hands knotted to fists around the reins. "Are you making a point here or just trying to piss me off?"

"I'm being serious. The damned cannot be cursed by anything

mortal, and goblins—despite being ugly little monsters—are mortal. You're immune."

"Fuck. Is that supposed to be a comfort, you incredible ass?"

"Life's hard, brother," said Tuke. "Your life sucks, I'll grant, but we're at war and if an advantage presents itself, why not take it?"

They rode on, and Kagen composed several crushing replies but left each unsaid because Tuke made sense. Kagen hated that Tuke made sense, but the big Therian did more often than not. A very hateful trait, the bastard.

"I'm not saying I buy any of this nonsense," said Kagen carefully, "but what powers is this hypothetical sword supposed to possess? I mean, how will it help me kill the Witch-king?"

Tuke tried his best to hide a smug little smile, but his face was too mobile, too expressive.

"The sword *Caladbolg* can kill anything that uses magic, is created by magic, or is *of* magic." His face grew serious, and now he met Kagen's gaze. "It cannot be thwarted by magic weapons, magic armor, or magic spells."

"You're saying—"

"That the sword can kill the Witch-king and any monsters or demons he conjures against you."

The only sound was the soft *clop-clop* of the horses' hooves in the loamy dirt.

"Gods of the fiery Pit," murmured Kagen.

CHAPTER SEVENTY-FIVE

The Vale twins and their party made their way across the Winterwilds, sometimes on snow, others on ice, and now and then on patches of iron-hard permafrost. Given that they were all injured, it was a labor to keep the skids of their sleds moving, but they prevailed.

Before them, the glacier—enormous even when viewed from a distance—rose high as if it was what kept the sky itself from falling. Mist clung to the base and dense fog at the top, but most of the ice was visible—blue-white and unbearably imposing. Conversation dwindled as they drew close to its foot because each of them was feeling that sense of scale—they were like ants at the base of a mighty oak. Even the Cathedral Mountains were not ambitious enough to reach this high, and yet the scholars of the Garden reckoned that thousands of years ago a sheet of ice as high as this covered most of the continent. Miles and miles of dense ice. It made them all feel not only minuscule, but strangely young, when the span of their lives was measured against something this old.

On one break—the last before they would achieve the base and end this part of the journey—they stopped for a hot meal. Alibaxter had become the group's cook. He made another of his soups that sent warmth through the body and to every finger and toe, nose and earlobe. When the Twins caught him sprinkling in some unusual herbs and muttering prayers over them, he gave them a wink. The brothers understood that the young wizard was using some kind of minor magic to bolster the food's natural healing qualities, and they were fine with that. The others in the team seemed to benefit from whatever it was Alibaxter added. There was even some quiet laughter and a kind of returning normalcy to both movement and conversation.

Jheklan, Faulker, and Cat sat with the young wizard to eat, and for a while the silence continued except for common things like asking for the salt cellar or a fresh cup of tea. Then Faulker tapped his brother's arm and nodded to the glacier wall, where the shadows of passing clouds made strange shapes.

"Looks like a bear," Faulker said, pointing to one. "See, the irregularities of the ice as the shadow moves make it look like he's walking."

Jheklan smiled. "It does, by the gods. Oh, and there—see that small one higher up?"

"The one that looks like a falcon?"

"Yes."

Faulker grinned. "Nice. And over there, see it? A fat old rat scurrying just above the mist."

The wind was steady enough to keep the parade of shadows moving constantly, and the Twins added to their shadowy menagerie all through second helpings. Cat, watching with amusement, shook her head.

"You boys never really grew up, did you?"

Jheklan looked at her. "Gods no."

Faulker nodded. "What possible incentive would we have to do such a thing? Oh, see there—that one looks like a cat."

Cat turned, found the shadow, and laughed. "How about that?"

Alibaxter, who had been sitting facing away from the wall of ice, glanced over his shoulder, smiled, nodded, and turned back to the soup pot. Then he paused and turned again, stared at a section of wall farther to the north. A frown grew over his features.

"What's bothering you?" asked Faulker. "Don't see your boyhood puppy?"

Alibaxter's lips opened but he did not speak, and instead stared with eyes that grew gradually wider. Then the brothers and Cat followed his line of gaze and their chatter fell away. They gazed at a huge, dark cloud-shadow that moved with slow, inexorable steadiness across the face of the glacier. It was not a dog or bear or jackrabbit or elephant. It was not a falcon or eagle or albatross.

"Gods save this sinner's soul," breathed Jheklan.

The shadow that moved relentlessly across the wall had vast wings, but they were not feathered—they looked more like the spiky wings of some great bat. The body, though, was bulky, with a pair of huge legs ending in long talons, a long neck, and a head that was monstrous and hideous, with a mouth fifty times bigger than that of a river hippopotamus and filled with teeth longer than the longest spear.

The shape was that of something that they all knew did not belong to this world. Something huge and alien. Something they had seen only in old paintings and tapestries. Something whose very nature was at the heart of their quest and the future of the world.

It was the shadow of a great dragon.

Impossibly huge. The span of its wings reached miles across the glacier.

They stared at it, and then one by one they turned to look at the cloud that cast such a strange and vivid illusion.

Except there was no cloud. The winds had blown all of the clouds to the south, and above them was a hard shell of dense blue.

When they turned back to look at the ice wall, they caught only a hint of a coiling tail at the near side, as if the shadow had flown around to the far side of the glacier. Faulker leaped to his feet and ran as far south as he could, trying to follow the shadow, but the southern face of the glacier was washed in soft, unmoving darkness. He stopped and stood there, mouth agape. The others joined him.

"Was that—?" began Jheklan, but his words were cut off as a flare of light—bright as the sun and with no visible or possible origin—flared in the middle of the southern wall. This was followed immediately by a huge *crack* that was louder than thunder. And then a titanic chunk of ice leaned out from the wall and collapsed with strangely slow grandeur. Uncountable tons of ice crashed down, splintering, throwing spears and boulders of ice, some as big as a castle, across the fields. The impact sent furious shockwaves across the land, cracking the ice beneath them, knocking plumes of powdery snow high into the air. The sleds toppled over, spilling their contents. Everyone was screaming and running away from the falling ice.

A huge chunk of deep blue ice seemed to chase the Twins as they ran west as fast as they could. The shadow of it above them made them split apart and not a moment too soon because it landed where they would have been had they stayed together. They skidded to a stop, staring at it and looking back at the glacier.

No more ice fell but a crushing silence stilled every noise.

Cat, who had dragged Alibaxter to safety, was fifty yards away. The wizard was shivering badly but not from the cold. Cat's veneer of calm was totally gone. All of the other members of the team rose from where they had fallen or fought free of new piles of snow. They were all there. Somehow all had survived.

There was no celebration for this escape, though. For there, on the side of the glacier, was a scar in the ice. It was not a crude gouge left by the falling ice, but instead looked like the rough art left by primitive peoples thousands of years ago. Rough, but eloquent for all that.

It was of a beast rising with spread wings and a trailing tail and a head turned to the west, mouth stretched wide as if roaring.

It was a dragon.

Down, beginning at the base of its tail, were a few cracks in the ice. Narrow at the top and only widening a little where it touched the ground. Big enough for a man to enter.

The Twins walked slowly toward it. Cat and Alibaxter fell numbly into step with them, and soon the entire party walked like sleepwalkers to the base of this new crack. It was too dark to see how deep it was, but Faulker stooped and picked up a fist-sized chunk of ice and threw it overhand as hard as he could.

None of them heard it strike a dead end. They heard nothing.

And a breeze blew out of the crack. It smelled of old ice. And of something else. There was a strange, vital, unpleasant, uninviting odor of strangeness. It smelled of something alive.

"Gods of the Harvest," whispered Alibaxter as he made a warding sign. After a moment, so did Jheklan and Faulker. And then all of them did.

CHAPTER SEVENTY-SIX

It took them the rest of that day and well into the following afternoon before they found the place marked on a map Tuke carried. The map was inked onto a piece of leather so old it might have come from the Dawn Calf out of the creation legends. Or, Kagen mused privately, some old goat whose skin had been cured, boiled in tea, and sold as an artifact. His older brothers, Jheklan and Faulker, had tricked him more than once with such maps.

Yet Tuke, who Kagen privately respected as both learned and wise, believed in it.

Kagen's own doubt cracked and crumbled when Tuke held up the map and pointed to a series of rocks and hills whose contours were close matches.

"Those two hills there," said the Therian, "are all that's left of the Great Gates of the Goblin Kingdom. That hillock there is the mound in which Prince Vorlon buried his own knights along with ten times their number of goblin warriors."

"Looks . . . similar . . ." said Kagen diffidently.

"Well, it wouldn't look exactly the same," said Tuke. "The map is over a thousand years old. The landscape's changed."

"Sure," said Kagen. "Whatever."

They rode until they reached the hillock and then dismounted. The sun was drifting toward the western hills, throwing long shadows behind it. There were a couple of hours of daylight left, but that place was deep in a valley and false twilight was nearly upon them. The air was chill and damp, and both men pulled heavy wool cloaks around their shoulders.

"By the icy balls of the god of winter," muttered Tuke, "but it's bitter down here."

"And thanks for bringing me to such a garden spot," said Kagen. He looked around. "There's supposed to be some kind of door into these hills?"

"Yes."

"What's your plan? Find it now or wait until morning?"

Tuke shivered in the cold. "Now."

"Then let's be about it," said Kagen curtly. "I do not like this place and want to be quit of it sooner than later."

They studied the map again and then began their search, though even Tuke's enthusiasm seemed to have dwindled with the failing light and falling temperatures. There was a biting quality to the wind that seemed able to find every opening in cloak and clothes.

Kagen paused in his searching and stood looking at the trees. Tuke came over, following Kagen's gaze.

"What is it?"

"The nightbirds," said Kagen. "They did not follow us here."

Nightbirds was a general term he had given to flocks of birds—crows, grackles, red-winged blackbirds, and others—that had been dogging his steps ever since he fled the fall of Argentium. The fact that no ravens were among them had made Kagen believe they were somehow his allies, for the raven was the state bird of Hakkia. He was often annoyed by the inexplicable presence of the hundreds of dark birds, but now that they were gone it made him feel strangely vulnerable and abandoned.

"Maybe they lost interest," suggested Tuke, though from his tone it was clear he did not believe it.

"No," said Kagen. "I think it's this place. I think they're wiser about it than we are."

Tuke began to speak, thought better of it, and loosened his

weapons in their sheaths. With one hand he touched the pouch in which he kept his icon of Dagon, and with the other made a warding sign in the air.

They spoke no more as they continued their search.

It was Kagen who found the entrance.

"Here," he called, and when Tuke came over to join him, they squatted on a rocky lip of a steep slope hidden by overgrown hawthorn bushes and stunted scrub pines. The half-eaten carcass of a rattlesnake lay at the top of the slope, and all around were the shredded skins and gnawed bones of countless animals. Tuke picked up the femur of a wildcat and studied the bitten end. He turned it over in his hand, showing Kagen the marks of short, sharp teeth and long scratches from savage claws.

"What did that?" asked Kagen, but Tuke could only shake his head. He tossed the bone down the slope, and they listened as it entered a weed-choked hole. The bone rattled and clattered. Beetles and sand mice scuttled out of the way.

Tuke shifted to allow the waning sunlight to spill down onto the opening. He pointed with a long finger. "See there? There were steps here once. And over there? That's part of a wall. You can still see something carved into it. Can you make it out?"

Kagen edged down the slope and looked at the ancient fragment of stone. He spat on his fingers and used them to brush away caked dirt. The image they saw was badly eroded, but as he worked a face emerged, carved in ages past. The face was small and misshapen, with too much brow, not enough chin, and far too many teeth. The eyes were tiny, glaring from pits of fat. The overall impression was that of some unholy mix of pig, ape, and human child.

"Gods below," gasped Kagen, recoiling. The scar on his chest suddenly flared with pins and needles. He rubbed it.

"What is it, Kagen?" asked Tuke. "Are you unwell?"

Kagen debated whether to tell Tuke of his encounter with the elvinkind, and nearly didn't, but then relented and gave him a terse account.

Tuke made the warding sign again, and far up the slope the horses suddenly whinnied with fear even though they could not see what the two men saw.

"Magic follows wherever you go," he said.

"Nice to remind me as I'm about to step into a goblin cave."

They studied the grotesque features carved into the rock.

"That's foul, and no mistake," said Tuke, his expression falling into sickness. "A goblin of the old world."

The old tales of those monsters rose up in Kagen's mind. His brothers Faulker and Jheklan had used those stories to terrify him as a lad, and those memories returned. He remembered running screaming to the chamber of his elder brother, Herepath—wisest and most learned of the Vale children—hoping to find comfort and even a complete dismissal of all that Jheklan and Faulker told him. But Herepath had not laughed it off. Instead, he sat all three boys down to tell them what *he* knew.

"They were children once," he said. Herepath was tall, thin, ascetic, and seldom spoke, but when he did, he told truths. Seeking him for comfort had worked against all three boys at different times. "They were stolen from their beds by the *Baobhan sith* and taken deep into the faerie grottos in the deepest woods. In those places they were experimented on, tortured, changed. Why this was done remains a mystery, for who can understand the minds of those ageless creatures? Through darkest magicks they forced and twisted nature to their will, blending the innocence of children with the viciousness of swine and the thieving cleverness of weasels and wolverines, apes, and other beasts. No two are alike in form except in that they all share a similar face—the snout of a pig, with the shape of an ape, but the innocent and terrified eyes of human children. To look upon them in the flesh is to have your mind shredded. To encounter them in the dark is to know that doom is upon you, for you will lose your very soul and fall into eternal damnation no matter when or how you die."

Jheklan had laughed at that, while Faulker begged Herepath to say that he was just joking. But Herepath seldom joked, and never about matters involving the old ways of magic and sorcery. The three boys got no sleep that night but instead huddled together in bed, each armed with a knife, and the family hounds clustered close.

Those words came back to Kagen in that moment—precise, exact, and complete—and he recited them to Tuke, who—despite the cold—began sweating profusely.

"I . . . I . . ." began Tuke, but seemed unable to find anything to say.

"You can't go in there," said Kagen.

"Look, brother," said Tuke, "this is a bad idea and I'm a fool. Let's just go. There's enough light for us to get a couple of miles back the way we came. There was that grove of young oaks. We can camp there and in the morning head out."

"And go where?"

"Anywhere but here."

Kagen squatted above the black entrance. "You can't go in there," he repeated, "but we both know that I can."

Tuke shook his head. "What if this whole 'damned' thing is wrong? A mistake. You said that you woke up drunk during the invasion and were probably drugged. Then you fought for hours, saw your family butchered, and only barely escaped the palace. What you saw in the sky—your gods turning their backs on you? That could have been a dream brought on by heartbreak, exhaustion, and whatever drug was still in your system. Maybe you're *not* damned. I'm a fool for even suggesting this."

He grabbed Kagen's arm and tried to pull him up the hill, but Kagen resisted and pulled his arm free.

"A sword that can defeat magic," murmured Kagen. "A weapon

that could slay the Witch-king." He shook his head. "I'm not sure I can go without trying to find it. Everything in my life could turn on this."

"Or you could die and lose your soul for real."

"What does my life mean if I walk away? If I *am* damned, then what other chance will I ever have to redeem myself? How else can I honor the members of my family the Hakkians slaughtered? How else might I redress the wrongs—the rape and torture and slaughter of the empress and her children?"

"Kagen, you're rationalizing this beyond sense."

"No, Tuke, you were right to bring me here. This is a chance. This is maybe my only chance to do some measurable good while I still have breath."

"And if you die in there?"

"Then I will have died trying," said Kagen. He shook his head slowly. "That has to matter to the gods, even if it's not enough to restore my soul."

Tuke's face was drawn and filled with agony. "You're mad."

Kagen suddenly smiled. "'Kagen the Mad' has a nice ring to it, don't you think?"

With that he rose, slapped the handles of the matched daggers he wore, and nodded. Those daggers had once belonged to his mother, the Poison Rose, feared throughout the empire as the deadliest knife fighter of the age. It had been a terrible bit of dark magic that had brought her down, and now those knives were his.

"Wait for me until morning," he said. "If I am not back by first light, then ride off and never look back."

"Kagen, I implore you. This was a foolish idea and I apologize. Let us be gone."

But Kagen held out his hand. "You are a good man and a good friend. My only friend. I thank you for giving me at least a chance to redeem myself."

Tuke continued to protest, but Kagen turned and slid down the slope into the darkness and was gone.

CHAPTER SEVENTY-SEVEN

"Your Majesty," said King al-Huk, bowing to Queen Theka, "it is a pleasure to finally meet you."

The queen, who was nearly thirty years younger than the Samudian, returned the bow and then accepted the king's hand. They shook briefly and he led her over to a pair of comfortable chairs by a bright fire. Aside from a pair of aged and retired hunting hawks dozing on perches, they were alone.

"I am glad to see you well, cousin," said the king. "Naturally I heard about what happened. My condolences on the loss of so many of your countrymen during that attack. Tell me, have you responded to it in any way?"

"What do you mean?" she asked. "Have I sent a fleet into Haddon Bay? Then no."

"I was referring to a letter of protest."

"Ah," said Theka with an edge of contempt in her voice. "Diplomacy."

"It is expected, even in such times," said al-Huk.

Theka looked faintly amused. "I wonder," she pondered, "what the proper diplomatic letter of protest would be had my people been slaughtered to the last and I raped by a ship-full of Hakkians. Phrased in strong yet civil terms, no doubt."

"It did not come to that."

"It very nearly did," said the queen. "Had it not been for aid unlooked for, it would undoubtedly be the case. Tell me, *cousin*, how would you have phrased your own letter of protest had things turned out differently? How *diplomatic* would you be?"

"That is unfair," said al-Huk.

"But allowing my people to be killed, my ship burned, and my person abused would have been . . . *what*? Fair because such things happen in troubled times?"

"You're young, lady," said the king. "You do not understand the subtleties of politics."

"And you are a man, sir," she fired back, "and you do not understand the realities of being a woman. Do not sit there and tell me that I am wrong for my anger and outrage, or that I should be content with a strongly worded letter. The Witch-king would not wipe his ass with it."

"Let us not be crude."

"Then let us not be weak. Or, if not that word, how should I phrase it? Shy? Or is cowardly closer to the mark?"

Al-Huk's face was blank—a practiced artifice—but there was tension in the corners of his jaws and fire in his eyes. "I would be very careful, my lady, with the words you choose while you are a guest in my house."

One of the old falcons rustled its feathers and then continued to doze.

"I have sent word to my people," said Queen Theka. "By now it has reached the capital and my admirals are preparing the entire Therian fleet for an invasion of Haddon Bay. My armies will be readying themselves to march on Argon. Tell me, cousin king, what will you do once the arrows fly and the cities burn?"

The king kept his face composed. In a quiet voice he said, "Samud is not ready to declare open war."

"I thought as much," said Theka in a tone heavy with contempt. "Will you wait until your palace is burning? Or will it take the murder of your son and heir, el-Kep, or the rape of your queen and the ladies of your court before you remember how to string a bow?"

"You are too young to understand war," said al-Huk. "Even if

Samud allies itself with Theria, we do not have enough power to defeat a nation of sorcerers."

Theka stood up slowly and smoothed her skirts. "My father had great respect for you, Majesty. He said you were a great king and a great warrior. I used to believe that."

She walked away from him but paused at the door.

"I expected so much more of you," she said. "Cousin."

With that she left.

CHAPTER SEVENTY-EIGHT

Jheklan and Faulker stood at the mouth of the crevasse that had been opened by the avalanche. Cat and Alibaxter stood with them, and the four of them said nothing for quite a while. The raw meat stink from inside was daunting on every possible level.

"We'll have to be careful," said Alibaxter. "There are bound to be more Hakkians inside."

"There are," agreed Faulker. "Sixty at least. So, yes, being careful is at the very top the list of things I will bear in mind."

Jace came over and quietly asked, "How exactly will we handle that many Hakkians?"

Jheklan smiled at him. "You heard my brother. We'll do it carefully."

"Gods above." Jace turned away and simply stood there, shaking his head.

Then Cat, gray with pain and fatigue, said, "Listen, lads, Mother Frey paid me to get you here, lads, but she didn't pay me enough to go in there."

Without looking at her, Jheklan asked, "And what amount would it take to have you accompany us?"

"Do you have half a hundred weight of gold?"

"Not on me," said Faulker.

"We could get it," agreed Jheklan.

"Well it's a damn shame you didn't bring it." With that she turned and limped back to the sled, then yelled over her shoulder, "Don't let the dragon eat you."

"Say hello to the snow apes for us," Faulker fired back.

Alibaxter cleared his throat. "That could have gone better."

The Twins resisted the urge to slit his throat.

CHAPTER SEVENTY-NINE

"Well," Kagen said to himself as the shadows closed around him, "this is insane."

The sound of his voice was uncomfortably loud, and he bit down on other commentary. He also did not like the notes of fear and anxiety he heard in his words. Brave words to Tuke did not grant equal amounts of courage. The truth was that he was terrified.

For a thousand years the Silver Empresses and their armies had maintained the ban on magic in all of its forms. Somehow, early in the history of the empire, the first empress had forced all manner of magic out of the world. Vampires and elves, demons and witches, sorcerers and faerie folk all vanished in the space of a single decade. No history book ever said how this was done, and even Herepath did not seem to know—although he threw himself into that field of study in order to understand it. For Kagen, the fact that magic was gone was a comfort, for he had learned to fear it greatly.

Then the Witch-king rose in all of his unnatural power and, as he stretched his dark hand across the length and breadth of the empire, magic had begun to flow back. In great ways, as with the sorcery the Witch-king used to conquer the empire in a single night; and in small ways, like blooming flowers of a color that was so alien it could not be described and could fracture the mind of any who tried to understand it. And countless other ways.

What of goblins, though? he wondered. Most magic still slumbered or was groaning in its process of awakening. There were rumors of a vampire in Argon and a unicorn in Vahlycor. Actually, weird things were being seen everywhere. Kagen had even met a woman who claimed to be a witch and who had spoken prophecy to him.

Madness. Horrors. That's what magic was.

Did the goblins slumber still, down here in this endless dark? Or had the presence of living men stirred them from their sleep and awakened their dreadful hungers?

Kagen patted the wall inside the entrance and found the shaft of an ancient torch, its tarry head wreathed in cobwebs. He sheathed his knives and used flint and steel to strike sparks onto the torch. His relief when the centuries-old pitch caught and blazed was enormous.

And short-lived.

Everywhere he looked—all along the corridor, crowding the walls, hanging from stalactites—were creatures. Pig-snouted, ape-faced, child-eyed. They were ahead of him, on either side of him, and as he turned, they closed ranks behind.

He was surrounded by goblins, and there was no way out.

"Gods of the Pit!" cried Kagen as he spun and crouched, flaming brand in one hand and a dagger in the other.

The goblins hissed at him. Their faces were something out of the deepest nightmares, worse than the description Tuke had given. The blend of pig and ape was horrific, but that alone was endurable; that alone could be accepted by the human mind as merely some new kind of animal. Kagen was not well-traveled, and so there were always new natural wonders.

Those eyes, though. There was nothing natural about them. The fact that they looked so definitely human made them unnatural in the worst possible ways because of what he saw in them. There was a mix of emotions burning in each set of goblin eyes. He saw the hatred, the rapacious hungers of the monster there, but that was not the worst part. Inside those stares he saw something deeper.

He saw the children that each had been before sorcery and corruption. Worse still, he saw their awareness of what they were and what had been done to them. He saw the horror that each of them felt because of what they had become and what they would always be. Children's eyes in monsters' faces, with hope still flickering but forever out of reach. The desperation, the stress, the shame, the pleading that hovered at the precipice of sad acceptance—he saw that in a thousand subtle shades as he looked around.

Monsters who knew that they were monsters, but with the terrible clarity of knowing what they had lost. What had been stolen from them.

And the anger. The frustration that had become rage. The horror that had become malice born of hurt.

Kagen's heart broke for them—for all those stolen children—and yet his fear was a towering thing that threatened to collapse and crush him. He held the torch high but lowered his dagger.

"I am not here to harm you," he said, fighting to keep his fear from his voice. And failing. "I have no fight with you."

"*Human . . .*" said one of them, drawing the word out into a snarl, a hiss. "*You dare come into our home with bright steel and fire.*"

The others whispered words in a language he did not know. Ugly words not made for human tongues. Words that sounded painful for them to speak.

"Let me pass," said Kagen. "I am not here for you. I have no wish to fight you or do harm here."

The goblins laughed at that. Their laughter sounded like weeping, and it came close to breaking Kagen's heart.

"You bring us fresh meat and heart's blood," said the goblin. *"And we accept this gift."*

They shifted, closing in around him though not yet within reach. He saw that their fingers were tipped with black nails that were chipped and broken from scrabbling in that darkness. Many had open sores on their bodies, and the scars from bites old and new. They stank of rotting meat and wormy dirt.

Kagen knew that he had made a terrible mistake by coming in there. Tuke could not help him, but even if he could, there were so many of the monsters that doom was the only outcome of this fool's adventure.

"We will feast upon your soul, man of the sunlight world."

"No," said Kagen. "You may kill me—though you will earn that at a terrible cost—but my soul is not for you. My soul is forfeit to the Gods of the Garden, who have damned me for all time."

More of the ugly whispering. Uncertainty flickered in their eyes.

"Why have you come here?" demanded the chief goblin.

Kagen saw no reason to lie. Things were going to shit anyway.

"I have come for the sword of the Prince of Dust and Shadows."

"Speak not that name in our halls," growled the goblin. *"Speak not of the devil who slew our great lord and was damned for it."*

"If he is your devil," said Kagen, "then let me take his blade and his bones out of here and you will be free of his shadow."

The goblins let loose with a wail of hatred, despair, and derision—each emotion in equal measure. They slashed at the air with their talons and snapped their porcine jaws in his direction.

"Stay with us," they whispered. *"Die with us. Feed us. Haunt our halls and entertain us with cries for pity and release. We will laugh as we eat your flesh. We will crack your bones and suck out the marrow. We will make masks of your skin and wear them as we copulate. Stay with us, O man of the sunlit world. We will suck the soul from you, and your screams will echo here forever."*

Kagen saw a crack in the floor and abruptly drove the end of the torch down into it so that brand stood tall and bright. He quickly drew his second dagger and tapped one blade to the other, creating a single high, sweet, ringing note that floated above them all and rebounded from the stone walls.

"You did not hear my words, you ugly little bastards," he snarled. "I have no soul to take, and any who stand in my way will feel the bite of my knives. I am Kagen of Argon. I am the son of the Poison Rose. You have no power over me. I have no soul to steal, for I am Kagen the *Damned*."

He spoke these words loudly, with force, and again rang the blades together. The goblins winced and recoiled from the sound.

The chief goblin glowered at him, his eyes feral and his hunger naked.

"You are meat, and you are ours."

Kagen, knowing that this was his death, felt his fear crack and fall away. After all that had happened since Hakkia rose up, this was how he knew his path should end. In darkness. In pain and death and endless nothingness beneath the world. Tuke would not even be able to bury what was left of him.

"So be it," he said. His body shifted into a fighting posture, with his weight balanced on the balls of his feet, knees bent, body angled, jaw set, and a killer's smile on his lips. "If you want me, you ugly little bastards, then come and get me. Hell will not take me alone."

They stared. They paused.

And then with a mingled, thunderous howl of red delight, they swarmed at him.

Kagen slashed out left and right, his blades meeting the scabrous flesh and tearing through it. The Poison Rose's knives were forged on Tull Heklon by the priestesses of the Sacred Trust. They were finer than the best Bulconian steel, and no blades took a sharper edge or held it longer. He took the chief goblin first, crossing his knives and then whipping them apart so that they bit all the way to the bone. The creature spun away, clutching at a throat that was little more than threads and rags. The force of its heart shot red-black blood out into the faces of a half dozen others. Kagen ignored those for the moment and half turned, kicking out with the flat of his foot to catch a goblin in the stomach, folding it in half and driving it back into the path of others who were surging forward.

He charged into the center of the goblins behind him, parrying the raking claws, making dozens of fast, small cuts to arms and shoulders and thighs, severing muscle and tendon. The wounded goblins screamed and fell away, crashing into their fellows. In the confusion of that crowded tunnel, Kagen fought to wound and maim more than kill. The screams of the injured were one of his weapons, the spurting blood a tool. This was a strategy his mother had taught all of her sons and daughters: to be a storm of blood and pain. Killing mattered less than confusion, sudden agony, crippling injuries, and the pleading of the mangled.

Then he surged forward, using blades and pommels, elbows and knees to bash a hole through the goblins that stood between him and the deeper part of the tunnel. He wanted that gods-damned sword and would have it at any cost. There were but two possible paths out of that moment: victory or death. Retreat was its own defeat, and Kagen was tired of losing.

As he fought, he wondered if his gods were watching. They had brought him to this, and maybe he would shame them for abandoning him so completely.

"You bastards!" he roared, though in that moment he did not know if he cursed the goblins or the gods.

The monsters reeled and stumbled as he charged forward. They had the numbers, but they did not have his skills. They slashed with claws, and he answered with steel. They crowded him, snapping with their pig teeth, but he chopped at them with a savagery that was their match and more.

He slashed and stabbed, chopped and sliced, kicked and even bit when his hands were too busy. His flesh burned from their nails, and his limbs ran with his own hot blood. But Kagen did not care. There was a purity to this kind of mayhem that was satisfying, even healing in some strange way. This fight—beyond the sight of any human eyes—made him remember who and what he was. Son of the Poison Rose was more than a remark; it was a statement.

The goblins ahead rushed him, but his onslaught made them falter, and finally, with howls like children in agony, they scattered, and the way ahead was clear.

Kagen saw this and broke into a flat-out run.

The goblins howled and gave chase, and for an unknown time—minutes, hours, or even years, as far as Kagen knew—they all ran. The corridor split into two, and he followed the one that looked most well-traveled, hoping it would lead him to the chamber where the dead prince rested. Though he was aware that it could just as easily have been the one the goblins used. But with no map to guide him, he followed instinct, hoping all the while he was not making a fatal error.

Kagen ran and ran until sweat boiled from his pores, his lungs burned, and he thought his heart would burst in his chest. And then the corridor spilled out into a chamber, and he skidded to a sloppy halt, losing balance and dropping to his knees.

There, as if in mockery of supplication, he beheld the thing that had brought him to that cave. The creature that Tuke had believed in enough to bring them all this way into the wilderness.

He sat there.

Him.

A figure in armor that was so badly pitted and rusted with age

that it was more like lace than plate steel. Beneath it was a surcoat of chain mail that had withered to a red-brown latticework.
His face was a sunken and withered mass of wrinkles that had
faded to the color of old dust. Spiders had spun webs across his
eye sockets, but those webs drooped now with disuse, and those
spiders had long since died. The skeletal hands gripped the arms
of a throne-like chair cut from the living rock, but that cold stone
held more vitality than anything belonging to this Prince Vorlon of Old Shimele—a kingdom lost so thoroughly in the past
that it was referenced on no map Kagen had ever seen. Not even
Tuke's map pointed that way. If prince he had truly been, then
his princedom was this hole in the ground, and his killers were
the ancestors of the goblins who made up the population of this
realm of shadows.

Kagen got slowly to his feet and walked over to the foot of the
throne.

Across the thighs of the dead prince was a naked blade. If he
had expected it to glow with some inner power or to hum with
magical potential, Kagen was disappointed. The centuries had not
been kind to the steel. It looked like the kinds of relics disinterred
from burial mounds at the edges of old fields of battle. Or, perhaps, like the fragile weapons dredged up along with shipwrecks.

"Magic sword . . . ?" he said aloud. "Gods damn it all."

He looked into the eyes of the dead.

"It did not save you, did it, my lord?"

A sound made him turn, and he saw that in the mouth of the
tunnel the goblins had returned. Scores of them choked the only
exit, and many were marked by his daggers or were splashed with
the dark blood of their kin. He waited, ready to renew the fight,
but none of them entered the chamber.

Kagen sheathed his blades, wondering if that would spark
them to enter, but they stayed where they were. His heart was
still pounding. The fact that a horde of monsters were afraid of

drawing near to a corpse dead more than a thousand years did nothing to ease his fears.

Through sheer force of will he turned away from the monsters and faced the prince. He began to reach for the sword, paused, stopped, and then cleared his throat.

"Look," he began awkwardly, "Your Highness, I don't know how much of the old legends are true. Maybe you're Prince Vorlon and maybe you're just some knight who got lost and had the bad luck to come in here. Why, though? Were you being chased? Had you lost a battle and come here to hide out? Or . . . hell . . . maybe you were drawn here with some absurd story of buried treasure. I don't know, and I never will, I'm sure. But listen to me: if there is any part of you still here—ghost or ghoul or whatever—a new power has risen in the south. Magic, outlawed for a thousand years, has returned to the world. It's awakening the monsters and spirits and other things. Dark magic that threatens the entire world of men. We are on the brink and probably going to lose."

He paused, trying not to feel ridiculous and self-conscious talking to old bones.

"The Witch-king of Hakkia has conquered everything west of the Cathedral Mountains. Everything. His power is beyond understanding. I walked through lakes of blood the night the Hakkian Ravens invaded. I know that people like me can't win this war. I'm a man. Not a prince, not a champion, not a hero from some old tale. I have no magic weapons, no impenetrable armor. Nothing like that."

The chamber was utterly silent. Even the goblins were still.

"If you are what the legends say, and if that sword holds some kind of power—hell, *any* kind of power—then I have to take it with me. We need something with which to fight the Witch-king. Can you hear me? Can you understand?"

The eyeholes in the skull were black, and the fleshless mouth hung open.

"I will say one thing more," said Kagen. "No . . . two things."

He licked his lips.

"First, I mean no disrespect by coming here to take your sword. I would do anything, go anywhere, dare it all to stop this evil. If you truly were a prince and hero, then you will understand that."

Silence.

"And second, I offer my thanks to you, Prince Vorlon of Old Shimele. I hope that by my taking this sword you can rest."

There was a sound that made him turn once more, but it did not come from the goblins. Nor from the corpse. Kagen tried to make sense of what he heard, but it was soft. A sigh or a whisper.

"Only the passage of air," he told himself.

Then he steeled himself to reach out and take the sword. He stretched out one hand but paused, his palm inches above the ornate handle. He saw that there were small gemstones set into the steel of the crossguard and pommel, rubies and sapphires that were dulled by time and dust.

"I will say one more thing," murmured Kagen. "If this weapon is all that the legends say, and I am able to use it to slay the Witch-king, then when he is dead, I will bring it back here and lay it once more across your thighs. I am damned, but I am no thief."

Having made that vow, Kagen closed his hand around the handle of the ancient sword *Caladbolg*.

He braced himself for something nightmarish to happen, for the dead prince to resist him, or to come alive and fight him for ownership of the storied blade.

But nothing at all happened.

The sword was so light, its weight and density lost to time and rust. As he lifted it, the pitted blade trembled, and Kagen steadied it with the fingers of his other hand lest it bend and snap.

He held it upright, trying to sense or feel some kind of power. Kagen had no idea what magic might *feel* like. Maybe like lightning, or something of that kind of intensity.

But again . . . there was nothing.

"Oh, Tuke, you crazy bastard," said Kagen. "You've sent me to my doom for a piece of rusted junk."

CHAPTER EIGHTY

"Duke Sárkány," said the Witch-king, "things have been so busy that I have not had the chance to formally welcome you."

The vampire bowed. He was tall, slender, pale as all his kind were pale, and dressed in black velvet trimmed with silver. His boots were soft leather made from serpent skin, and they matched a belt cinched around Sárkány's narrow waist. That belt supported a sheathed sword of incredible age known as Dragon's Bane. There were a hundred stories that purported to tell the true story of the weapon's name. None of them were accurate.

"It is my honor to be invited to your court, Majesty," said the duke. "I am one of many who celebrate your victory over the Silver Empresses. And I am yours to command."

His tone was formal and proper, but there was a sly smile on his full lips as if all such oaths and courtly promises were lines from some play. Or, perhaps, that everything that occurred within the world of humans was beneath him in amusing ways.

Then the duke glanced at the figure standing to the right and slightly behind the throne.

"Do I see an old friend there in the shadows, my king? Greetings, Nicodemus of Jericho."

The Prince of Games took a step forward. "I have not used that name in a very long time. And it was not my real name even then."

Sárkány's smile did not change one bit, but there was a dark twinkle in his eyes.

The Witch-king looked at the prince. "You know each other?"

"Aye, lord," said the prince. "We have been players on the same board many times."

"And not always on the same side," agreed Duke Sárkány.

"If there is blood on the ground between you," said the king, "on either side or both, such debts of honor or vendettas have no place in my hall. We are allies here, and *only* my allies are welcome."

"Oh, fear not for my loyalty," said the prince in a particularly oily voice. "As for the *upierczy* who calls himself Sárkány, he must speak for himself."

The duke laughed. "Peace, my old friend. We are indeed well met and I spill blood in the name of Hastur the Shepherd God and his avatar on earth, Gethon Heklan. This I swear by my own blood."

Those words hung in the air for a moment and then the king nodded. "Let it be so. For war is upon us and my diviners cannot see a clear path to victory."

"Do they foretell defeat?" inquired the duke.

"They see fire and smoke," said the Witch-king. "They see the world drowned and all lands swept clear."

Sárkány made a face of disgust. "Bah. Clairvoyants can barely tell the time of day with any accuracy let alone predict the future. They fail far more often than they succeed, and when they are right, they are seldom completely so. No, great king, do not fear their predictions."

"I do not fear the future," said the Witch-king, "but I do not dismiss a caution, either. I, too, have seen the chaotic flow of events in visions. There *is* something coming and it *will* change the face of the world. Magic, in all its many forms, has begun to return. The common folk think it has returned in full, but we three know different. What has passed since I conquered the Silver Empire is but a bud on a green stem, and none live who can guess what flower will bloom from it."

The duke's disapproval did not vanish. "I do not fear a Gardener's analogy, my lord."

"Ah, the bloodsucker is wrong this time," said the prince with dark amusement. "His Majesty quotes his own ancestor, Vellismia Heklan."

Duke Sárkány recoiled, his hand clawing for the hilt of his sword. "You dare speak that name in my presence, you specter of discord?"

"Why?" taunted the prince. "Are you afraid of ghosts?"

"Peace," cried the Witch-king and both men fell silent. The king settled back against his throne. "The past is the past and even we cannot change it. The future is in motion. That is what matters. We three, and our allies, have the power to force the winds of chaos to blow fair for us and ill for our enemies. Let us agree on that and leave old hatreds and feuds behind us."

The prince descended from the dais and walked over to Sárkány. They stood for a long moment measuring each other by many different kinds of yardsticks. Then the Prince of Games took a step back and bowed.

"I offer my apologies, your grace," he said.

Duke Sárkány let go of his sword handle and in a calmer voice said, "We were brothers once. We fought together more often than on opposing sides. I, too, regret my words."

The duke bowed and then went a step further and held out his hand. The Prince of Games looked momentarily surprised and his mocking expression faded. He stepped forward and clasped the duke's forearm.

"It is good to see you, brother," the prince said.

Then they both turned and bowed to the King in Yellow.

"It is well," said the king. "Now . . . let us talk of how we will build the future that suits our hearts' desires."

"We are yours to command, Majesty," said the lord of vampires.

"War, as I said, is coming. It is inevitable. Had the coronation gone as planned, there would already be peace. That hope is shattered and we must accept it. But the Yellow Empire will not be denied, even if we have to serve as midwives and deliver it in screams and blood."

"You have my complete attention, sire," said the prince.

"Answer me this, then," said the king. "What is the surest way of killing a serpent?"

Sárkány shrugged. "You cut off its head."

"And if it is a serpent with many heads?"

"Then," said the prince, "you keep cutting heads until there are none left."

The Witch-king said nothing but watched them through the lace of his veil.

After a moment the Prince of Games began to smile a great smile of delight. "Ah," he said.

"There is red and wild work to be done," said the King in Yellow. "Your grace, this is the time where your knights will write in blood their names into the future history of this world."

Duke Sárkány bowed low. As he straightened, his pale tongue snuck out from between sharp teeth and slowly licked his bloodred lips.

"Tell me how I may serve the beloved of Hastur," he said.

CHAPTER EIGHTY-ONE

"I'll go in there with you," offered Alibaxter.

The Vale brothers glanced at him.

"It could be very dangerous," said Faulker. "Dragons, Hakkians . . . the lot."

The young wizard looked at them. "You actually think it's more dangerous than it is out here?"

"Yes," said the Twins at the same time.

Alibaxter blinked slowly, like an owl. "Well . . ." he said nervously. "I'll come anyway."

Faulker glanced over his shoulder to where the three least injured members of their team—Jace of Argon, il-Vul of Samud, and Lehrman of Zehria—were stuffing food into packs and unwrapping quivers of arrows and soaking torches with pitch.

"Then let's be about it," said Jheklan. "We didn't come all this way to stop here."

If he said that loud enough for Cat to hear, she did not seem to care. She was wrapped in furs on a seat made from crates, her back to the side of the sled. A fire burned in front of her and her sword lay across her thighs. Despite her injuries, she looked quite comfortable and decidedly unwilling to move.

Jace and Lehrman lit six torches and handed them around.

"I'll lead," offered Faulker.

"Oh, I think you should," agreed Jheklan.

And in they went.

The crevasse was narrowest at the opening, but once they were a dozen paces inside, it widened considerably. The walls of ice rose above them and vanished into shadows beyond the reach of the torchlight. The ground was littered with debris from the avalanche, but even that thinned out and soon they were following a path that was flat and generally unobstructed.

When Jheklan, who was at the rear of the line, looked back, he saw barely a glimmer of daylight reflected on the wall at the last turning. When he glanced back again five minutes later, the only thing to see was a black nothing.

Alibaxter was a half step behind Faulker.

"This path looks almost hand-smoothed," he remarked after an hour.

"Yes," said Faulker softly, "I noticed that."

"My guess," said the wizard, "is that the avalanche opened up a crevasse that joins with the tunnels cut by generations of scholars. This floor seems to prove that. And I wouldn't be at all surprised if we didn't find those other tunnels."

Faulker patted his shoulder, "Let's hope that's the case."

As they went deeper into the glacier it became obvious Alibaxter was correct. They began finding tool marks on the walls and floor, and then some litter here and there—discarded torches that had burned down to stubs, a neatly stacked pile of fish bones, and a piece of parchment torn from some larger document. Faulker picked this latter item up, studied it, then handed it to Alibaxter.

"What do you make of this?"

The wizard examined it by torchlight, nodding as he did so.

"This is very interesting," he said as the others gathered around. "See here? It's written in the kind of shorthand used by field researchers for the Garden. It's only a fragment, but there's part of a date . . . yes, see there? It's old. Sixty-eight years."

"What does it say?"

"Oh, nothing of real importance. It's part of an inventory of artifacts being placed in numbered crates for shipment back to a Garden office in eastern Zaare. Bones and some ancient weapons removed from the ice."

Jheklan brightened. "Magic weapons . . . ?"

"Not as far as I can tell. It merely says 'old swords, arrowheads, and a spearpoint.' The rest is missing. I'll hold onto it, though," said Alibaxter. "In case we find the rest of the document."

They moved on.

Two hours later the corridor opened into a chamber that was crowded with wooden crates and littered with tools. The crates proved to be mostly filled with bundles of seal furs, various kinds of tools used for chipping ice, the bones of unknown animals carefully wrapped in sheets of cotton, and dried fruits that were as hard as rocks.

Beyond that chamber, though, was a much bigger one. They moved into that and spread out to let their torchlight reach as far as possible. The room had rough walls, but two of these had been cut into to get at artifacts frozen there. Those details were interesting and the party moved around to examine the whole of the space, including several small side chambers. It was one of those that caused il-Vul to yell out and beckon the others. They hurried over and stopped, staring at a tableau more chilling than the surrounding ice. It was immediately clear that they had found the group of Garden scholars who had been working in this part of the glacier.

They were all dead.

"Gods of the Pit . . ." breathed the Zehrian, Lehrman.

There were nine bodies in a group. All of them were naked. None of them were whole.

Each of them had been comprehensively and brutally tortured. Fingernails were missing from some, but they were the least of the horrors visited upon the scholars. Many had burns, most displayed stumps of fingers and toes. Several had been flayed. Eyes had been pierced or gouged out, along with ears and noses and genitalia. It was evident that none of the Gardeners had died quickly.

"Whoever did this knew their trade," mused Jheklan.

"Aye, and they enjoyed their work," said Faulker bitterly.

Alibaxter said nothing. He was on his hands and knees in a corner, vomiting loudly.

Faulker knelt by one of the bodies. "This wasn't done sixty years ago. I think this is much more recent. See there? That tattoo this one had on his shoulder? That was from the anniversary of Empress Gessalyn. A lot of people in the faith got that when she turned forty."

"Five years ago," said Jheklan. Then he turned sharply toward his brother. "By Mother Sah, Faulker, that was when Herepath was supposed to be here."

They gave the bodies a closer inspection, but none of the mutilated corpses were Herepath's. Faulker went and fetched Alibaxter, who looked glassy and gray.

"How many Gardeners were on the expedition with Herepath?"

"Um . . . ah . . . thirty . . . ? Perhaps more," said the wizard. "Gardeners, I mean. As for guards and camp followers, I have no idea. Maybe another score."

"Can you tell how long these people have been dead?"

Alibaxter shook his head. "Frozen like this? It could be a month or ten years. Nothing thaws here. Herepath wrote about finding corpses—many hundreds of them—frozen into the walls, and he thought some of them might have been there for hundreds or even thousands of years. With no thaw, no real change in temperature here inside the glacier, there really is no way to tell."

"And," said Jheklan quietly, "we know that there are Hakkians about. I'd like to think we killed the lot of them, but . . ."

They turned and looked across to the far side of the chamber. There was another corridor leading deeper into the mountain of ice. Jheklan and Faulker drew their swords. After a moment so did Jace, il-Vul, and Lehrman.

Alibaxter looked ready to faint, but when the group began to move, he squared his shoulders, set his receding jaw as best he could, drew a small ceremonial dagger, and followed.

CHAPTER EIGHTY-TWO

The sighing sound came again, and Kagen turned sharply, knowing with instant terror that it *had* come from the dead prince.

There, on the rocky throne, the figure was trembling.

Moving.

Slowly. So painfully slow.

Kagen stared in total horror as the withered chest of the prince expanded as he took a breath. How, without lungs or flesh, such a thing was even possible, was beyond him. He stumbled backward, hearing the alarmed cries of the goblins but hearing his own sharp yell of terror all the louder.

The helmet rattled against the bones of the skull. The pitted armor juddered as the creature raised its hands, gripped the arms of the chair, and pushed itself erect with painful, impossible slowness.

Kagen moved backward one stumbling step at a time as the prince rose to his full height. Because the throne was on a small dais and the helmet had a spiked crown, it made the thing appear huge, a giant from old stories. Dust puffed from every joint and link of the chain mail. Spiders scrambled from under the seat and cockroaches dropped from under the surcoat.

Kagen tripped and fell, landing hard on his buttocks, *Caladbolg* out in front of him. Not as a weapon, but as some kind of talisman against this thing.

"By the g-gods . . ." he stammered, tripping over the words.

Prince Vorlon of Old Shimele turned his ghastly head toward Kagen and in that moment the empty eye sockets flared with inner light, a red and hellish glow that exuded such heat that Kagen could feel it. The monster raised a hand and pointed a skeletal finger at Kagen. At the sword.

The prince's jaws worked, and Kagen knew that this thing was trying to speak, to condemn the theft or pronounce some deadly curse. Kagen nearly threw the sword at him. It felt heavier than it had before, and when he looked at the blade, he felt his mind toppling. The blade was rebuilding itself—closing pits carved by rust, taking on weight and substance, becoming whole again.

"Magic!" cried Kagen. "By the gods, this is true magic."

Within moments the weapon he held was whole, the blade long and bright as if newly polished. The edge was like that of a razor, the tip a dagger point.

Kagen looked from the blade to the prince.

He ached to take *Caladbolg* and simply run. With it he could carve a path through the goblins. And yet . . .

The prince was real, too. Would the sword restore him to life and vigor? Was that the secret here? Not to steal the weapon, but to restore it to its rightful owner? Would that complete some time-forgotten spell? Would it restore this champion of the elder world to life? If so, would this legendary hero choose to stand with Kagen and Tuke against the Witch-king and his forces of darkness? Or was this more evidence of magic returning to the world in the service of the Hakkian usurper?

Kagen was torn. Need said one thing, but honor—even the honor of the damned—said something else.

But he took a chance. He reversed *Caladbolg* in his hand and extended the handle toward the prince's outstretched hand.

"I will not steal from you, O prince," he said reverently. "*Caladbolg* belongs to you, and I offer it once more to your keeping."

The prince stared at him with his flaming eyes. The hilt of the sword was inches from those skeletal fingers. For a moment Kagen thought the prince would take the handle and thereby be restored. That moment stretched and stretched.

And then Prince Vorlon threw back his head and laughed.

It was a crashing, crushing, deafening sound. A peal of laughter boiling up from the very pits of hell. It smashed into Kagen, sending him reeling backward. Cracks whipsawed along the walls, and chunks of stone broke loose from the ceiling as the laugh rose and rose and rose.

"*Free!*" cried the dead prince. "*By the gods of light and thunder, I am free!*"

Immediately the skeleton inside the armor began to collapse, bursting into clouds of dust. The armor split apart and fell, disintegrating into metal powder. The skull was the last thing to fall, and, in the moment before it struck the floor, the flaming eyes flared with blinding and painful intensity. Then they abruptly winked out.

Kagen lay there, dazed, covered in dust, the sword heavy in his sweating hand.

On the seat and all around the dais, there was nothing left of the prince but dust.

"G-g-g-gods . . ." was all Kagen could say.

He stared for a very long time, unsure of what to say or even how to think about this.

Then he was on his feet, heart slamming painfully against the inner walls of his chest. He held the great sword, and now it hummed with power so rich, so potent, that it rippled through his arm and outward to every part of him.

Kagen staggered toward the exit, ready to cleave his way out of this mad place, ready to fill hell with goblin dead, but they saw the sword in his hand, and they screamed as they fled.

He stalked along the corridors, not at all sure he was even going the right way. It was only when he saw the pale flicker of his torch in the black distance that he knew he was on the right path. Kagen broke into a run, aware of the darkness growing thick behind him. Aware of goblin eyes—terrified and hateful—watching from niches and holes in the walls. They hissed at him as he passed. Some wept, and some cried out in their guttural tongue.

He ran and ran.

And then he burst out into the thickening twilight.

Tuke was there, and as Kagen crossed the threshold, his friend grabbed him and pulled him into the cold, clean spill of newly risen moonlight.

"I have it," gasped Kagen. "I have the . . ."

His words died on his lips.

He and Tuke stared at the sword of Prince Vorlon.

At the pitted, broken, twisted length of time-rotted metal. As they stared, it began to crumble into dust once more. In the space of a dozen heartbeats, all Kagen held was debris, and when he opened his hand, the night wind blew it away.

Kagen's knees buckled, and he dropped down again. Tuke knelt with him, his body seeming to deflate as the reality of it all struck him.

"Magic sword . . ." said Kagen, gasping and blinking.

"Magic sword," agreed Tuke, looking stricken.

They turned as a deep rumble thundered beneath them. The mouth of the goblin barrow belched out a cloud of gas and dust, and then that whole section of the landscape shuddered and fell inward. Tuke shot to his feet, caught Kagen under the armpits, and hauled him away. They broke into a fierce and desperate run as the whole world seemed to collapse beneath them. Trees cracked and crashed down. The rumble felt as if it reached down to the halls of hell itself.

They ran half a mile. Their horses, panicked, ran on ahead.

And then the two men collapsed against the rising wall of a slope beyond the field of destruction. There they lay, panting, gasping, bathed in sweat, their minds shocked and filled with horrors.

It was a very long time before either of them could speak.

Tuke said it first, repeating the same words. "Magic sword."

Kagen looked at him and then up at the moon. "Magic sword."

It was Kagen who started laughing first, but Tuke followed close on his heels. They laughed as the moon sailed above them.

They laughed like madmen far into the night.

CHAPTER EIGHTY-THREE

The Vale twins searched for hours but found no additional bodies, nor a trace of anything even remotely associated with dragons.

"How sure are we that this whole dragon thing is real?" wondered Faulker aloud.

Jheklan stared at him. "You come six thousand miles, cross a frozen sea, brave every kind of danger, nearly get your throat cut by Ravens, and *now* you ask that?"

"Well," muttered Faulker, "it's not like it hasn't been on my mind for a while now."

Jheklan turned away, flapping his arms in disgust. "Why wasn't I an only child?"

They pressed on, following miles of ice corridors and finding chamber after chamber.

"No damn books of magic either," said Faulker sulkily.

"But no Hakkians either," said Alibaxter. "That's good news."

They found Hakkians in the very next chamber.

In the fourteenth chamber they entered, there were several corpses dressed in Hakkian yellow. They lay sprawled in death, their hands frozen to the hilts of swords or the shafts of spears. But their bodies were ruined—torn to pieces so that it was difficult to count the dead.

Faulker knelt to study the wounds of one group. "Look at the cuts," he said. "They're wrong."

Jace and Alibaxter came over. "Wrong how?" asked the wizard.

"Some of these are sword cut, sure enough," decided Jace. "But see here and here? Those are bites."

"Yes, they are," said Faulker. "Bites with dull teeth." He looked at the others. "So tell me why the sword cuts were made *after* the bites?"

"After?" cried Alibaxter. "Are you sure?"

"He's sure," said Jheklan, and the other members of the team nodded. "You can read battle wounds as clearly as tracks on the ground if you know how. All of these men were bitten first—and bitten a lot—and then someone hacked them to pieces with blades."

Il-Vul said, "I've heard about that sort of thing only once. They taught us about it in school."

The wizard licked his lips nervously. "Actually, I think I know what you might mean. I've never seen it, of course, but I read about it. The Blood Curse of Samud."

All of them rose and backed away from the bodies. They all knew the story.

A terrible disease called the Blood Curse swept Samud nearly fifteen hundred years before. The disease drove people into states of mindless rage and, worse, turned them into cannibals. Wherever the plague struck, whole towns were wiped out. There was no cure save for sharp steel and fire.

"It was spread through bites," said il-Vul in a hollow voice. "The infection took hold fast. Hours for some, but minutes for others. People who were bitten would collapse into comas, then wake up and attack anyone around them—family, their own children, friends, and neighbors. One version of the story says that those bitten people actually *died* and then came back to life as cannibal ghouls. Either way, had it not happened in one of the more remote parts of my country, the plague might have spread everywhere. The king sent an army to fight them, and more than half of them died. Then the king had the entire region set to burn. Even uninfected towns were sacrificed to save the nation. To save the world, I suppose." He nodded to the corpses. "In the history scrolls they talked about how some people survived by cutting their friends and family to pieces. Cutting heads off worked best, but I guess most people facing that went a little mad themselves and just kept cutting."

The bodies on the icy floor showed that level of savagery or, perhaps, desperation. And the fact that frozen bodies looked so fresh, so recently killed, made all the capering shadows thrown by the torchlight seem immediately and completely ominous.

"Don't touch a gods-damned thing in here," warned Faulker. "Nothing. If you see a fucking gold piece, leave it where it lies."

From the looks on their faces, no one needed that warning.

They left the chamber, each of them gripping a torch in one hand and naked steel in the other.

CHAPTER EIGHTY-FOUR

Duke Sárkány met with the officers of his small army.

They met in a high room in the west tower of the palace. Heavy brocade tapestries had been hung over every window, completely blocking the harsh light of early twilight. There were nine of his kind with him, each with long, pale hair that had once been dark brown or black. The years had bleached them so that they looked like kinsmen, though in truth it was the hunger for blood that made them family and not blood lineage.

They had begun the meeting with a meal, and it lay on the floor. Two of them dead, and one—a young boy—clinging to death's steep edge. Rats clustered around the dying boy, licking at the blood that leaked sluggishly from many bites.

Sárkány bent and picked up one of the rats—a bloated one with sleek gray fur—and when he sat he placed the animal on his lap. The rat nuzzled against his hand until the duke began to stroke it with affection and surprising gentleness.

The officers carried heavy chairs over, lifting them as if they were made of boxwood instead of oak, elm, or maple. They sat and leaned in, for the duke spoke softly.

"We have work to do, my children," he said.

He drew a map from a pocket in one voluminous sleeve, handed it to the most senior of the knights, and bade him spread it on the floor in the center of the space formed by the chairs. The map showed the west, from the ocean to the mountains. Each of the nations of the former Silver Empire was marked in blood with the duke's thumbprint.

"Much work . . ." he said, smiling as he stroked the rat's humped back. "I will leave one third of you here in Argentium to wait upon the pleasure of the king. The smallest thing he asks of you will be done as if Hastur himself has commanded it."

The vampires bowed.

"Ten of you will go hunting for me," said the duke. He named the knights and told them who they were to hunt. "Fail me and may the gods have mercy on your souls for I will have none."

But this he said with a smile, and their returning smiles were filled with delight and hunger.

"And the rest of you will ride with me to the town of Arras where I have a very special rendezvous with a lady in a tower."

His knights hissed with red joy at this.

CHAPTER EIGHTY-FIVE

The corridor through the ice ran straight on for a long way, and there were long stretches where it was evident that some natural event had created the tunnel. In many places, though, the walls had been widened and the floors smoothed by hard labor with tools.

Faulker brushed his fingers over some chisel work and turned to Alibaxter. "How long have Gardeners been poking around up here?"

"The first expeditions were sent north six hundred years ago, following old maps found in a library in Nehemite," explained Alibaxter. "But the really serious investigations have been over the last two or three hundred years. Plenty of time for Gardeners and the laborers they brought to have done all this."

"What the hell else could they have had to do," muttered Jace.

"Gods above, how could anyone live up here for any length of time without running mad?"

"From what we've seen," said Jheklan, "I think the answer is obvious."

A few hours later they found a side chamber that had a few worktables, barrels for chairs, and even a stack of furs.

"We can camp here overnight," decided Jheklan. He pointed to a couple of braziers. "Let's build a fire and get some hot food in us. Clear off some of those crates. They'll make better beds than the ice floors."

Every surface was covered with ice-crisped parchment. When Jace and Lehrman began sweeping the papers away, Alibaxter yelped like a small, cross dog.

"No! Let me, for the love of the gods."

He shouldered them out of the way, gathered up the documents, and began laying them on the floor in stacks approximating where they had been. As he worked, he paused often and made small noises and exclamations. "Hmmm. Ah! That's interesting. Oh, look at this." But he wasn't actually asking anyone to really look.

"Let us know if you find something that might tell us what happened to Herepath," said Faulker.

"Until then," said Jheklan, "we'll give you and those papers some private time."

"Mmmm . . . what? I daresay," said Alibaxter distractedly.

The wizard had made a large pot of his special stew before they entered the crevasse, and it had frozen nicely. Jace chipped off a large chunk, put it in a pot, and built a fire in the largest brazier using some wood from an empty barrel. While it heated, they settled down to rest and check their wounds. The stitches on il-Vul's hip—the result of a Hakkian spear—had torn, and Lehrman, who had spent time aboard a coastal trade ship, used his sail-making skills to sew it back up neater than before.

They ate in companionable silence, though each of them cast occasional glances at the corridor from which they'd come. The chamber with the slaughtered bite victims was a good half-day's walk behind them, but after they finished their meal, Jace, Faulker, and Lehrman—without even having to discuss it—dragged a number of heavy boxes over to block that entrance.

Jheklan took the first watch, and he sat up with Alibaxter for several hours.

"What has you so damned enthralled?" he asked, and the young wizard came over with a sheaf of documents. It was obvious, though, that his earlier excitement had given way to an entirely different emotion.

Alibaxter sat for a moment, lips pursed, before he spoke. "First, let me begin by saying that the expeditions here to the Winter-wilds were not generally spoken of, even in the Garden. Everyone knew there were scholars up here, but the information we received from *within* the Harvest Faith was scant. When the Garden did not want to share information then doors and mouths were shut."

"How like politics," observed Jheklan.

"It has much of the same process and dedication to obfuscatory policies. I think it's fair to say that there was deliberate disinformation that fed into false rumors that nothing much of import was happening here."

"That sounds ominous."

Alibaxter nodded, his face unsmiling. "While I have yet to find anything directly relating to Herepath, I have found some unusual references. Mind you, these papers here are not what I hope yet to find in the chief Gardener's records—which I presume will be in one of these chambers. So, I am inferring much from small notes, comments scribbled in the margins of documents still in draft form, and a partial diary that someone had begun and then abandoned."

The wizard produced a small book with leather covers and held it in his lap.

"This diary," he continued, "is quite old, and was not written by a Gardener. Nor is it written in either the common tongue or the ecclesiastical language used by scholars."

"Oh? Don't tell me it's in that old Skyrian hieroglyph picture language."

In the torch's glow, Alibaxter's eyes seemed to be filled with strange lights. "No. It's in a very old dialect of Hakkian."

"So? We know the Hakkians have been here off and on for years. The Witch-king himself, Gethon Heklan, was supposed to have come up here. Mother Frey said so."

The wizard turned the diary over so Jheklan could see the cover. Engraved into the leather was the symbol of an eclipse. It had been painted long ago, but the sun's corona around the moon was not yellow, as were all other Hakkian symbols.

Jheklan took it and peered closely at it, then looked up at Alibaxter. "I don't understand. Has the cold faded the color?"

"No," said Alibaxter, and he used a thumbnail to chip off a flake. It was the same color on either side.

"Why on earth would an old Hakkian diary have an eclipse edged with *silver* fire?"

"Why indeed."

"Silver isn't even allowed on any artwork in Hakkia," protested Jheklan. "Not since my own ancestor, Bellapher the Silver Thorn, crushed their religious uprising centuries ago."

"Correct," said Alibaxter. "The priests and royal family forbade it ever since the Silver Empire was born. Remember, Hakkia never willingly joined the empire. They were a conquered nation. Had Hakkia been located on the edges of the empire, as is Bulconia, they might have been spared that conquest, but they are in the empire's heart, bordered by Ghenrey, Nehemite, Zehria, Ghul, and the Waste. That nation squats on the hubs of a dozen key trade routes, and it commands a key portion of the Golden Sea. The first empress forced it into the empire in order to control that trade and to prevent Hakkia from being a threat from within the span of the Silver Empire."

"Which makes it even stranger that someone—a Hakkian—would paint his national symbol in the color of the empire."

Alibaxter ran his finger along the rim of silver fire. "This diary speaks of a journey to this glacier many generations ago. It took me a while to figure out how old, but there are references to Mithlindel—do you know it?"

Jheklan shook his head.

"I'm not surprised. It isn't mentioned in the standard history books. Certainly not the ones written by the Gardeners. Mithlindel was a small but important region of Hakkia. No one knows exactly where it was because it has been so comprehensively edited out of history. Countless maps were burned and new ones drawn that did not include it. There used to be a department within the League of Historians, which as you know was always one of the most powerful groups within the Garden, and the priests of that department were charged with erasing all mentions of Mithlindel. They were diligent and very effective, for it isn't even a rumor anymore. It has effectively ceased to exist."

"Why? Was it an abode of dark sorcerers?"

"Not at all. In point of fact it was a place of great learning, art, high culture. But it could not be allowed to exist."

"Again . . . *why?*"

"For a number of reasons, my friend," said Alibaxter. "One is that many of the kings and queens of the Silver Empire's nations can trace their bloodlines to families from Mithlindel."

"Bullshit," laughed Jheklan. "That would make them Hakkians."

"Oh, it's worse than that." Alibaxter opened the diary and found a page. He read from it. "*Before we set out, our company received blessings and gifts for the High Lady of Silver Hall. She hung garlands of roses around our horses' necks and gave Krenleigh, the leader of the expedition, a pair of beautiful daggers that had been forged by the priestess of the Sacred Trust on Tull Heklon.*" He looked up. "And there is a drawing."

Alibaxter opened the diary wide and angled it to the torch so Jheklan could see the drawings. He heard the catch in Jheklan's throat and then a very soft word—just the one—spoken in wonder and horror.

"No . . ."

The wizard closed the book.

"Do you want to know the name of the High Lady of Silver Hall?" he asked. "Or can you guess?"

"It's impossible," whispered Jheklan hoarsely.

"The High Lady's name was Theselyanna," said Alibaxter. "Mother of the first Silver Empress. This is a secret long kept by the Garden. It is a secret drenched in blood and born of oppression and subjugation. And as for Theselyanna's last name . . . can you guess it? After all, they named an island after her family three thousand years ago. The island where those daggers were forged. But she abandoned that surname when she first sat upon the imperial throne and now it is hated throughout the west."

Jheklan stared at him.

"The Silver Empresses . . . were *Heklans?*" he cried.

CHAPTER EIGHTY-SIX

Ten men and women knelt in the dirt.

Twenty thousand men and women stood around them. A sea around an island.

Tuke Brakson and Filia alden-Bok stood facing the kneeling soldiers. Redharn and Gi-Elless flanked them, and Horse the dog sat at Filia's left side, his dark eyes filled with hunger. Selvath stood apart, watching with pitiless eyes.

"Unbladed," Filia said to the ten prisoners. "That's what you are. You joined the Brotherhood of Steel, sponsored by your saints. You are oath-bound. You are trusted."

They said nothing. A few met her eyes with looks of pleading, resentment, and anger. The rest stared down at the dirt.

"And now," continued Filia, her voice as hard as steel, "you are revealed as traitors. As spies of the Witch-king. As the enemies of your own sworn brothers and sisters."

She walked up to one of them, a lean and wiry man with side whiskers and icy blue eyes. "Gelfun, you were at Ghuraka's camp when Tuke and I brought Kagen there and stood up as his saints. You witnessed the betrayal of Ghuraka. You saw what Kagen did to Branks. And you stood with the others and threw your axe at his feet and declared that there was blood on the ground between you. You accepted the blood oath that has endured as a true bond for thousands of years. You *swore* then, just as you swore when you joined the brotherhood. How is it that a Nelfydian warrior of repute has come to this? What coin was used to buy your soul?"

Gelfun leaned forward and spat full in her face.

Horse began to lunge, but she stopped him with a small click of her tongue. Then she plucked a rag from her belt, wiped her face, and let the cloth fall.

"The Witch-king will eat your heart," snarled the spy. "He will kill you and everything you love. There are more of us than you think. We will kill you in your sleep and the Witch-king will reward us with mountains of gold."

Only two other prisoners growled agreement. The rest were caught in a shocked and despairing silence.

Filia walked away from them and made a slow circuit of the space surrounded by the army. She met the hard eyes of men and women whose faces slowly transformed from the shock of the man's insult and words and into masks of anger that ranged from red hot to bitter cold.

Filia stopped beside Tuke.

Then she turned to address the troops.

"Many of you are Unbladed. The rest are soldiers from across the empire. Soldiers of great houses and soldier volunteers from farms and hamlets. This betrayal is yours to judge. I will leave them to whatever justice you feel is merited."

With that she left the circle, walking down an aisle quickly formed for her. Horse trotted beside her. After a moment Redharn, Gi-Elless, and Tuke followed.

They made it almost to their tent before the screams began.

Those screams lasted for a very long time.

Selvath lingered to watch.

CHAPTER EIGHTY-SEVEN

The news rocked Jheklan and he woke his brother to tell him.

Faulker listened in silence, then grinned. "Go fuck yourself, you lying piece of moose shit."

When Jheklan did not smile or even riposte with his own vulgarity, Faulker's grin faltered, cracked, and fell away.

"No," he said. He looked at Alibaxter. "No. No, no, no."

The wizard merely spread his hands.

Faulker sprang up and snatched the fragment of parchment from Jheklan. It made no sense to him and he flung it away into a corner.

"No," he insisted.

He walked away, then sat down hard on a crate, put his head in his hands, and kept saying that word. No.

But from his increasingly wretched tone, it was clear he believed it.

CHAPTER EIGHTY-EIGHT

Jendor Fint had spent the last twenty-seven years of life as a watcher for the city of Arras in Vahlycor. It was a very quiet town, even after the coming of the Hakkians, and there simply was never much to watch.

But Jendor was a conscientious man and he walked his regular route, which covered about an eighth of Arras, from the courthouse to the bluffs over the ocean. About three times a month he arrested drunks—usually sailors from one of the merchant vessels, and there were never many of them because the cliffs made Arras a tricky port. Once in a while he would catch some lads trying to break into the back of a bakery or a wine merchant's store at night and send them packing with a thump from his staff or—if they were lads whose parents he knew—a scolding.

Only twice in all those years had he needed to deal with anything serious. One was when Old Rabe, the butcher, went mad after his wife left with the cabbage farmer and decided to take his hurt and anger out on everyone he met. Jendor thumped him, too, and more than a few times. The other was when a pair of ruffians from Zaare drifted in and tried to force themselves on a barmaid walking home late. Jendor, who had three daughters of his own, beat the two men insensible and then arrested them. He was present at their hanging.

But those events were years back, and things had been quiet since then. Mostly quiet. There was the Night of the Ravens, but it was more about controlling local panic than violence, since there was no actual Hakkian invasion force in a place like Arras. Then there was a fuss when a platoon of Ravens came through looking for the Argonian fugitive, Kagen Vale, and his confederates. The Ravens found nothing and eventually left. Since then, nothing at all.

Until the night of the half moon.

Then a dairy farmer friend of his rode into town on a fast mule to report that there was potential trouble coming up the road from the south.

"What kind of trouble?" asked Jendor.

His friend, Nip, made a warding sign and then leaned in close to answer. "I was just finishing up for the day, settling the cows down for the night when I saw a company of riders coming up the old Sycamore Road."

"Nobody uses that road anymore," said Jendor. "It only goes to the old copper mine, and that's been played out these ten years and more."

"I know," said Nip. "And that's why I thought it was so queer. They came *out* of the mine, horses and all, and I saw them looking at a map and pointing toward town. I didn't like the look of them, I can tell you, so I saddled up old Bernice here and came to tell you." He patted the mule affectionately.

"What'd these fellows look like?" asked Jendor. "And how many of 'em were there?"

"There was at least a dozen of them, and maybe more, I didn't see who were still in the mine. As for what they looked like . . . well, mate, they looked wrong, and that's the truth." When Jendor pressed him for details, Nip described a company of tall, slender, and very pale riders. Mostly men, but with a few women with them. They wore black armor with only an odd version of the Hakkian eclipse on it—a sun in full eclipse, with only some curls of yellow fire around it. Each of them had swords or spears, and some had bows. They wore cloaks with hoods, but he could see their faces well enough by the moonlight—very gaunt and extremely pale, with dark eyes.

"Albinos?" queried Jendor, but Nip shook his head.

"No, for their hair was normal—black or brown, though a few were blond," said Nip. "But as for their skin . . . they had that pale, wasted look you see on prisoners who were in dungeons with no windows. Faces the color of mushrooms, and I swear—

hand to the gods—that they looked more like corpses than living men and women."

Jendor did not like the sound of that. Not at all.

"And you said they were pointing this way?"

"Aye. They were just saddling their horses when I hopped on Bernice and came here to tell you." The dairy farmer paused. "What do you think ought to be done?"

Jendor considered. The entire group of town watchers amounted to eight men, none of them younger than forty and most—like him—considerably older. There had been a garrison of soldiers before the Ravens came, but they were all gone now. And not even a group of Hakkians to keep watch.

So, seven men against at least a score of heavily armed strangers.

"Maybe they'll pass through and move on," said Jendor doubtfully. In truth there was only one road through Arras.

"Maybe," said Nip doubtfully. "And maybe they'll—"

He stopped midsentence and the watcher saw him staring over his shoulder. Jendor turned to see what he was looking at, and that's when he saw the riders.

There was not a dozen.

There were at least thirty of the riders in black armor. Each wore cloaks and had their hoods up, yet Jendor could see their faces—burning a sickly white in the bright moonlight. And *he* did not like the look of them, either.

The riders must have made remarkable time because they had reached the town only minutes behind Nip. And what was odder was that their horses' hooves made almost no sound. Even on the cobblestones of the main road there was a muffled quality about them as if they were miles away, yet they were no more than thirty yards from where Jendor and Nip stood. Axes, coils of rope, and heavy sledgehammers hung from the saddles, and knife handles sprouted from every belt and sash.

Behind the line of horses were two animals yoked to a wagon.

At first Jendor thought they were oxen, but with huge horns that curled up from their heads and down over their faces. With a terrified start, the watcher realized that they were *goats*. But incredibly massive black goats—creatures as large as any rhinoceros. The paving stones cracked beneath their cloven feet.

The leader of this grotesque company had a face that made Jendor want to run away and hide. High cheekbones, a high brow, full lips, a long patrician nose, and a sneer of cold disregard. There was no humor, no kindness, no trace of affability. What Jendor saw was the kind of haughty superiority that reduced everything the man looked at to something more worthless than dirt. Plus there was some other quality to the man's dark eyes. A predatory gleam and a hunger that made the watcher's blood run cold.

For a fragment of a moment Jendor considered challenging him and demanding to know his business, but that impulse was a reflex and the watcher forced it out of his mind. He stepped out of the rider's way, using his arm as a bar to push Nip back as well.

The pale-faced leader flicked a single glance at Jendor and in that moment, the watcher felt more than fear. The impact of those eyes was penetrating, invasive, violative . . . and Jendor staggered back, his bladder failing him, his breath turning to poison in his lungs. He fell back against Nip and the two of them pressed against a wall, trying not to be seen. It was the most dreadful sensation Jendor had ever felt, and his knees buckled. He dropped to all fours and vomited onto the stones. Then he cried out as he saw that there, crawling in the stew and ale he'd had for his dinner, were maggots. Beside him, Nip was gagging and then he, too, threw up. When the watcher looked at his friend, he saw pale maggots clinging to the slop on his chin.

Then the rider was past, and his followers with him.

When Jendor looked down once more at his vomit, the maggots were gone.

He covered his face with his hands and prayed with silent desperation for salvation from the Harvest Gods. But that was disturbed by a sound overhead, and when he looked up, the sky was filled with a flitting, snapping, fluttering mass of bats. Hundreds of them. Thousands. Following the riders in black as they made their way through the town of Arras toward a tower perched on the outermost bluff. Toward the Tower of Sarsis.

CHAPTER EIGHTY-NINE

Lord Nespar stood waiting a long time for the Witch-king to acknowledge his presence, and when it came it was only the lift of a finger. Nespar came to the foot of the dais and bowed.

In the weeks since the Witch-king had revealed his face, the monarch had rarely been in his throne room. Much of his time was spent in secret meetings with the Prince of Games, Duke Sárkány, elders from the van Kelton clan who were rumored to be werewolves, or one of the many thaumaturges brought up from Hakkia. Or the king was in one of the many restricted courtyards where he kept an increasingly bizarre and disturbing collection of animals of kinds Nespar had never seen. Some of these looked like monsters from old myths, but others seemed new and strange, and all but the King in Yellow were forbidden to touch them.

Nespar's friend, Jakob, had been equally frustrated in obtaining an audience. Privately they wondered if the unveiling had somehow driven the Witch-king into some form of depression. Or, possibly, he resented his two chief advisors for even suggesting it.

The royal generals and admirals were allowed audiences, but Nespar was seldom invited to those, which troubled him very deeply because it meant that he had lost touch with the plans for the coming war. Yet he pressed his request that day because he had valuable strategic information.

"My lord," said the chamberlain, "I thank you for this audience."

"Whatever you have to say, Nespar, say it and skip the groveling. I'm in no mood. There are enough vermin in the palace as it is."

This shocked Nespar. The king had always been stern but never rude, not to Nespar, who had been with him during the entire preparation for the conquest of the empire. He felt hurt but did not dare to let it show on his face.

"My network of agents has brought word of forces gathering in the north and east."

"Kagen Vale's army?" mused the king. "And now you will tell me how frightened I should be."

"Fr-frightened . . . ? N-no, sir," stammered Nespar. "However, I felt it was important to know the latest details."

"Speak, then."

Nespar produced a scroll from a pocket and read off the lists of troop numbers and probable locations, names of collaborators among the nobility, and estimates of the size of Therian, Samudian, and Vahlycorian navies. He also mentioned that troop ships were being built at an alarming rate in Sunderland, Behlia, and on various of the many Dragon Islands. The sum total was impressive, and yet the Witch-king seemed unmoved.

"Is there more?" he asked.

"Not at the present time, sire."

"Then give those numbers to Lord High Marshal Mari Heklan. You may leave now."

Nespar bowed himself backward, turned, and left.

He delivered the scroll to a clerk to have a copy prepared for Mad Mari, then fled to his tower where Jakob was waiting. The historian took one look at him and thrust a large goblet of wine into his hands.

"I won't ask how it went," Jakob said. "It's written on your face."

Nespar sat uneasily in his chair and drank down half the wine.

He did not seem to notice that a few drops fell onto his breast. Then he looked at Jakob with such deep despair in his eyes that the historian leaned forward, took the cup from Nespar and set it aside, then held his friend's hands.

"He just did not seem to *care*," said Nespar, his voice trembling at the edge of tears.

CHAPTER NINETY

Kagen rode through the day and used that time to consider what had passed between Clementius and him a few days ago. The silk flag was in his saddlebag, and he found himself alternately wanting to throw it away and wanting to take it out and look at it.

The concept that he wrestled most was that tens of thousands of soldiers, villagers, and nobles were willing to march to war under that flag. Under a flag meant to represent *him*.

"The whole damn world is mad," he said aloud, and Jinx nickered.

The road that day took him to a small village near a crossroads, and to an inn that catered to traffic going toward and away from the busy harbors on the coast, down to Theria and Argon, and to the vineyards of Zaare. In the relative quiet in the recent months since the Night of the Ravens, trade had resumed and there were always strangers in that town and that inn. There was no Hakkian garrison in the town, though Kagen wore a soft felt cap to hide his dark curly hair, and he had grown a beard during his journey to see Frey and the nobles. He worked some pale pipe clay into his beard to turn it gray, and when he dismounted, he walked with a stoop, favoring one leg.

He found Filia already in the bar attached to the inn, sitting in a corner with her ugly dog, Horse, pretending to doze at her feet. The dog's eyes were closed but his scarred ears swiveled this way and that, and his nostrils sniffed the air. When Kagen approached,

Horse's crooked tail thumped twice, which—for him—was a sign of great affection.

Filia stood to embrace him and kiss his cheek. Then they sat.

"It's damn good to see you," he said. "I have much to tell you."

"Tuke told me some of it," she said. Then gave him a lopsided smile. "Goblins?"

"Goblins," he said. "And be aware, my dear, that once we get this war settled I intend to beat Tuke to death for dragging me into that adventure."

She laughed. "He's so distraught. He was convinced he was going to help you win this war and earn you both a place in the kind of tavern song they'll sing for the next thousand years."

"He's a bastard."

"He loves you," she said.

Kagen sighed, long and slow. "Aye. I know it. I love the big bastard, too. And his heart's in the right place."

"Although," said Filia, "he really *can* be a pain in the ass."

"And this is the man you fell in love with."

"Well . . . he does have other qualities."

"Apart from an obsession with balls . . . ?"

Filia kicked him under the table. They drank to Tuke.

"Tell me about Selvath and the spies," he said as he set his cup down.

Filia went through all of it, including the executions of the men and women Selvath named. Their belongings were searched first, and there were code books and pouches of gold in each of their kits.

"I can't say that I'm surprised," said Kagen when she was done. "Spies are inevitable. When I was a lad my best friend's mother was deputy spymaster for the empire. Lawyers, politicians, and spies are like cockroaches . . . no matter how diligently you clean your house another scuttles out from under the bed." He signaled for more beer. "I assume you interrogated them?"

"I did," said Filia. "With Gi-Elless to help."

"Did we learn anything?"

"Nothing of great moment. Enough to make us more cautious. Selvath is now working with our recruiters."

Kagen nodded. "Is she well?"

Filia smiled at the question. "She is. And she's grateful for what you did for her."

"It's what anyone would do."

She kicked him again.

"Oww! What was that for?"

"For being a decent, well-intentioned, good-natured idiot," she said and rolled her eyes. "*It's what anyone would do.* By the intangible balls of the saints."

Kagen snorted beer out of his nose. "Ha!" he laughed, pointing at her. "Tuke's infected you with ball fever."

"I could kick you harder and in a different place."

"No thanks."

"But as for Selvath and what you did," said Filia. "Kagen you are so naive. But I love you for it."

"How hard would you have kicked me if you didn't?"

"I'd sic Horse on you."

The big dog made a low growling sound, then thumped his tail again.

They drank and Kagen said, "Let me catch you up on what I've been doing."

And he told her about the estates he'd visited, the conversations had and promises made. As he recounted the numbers of fighters promised by each noble, Filia did some quick math.

"If all of them show up," she said, "and counting the fifteen camps we already have, we could conceivably put ninety thousand in the field against the Hakkians."

Kagen goggled at her.

"Surely not!" he cried.

"And that doesn't include any formal armies from the various kingdoms. Hannibus Greel is on his way to meet with Tuke and me in a few days. He should have a better idea of who will join the fight on our side, and what forces they might bring."

"Will he have an idea of how many will side with Hakkia or simply sit it out?"

"Of course," said Filia, "but I doubt many will remain neutral. Let's face it, Kagen, it's not that kind of war. It's not a border or trade dispute. It's going to be a long war, and costly in terms of gold and lives."

"I agree with the latter—it *will* be costly—but," said Kagen, "I don't think it will be a long war."

"What makes you say that?"

"I've had a lot of time to think about it. Unless several nations side with the Hakkians, we have a real chance in the field. I did not think we would—not at first. But after talking to the nobles, they are doing our work for us. They are setting the stage for a mass uprising. The fact that the Witch-king has not used much magic since he conquered the empire is suggestive. That effort drained him, and maybe he's rebuilt his power, but what other big move can he make this time? Sending troops into the capitals was a coup, but it won't work again. Everyone is vigilant, and every palace is packed to the rafters with soldiers. No one will be surprised again. Oh, and as for the Hakkian fleet showing up to burn every warship in Haddon Bay a second time . . . they have closed the bay to warships, which tells me that Theria and Samud, who have the biggest navies, are keeping their fleets away, hiding them in the islands, most likely, until the war starts."

"The Witch-king is a sorcerer," countered Filia, "he could find those fleets."

"Can he, though? Why would he need a network of spies if he had such vision? Why are we—you, me, Tuke, all of us—alive and not rotting heads on pikes? No, Filia, he has his limits and we need to keep perspective. Besides . . . Herepath is devious but he was never a student of military science."

"I take it you've not heard about the new lord high marshal?"

"No. Who is he?"

"*She,* actually." And Filia told him about Mad Mari Heklan.

It was not good news, but Kagen did not let his heart sink. He said, "We have some powerful allies of our own."

"You're going to see Maralina, I take it?" asked Filia.

"It's where I'm off to. I leave at first light."

They spent the rest of the evening talking about the coming war. If there was a reserve in Filia, Kagen could accept it. In her place he would have the same doubts, and at one point he even mentioned that the Hakkian propagandists were doing their own best to win the war.

"Oh, by the way," he said as they were getting ready to head up to their rooms. "I almost forgot to show you this."

He picked his pack off the floor and rummaged in it, asked her to clear the table, then spread the turquoise silk across the top. Filia traced the various symbolic elements with her fingers.

"This is beautiful," she said. "And terrifying."

"Yes," he said, understanding the many subtle meanings implied by her comment. "Take it with you. Have more made, I suppose. People need a visible symbol, so let them rally around this."

"A flag for war, and a general to wave it."

"I'm not a—"

"—general. Yes. You keep saying that. I wish you'd just accept it, even if for convenience sake."

Kagen began folding the flag. "It makes me feel just a bit like a pretentious jackass."

"Well, you *are* a jackass at times," said Filia judiciously. "Though pretentious? No. That would be true only if you had designed the flag yourself."

"Still makes me feel strange."

"We live in strange times, my dear."

They went to their rooms and slept. When Kagen came down in the morning, Filia was gone.

Kagen ate a quick breakfast and was gone before the first cock crow.

————————————————➤ **CHAPTER NINETY-ONE**

The Prince of Games drifted like a ghost through the halls of the great palace where the last Silver Empress died.

He often walked aimlessly, drawn by the ghostly echoes of suffering and death. The screams of the Seedlings as the Ravens cut them to pieces, and of the eldest, who was held down to her bed and defiled in every possible way, even as she sought refuge beyond the doors of death. He could feel each individual arrow shot into the body of Empress Gessalyn. There was the defiant roar of the giant Hugh Vale, who had killed even as he was killed. The despairing cry of Lord Khendrick Vale as he watched his son die and knew his own death was at hand.

And then the death of the Poison Rose, torn to red rags by the razor-knight.

He visited each room where important lives ended. Most of the rooms were sealed, left as they had been when the murders happened. Nespar had pleaded with the Witch-king to allow him to empty and scour those rooms, to remove the stink and, perhaps, the very echoes that the prince could hear. But the yellow king had been adamant. They were his proofs of victory. His trophies.

And so the rooms remained as they were. Only the wall of the empress's bedroom had been rebuilt, repairing the damage from the banefire Kagen used to slay the razor-knight.

It was here that the prince stopped his wandering and stood in long contemplation.

His visit to the Witch-king's zoo had unnerved him, and that was something he rarely felt. Maybe once in a century, and never before as profoundly as this.

"You risk a war in heaven," he murmured to the empty room. "In your madness to conquer the world for your god, you risk *all* the worlds. The veils between this world and the many that make up the larger world are so fragile. I don't think you ever understood this, my king."

The smell of blood had long since faded. Now what remained was a less pungent but far more specific stink of death. The sacrificial chambers in Skyria and Vespia once smelled like this, even centuries after those cultures tumbled into barbarity or dust.

The prince walked over to the wall and traced the edges of the new masonry. Then he turned and looked at the furniture, infested now with cockroaches and littered with rat droppings. There were splotches of dark brown that looked like old mud but were not.

The Prince of Games knelt in a corner fifteen feet from the repaired wall. There were many spots of that old brown here. Insects had dwindled them, but flakes of dried blood still lingered.

He drew his dirk and carefully scraped those flakes into his palm.

Rising, he left the room and went to the far side of the palace, climbing the back stairs into one of the towers. Nespar and Jakob Ravensmere had suites there, as did several of the more senior generals. Even Mad Mari had rooms there, though she was in the field, hunting through Argon and Vahlycor for pockets of Kagen's growing army. Her delight in killing kept her far away, and the prince was glad of it. She was not *his* kind of fanatic. Her loyalty was to the Witch-king and no other. There was no conflict in her heart or mind that could be manipulated.

He stopped outside of Kestral's room. A single sentry stood guard.

"My lord," said the soldier, "all are forbidden to enter here."

"Shhhh," whispered the prince, and the soldier puddled down onto the floor. He emitted a soft, buzzing snore and even looked content.

The prince was amused. Once the soldier woke up, he would tell *no one* of this. He would not remember the prince and only know that he had fallen asleep on duty. To admit it would be to invite a public flaying.

The door was locked, but the prince merely stroked the plate and the inner mechanism turned and clicked open. He slipped inside and closed the door.

On the floor was a circle made of salt and sand mixed with the finely ground bones of crows and starlings and grackles. A circle of protection. The prince had seen many thousands of these and had crafted countless of his own over the years. Even a chaos trickster needed protection, and he saw that Lady Kestral had done everything right.

There was the cold stub of a single candle standing in its own small protective circle. Once lit, no wind could blow it out, and it would burn slowly and never burn all the way out. A nice bit of practical magic.

Against one wall, rotted and gnawed by vermin, were the bodies of soldiers who had died fighting Kagen, Tuke, and Filia on the night of the failed coronation; and others who had survived that battle only to be ritually murdered by Kestral as she sought to learn everything that had happened there before the throne. Kestral's task, set by the Witch-king, was to identify which splashes of blood on the floor of the great hall belonged to Kagen Vale. By conjuring the dead, she was able to force them to reconstruct those frenetic moments for her, allowing her to scale down her task from impossibility to merely suicidal. She had needed to conjure many spirits, and each of these drained more of her life force away. Once she discovered Kagen's blood, the process of then invoking a razor-knight had pushed her to the very edge of death.

Had she stopped there, she might have lived. The prince thought it possible, though she would have been a withered crone for what few years were left to her. Instead—perhaps driven mad by her efforts or to rage by the Witch-king's total disregard for her life—Kestral had done something to change the razor-knight's nature. It stopped hunting Kagen and began to hunt the Witch-king. Now that monster was in a pit of spikes, lured there by the prince and Mad Mari Heklan.

The razor-knight intrigued the prince. Once its target had changed, so, apparently, had its nature. Where a regular razor-knight would kill literally anyone that got between it and its target, this one did not seem to have that same absolute disregard for human life. In its long journey from Vespia to where Mad Mari trapped it, the thing had walked through villages and towns and did no harm to the people living there. Instead he sought out Hakkian outposts and butchered them. That made no sense to the prince. None.

He squatted down and looked at the conjuring circle. "How did you change its nature, my lady?" he mused aloud. "Did you find a kindly demon to occupy its monstrous form?"

That was the question. Razor-knights were golems whose animating life force was provided by a demon conjured through necromancy and forced into the knight's body until the desired mission was accomplished. Demons were never merciful at the best of times, and certainly not when forced to serve the will of a necromancer.

"What oh what did you do?" he wondered.

A very old memory flickered through his ancient brain and he snatched it from the shadows, turning it over in his mind.

He knew that the razor-knight's animus was created by some fragment of a living person imbued into the golem form, so that the demon had a clear focus—kill that person and be freed to return to hell. Which meant that Kestral had redone her spell with something of the Witch-king's.

There was a small bowl fashioned in the shape of a pond lily, and in it was a dried paste. The prince sniffed it, and his subtle senses registered everything Kestral had mixed together—salt water from the ocean, the heart of a dove, moth cocoons, ground bone, mugwort, hellebore, and salt from the deserts of Skyria. He poked around in it and, indeed, found strands of hair. Yet there was nothing that explained the greater mystery.

Kestral would have combined these items and then spoken a certain prayer to Nyarlathotep, one of the Outer Gods, a creature from a pantheon even older and greater than that of Hastur and Cthulhu. The prince had no doubt Kestral had done it all just so, else the razor-knight could never have come into existence at all.

But, save for the circle of protection, what kept the demon in check?

Not much at all, he decided. The circle was so fragile. A moistened finger could draw a line through it and cancel that protection. In ordinary situations, that would mean releasing a demon into the world with nothing to check its aggression.

Kestral had changed her spell, though. What would that mean if this circle was cut?

He thought about that. If chaos was the result of such a cancelling of protection, he might have licked his own finger and made the cut.

The prince sat cross-legged on the floor and thought about what he was considering doing. He thought and thought for a very long time. But demons were tricky. Some were even dangerous to one such as he. That had been a lesson hard-learned.

Yet the temptation was there.

He cocked his head and thought about another circle like this one elsewhere in the castle. Drawn on the floor around a block of ice.

He was more than a little sure what was trapped in the unmelting ice. But, what was the nature of *that* spell? What would happen if *it* were cut?

"So many wonderful things to think about," he told himself.

Had anyone been in that room, they would have seen a change come over the Prince of Games. His eyes swirled with strange and ugly colors, much as they had when the Witch-king had revealed his true plans in the zoo. But his form also transformed. Instead of the lean and wiry body, his limbs grew longer and thinner, his spine cracked and curled forward as spikes rose, pressing each vertebra visibly through the fabric of his tunic. His ears rose into points, his chin became sharper, his cheekbones far more pronounced, and his nose became hooked and beaky. The air around him crackled with small capering arcs of electricity and the air stank of sulfur.

The thing that wore the countenance of the Prince of Games opened his palm and regarded the flakes of blood. And in that forbidden room, under the watchful eyes of murdered ghosts, he played a new game.

CHAPTER NINETY-TWO

The Vale brothers and the young wizard sat huddled around a fire that burned brightly but seemed unable or unwilling to provide useful heat. The air was redolent with the mingled smells of frozen meat and something else—a vital animal smell that all of them could put a name to but none wanted to. That would have made things far too real. Nor were any of them ready for such a burden.

The other three were asleep and they slept so deeply and so quietly that Faulker could not help thinking that they looked dead. He hoped it wasn't this newly magical and deeply twisted world sending him a vision of a terrible future.

He almost said as much to his brother and Alibaxter but held back. They already looked like they were close to screaming. Or crying.

Or running the hell away.

Alibaxter produced a pewter-and-glass flask and handed it across to Jheklan, who took it, sniffed, took a sip, winced as if it was acid, took another sip, had the same reaction, and nodded in appreciation. Without a word he handed it to his brother. Faulker sipped it but had no thirst for more. His stomach felt like it was filled with sour milk and filth. He handed the flask back to the wizard.

The fire cast strange shapes onto the walls in colors, and they capered in tones of hot yellow and bitter blue.

"Are we not going to talk about this?" asked Faulker.

Alibaxter glanced at Jheklan, who simply stared at the fire.

"The world is broken," he said. "What is there to talk about?"

"Um . . . *everything*?" Faulker said. "This calls into question everything we know about our own history. If the empresses are descended from the Heklans of Hakkia, then the Witch-king's claim to the throne is absolute."

"So it seems," said Jheklan without emotion.

"So it means that the war we're all planning to fight is, by definition, illegal."

"Aye. Which is a shame, since we have always walked the straight path of law and order."

"No, no, don't go there, brother. Our occasional dalliances with bending the odd rule or two is hardly the same as . . . as . . ." He faltered, trying to find the cleverest end to that sentence. "It means that we're fighting on the wrong side."

Jheklan looked up. His eyes were haunted but not defeated. "Dear brother, *we* are not Heklans. We swore our allegiance to the Silver Empire. Remember the oaths we took when first we were bladed."

"I remember, and what of it?" demanded Faulker. "We swore an oath to a false empress."

Jheklan shook his head. "You don't remember clearly enough," he said. "We swore on our hearts and blood and on our souls to protect and defend the Silver Empire and to obey—"

"—the will of the empress," interrupted Faulker. "I know, damn it, I was there. I spoke the words."

"If I may," said a hesitant Alibaxter. "Master Faulker, I believe your brother is making a point that, in your distress, you are missing."

"Oh, then pray illuminate me."

"It is right there in the oath," said Jheklan slowly. "We swore hearts, blood, and soul to the Silver Empire. Not to the Silver Empress."

"But . . ." began Faulker, but Jheklan held up a hand.

"We swore to obey the will of the empress. That's it. We were oath-bound to her, yes, but only while she lived. Our enduring oath was—and I feel *is*—to the Silver Empire."

"That's the same thing," Faulker protested.

"It is not," said the wizard. "Not at all. An oath made to a living person ends with their death, unless it is a promise made to carry out a specific task after that person's death. Your oath to Empress Gessalyn was legally satisfied and ended at her death. Your oath to the Silver Empire yet endures, for there is wording in the full oath that requires that you protect and defend it against all enemies, whether they be from foreign lands or from within."

Faulker stared at him but said nothing.

"Gentle sirs," continued Alibaxter, "I think we need to assess where all of this leaves us. You are still oath-bound to the Silver Empire but have sworn no oaths to any living empress. Or emperor, for that matter. You are what they used to call 'free bondsmen'— soldiers of the empire who serve no person but yourselves and no law but your own sense of duty to the institution of the empire.

By this I mean it is your sworn and unbreakable bond to protect the empire. It may be in ruins, but unless a new ruler is officially and legally crowned, you must continue to follow what you feel is the best path to defend that empire and, by inference, to see it rebuilt."

"More to the point, brother mine," said Jheklan, "we are under no oath to any Heklan, alive or dead."

They allowed Faulker time to process this for a bit, and the flask was passed around several times. At one point Jheklan shook it and weighed it in his hand. Then he gave Alibaxter a suspicious squint.

"Either I'm drunk or you did some sleight-of-hand and refilled this."

"Oh," said the young wizard, "just a little bit of magic."

Jheklan smiled and drank. "Funny, but I used to hate magic."

"Give it here," demanded Faulker, and once in hand he tried to drink it dry. But as soon as it left his lips the flask's weight increased. "By the gods of joy and bounty."

"We need to decide something very important," said Alibaxter. "And I daresay we should do that sober rather than drunk."

Jheklan took the flask from his brother and handed it to the wizard.

"We need to get back home to tell Mother Frey this."

"I daresay she knows," observed Alibaxter. "About your oaths, I mean. Not about the empresses being Heklans. If I may, I think we need to complete the mission she set for us. If there are books of magic here, we need to locate them—both to take for her and to keep them out of Hakkian hands. And we must find the dragon and decide what to do with her. Kill her to end the Witch-king's magic, or free her so that magic can follow the course nature intended." He looked at the brothers. "What is your thought about this? Kill or free?"

Faulker said, "I say we—"

And his words were erased by a sound that burst, seemingly, from every corridor, every chamber, every part of the endless glacier. It was a massive sound that troubled the air, rustled the stacks of papers, and made the flames of their meager fire leap up as if in fear. The sound went on and on, waking the sleepers, making the three men around the fire clap hands to their ears. The force of it sent cracks running up and down and across the walls of ice.

Then it faded . . . faded . . . and died away.

All six men were on their feet now, weapons in hand, except for Alibaxter. They stood in a circle around the fire, facing out, ready to fight whatever awful thing made that sound, for it was not the roar of an earthquake or the grind of shifting ice. It was an animal roar, amplified by the strange acoustics of the ice caverns. But even made louder, the source of that roar had to have come from some enormous beast.

As silence fell slowly over them, the fighters remained still, their weapons clutched in tight fists.

"What in all the hells *was* that?" breathed Jace, his face running with fear sweat.

"That," said the young wizard, "was the dragon."

They turned sharply to look at him.

"She is close," he said. "And I fear she may have heard us and everything we said."

CHAPTER NINETY-THREE

Duke Sárkány sat astride his horse while the others dismounted and approached the tower. A few bats had landed on him, and they crawled into the folds of his night-black cloak.

The others of his clan stood outside of a stone wall that surrounded the Tower of Sarsis. On the other side of the wall was a large formal garden that had become wildly overgrown. Where once there had been neat rows of flowering plants, ornamental shrubberies, and sentry trees at each corner, there was now a confusion of weeds turned deathly by the winter's assault. Yet, even as everything around them had died, several rose bushes, heavy with flowers, yet endured. The roses were a red so dark they were nearly black, and their delicate petals were edged with moonlight so that they looked like the cutting edges of strange knives.

Sárkány sniffed the air, taking the rose scent and scowling. Like all vampires, he hated roses. They, along with garlic and some species of holly, were poisonous to his kind. He decided that he would burn them before he left this place.

One of his knights, a young man less than a century old, came over and bowed. "Your grace," he said, "there are no doors down here. We've thrown grappling hooks up to the walkway and will climb as soon as you give the word."

Sárkány did not bother with a spoken order but merely lifted one finger of the hand resting on the pommel. The knight bowed, whirled, and ran off. The duke kicked his spurs into his horse's sides and steered the animal around to the cliff side, where three of his soldiers were just beginning to climb.

"Once you get inside," he said, "if there are any guards, kill them. And I mean just that. Kill them. You can feed later."

The knights all nodded.

"We are here to find the Hsan scrolls," said the duke. "That is the most important part of this mission. Kagen Vale has almost certainly brought them to Lady Maralina. Who else could possibly read them? The Witch-king wants the books brought to him. We cannot allow the living to possess such power. All other concerns are secondary."

They bowed again and each beat a fist against an armored chest.

"Leave Lady Maralina to me."

"Do you not want us to restrain her, your grace?" asked the boy.

The duke laughed. "She is beyond. Beyond *any* of you. If there is no other choice, shoot her in the leg or shoulder with an arrow. But woe to you if you kill her, for she is mine. She has been mine since before this world was made. Fail me in this to your peril and eternal damnation."

"By our blood we swear," they all said, and moonlight sparkled on pale skin and sharp fangs.

"Then go and do what I have asked of you," said Sárkány in a gentler voice. "You are my beloved children. Do this for your love of me."

Three were chosen as climbers. One was the young knight, and Sárkány sat back and watched. The young one was handsome, but the duke could not recall if he had ever been invited to bed. Probably. Certainly the woman climbing next to him had been. He had first taken her when she was alive, raping her with cock and fangs at the same time; and then many, many times since. A delicious wench, and she had become one of his most trusted fighters. The third climber was an ugly brute with a sword cut that bisected his face in a diagonal line from right eyebrow to left jaw. The wound was terrible, but Sárkány liked the way it amplified his apparent cruelty. Maybe he would bed all three of them once this night's work was done.

Though in truth he hungered more for the woman who lived in the tower.

She was someone he had known—in every beautiful and ugly way—uncountable years ago. Had it been in Kamahaloth—a thousand or more years before the end of the old world? No, he decided. Further back. Perhaps in Ur. He could not remember the exact location, but he remembered how she tasted.

Sweet and delicious Maralina.

Even the thought of her name aroused him.

She had been a young princess. Pure, untouched, naive about the world. When he came to her, Sárkány had worn a younger face. Partly glamour, for he could do some minor spells, but mostly the younger version of his own face. Graceful and elegant, almost pretty. Maralina had seen him and, like so many young women over the years, had fallen for him like a rock dropped from a mountaintop. He had played the game of patience, even of reluctance, yet with each word, caress, poem read, or song sung, she had become more his. When he had finally made her beg for it, he had taken her in every way. Some of what he did to her even shocked himself. But then again, he was so much younger then. His greatest excess lay before him.

He used her like a lover, and she craved it. He used her like a slut, and she begged for more. He used her badly and she apologized to him.

It was so delicious.

And *she* was delicious. Her skin, her womanhood, her tears, and her blood. Delicious beyond words in any mortal tongue.

As his knights climbed, Sárkány felt his loins stir and his cold blood boil.

"Ah, sweet Maralina," he said to that tower, "I will show you wonders and horrors of the like you have never seen. Not even in your magic mirror. You will scream for more, and then you will scream for death. You will have both."

His tongue sought one sharp fang and he dragged it across the point, lacerating it so that the rich, delicious blood filled his mouth.

The knights were halfway up to the top. Other soldiers stood back, some to steady the climbing ropes, and the others stringing their bows. The archers were careful not to touch the hawthorn barbs on their arrows, for it was as deadly to them as it would be to the violated and disgraced daughter of Titania à-Mab, queen of the *Baobhan sith*—oldest clan of the faerie folk of earth.

"Stop dawdling," he growled, and the climbers immediately increased their pace.

Sárkány turned to look at the town, curious to see if there would be any protest or even an investigation as to what his company was doing. But every window was closed and shuttered, and the streets were completely empty.

Depending on how things went in the Tower of Sarsis, he considered letting his followers free to have some fun. Discretion no longer mattered now that the war was about to start.

A sound dragged his attention back to the tower and he looked up in astonishment to see that the burly, scarred knight—who had climbed faster than the others—was screaming. Light flared around him and suddenly the man was ablaze. The climbing rope was on fire, but the fire crawled *down* rather than rose. It ignited the soldier's leather gloves and then leapt instantly to his hood. Within the space of two seconds the knight's entire body was wreathed in fire. His second scream was terrible because between the two he had drawn a deep breath, and fire had surged into his mouth.

The other two had paused, watching in shock and horror, then their ropes began to burn.

"Come down," cried the soldiers steadying the ropes, but it was already too late. The strange fire seemed to rush down the ropes and leap onto the climbers. The beautiful boy and the woman were enveloped in flames faster than was possible.

The three of them fell as their ropes parted. Like dropped torches they plummeted down to the weeds and rocks. The shock of the impact burst them apart, flinging blood everywhere that ignited, too, and kept burning until the bodies were ash. Even the bones and their weapons crumbled to cinders.

Duke Sárkány stared at them with lifeless eyes and no expression on his face. He looked up at the tower to where the last of the rope was still burning.

"Very well then," he said quietly. "There are other ways to breech these walls. Fetch Chernobog and Baphomet."

The closest knight laughed with red joy and ran to fetch the two monstrous goats.

Jendor Fint had not fled the district after his trauma but instead hid in the unlighted doorway of a dress shop halfway along the street. Nip was nowhere to be seen, so the watcher had no companion to verify what happened next.

The pale knight and two handlers led the goats from the rear of the column to the embowering wall around the space of overgrown flowers. They were massive creatures and could not leap the wall like ordinary goats. If, indeed, goats they were. Jendor had seen many kinds of goats and also mountain sheep with powerful curled horns. The kind of animals that declare their power by butting heads with rivals, often with such shocking force that a weaker opponent's neck is shattered. Many an unwise mountain traveler had been cruelly wounded or even killed by running afoul of such animals. But these brutes were some twisted version of those.

They were definitely goats, despite the fact that their horns were curled like bighorn sheep. Beneath their black hides muscles bulged and flexed, and sparks flew with each hoof-fall on the cobblestones. Worse than that, their eyes were alight as if fires burned inside their skulls. Jendor could almost feel the heat when one of them glanced his way. He cringed back. Drool dripped from the creatures' mouths and it sizzled like bacon grease on the ground.

The handlers brought them to the closest side of the stone wall, then they removed heavy chains that were attached to steel collars. The black goats tossed their heads and cried aloud in voices like souls in torment.

Upon his horse, the lord of this strange company blew them a kiss and laughed as the creatures immediately hurled themselves at the wall. The barrier was shoulder height to a tall man and eighteen inches thick. Old stone cut from the heart of a mountain, and it had endured for years without number.

Until that night.

The two monsters slammed their curled horns against it and burst through at once, sending a hurricane of flying stones everywhere. It was as if the wall had been made of plaster and straw for all that it impeded them.

"Make me a door," said the lord on the horse.

The goats cried out again. They crouched, braced themselves, huge muscles bulging and fiery eyes blazing, and then they launched forward, striking the base of the tower. That wall did not so easily yield, even to their titanic weight and force.

But a crack appeared.

They reeled back, blowing hard, growling in anger, slashing at the ground with their cloven hooves, and struck again.

And again.

While the Tower of Sarsis trembled.

CHAPTER NINETY-FOUR

Helleda Frost stood in her doorway, watching as Mother Frey was handed down from her coach. It was a slower process than it should have been, and the fragility of the old nun was heartbreaking to see. The Frey who had left the estate weeks before had been frail, but the one who returned seemed to be made of dry sticks and old straw.

Frost touched the green leaf pendant that hung in her décolletage with one hand and made the warding sign with her other, for she knew that good news would not have done this kind of damage.

Then she hurried down the steps and across the paved drive, reaching out to help, but Hop shook his head. The squat Therian and his lean Samudian companion half carried Frey into the house. Lady Frost followed, her heart turning to winter ice.

The Unbladed guards settled Frey onto a couch they dragged in front of the fire, doing everything with a gentleness and care that surprised Frost. Once she was covered in blankets and tea was ordered, Frost gestured for the two bodyguards to join her in the hall.

"What happened?" she asked with quiet urgency. "Is she ill? Were you beset?"

"Neither, milady," said Brace. "She was fine, though her meeting with Captain Vale wore her out a bit."

"And it's colder than a snow ape's tits," said Hop, then he yelped as Brace kicked him.

"Excuse my friend, my lady," said Brace. "He was hit frequently as a child."

Helleda Frost affected not to hear any of that. She said, "I will have one of the cooks make you both a hot meal. Rooms will be prepared for you on the third floor. If there is anything at all you need, ring the bell for a servant."

She began to turn, then paused.

"Mother Frey is old, but she is still strong."

With that she left hurriedly upstairs.

The two Unbladed shared a look.

"Was she saying that to reassure us or herself?" asked Hop.

Brace merely shook his head.

CHAPTER NINETY-FIVE

"Your Majesty," said the wet nurse as the queen hurried down the hall.

"What is wrong?" demanded Lliaorna. She ruled Nehemite in equal partnership with her brother, Adrell. He had no children, and she had a nine-month-old baby. "Is the princess unwell?"

The wet nurse looked pale and stricken. "Something bit her, Majesty," she said quickly.

"*Bit?* In the palace? By the green Gods of the Harvest, was it a rat? Did you not check before you put her down for the night? Damn your eyes, how could this happen?"

Before the wet nurse could manage a reply, the queen shoved her aside and rushed into the nursery. There were four guards there, all of them clearly in the middle of searching the corners, knives in their hands. They snapped to attention.

"What have you found?" demanded Lliaorna.

"Nothing yet, Majesty," said the sergeant.

"Then why are you prattling on instead of looking?"

They bowed quickly and returned to the search.

A night nurse held the baby in her arms, and the blankets glistened with blood.

"Is she all right?" begged the queen.

Before the nurse could answer, a doctor in black robes hurried into the room. "I came as soon as I heard, Majesty."

He was old but still he ran across the room and bade the nurse lay the child on a changing table. With the nurses and the queen leaning over him, he peeled back the blankets and unlaced the little nightgown around the child's body. There were two large and ragged punctures on the tender throat around which fresh blood glistened. The baby's eyes were open but glazed and she was utterly silent.

The doctor's face went pale and he bent to press his ear to the child's chest. He was there for a very long time. Too long.

"Does she live?" cried the queen.

The doctor straightened and pressed his fingers to the baby's throat. And then the inner thigh. His stricken face turned to shock and then sadness.

"My queen," he said in a fractured voice, "there is no sign of life."

Lliaorna stared at him as if he had spoken in some unknown language. Her mouth formed a single word.

"*What . . . ?*"

"He said that the little bitch is dead," said a voice and they all whirled to see a figure step out of the shadows in the far corner of the room. Three soldiers instantly shifted to form a line in front of the queen. The fourth, who had been searching that part of the room, grabbed the man by the front of his tunic and slammed him against the wall and pressed the edge of his dagger across the stranger's windpipe.

Lliaorna's face went white and then red and she screamed at him. "*You killed my baby!*"

The man laughed.

It was a high, shrill, piercing laugh that chilled the blood of everyone in the room.

He laughed as he caught the hand that held the knife to his throat and crushed the bones to pulp.

He laughed as the other soldiers charged at him, and he laughed as he tore them to pieces with his bare hands.

He laughed as Queen Lliaorna attacked him with fists and fingernails, knees and even her teeth. And he laughed as he hurled her through the window to her death.

He laughed as he killed the doctor, the nurses, and the five other guards who came running at the sound of screams.

And he laughed as he flung himself out into the night.

CHAPTER NINETY-SIX

Alleyn and Desalyn loved playing in the corridors and hidden rooms in the unseen ways. Mostly it was just that—play, for they were but six years old. However, there were some moments that drew their attention and held them, even though a few of these were also inexplicable.

Late one afternoon, when many of the court nobles—including the Witch-king, that nasty Prince of Games, and the scary Duke Sárkány—were all away, they ventured to visit a room they had seen but hadn't dared visit before.

They had heard it called by various names—the potions room, the alchemy room, among others—and it was filled with strange things. They had been there only once before, to fetch something for Lady Kestral so she could turn the razor-knight she'd conjured away from Captain Kagen and instead send it off to try and kill the Witch-king.

The room scared them to the marrow because it was in there that they *felt* the Witch-king more clearly than anywhere else in the palace. Everything in that chamber was something he had found or stolen or made.

They eased open a small door that was so skillfully made that no trace of it was visible when closed. They knew the secret because Captain Kagen had shown it to them once, though he warned them not to go inside because it was Herepath's room.

The twins had resisted going back even though there was something about that awful place that seemed to call to them. Finally, that call became irresistible.

Desalyn stepped out first, her slippers making no sound. After a moment, Alleyn stepped out of the wall, too. Neither wanted to look at the countless books, bottles of chemicals, stuffed creatures, or other items that whispered of a world beyond the seen and known.

What drew them was a thing that stood in the far corner of the room. It was a block of ice that stood in the center of a conjuring circle identical to the one Lady Kestral had used to contact the demon. They crept toward it, careful to stop well outside of the circle, which was made of salt and sand.

Alleyn reached out with one hand, mindful not to touch the thing.

"It really *is* ice," he said.

"Can't be," said Desalyn.

"Feel for yourself. No . . . don't cross the circle. There," said Alleyn, "can't you feel the cold?"

She snatched her hand back. "It's ice . . . but that makes no sense. It's been here for months now. Why hasn't it melted?"

"Magic," said Alleyn, and that, of course, explained everything.

They stared at it. Inside the block of ice was a figure—clearly a tall man—but the surface of the ice was frosted and they could make out few details. He wore some kind of robe. His skin was pale and he had dark hair.

That was all they could see with any certainty.

"Who is it, do you suppose?" asked Alleyn.

Desalyn shook her head.

Motes of dust floated slowly through the air, and when they reached the space above the circle they veered off as if from a breath of wind.

"I want to try something," said Desalyn, and she looked around, saw a dish of small pebbles, took one and—holding her breath— tossed it at the ice.

It passed through the circle but as it crossed the line the pebble burst into powdery sand and fell to the ground.

"Glad we didn't try to touch it," said Alleyn.

Desalyn nodded.

They watched it, saying nothing.

"It's creepy," said Desalyn. "I can feel it watching me."

"That's stupid," said her brother, though it was clear he agreed with her.

"Who are you?" asked the girl.

There was only silence in the room.

On silent cat-feet they left and sealed the hidden door behind them.

CHAPTER NINETY-SEVEN

The Tower of Sarsis fought the vampires.

It was built by magic and fashioned to imprison one of the most powerful beings in all of the larger world. Maralina, princess of the *Baobhan sith*. Daughter of Queen Titania à-Mab and King Oberon Erlking. The blood of the two oldest and most powerful families of the faerie folk was like lightning in her blood. With it was the taint—the supernatural poison inflicted upon her by Duke Sárkány during his seduction and destruction of her. The faerie queen herself had cast those spells and in one form or another, as the shape and nature of the tower itself changed with the changing tides of time, the spell adapted and corrected and remained unbreakable.

Armies of men had broken themselves upon those walls. Siege engines had splintered to matchwood against it. For they were things of the mortal world, but the larger world held far greater power. Even the treacheries of the Silver Empresses and their secret sciences had failed to topple the tower.

Its greatest strength—the true core of Titania's magicks—was to keep Maralina in. To prevent her from walking free in the world as both faerie and vampire, and as whatever those two things had made of her. There had never been something like her, and even her mother feared what Maralina might become if freed. And so those magicks worked to their greatest effect inside the walls.

But the great black goats, born of nature but corrupted and ensorcelled by the Witch-king of Hakkia, were something new to the earth. In the zoos and houses of surgery and blasphemy hidden beneath the stolen palace in Argentium, nature was torn apart and rebuilt according to the darkest of visions. The blood of thousands of innocents—mostly virgin children of either sex—had been spilled for the purpose, and that was among the very strongest of transgressive magic.

It was what the Widow felt across hundreds of miles.

It was what made the razor-knight feel it in the fires of his heart.

It was what made the elvinkind of the woods and the redcaps of the mountain pause and stare in horror in the direction of the great palace of Argentium.

And it was what drove cracks into the ice walls of the Winter-wilds, where, deep in the heart of the glacier, the ancient, tortured, dying dragon, Fabeldyr, howled in outrage.

It was this that made the earth itself shriek in horror and groan in agony.

Creatures such as those two goats, and the other abominations in the Witch-king's menagerie, did not belong here, not even in the larger world. There were rules even among the many races born of magic, and this was blasphemy. It obeyed no natural or supernatural laws except those established by the Witch-king.

And it was why the King in Yellow himself stood gazing out at the starlit darkness, his body tingling with excitement and crackling with power as he spoke to the midnight wind.

"You think you know me," he said to those voices he knew could hear him even through the veils between worlds. He spoke even to his mortal enemies who could not hear him but would writhe and tremble in that night's unquiet sleep. "You think you know me by what you have seen. The conquest of an empire in a single night. But I will soon reveal more than my face. I will show the King in Yellow to all of you—what power truly is."

He laughed quietly to himself, knowing that everything he had crafted and on which he had labored these many years was coming to fruition.

In her plotting and planning, Mother Frey believed that the greatest threat facing the west were the armies of the Witch-king. King al-Huk and his royal cousins believed that force of arms was what mattered in the coming war. They all knew they were facing a sorcerer, but since the yellow king had used so little magic since the Night of the Ravens, they had fallen into a complacency born of having lived in a world without magic. The use of banefire and razor-knights and the Red Plague of the Hollow Monks were all merely feints, distractions. And each had worked in its time and in its way. The skirmishes and battles since the conquest had solidified their view, even if they spoke of preparing to use magic against magic. Their hearts and intentions were good, but they had all made one critical and unforgivable mistake.

They underestimated the Witch-king of Hakkia and his patron god, Hastur. And he took great delight in that lack of vision.

The use of the brothers Baphomet and Chernobog was the true start of this war. Of the Witch-king's war. This was new magic. Twisting nature into new and perverted shapes; imbuing things of the natural world into creatures that belonged neither in the material nor larger worlds—*that* was the opening salvo in a war of conquest. Not merely of the fallen Silver Empire, but of the whole world.

After all, who or what could stand against such power? Kagen the Damned and his army of mercenaries? Old Mother Frey and her cabal that whispered plans in the dark? Or even an ancient and dying dragon in chains?

By banishing magic a thousand years ago, the Silver Empresses had chased away the greatest powers on earth and now bared its throat to the teeth of true conquest.

Duke Sárkány knew all of this, for it was the mission to which the Witch-king—the only master to whom he had ever bent his knee—had set for him.

"Take my children Chernobog and Baphomet, my dear duke," the King in Yellow had said as he kissed Sárkány on each cold cheek, "and start me a war. Send your knights abroad on the wings of the dark, dark night and raise my battle flag for all to see. Start for me the greatest war that has ever been and ever will. I give you this honor, your grace, for you are beloved of Hastur and I am proud to call you kinsman and heartfriend. Start the war that will change this world forever. Do this for me."

And Sárkány—even the icy lord of the vampires—had wept. Tears of blood coursed down his cheeks as he knelt to kiss the hem of the Witch-king's robe.

Now, Sárkány sat upon his horse and watched the black rams smash and smash and smash the walls of the Tower of Sarsis.

Smash into it, and through it.

The stones that had been set in place sixty thousand years ago by masons of the *Baobhan sith* and sealed by Titania à-Mab, burst inward and the Tower of Sarsis stood no longer impregnable.

A huge section of the curved wall collapsed inward, belching out a great cloud of dust. In the sky above, the bats screeched out and their flight became even more frenetic. The sound of the implosion was like dull thunder that was immediately drowned out by the triumphant roars of the two gigantic goats and the cheer of the vampire knights.

Sárkány laughed aloud for the sheer joy of what he had accomplished. What no one else had ever done—to break through the enchantment and gain entrance to the Tower of Sarsis.

His soldiers paused as the entire tower seemed to shiver. Its shape shimmered in the night air as if surrounded by a hellish wind. Cracks appeared all along the walls and whipsawed upward. Nightbirds in the trees cried out as one, and the sheer volume of their voices drowned out the cheering of the vampires and the squeaking of the countless bats. They did not attack, though, but gripped their tree limbs, leaning forward, watching intently with Stygian eyes.

Sárkány narrowed his eyes as he watched the swirls of dust in the opening. He had been about to send his knights in, but that bird cry changed his mind, for he suspected some kind of trap. The princess was, after all, still a great sorceress.

"It is your honor to be first through the breech," he said aloud and raised one hand high into the air. Long white fingers snapped once, as loud and sharp as a thigh bone breaking.

There was a moment's pause and then, running from every corner of the town, from the nearby forests, from granaries and warehouses, and over the edges of the sheer bluffs came vermin. Rats—black and brown and sickly gray—chittering with mad hunger as they raced across the ground. And with them were countless cockroaches. They swarmed toward the breech and entered in through the clouds of dust.

From somewhere within the tower, he heard a single piercing scream.

A woman's scream.

And it painted a great and terrible smile on the face of the lord of the vampires.

CHAPTER NINETY-EIGHT

"I will retire early, I think," said King Vulpion as he rose from a table on which were maps, lists of troops, and quantities of supplies. "I think Zehria can manage without me for the rest of the night."

His generals all stood at once and bowed. They still had much work to do, but the mundanities of this part of war preparation really did not require any royal opinion or orders. Vulpion, though, was typically very involved with every stage of such preparations, having served his own father as an officer in the cavalry—a tradition common to many small nations. His retiring early was uncommon, but his officers knew that the king was under great strain. After all, preparing to declare war against the Witch-king of Hakkia was hardly a normal thing. Sleep and a clear head, though, were every bit as important as sharpened swords.

He left the room, waving them back to their seats. Two guards accompanied him along the halls toward the royal suite. When Vulpion paused, so did they, watching him as he stared up at a painting of Tupelion the Red, an ancestor from older times—as much a brigand as a king, who had waged many small wars against Nehemite and Narek.

The king studied the face, looking for traces of himself in his ancestor. Although history was often critical of Tupelion's motives for the frequent wars, no one had ever questioned his bravery or his military acumen. Tupelion had always ridden into battle at the head of his own troops. That king's ancient sword hung now in the king's sitting room. Vulpion knew that soon he would have to take it down, sharpen the edge himself—a tradition of Zehrian monarchs—and strap it on. He knew that he was too old to lead many charges, but what of that? If he died to win freedom from the Hakkian usurper, then it would be a fine way to end a life. He had always been more statesman than warrior, despite his own days with a sword in hand and an armored warhorse between his thighs. He had hoped—vainly, perhaps weakly, he was never sure which—that he would die in bed, in the arms of his chief concubine.

That dream was gone, and in retrospect he felt foolish for even imagining such ease was ever his fate.

He sighed and continued down the hall to his suite. One guard opened the door and stood there while the other went inside and checked each room.

"All clear, sire," said the guard. "May the gods grant you a peaceful night."

"Thanks lads," said Vulpion as he went in. The door closed behind him softly.

He undressed, poured fresh water into the basin on the washstand, and cleaned himself thoroughly and carefully, thinking about the many letters he had received that day. A scathing one from the young Queen Theka of Theria, a cautious one from King al-Huk, and others. Only Theka was openly speaking of declaring war. Al-Huk, dangerous but shrewd, was far more calculating in his note, saying that the monarchs needed another meeting to decide once and for all what to do.

Vulpion was personally in favor of war, but Zehria was such a small country and in a dangerous geographical position, with Bulconia—always a state to be watched—to the northeast and Hakkia to the southwest.

He ached to ride out and put his sword through the black heart of the Hakkian usurper. But reality chained him to passivity. He knew he was doomed to wait and watch. Those cousin monarchs who rode to war would despise him for his weakness even if they understood his unwinnable position. History would vilify him. Perhaps, he mused darkly, he would be remembered not as Vulpion the Gray but Vulpion the Shy. Vulpion the Unwilling.

Vulpion the Coward.

It was during this moment that he heard a discreet *tap-tap-tap* at the window. He turned quickly, frowning. Who could possibly be knocking at so high a window in the dead of night? He stood and plucked an axe from the pair that were crossed above the fireplace. With it in hand he crept to the window, but even as he reached for the latch, he realized who it might be—Islak Horchleberg, his spymaster general, known privately as the Mantis.

"Mantis," he whispered. "Is that you?"

"Let me in, Highness," came the reply. A whisper, barely heard. "I have important news."

Vulpion lifted the latch and threw wide the window.

"Why in the many hells didn't you simply take the hidden stairs?" He laughed. "You're getting too old for antics like—"

The rest of the words died in his throat.

The figure who crouched on the sill was not the Mantis. It was a slender woman dressed all in black, with snow-white hair flapping in the night breeze, and a face pale as winter moonlight. Eyes that were black within black glared at him above a smiling mouth filled with far too many teeth.

Vulpion brought up the axe, swinging it even as he opened his mouth to cry out for his guards. Icy hands shot toward him and grabbed him by the front of his tunic, jerking him forward with terrible force. The scream died to a wet gurgle as the creature on the sill buried those dreadful fangs into his throat.

That dying scream had been enough for the vigilant guards to hear. They banged on the door, shouting for their king. When there was no answer, they sent for a sergeant who returned with the key and half a dozen soldiers with spears. They opened the door and charged into the room.

And froze in horror as they beheld the thing in the window. Their king lay on the floor, his throat so savagely torn that only the spine kept the head from rolling away.

"Kill it!" screamed the sergeant, and they rushed forward.

The assassin smiled her awful smile and turned away, hurling herself out onto the night wind. When the sergeant reached the window, he saw no one below. Instead he saw a shape like a great black bat flap into the night, crossing the shocked face of the winter moon.

━━━━━━━━━━━━━━━━━━━━▶ **CHAPTER NINETY-NINE**

The rats and roaches swarmed over the rubble until they reached the foot of a great circular stair and here, they paused for a moment, the rodents rising onto two legs as they sniffed the air. It smelled of dust and cats and candle wax.

And something else.

Find her, my children, whispered the lord of vampires. *Tear her down but do not kill her. When I have had my fill of her blood, then I will leave the meat to you. Go!*

And then all of the vermin went, chittering with madness and hunger as they began to climb the steps. Up and up, around and around, they climbed. Past skeletons of great creatures that hung from wires. Past rooms stacked to the ceiling with embroidered tapestries. Past libraries filled with books so old that no one lived who yet spoke their languages—books that the Witch-king would have given over the whole of his kingdom to possess.

Still the rats and cockroaches climbed as candlelight threw their shadows against the curved walls.

When they were halfway to the tower's apex, they suddenly stopped.

For there, above them and on every step beyond, sat cats.

Not one or two, or even a handful.

Hundreds of cats.

Thousands.

Patient. Quiet. Watching with luminous eyes.

The rats shivered and the cockroaches hissed.

The cats merely waited. One of them, a smoke-gray one with eyes the color of an October moon, looked up, turning and raising its head to see the very top step. To see the tall figure standing there, silhouetted to total blackness by a thousand candles.

"*Ní i mo thigh seo,*" said a voice that was not even remotely human. It was long a dark song whispered on the night wind.

Not in my house.

And the cats leapt down the stairs at the rats.

The screams tore the air. The sound of a single swipe of a cat's claws was nearly silent. The slash of thousands of claws added its own unique and peculiar tone to the symphony of murder and death that filled the tower.

The tall shape began to descend. Bare feet, pale except for sharp black toenails, stepped down without hurry. First on cold stone, then on warm blood.

Her feet stepped on gore and torn fur and crushed carapaces, they stepped on savaged bodies and cracked bones. She did not look down, but never once did she step on any of the cats, not even the dead ones.

The tide of vermin reeled back from the onslaught of savage felines, falling over themselves, biting each other in panic, hundreds caught between their fellows who could not flee fast enough and the animals who could not kill fast enough. They died by the score, by the hundreds, and still the cats attacked.

And still the lady of the Tower of Sarsis descended, one slow step at a time. Behind her came flights of nightbirds who had flown in through the open doorway on the top floor. They fell upon the roaches, crushing them with clawed feet and snapping them up with sharp beaks. It was an orgy of feeding, an orgy of killing.

Outside, with his pale hands touching the ragged hole in the wall, Duke Sárkány watched the battle. His smile did not fade as his vermin were torn to pieces. What were their lives to him? Sárkány knew who held the real power here.

He turned to a group of his knights.

"Bring her to me," he said softly.

Then he stood aside as a dozen of the fiercest and most powerful vampires alive in that world drew their black and poisoned blades and rushed inside. They saw the slaughter on the stairs, and it gave the knights but a moment's pause. They wore armor—ring and plate, leather and brass fittings. They could heal from cuts or stab wounds or spear thrusts. Each had taken mortal wounds beyond counting in wars to the east of the Cathedral Mountains, and down through the long tale of centuries.

They laughed as they charged up the stairs, turning inside the cylinder of the Tower of Sarsis. When they saw the lady, though, they paused and stared in wonder.

She stood thirteen steps above them.

The lady was tall—as tall as the tallest of them—and her posture was queenly, regal. Powerful. Her face was incredibly beautiful in the ways that creatures from the larger world are beautiful. She had high cheekbones and a clear brow, strong jaw and very full lips—but the composition was not really human. The face was a bit too long and the eyes too slanted for even the disguise of humanity to flourish there. Her mouth was wide and the lips too intensely lush and full and red. So very red.

Her eyes were so pale a blue that they looked like moonlight on the coldest night in winter. There was wisdom there, and age. Great age that was at odds with the timeless and unmarked perfection of her face. There was great sadness in those eyes, and it was a sadness born of knowing, of seeing the ages of man rise and fall. Eyes that had seen the first empires built by human hands and feet that had walked in the dust of those forgotten nations. There was wisdom there of a kind that could not be learned in a single lifetime, or even ten thousand lives of men. There was a knowing that went with the knowledge, and it made the thorns of her sadness bite deep.

She wore a gown of black velvet that was so dark that it looked like moving shadow. Around her waist was a belt of silver that matched her eyes, and from this were suspended a knife, crystals of various kinds and cuts, and small bottles whose contents were known only to her. The belt itself was a complexity of interlocking links and chains that created the effect of delicate filigree. At intervals along the belt were heavy garnets, each with a different number of precisely cut facets. The center of the belt dipped into a vee that supported a square cut into geometric patterns, and from this dangled a single rose with one ruby as rich and dark as welling blood.

The sleeves of the gown came to her wrists and were caught by loops attached to heavy silver rings. There were rings on each of her fingers, each set with a different stone and inscribed with words of power that predated that first moment when mankind learned to strike fire from flint and stone.

Upon her head was a headdress made for war. It was a skullcap of gray velvet over leather, and in the front was another complex assortment of delicate patterns with the skull of a crow that had been dipped in gold. All around the skullcap were the shells of scarabs in shades of electric blue and green. Curling out from the sides of the cap were rams' horns coated with silver and set with onyx and osmium.

The sight of Lady Maralina gave the vampires serious pause.

But the smile—small and subtle though eloquent in the evident hunger—made them afraid.

"Tháinig tú anseo chun fola," she said. *"Báthaigh mé tú i n-abhainn choradhearg."*

Only one of the knights was old enough to know that ancient tongue. His lips moved as he translated it silently, only for himself.

You have come here for blood. I will drown you in a river of crimson.

He raised his sword and bared his fangs.

All the lady did was smile as she walked down those thirteen steps.

CHAPTER ONE HUNDRED

They struck camp in silence, each of them chewing on the gristle of what they'd learned about the Silver Empresses and their Heklan connection. It was not a very nourishing meal and none of them had much of a taste for it.

When they were ready, they moved on, happy to quit the chamber.

Within a thousand paces they found that the corridor was

blocked by stacks of heavy crates. Faulker pushed on it, felt it give but slightly and stepped back.

"At a guess," he said, "the Hakkians did this after the outbreak of the Red Plague."

"You mean they left their own people to die like that?" asked Jace.

"You have any other theories?"

"No," said Jace. "But . . . damn."

Jheklan unslung his pack. "We need to get past all this."

Lehrman grunted. "How come the infected didn't just bust through the crates? Even if they're packed with lead bars it won't take but a few hours to bust up the crates and empty them into this room."

"Because that involves thought and planning," suggested Alibaxter, "and the living dead are capable of neither."

"Oh."

"Let's be about it," said Faulker. "But let's do it quietly. No axes. We'll pry the crates apart and empty them. Stack whatever's inside."

"Exactly," said Jheklan, nodding. "We have to be getting closer to wherever the rest of them are. Let's not announce ourselves."

They set to work with the crowbars and cold chisels. It was hard work, but once the first crates were opened—they were filled with thousands of ceramic canisters and very heavy glass jars— the process became routine. There were three layers of crates blocking the way and in under two hours the path was clear.

As Jace, Lehrman, and il-Vul worked, Alibaxter edged over to Jheklan, and in a very quiet voice asked, "What were you going to say? Before that roar, I mean. Do you think we should kill Fabeldyr or set her free?"

Jheklan gave him a stern look. "What do you think?"

Then the way was opened, and the whole group packed up their tools, took up their torches, drew blades, and crept into the next chamber.

The corridor ran straight for a quarter mile and then began to curve as it sloped down and widened. There were many more signs of human presence there, particularly from Gardeners and their staff. There were tools, bundles of unnamable artifacts wrapped in cloth, a book of common prayers from the Harvest Faith, clothes, and more. Alibaxter picked up several leather-bound books that proved to be diaries of various Gardeners, some dating back more than a century. Each had a different kind of leaf embossed on its cover—oak and maple, begonia and trachyandra, no two alike—marking them with the sigils of individual Gardeners. The wizard stuffed these books into his pack for later study.

They also found more corpses.

In five separate side chambers they found frozen bodies. One chamber was clearly set aside for any member of the various expeditions who had died of natural causes, including being crushed by falling ice. That much was clear from the condition. Many were on biers cut from ice, while the bodies of more elderly and notable Gardeners were in the slots from which the biers had been cut. It was evident that these noble corpses had been searched and looted, for none had the silver ornaments commonly placed for burial, and none had any rings or jewelry.

Alibaxter said a quick prayer over these honored dead and they hurried on.

In other chambers there were bodies sprawled in more haphazard postures, and it was clear they lay where they died. All of them had belonged to the last Garden expeditions, and all had died very badly.

The group moved on.

Once, when Jheklan and Faulker were well ahead of the party, they spoke in low tones about that.

"I know we came all this way to find a dragon," said Faulker. "We know it's here. Hell, we *heard* it and we can damn well smell it, but . . ."

Jheklan nodded. "I know. I can't make it real in my head, either. I keep thinking we're going to find Herepath sitting on a stool having a chat with some kind of overgrown but otherwise docile crocodile."

Faulker snorted. "Either you've had too much of Alibaxter's liquor . . . or not enough."

"Not nearly enough," said Jheklan.

"Aye," his brother agreed.

They pressed on. Moving in the direction where the strange animal stink was strongest.

━━━━━━━━━▶ **CHAPTER ONE HUNDRED ONE**

"I won't hurt you," said the Widow.

She crouched on the muddy bank of an inlet near the ocean. The water this far upstream was brackish, but she saw both sea and freshwater fishes swimming around one another. Turtles hid among the bulrushes, and frogs croaked from piles of sodden leaves. The water was cold, but warmer than the air, which had the bite of frost in it.

Ten feet from the shore, with all of its bulk beneath the water and only a pair of huge, luminous eyes visible and round ears fringed with brown hair. Those eyes watched her with mingled curiosity and apprehension. Bubbles brought a low growl to the surface, but Ryssa did not recoil or even flinch.

The growl concerned her, though. Since her experiences on Tull Yammoth—and the changes that had begun inside of her body and mind—she had a strange new insight into the noises animals made. There was none of the fairytale nonsense of being able to speak in "snake" or "whale" or even "bird." It wasn't like that, because they did not think in the words, phrases, or even concepts that had any corollary to human thoughts. It was more a matter that their movements, their clicks and growls and songs and cries painted pictures in sound that informed empathetic understanding in her. Try as she might, even with her evolving understanding, it was nearly impossible to translate for herself into human thoughts. But instead came empathic awareness of fears and joys, hungers and satisfaction, urges to procreate and incentives to flee. From those broader concepts she intuited subtler meanings.

This thing in the water—something whose body she had not yet even seen—was in distress. It was afraid and it was confused. It was not hurt but it feared being hurt, and that was odd. Few animals could hold the concept of a future possibility in their minds.

And yet this one was certainly afraid of something that *might* happen to it. The fear was intense enough that it had come to believe that the injury was not only likely but certain. Very complex thoughts for animals, who live mostly in the moment.

"What are you afraid of?" she asked, not knowing if it could understand her. After all, when she had wanted the sea creatures to come and save her and Queen Theka's crew, she had not been specific in her prayers. Fear had gripped her very deeply. It may not have shown to the Therians, but it was there, and from that fear had come a voiceless, wordless, cry for help. And the sea beasts had come. The whole thing had been perhaps ten percent focused thought and ninety percent something so abstract that Ryssa did not know how to think about it.

This was different because she did not have full command of how to send out such calls for help. Nor would such a call matter now.

The thing in the water growled regardless, the water frothing in agitation.

"What are you afraid will happen?" she asked, hoping with her spoken words that somehow her mind would translate it into some form the animal could understand.

The eyes immediately vanished and after a moment the surface water was calm and still.

Ryssa felt a pang of loss, fearing she had scared it away, and she sat down on the bank and stared around her in helpless defeat. It was maddening that sometimes—when Miri, or her ghost, came to the forefront and shared consciousness with her—this all made sense. But when Miri was back in the shadows Ryssa's understanding receded, too, leaving no lexicon behind to study.

The water was completely still now, smooth as glass, and the shadows of trees moved unhurried across the inlet. The sun was getting close to its zenith. Ryssa felt lost—she had been compelled to have the Therians leave her near here, and then her feet seemed to know which way to take her. But there was no inner guidance at all.

Ryssa felt alone and also felt her age. Sixteen was not old enough to accept the world as it was or know what to do next. The façade of calm confidence was a mask that slipped when she was alone.

"I would never hurt you," she said, hoping the animal could hear her. Hoping every animal could hear her. Those in the water and those all around her. "Never."

The hungers of winter tried to steal her precious body heat, and Ryssa pulled her cloak around her, huddling there. Lonely and lost, with no idea of what to do next. The sleep of fear and weariness coaxed her down into a doze.

It was a soft splash that woke her hours later.

Very soft, but it teased her to the surface of awareness. The sound was tentative, bordering on secretive. And she did not move right away, knowing that whatever had made that sound was watching her, gauging her reaction.

She sat very still.

After several minutes there was another sound. Wet, squishy. The noise of water dripping on sand and mud. A pause. Then the damp sound of a heavy footfall in moist and yielding ground. But there was a second sound with it. A hissing noise and it took her a few moments to make sense of it, then she understood—something was walking slowly and dragging something else.

Coming toward her.

Fear spiked again in her, but Ryssa pushed it down.

If you are a beast, she thought, *and if you are starving, then I will give myself to you. Better to be sustenance for something natural than become another victim of evil men.*

Although she did not want to die, she could accept such a death. It would end her ongoing pain, and perhaps allow her to see Miri again.

The footsteps drew closer, and now she could hear the thing breathe.

Labored.

Somehow, she knew it was because of effort and not age. Not illness or injury, either.

There was a soft, heavy thud directly behind her, and then the breathing as the thing waited.

For her.

Understanding dawned slowly.

Ryssa raised her head and turned slowly to see what was behind her.

There were two things.

The animal that stood behind her was massive, at least fifteen feet from its broad, soft snout to its rump, not counting a foot-long tail. The thing had short, heavy legs and a barrel of a body that was enormously bulky, and at first she thought it was simply fat, but as it breathed Ryssa could see huge muscles beneath a coating of surface blubber. It was a dark gray and had to weigh at least three thousand pounds. It stood panting, and between its jaws there were enormous teeth that were chipped and jagged as if worn from combat.

Seeing it filled her with awe because she had only seen animals like this—a river hippopotamus—in books. Never in real life. She knew that they were much faster than they looked. If its intention was to attack her, Ryssa knew there was nothing she could do about it.

She stared into its eyes and saw hatred, but not directed at her. She saw hurt there, too. So much of that. Ryssa leaned slowly to one side to look behind the animal. Seeing what it had dragged up onto the bank.

It was another hippo. A smaller one, barely half the size of this one. It was dead.

And it was wrong.

Every part of it was wrong. Where the tusklike teeth should have been there were curved fangs as sharp as daggers. In place of the gray skin there was a mottled armor more like that of a rhinoceros, and from its plates sprouted dozens of spikes of various lengths. There was a crest of spikes as well, and the four feet had retractable claws where its blunt toes should have been.

Only the eyes, half open and cloudy with the onset of decay, looked like they belonged to the kind of animal that stood above it. The animal was a younger version of the hippo, but something had caused these radical and horrific changes.

The bigger hippo stamped the ground and uttered a high, plaintive cry that was filled with terrible pain, and the sharper pain of loss. Ryssa immediately understood that this was a mother's cry.

"No . . ." Ryssa gasped as she got quickly to her feet. The hippo shifted her stance, reflexively protecting her young. Then it seemed to understand and its ears drooped, and its large, brown, liquid eyes filled with a despair so eloquent that it brought tears to Ryssa's eyes.

She took a step toward the animal, holding her hands up, palms out, willing the creature to know that no harm was meant. The hippo shook its head in frustration, but it did not charge. Nor did the cow shift again to block its child even as Ryssa came close to examine it.

"What did they do to you?" she said softly, kneeling beside it.

Like an echo she heard her own words.

What did they do to you?

They.

Inside her heart Ryssa could feel Miri's presence, but her lover was hanging back. Watching. Not struggling for control.

Ryssa leaned forward and placed a gentle hand on the cheek of the dead calf. The flesh was cold but there was a subtle tremble of energy there. Ryssa closed her eyes.

Show me. It was a thought that required no words.

Images came slowly, and they were vague. Some half-formed so that they were little more than meaningless shadows. Others were sharper but they came and went. Ryssa saw a human shape, but no skin. It was covered in concealing cloth from head to toe, even to the point of wearing gloves and a veil over its face.

A yellow veil made of intricate lace.

Somehow Ryssa sensed that she could see beyond that lace, and she tried to force her mind to go deeper, but the image immediately faded, becoming indistinct.

Yield to it, my love, whispered Miri from the shadows.

Ryssa made her breath slow and one by one she pulled tension from her muscles. Her body sagged and her head drooped.

The image sharpened reluctantly, slowly.

A man in yellow did things with potions and knives and muttered spells. Ryssa could hear the voice but not the words of those spells. She felt every sharp or subtle, sweet or bitter taste of the potions. She felt the knives he used to cut into infant flesh, and the needles that dragged catgut through incised flesh to seal it. The pain was so real, so specific and terrible, that Ryssa felt it on her own skin. She became the young animal in every way that mattered and what was done to it was done to her. The brutality, the violation, the unbearable *wrongness* of it.

She could have let go, broken the contact, refused to go the whole way into horror. But that would have been the action of some other person. Someone who was not Ryssa. Miri might have done it because although she had more knowledge and power, she was not the empath that Ryssa was.

And so Ryssa endured it all. Months of surgeries and magicks and potions were condensed into minutes, though it felt to her like centuries. Only when the sorcery caused a rupture in the young calf's heart did Ryssa fall back, sobbing with pain and anger, covering her face with her hands, rocking back and forth in the mud.

She felt something heavy and warm and soft press against her and she slowly opened the trembling gates of her hands and looked up through them. At the mother hippo who stood above her.

The animal's eyes pleaded with her. For understanding. And for something else.

Ryssa got to her knees once more and reached for the cow, wrapping her arms as far around the huge neck as she could manage. Clinging to her. Weeping against that massive form.

"I know," she said. "I know. I saw."

Those words, meaningless in that form, were conveyed on other levels. The hippopotamus understood. Ryssa could feel Miri move all the way forward now, and between the two minds insights bloomed, bright and terrible.

The monster in yellow who did this was doing it to many other kinds of animals. Many, many kinds. He was warping nature in the worst possible ways. The harm being done was not only on an individual level, as with the calf and cow here, but was slashing wounds in nature itself. Twisting it. Perverting it. There was nothing about this that aligned with the physical world or in the infinite realms of the larger world.

This was horror.

This was blasphemy beyond words.

Ryssa and Miri wept together.

But it was the Widow who rose from that embrace and looked northward with burning eyes. North toward Argo. North toward the city of Argentium, and into the palace there. To where the Witch-king sat on his throne of sins.

The Widow threw back her head and screamed.

It was so loud that it stilled every bird and animal and insect in the woods. It rose into the air and was taken by the winds, blowing across the ruins of the Silver Empire and through the holes torn in the veils between this world and so many others.

The hippo howled, too.

Soon the silenced creatures of the forest threw off their shock and cried out in sympathy and empathy, in a shared rage. With awful promises.

And so the Widow rose and went to wage her war with the Witch-king.

CHAPTER ONE HUNDRED TWO

The pale knight laughed with wild joy as he charged up the steps to meet Maralina.

His sword was known as Death's Kiss in songs and stories. Though, in truth, there were few alive who remembered the ballads that were old when their grandfathers were not yet breached. He swung it at her middle, wanting to gut but not kill her. The terrified rats below him on the stairs screeched as he attacked.

Death's Kiss was forged from metal smelted from a falling star. It was so heavy that only a powerful human could even lift it, but it moved with silver lightning in his hand. That knight had used it to kill hundreds of warriors. He had decapitated horses with it, and once slaughtered an entire field of oxen in order to punish a family who had smeared garlic around their doors and windows to bar him entry. The blade whistled death's own anthem as it cut through the air toward Maralina's stomach.

And time itself seemed to stop when the lady of the tower caught it in her bare hand.

The knight froze, his face transformed into a mask of total shock. The other vampires behind him gaped, some frowning, because they could not understand what they were seeing.

Maralina smiled at him.

And with no apparent effort she tore the sword from the knight's hand, doing it with such hideous speed and force that finger bones broke. She held the weapon by its blade, and not a single drop of blood fell from that hand.

"My garden is filled with the bones of heroes and champions far greater than you," she said mildly. "Was it haste or arrogance or plain stupidity that allowed you to tread upon their graves and take no warning?"

She raised the sword and looked at it with cold disdain.

"And you bring a toy such as this into battle with the princess of the *Baobhan sith*?"

With slow deliberation she closed her hand into a tight fist. The steel shrieked as it bent and folded and then finally snapped in two. The pieces fell clattering to the stone steps as the cats all around her howled. Maralina opened her hand and let a thousand silver splinters fall like dirt.

The knight tried to back away as she descended another step. But there were too many other knights behind him, all of them dumb and immobile with shock. Maralina's left hand shot out, faster than thought, and caught him by the throat. With no flicker of effort, she raised him up so that he was face-to-face with her.

"You were nothing before you came—a leech, a tick, a mosquito," she said. "You are less than that now."

And again her hand closed. Flesh burst and arteries shot red blood against the walls. The vertebrae crunched like winter-dried twigs, and the knight shuddered and kicked and died.

Maralina tossed the body at the other knights, knocking them back, driving them down the stairs. Some fell among the rats, crushing many. Others clung to the handrail for balance. A few evaded the grisly bundle and they drew their swords.

Ten steps above them Maralina looked at the blood on her left hand and touched it with her right; then she spread her hands apart and between them a line of darkness appeared in the air. It grew and thickened and formed into a sword that was so densely black there was no visible definition. She took the sword in her right hand and pointed it down at the vampires.

"As you die, each of you should curse the name of Duke Sárkány," she said, "for he has sent you to your doom."

With the shadow-sword in her hand and a smile that was filled with joy, Maralina stepped down toward them.

━━━━━━━▶ **CHAPTER ONE HUNDRED THREE**

"My lords," called Alibaxter, "wait. Wait, please . . . I've found something."

The wizard had lagged behind the others, drawn to places where bodies were frozen into the ice. They had all seen them—quite a large number—but Frey had warned them at the outset that it was an agreed-upon theory by the Gardeners that a great wave had swept across parts of the civilized world ages ago and then it froze, trapping those who could not escape. Many of these figures were little more than hazy shapes far back into the ice walls, while others were closer and their clothing, hair styles, and accoutrements were very strange. Nothing at all like modern dress.

But that was not what caused Alibaxter to cry out.

"Look," he said, touching a depression in the smoothness of the ice. He held up his torch and its light penetrated the wall and illuminated something frozen about ten inches deep.

Faulker and Jheklan stared at it and then each other. Then they were fishing in their bags for tools.

"What have you found?" asked the Zehrian, Lehrman.

Il-Vul peered close. "What's the fuss? Looks like a book."

"Look at the damned cover," snapped Faulker as he removed a small ice-axe from his pack.

"Well, hell," breathed Jace. "I know that sigil as well as I know the back of my own hand. That's the sign of the Poison Rose. That's your mum's sigil, sure as I'm standing here."

The book was similar to the other diaries Alibaxter had found, but instead of a symbol of a leaf engraved on the leather cover, this one had the two crossed daggers entwined by a climbing rose.

"Not exactly," said Jheklan. "Look closer."

They did. It was il-Vul who noticed it first. "The leaves on the rose aren't rose leaves," he said. "My grams raised a yard full of roses. Those are holly leaves."

"Yes they are," said Faulker, retrieving his own axe.

"But what's it mean?" asked Jace.

"That's Herepath's sigil."

Jheklan took a small ice-axe and set to work and soon had the book clear of its frozen prison. Then he drew back and allowed Alibaxter to actually remove it, which the young wizard did with great gentleness and reverence, then turned it over in his hands before opening it. "Appears to be bound in seal skin," he murmured. "Very good quality work."

Everyone held their breaths as he opened it.

"Maybe we really shouldn't read it," suggested Faulker.

"I know," agreed Jheklan.

"But we're going to, right?"

"Of course."

Alibaxter flipped through the pages, making small grunts as he did so. "Now that's interesting."

"What?"

"It's written in one of the most ancient languages of the lost people of Skyria." He turned it to show them pages filled with pictograms and hieroglyphs. "A rare enough language that would limit who could read it. He was a careful man."

"Can you make sense of it?" asked Jheklan.

"Oh yes. I grew up on Skyria," said the wizard, "and I flatter myself that there is no one who is more skilled at reading the nine languages of the ancient priests and kings of that land." He chuckled. "It's almost as if this was written just for me."

"What does it say?" asked Faulker.

The wizard browsed through the book. "Well, a lot of it is day-to-day stuff about the expedition. Lists of people, some cataloguing of artifacts, speculation as to their function. But . . . these pages are odd."

The others crept closer and peered over his shoulders at the open book.

"Odd . . . *how?*" asked Faulker.

"Well, they concern your other brother—Kagen. And they are Herepath's recollections of a series of dreams Kagen had as a lad. There are . . . well, many pages of them, and . . . oh! Oh my."

Faulker leaned back a bit. "I'm not at all happy when a wizard says 'oh my' in that tone of voice."

"What does 'oh my' mean?" demanded Jheklan.

"It seems," said the wizard, "that Kagen was dreaming about Fabeldyr the dragon all his life." He looked around at the Vale brothers. "And it's clear that this is the main reason Herepath wanted to come up here. He believed Kagen's dreams were prophetic, and that the fate of the last dragon was irrevocably tied to the sons of the Poison Rose."

CHAPTER ONE HUNDRED FOUR

Samud at night.

The balmy wind off the ocean sold the lie that warmth and comfort still existed in the world. The big fireplace in the grand hall conspired with it, burning brightly and crackling cheerfully.

But it was all a lie. Every flicker of warmth, every whisper of hope.

All lies.

Hope for King al-Huk was his son, el-Kep. His only son. His heir. His beloved child who was growing into a strong, confident, wise, and kind young man. Fifteen summers with most of his life before him. That was hope. That was the king's comfort in these troubled days. The easy smile, the joyful laugh, those eyes filled with trust and love.

The ocean wind blew and the fire crackled and it was all lies.

King al-Huk sat on the lowest step of his dais, his crown lying where it had fallen. He sat there, holding the dead body of his beloved son to his chest. The boy's arms hung limp, his legs twisted into impossible angles, his clothes rent to expose torn flesh. When al-Huk bent to kiss the boy's head, he found el-Kep's skin already cool.

Seven guards lay on the marble floor in pools of dull red, their bodies torn and broken, eyes wide with the horror of what had killed them. Swords were shattered, spears broken in half, bows snapped. The metal of their armor had been peeled back and split apart to expose veins and arteries.

All al-Huk saw, though—all he *could* see was el-Kep. His son, and the hole in the world in the boy's shape.

His vizier stood a few yards away, the hem of his robes soaked with blood, his face gray with shock.

"Sire, I have called the priests . . ." he said, his voice tentative, weak, knotted with grief.

"Priests?" murmured the king in a voice that was distant and hollow. "What use have I for prayers and platitudes, damn your eyes."

"But sire . . ."

Al-Huk raised his face to look at the vizier, and the impact of his stare drove the old man back several steps. The king's eyes were rimmed with red and his face streaked with tears and his child's blood. "Priests be damned," he said in a low, dangerous, hate-filled voice. "Call my generals. All of them. Call every admiral of the fleet. Do it *now*."

The vizier whirled and fled, his feet slapping and skidding in the blood.

The king clutched his son to his breast and wept. His chest labored and his whole body trembled. But his mind was an inferno.

There was no path left open to him in which peace beckoned.

And so King Hariq al-Huk, thirty-second of his name, lord of Samud, master of ships, divinely appointed Archer of Heaven, and divinely ordained protector of the realm prepared to make war on the Witch-king.

CHAPTER ONE HUNDRED FIVE

Duke Sárkány heard the screams, and this time they made him frown.

This time they were not a woman's screams. They were cries and shrieks torn from the throats of his own knights.

"Gods of fire and death," he swore and dropped from his saddle onto the ground. As he approached the hole in the wall, he heard one knight beg for mercy. Another called out to a god that no one alive even remembered. Yet another pleaded for his own mother to save him.

"What madness is this?" he growled as he drew his sword, God's Thorn, and a dagger that had a sword-catching serration on the back. Thus armed Sárkány stalked into the Tower of Sarsis.

And stopped short.

There were bodies at the foot of the winding staircase. The mangled bodies of vermin and the dismembered bodies of vampires. His own knights—the ancient warriors with whom Sárkány had haunted the lands of living men for tens of thousands of years.

Dead.

Arms and legs and heads cut off. Bodies sliced open. Sprawled in heaps there and up the stairs.

With a snarl of hate, Sárkány leaped over the dead onto a higher stair and began climbing. There was no part of that long stairway that was not splashed or smeared with blood. He saw a few dead cats among the corpses, but for each of these there were a score of rats. A few living cats looked up at him from above, their whiskers dripping with vampire blood. They hissed at him and retreated, and he chased upward, roaring challenges to whatever knights-at-arms the faerie slut had gathered to her. Was it Kagen up there? The damned Argonian and his friends—Tuke, the Therian giant, and Filia, the Vahlycorian caravan guard.

The thought of killing them, too, made him smile. There would be time to mourn for his knights, but in truth he did not much care. Some were friends, but he could always make more. The thought of turning Kagen, Tuke, and Filia into vampires delighted him. He would bind them in silver chains and bring them before the Witch-king as an offering to Hastur the Shepherd God.

"I will win this war myself," he yelled. "I will end this war by killing it in its cradle."

He rounded a curve and stopped, bringing his weapons up in a crossed guard.

There, on the next six steps, were headless corpses. And on the seventh were the heads. Arranged in a neat row so that their mouths gaped at him and their eyes pleaded with the persistence of the truly dead.

Sárkány looked into the eyes of his most powerful knights. Men and women who had been accomplished killers even before he gave them the red gift of eternal life. The air was thick with the smell of their blood, and the duke felt his stomach churn in mingled hunger and revulsion.

Then he raised his head and saw the dark figure a few steps above him.

She held her shadow-sword in one hand and the head of Ihlanique, Sárkány's oldest friend and most trusted warrior, in her other. Maralina raised the head to show him and then brought it close for a deep crimson kiss. Her face was smeared with blood already and Sárkány could see how long and sharp her teeth had grown.

He hissed at her and she let the head drop. It struck with a wet crunch and rolled bumping down the stairs. Sárkány stepped aside to let it pass.

"I am your doom," he said. "I took your maidenhead and stole your life and now you are nothing but one of *mine*. All of the family of blood must yield to me. You knew it then and feel it now. On your knees, faerie whore."

Maralina studied him with an icy detachment as she drew her finger through the gore on her chin and then licked that finger clean.

"Oh, my precious duke," she said. "I loved you once long ago. You did not *take* my virginity. It was offered out of love. And you repaid me by taking more than I could afford to give. My blood. My life. My family. My mother."

"You should have stayed dead," said Sárkány, rising two steps. Then he paused and smiled. "Tell me, Maralina . . . how did it feel when I threw you from that window long ago? How did it feel when your own kind drew back in fear of you? How did it feel, my lady, when your mother rejected you as unclean . . . as *doomed*? By Hastur's staff I hope you suffered. But I have come to end that suffering, for you are no longer amusing. You are nothing."

Maralina pointed her sword at him, but he mocked that, too.

"A shadow-sword?" He sneered. "Is that the height of your magic? Have these millennia dulled you so completely?"

"This is Nightsong," she said. "With it I have slain your army."

"You have slain friends and trusted companions," said the duke. "By admitting it without respect or remorse you speak your own doom."

Maralina lowered her sword. *"Chreachais tú féin nuair a chreach tú mise,"* she said in the old tongue, then repeated it in the modern language shared across the continent. "You doomed yourself by dooming me, your grace."

Sárkány laughed, and it was a laugh filled with unfiltered delight. "Long have I dreamed of this," he said. He feinted with his dagger and then lunged upward to drive his sword into her stomach.

Which she parried.

Easily.

It was a subtle flick of her wrist that brought the shadow-sword down on his, but the force of it drove the tip of that storied blade deep into the stone at her feet. Such was his strength and the power of the parry that the tip dug many inches into the step.

Sárkány was too canny to be shocked and instantly lunged with his dagger. He was so fast that the tip of it pierced her hand. Blood welled rich and scarlet around the wound, but as he jerked back on it to pull the weapon free, Maralina stepped down quickly, pushing her hand toward him so that the blade passed all the way through until the crosspiece slapped against her palm. Her long white fingers closed around the crosspiece and around Sárkány's hand. He tried to tear it free, but he could not.

With all of his titanic strength, he could not. Maralina held him fast.

He tried to pull God's Thorn from the stone step, but it was buried so deep that it would not budge. Maralina grabbed his right wrist with her uninjured hand. She held his hands in both of hers and with no visible sign of effort pulled his hands wide. That pull tore the sword free, but his hand flexed open, dropping it.

Sárkány tried to kick her, but it was like kicking iron. He twisted his hips and swung his spurs at her, tearing her skirt, but that was the only damage he did.

Maralina, though, did far more damage.

With a soft cry of delight she tore his arms from their sockets as easily as if dismembering a child's straw doll, and then flung the limbs over her shoulders to where half a hundred hungry cats waited. Blood erupted from the gaping shoulder sockets, but the duke's unnatural powers began at once to seal the wounds, to retain his blood, for that blood was his life. It held his magic and his immortality.

That only made Maralina's revenge last longer.

So much longer.

There were so many parts of him to rip away.

Maralina made it last a very long time.

She left Sárkány his tongue because his screams were so beautiful.

So very, very beautiful.

When she was done, there was very little left of Duke Sárkány. His flesh dried to a papery thinness and his bones to brittle sticks. She trod upon them until all that was left of him was dust. This she gathered up and when she stepped out of her tower, she flung it to the wind.

"No grave for you," she said as he vanished into the night. "No grave to be a womb for your rebirth."

The winds blew the dust of the ancient vampire out to sea where he would exist forever as a ghost, powerless and alone, but aware of his absolute helplessness.

Forever.

Maralina then walked down the steps, past the cats feeding on the last of the rats, stepping over what was left of the vampire army. Outside she saw the black goats, Chernobog and Baphomet, and stood looking into their eyes, saying nothing.

They growled and snarled and stamped their cloven hooves on the ground, growling threats and flaring with burning eyes. They bunched their muscles in preparation for charging.

She stood there, silent and unmoving until they *saw* her. Saw all the way into her.

Then the two gigantic black goats lowered themselves so that their front legs were beneath them and their great horns touched the ground. Maralina placed one hand on each of their heads. After a moment they pushed their heads against her touch. Like puppies needing forgiveness and acceptance.

Maralina turned then and looked at the tower. Regarding it. Seeing it with the objectivity of someone no longer imprisoned therein. It had been her home for years uncountable. It might have imprisoned her until the sun burned to cinders in the sky had Duke Sárkány not used magical creatures to break the walls. And break the spell. Nothing else could have done it. It amused her, because Sárkány never really understood the ways of faerie magic. Had he held that knowledge, he would never have used magic to breach her walls. Had he known, he would never have brought so many vampires for her to feed upon.

Perhaps if he had come alone and fought her, he might even have had a chance.

Perhaps.

Or perhaps not.

In any case, his foolishness and pride and arrogance had set her free. The princess of the *Baobhan sith* who was now the oldest vampire in the world, with all the power that such a state bestowed.

Maralina looked to the east.

"War is come," she said to the goats. "Rise and bear me thither."

She took a single step, then paused and looked down at the

ground on which she stood. She could see the outlines of old graves. She could see beneath the dirt.

The ground beneath her trembled. Maralina stepped aside as the soil churned as if pressed from beneath. A hand—with parchment flesh still clinging to the bones—stabbed upward into the cold moonlight. It flexed open and closed as if seeking to grasp something. Then the other hand tore free of the grave, and both hands pressed down on the ground as a bulky mass pushed itself up. Head like a skull, broad but withered shoulders, a torso, legs. It was slow and painful, but finally it stood there, still wearing the rags of its doublet and the rusted links of chain mail.

To the lady's left another form fought its way out of the earth. And another.

Midnight ruled the world and the lady stood in her garden with ragged figures out of a nightmare. They drew rust-eaten swords and battle maces and notched axes.

She said, "You were heroes once. Champions and princes, kings and warlords. Be heroes once more, my loves."

The knights—those pale kings and princes—hitched Chernobog and Baphomet to the wagon that stood empty. One of them, a great champion of a hundred battles, held his withered hand to help the lady up onto the seat. Another handed her the reins.

In the tower, the cats howled at the moon. In the trees around her tower a thousand nightbirds cried aloud. The army of the dead fell into lines behind the wagon.

And so Lady Maralina rode off to make war with the Witch-king and his god.

PART THREE
THE GOD OF FIRE AND TEARS

———

"I woke in the middle of the night to the sound of fury from above. I raced to my windows and threw back the shutters, fearing that the Gods of the Harvest and the gods of the pagans were finally at war, and that both judgment and redemption were at hand. But what I saw were monsters of such hideous alien forms battling among the clouds, trampling the planted fields and the towns at rest, and caring not a whit for what toll their conflict levied on simple men like me. Is this what we prayed for? Is this what we prayed *to*? None of these monsters cared to answer my questions or my prayers, and so I closed my shutters and went back to bed. If I died beneath their heels or if the battle passed me by—in either case, I no longer felt that this war was for or against me and mine. And that is the worst part of the war—knowing that we simple folk don't matter and likely never have."

—JANAL FIGG, APPLE FARMER IN ARGON. FROM HIS JOURNAL FOUND AMONG THE RUINS OF HIS FARMSTEAD.

CHAPTER ONE HUNDRED SIX

Kagen saw the smoke from a mile away.

It curled upward, thick and gray, lit from within by sparks and embers.

The Tower of Sarsis stood on the cliff over the ocean, and it was burning.

"Gods of the Pit—*no!*"

He kicked Jinx into a gallop, and although the horse was weary, it caught his rider's sense of urgency and broke into a fierce run. The other horses tied to Jinx's saddle whinnied as they raced with him.

They tore down the road into town and clattered over the cobblestones. There were scores of people standing in clusters around the stone walls that embowered the tower. They turned at the sounds of Jinx's hooves. Several had to jump out of the way.

"Sir!" cried one man wearing the sash of a beadle. "Don't go in there."

Kagen ignored him and leaped from the saddle as he jerked Jinx to a halt. He tore his daggers from their sheaths, pushed past a few slow-witted onlookers, vaulted the wall, and ran to the breach. There he paused, shocked by what he saw. There were corpses, many mangled to inhumanity, lying in heaps at the foot of the big winding stair, and more on the steps themselves. All around the bodies were rats that had been thoroughly savaged. Smears of blood were on the ground and splashed high on the walls.

The beadle hurried up to the edge of the wall. "Sir, *sir*," he cried, "you mustn't go in there. It is the abode of a demon."

Kagen turned to him with blazing fury. *"Be damned to you all."*

The beadle and everyone around him stumbled back, some making the warding sign.

Kagen stepped through the hole in the wall and began climbing.

He paused to check a few of the bodies, not sure what he was looking for. His initial assumption that they were Hakkians was immediately disproved. The dead in Maralina's home were of a kind he had never seen before. They were deathly pale and thin— almost albinos, but he did not think they truly were. The sense that their color had been somehow *drained* out of them came into his mind, though he could neither explain nor defend such a thought.

Their weapons lay where each had fallen. Some of the swords were shattered and a few looked oddly crushed.

He hurried on, though, fearful of what he would find.

The smoke he saw above seemed to be coming from a fire near the top of the tower, but the lower chambers were not even clogged with smoke. Nor was there any oppressive heat within the structure.

"Maralina!" he yelled.

There was no answer. At least not in her voice. And it struck Kagen that there was a difference to the atmosphere there than what he remembered. When he had been to the tower months ago—first as a prisoner and then as lover of the immortal woman— the place had felt substantially alive. By the end of that stay, Kagen had come to sense that it was the immense personal power of Maralina that imbued the walls and furniture, the books and everything else with that feeling of unyielding vitality.

That feeling was gone now, and the tower felt *older* than it had. More frail and with a sense of disuse. Or abandonment.

He ran up the stairs, past the point where there were any marks of combat or death. When he reached the level where Maralina's study had been, he stopped. Everything had changed, and his mouth went dry even as he was about to call her name again.

The tables were there, and even the books and crystals and candles, but they were covered with ages upon ages of dust and cobwebs. The huge mirror on the wall was cracked from side to side. The loom on which Maralina wove her magic tapestries was shattered, and the pieces, they, too, were covered in the dust of centuries. Thread in a thousand different colors and shades had rolled across the floor, covering it in a fantastical complexity of threads—but even as he watched, those bright colors were fading, losing richness, becoming older.

He heard cracking sounds and saw fissures open in the stone walls. Even the boards beneath his feet began to warp and splinter.

The only things in that room that seemed able to defy this pernicious process of aging were Maralina's tapestries. There were scores of them, each of various sizes and with unique designs, hung from the countless bookshelves. The tapestries were affixed to the wood with iron nails, but these did not pierce the image but were rather entangled with the colorful fringe.

Kagen stood there, his knives forgotten in his hands, looking at the pictures embroidered with infinite skill by the faerie princess. They showed places he had been, places he knew, but also places of which he was unfamiliar. There were no people in any of the tapestries. The only figures depicted were magical beings.

And of these there were two Kagen knew. He stopped and stared at these as dust swirled around him. One of them featured a creature he had met in actual combat, and the second was from a thousand dreams since he was a lad.

The razor-knight he had fought in Vespia.

And the chained and tortured dragon, Fabeldyr.

There was a sound behind him and he turned, crouching, his knives rising to defend or attack.

On the shattered frame of the loom stood a bird. A ragged old crow, and Kagen knew him, for this crow always seemed to be nearby when the larger world collided with the one Kagen was born to.

"Old Grandfather," said Kagen, lowering his knives. "She's gone, isn't she?"

The crow opened its mouth but its caw was nearly silent.

"Tell me, if you can, if she yet lives," begged Kagen. "Or is this dust all that is left of her?"

The crow rose up and spread its wings, beating them once, twice, then settling back down.

"Gods of the Pit, bird, I hope that is a yes."

With a squawk, the crow jumped from the loom and flapped across the room and out the door. Kagen followed quickly, pausing only to look up the spiral staircase at a strange sight. The fire was there, roiling and rippling like water as it clung to the ceiling, but it did not seem to consume what it burned. He could see the timbers through the intense golden glow and they were unmarked, as if the blaze was somehow kept in check.

A sense of urgency tugged at him, emphasized by a sharp rebuke from the old crow. He looked and saw that it had flown to the far side of a curving hall and landed atop a stack of crates. As Kagen approached, the fire cast a glow over two objects. One was a barrel—a three-and-a-half-gallon hogshead—upon which was a stencil of daggers crossed in front of a sword, with a rose vine wrapped round about, and the silhouette of a dragon in the center. Kagen gaped at this for it was the same sigil as on the flag Clementius had given him.

The battle flag of the war against the Witch-king.

Atop this barrel was a small crystal vial of a kind he knew very well. He could hear the echo of the words Maralina had said to him when she gave him an identical vial many months ago.

"It is something very old. It has no name in Argonian or the common tongue, but ages ago it was called eitr. In ages past, eitr was both the source of life and a certain means of ending it. Once, before the world was made, gods battled each other for the right to rule this planet. When fragments of a great kingdom of ice encountered the fires of a burning realm, that sacred ice melted, and the runoff was this. Some believe that eitr was the water of life that gave birth to all living things, but as it gives life so it can take it."

And he had asked her what it does.

"This poison was said to be deadly enough to kill gods," she said, "though I do not know if that is true. It is at its most potent, however, when it touches enchanted flesh. If you fight the Witch-king and can cut him with this, much will be revealed. If he is mortal, he will bleed and become sick. Perhaps he will die. But even if he does not, his mortal weakness will be revealed to anyone who sees him so afflicted. If he is a god or a demon, then his true form will be fully revealed. It may not kill him, but it may show him for the monster he is, and that may help your dreams of rebellion."

The crow stepped aside to let him take the vial and Kagen held it up to the firelight. The amber liquid seemed to boil and burn within the crystal. He put it into a pouch tied to his belt. Then he knelt and studied the hogshead. The crow tapped his beak against the top of it and uttered a shrill caw of warning.

That told Kagen much, and he bowed to the bird. It cawed again, now with a different kind of urgency, and flew down to the study. Kagen hoisted the barrel and followed.

Smoke was only just beginning to gather, spreading out across the ceiling. Kagen knew his time there was running out. The crow flew in a circle around the room, cawing as it passed each of the hung tapestries.

"Yes," said Kagen. "I understand."

Hurrying now, he took the hogshead down the stairs and set it in the ragged breach. Then he returned to the study and—making absolutely sure not to touch any of the images with his hands—he took the tapestries down, laid them one atop the other, and rolled them into a bundle so that the blank back of the bottommost one was visible. He lashed the cylinder of cloth with strips torn from a table cover and hoisted it onto his shoulder. It was a heavy burden, but bearable. As he began descending the stairs, he heard a loud crack and looked up to see flames breaking through collapsing timbers.

The Tower of Sarsis was dying, its time come to an end.

"Thank you," said Kagen. "If you can hear me, sweet Lady Maralina, know that I love you now and will always love you. I hope you are not lost to me."

It was then he saw something on the floor that he had not noticed before. It was a folded piece of parchment weighted down by a beautiful long-stem rose. He knelt, setting his burden down, but hesitated before touching either of the objects because he was certain they were not there before. The crow cawed and when he looked at it, the bird nodded.

Kagen carefully lifted the rose and smelled it. The scent of rose was there, but another scent overlaid it. Maralina's strange perfume, and smelling it now brought her so vividly to his mind that his heart began to beat like a drum in his chest.

He picked up the parchment and unfolded it, and found that there were actually two pages. Both were written in an elegant and flowing hand. One was long and personal and heartbreaking. The second looked like a page torn from a diary. It was written in the same hand, but there was a different flow to it, as if it was written at an earlier time, during Maralina's imprisonment. Where the first note was written to him, the second was written about the Silver Empire.

He read them both. One made him weep. The other stabbed him through the heart.

He read them, then read each through a second time. When he was finished, he folded the notes with great care and stowed them in his shirt over his heart. Then he rose, his mind filled with new understanding.

The crow cawed again and flew past him down the stairs. Kagen took the rose, tucked the stem into his belt, hoisted his burden, and followed.

Outside he carried the bundle to the far end of the yard, puzzled at the ground, which was greatly disturbed, with heaps of dirt everywhere. He returned for the cask and then hoisted them over the low wall and lashed them to his spare mounts. The people from Arras watched him, and a few—including the beadle—tried to engage him in conversation, but he warned them off with a harsh glare.

Once the horses were ready, he took Jinx by the reins and led all three animals away. The crowd parted to allow him passage, with no one daring to stop the fierce-looking warrior.

Kagen mounted and rode away. He paused only once, on a knoll east of the town, and watched as the Tower of Sarsis, now fully wreathed in flames, bowed toward the sea. The structure hung there for a long moment, and then it toppled over the cliff, trailing smoke during its long fall to the rocks below. A plume of smoke and flaring cinders rose up, then they, too, vanished. All that was left was the ruined garden and the stone wall, but all traces of the Tower of Sarsis were gone.

His heart was heavy as a great stone in his chest. What would all this mean? Lady Maralina was free of her prison. She was abroad in the world. Kagen knew that this was something she had both yearned for and feared. The yearning was that of any prisoner who could count more years in a cell than those out of one, and for Maralina she could count her sentence in centuries instead of years.

But she was aware of the monster she had become because of

Duke Sárkány's foul bite—his vampire's kiss. It had changed her into something that had never before existed—a faerie become a vampire. Her own mother had despised and feared this new state of existence and it was she who had built the tower and condemned her daughter to an eternal existence there. Maralina feared what the vampire's hunger might become if she was free.

And she was both free and gone.

Kagen turned his horse away, uncertain what to feel. There was love in his heart for Lady Maralina, but there was also dread. With her powers—faerie, vampire, and sorceress—she could pose a greater threat to the world than did the Witch-king.

How would freedom change her from the woman with whom he had shared love and secrets and passion?

He saw the old crow swoop down and land on the rolled bundle of tapestries.

"I will find her," he told the bird. "Or, perhaps, she will find me."

The crow cawed softly.

Kagen smiled sadly. "But I guess you already know that."

He rode off and the crow, in his own time, followed.

━━━━━▶ **CHAPTER ONE HUNDRED SEVEN**

Since they had been searching for hours now and the smell of the dragon was not very much closer than it had been, they decided to pause in that spot for rest and food—and to allow Alibaxter to continue reading the diary.

The young wizard was fascinated by it and read many of Kagen's dreams aloud.

"Wait, wait," said Faulker when Alibaxter was midway through one, "I'm confused. The way you're reading it is as if both young Kagen, the stripling, is speaking with the voice of the Kagen of right now."

"And that is exactly how Herepath recorded it. There are remarks in the margins to verify this—that the dreams, as related by young Kagen, contained elements that were out of keeping with a child recounting them. Instead, Herepath seemed to think that the younger and older—I suppose the *present* or, at least, *recent* Kagen—somehow merged in those prophetic dreams. Please don't ask me how this is possible, because it's completely outside of my field of knowledge. Even Herepath admits that it was a mystery to him."

"That makes no sense," said Faulker.

Jheklan gave him a pitying look. "And everything else that's happened lately does . . . ?"

"You know what I mean."

Alibaxter uttered a small cry. "Oh my," he said again.

"Now what?" asked the Vale brothers.

The wizard pointed to a passage in the book. "It says here that nearly two years ago a Hakkian expedition arrived here. Soldiers and . . . a sorcerer."

"A sorcerer?

"Very likely," said Alibaxter. "The name of the sorcerer was Gethon Heklan."

"Gods of the Harvest," breathed Jheklan. "The Witch-king came here."

And at that moment the unseen beast, the dragon deep in the heart of the glacier cried out in terrible rage and pain.

CHAPTER ONE HUNDRED EIGHT

His name was Unka and he had killed two hundred and two men.

He did not add the numbers of women to that count unless they were warriors, and then he grouped them as "men." As for children, they were not worth counting.

Unka was known as the Spider, and his skin was covered with spider tattoos. Black widows and brown recluses seemed to crawl across his face. Wolf spiders ringed his neck, and huge tarantulas crouched on his shoulders. There were funnel-web spiders and redback spiders and orb weavers and camel spiders and so many others on his arms, legs, and torso. One spider for every warrior he had ever killed.

And room for more.

Unka the Spider stood in a cleft formed by lightning-struck rocks, high on the crest of a mountain. Behind him was the endless green expanse of the Jungle Belt. Before him were the slopes that ran down to the Great Inland Sea. Cramming the road from where he stood down and around and far out of sight were his soldiers. The Spider had spent months going from city to town to village recruiting. He had spearmen from Yehtec and Kortha, archers from Inaki, light cavalry from Ashghulan, heavier cavalry from Wyndhoven, axe men from the forests of Kierrod Sund, and swordsmen by the thousand from the vastness of Bercless.

Fifty thousand mercenaries waited in lines that stretched for miles.

Waiting for Unka the Spider.

The road ahead ran south through the city-states of the Waste, and through a series of mountain passes that cut between Weska and Delios, all the way to the Great Southern Sea. Countless ships were waiting there. Uncountable numbers of troop transports that would skirt the rest of the mainland, sail up through the Dragon Islands, past dead Skyria, and into the blue waters of Haddon Bay.

And from there . . .

Unka smiled. By the time those ships reached the bay, word would have reached him from the Witch-king. By then the field of battle would be known.

He could almost hear the sound of all those thousands of blades clashing, the air above screaming with the flights of arrows, and the cries of the weak men of the west who had grown soft over their centuries under the heel of the Silver Empresses.

Unka the Spider thought about that and the images conjured in his mind were headier than the strongest ale. He could almost smell the blood on the air.

He turned and looked back, and nodded, content with what he saw.

Then he waved them all on, and those fifty thousand followed him into the south.

CHAPTER ONE HUNDRED NINE

It came like a wind, like the coldest breath of the god of ice and blizzards.

It blew across the face of what had been the Silver Empire. No corner of that vast land—from the frozen north to the warm southern sea, from the snowcapped peaks of the Cathedral Mountains to the foam-capped waves of the Western Ocean—escaped its frosty whisper.

Sárkány is dead.

It spoke in every language and in every way meaning is shared.

The king of the dead himself has died.

The wind whispered this.

It screamed it.

In Argentium, deep in the bowels of the palace, twenty sleepers woke with cries on their red lips. In rows of coffins, where each lay upon soil of the lands in which they had been born, they rose up, shrieking in psychic and physical pain.

They tumbled out of their coffins, breaking the wood or metal in their panic. They crashed to the stone floor, sending roaches and rats scampering for shelter. The vampires crawled blindly or curled into fetal balls and howled their confusion and grief into their own palms.

The unkillable king of their kind had been slaughtered.

It was impossible. It was unthinkable. It went against prophecies that had whispered of a kingdom of blood that was to come.

They wept red tears there in the lightless dungeon.

Duke Sárkány was dead.

And the world itself had broken.

In his throne room, the Witch-king staggered and nearly fell. He snaked a hand out and caught the arm of the Prince of Games.

"Sire," cried the prince, "what ails you?"

The King in Yellow was choked to silence by the sudden, clear, irrefutable knowledge that the duke was dead.

But that was only a small part of what made him so afraid.

"She is free," he gasped.

The Prince of Games, that immortal son of chaos who had seen civilizations uncountable rise and fall, went dead pale.

"No . . ." he breathed.

In Vahlycor, in the bedroom of Queen Egnes, a figure froze in the act of commission, his mouth wide so that his teeth could bite the throat of the sleeping monarch.

That yawning bite turned into uncontrollable gagging. The vampire reeled away, clutching at his throat and his heart. On the bed, the queen woke with a start and immediately began screaming. Doors banged open and guards ran to her aid with drawn swords and heavy glaives.

They saw the wan figure staggering toward the window, and they rushed at it, stabbing and chopping. Mangled, cut to the bone in a dozen places, the vampire threw itself from the high window. It tried to change, to become a bat, to fly away.

Instead it fell through the night air and dashed itself to ruin on the rocks that jutted up from the moat. Alligators snarled and bit at the cold flesh and the monster vanished beneath the churning water.

On a riverbank in Ghenrey, a young woman dressed in mourning robes paused and looked up into the night sky. She heard the whispers on the wind, and though she did not know who Duke Sárkány was, the magic in her blood whispered to her that a great thing had happened.

The lord of all the vampires who had ever lived, was dead.

And the Widow knew that this was the first great battle and the first victory of the war. Her smile was filled with an ugly joy, and she felt a hunger of her own. For blood, though not to drink it. She wanted to spill it, to bathe in it.

Perhaps to die in it . . . though not before the Witch-king lay broken at her feet.

In northern Argon, in a huge manor house where death had come to call, there were screams and shouts and the sounds of a deadly battle. But as the wind blew through a smashed window and roamed the halls of the manor, the noise of combat and murder ceased. For a moment, for a breath.

An Unbladed—Bracenghan ah-Fahr, known as Brace—lay dying on the floor. Most of his face had been ripped away by savage claws. His breast was torn down to the bone, and blood pumped from these mortal wounds.

His friend, Hop Garkain, stood over him, a chipped axe in both hands, and he, too, was bleeding. Two household soldiers were sprawled in artless heaps, their flesh in tatters. Near them, sitting with her back to the foot of a heavy bed, was Helleda Frost. Her eyes were open but her mind had gone dark with pain and shock. She yet lived, but that life hung by a thread.

On the bed itself, the old former nun, Mother Frey, was huddled back against the headboard, one hand holding a knife and the other pressing a pillow to the ragged wound in her throat. She was bathed in her own blood and that of Brace and Lady Frost.

By the window, frozen into a posture of listening, head cocked and ear tilted to the night wind, was the spy who had followed her from the meeting with Kagen Vale. Thin, small, pale—a shadow of the fourteen-year-old he had been when Sárkány took his life and then gifted him with immortality seven centuries before. His body was crisscrossed with knife, sword, and axe wounds and even his enormous and unnatural strength was waning. Still, he knew that he could finish his mission and kill the old woman who was one of the Witch-king's greatest enemies.

But then that night wind had whispered a terrible truth to him.

The king of the dead himself has died.

His pause, the moment in which he had stopped his slaughter to hear that news, and the horror that it sent through him, were his undoing, for it was one moment—one heartbeat—too long. He did not see the axe that sliced through the air.

He did not know he was in ultimate peril until he was dead, and then it was almost a blessing for without his lord, his sire, his king, what was he?

The vampire died.

Five heartbeats later, so did Brace.

CHAPTER ONE HUNDRED TEN

"By the startled balls of the god of surprises," said Tuke Brakson as he stopped in the middle of the road, fists on hips, a huge grin on his dark face. He turned to Filia. "It *almost* looks like Kagen Vale, though this one appears rather handsome and nearly intelligent, so I'm probably wrong about that."

The rider looked down from his horse. "Two things," he said.

"Which are?"

"Fuck," said Kagen, "you."

Filia smiled. "Sounds like Kagen, too."

Kagen slid from Jinx's back, wobbled on tired knees, caught his balance, then arched backward in a stretch that filled the air with a chorus of snaps and pops.

"Gods of the Pit," he sighed. "I've been in the saddle so long my ass hates me."

Then he laughed and caught both Filia and Tuke in a huge embrace. They hugged and laughed, and both Filia *and* Tuke kissed his cheeks.

As they all stepped back, Kagen looked past them at a massive field that was filled to bursting with tents, corrals with thousands of horses, and a row of wagons that stretched out of sight. "What the hell *is* all of this?"

"We fed and watered your little army and it's grown," said Filia.

"So it seems . . . but I'm amazed."

Tuke slapped him hard enough on the back to create a small cloud of road dust. "I hope you didn't think we were being idle while you were visiting your lady love."

That remark slapped the smile from Kagen's face.

"What?" asked Tuke quickly. "What did I say?"

But Kagen shook his head. "I need a chair with a cushion on it, a lot of food, and even more drink, for I have a story to tell you. Filia knows some of it, but there's more."

"Aye, Kagen," said Filia. "We have a fair bit to share with you. But first, let's get you fed. I'll have someone see to your horses."

Kagen touched her arm. "Listen, whoever unpacks my gear . . . make sure they are very damned careful. That cask is to be handled with the greatest caution. It is very dangerous. Let no one open it," he said. "Mind me now."

"Of course."

"And that bundle is of equal importance and dangerous in its own way. Have it brought to whichever tent I'll be bunking in. Again, handle it with the greatest care. Do not let anyone unroll it. Place both items in my tent and post a guard of six soldiers. Pick people you'd trust with your own life. Much will depend on how safely we keep those things. I'm neither joking nor exaggerating."

"It will be done as you request, brother," said Tuke. He signaled Hoth, the moody Ghenreyan poet and duelist who was a sergeant of the Bloody Bastards and had gone with them into Vespia. Hoth, never the most affable or garrulous man at the best of times, nodded and began yelling for the other five that would form his detail.

Tuke and Filia led Kagen to a big tent.

When hot food and cold drink had been brought, Filia tasked the Zehrian spear-fighter, Pergun, who was another of the veterans of the Vespia mission, to stand guard outside.

Kagen tore into a big piece of barbecued pork that was seasoned with white pepper, sesame oil, raw sugar, and white wine, and washed it down with good Argonian beer as he told his tale. Even though he had shared some of it with Filia when he'd met her a few weeks before, he went over all of it, adding bits of insights and opinions he'd formed during his long journey. He spoke of the Witch-king's ascension, and some theories on how to stop it. When he got to the part about the Tower of Sarsis, they leaned in and hung on his every word. He was working his way through a plate of nuts and cheese by the time he had all of it out.

They sat back and drank deeply as the information, and all its implications, were digested.

"By Dagon's balls," said Tuke, whistling.

Filia goggled. "Your lady killed a couple dozen vampires single-handedly?"

"That's how I read the scene," said Kagen.

"I had no idea she was so fearsome a warrior."

"Nor I," admitted Kagen. "Though I shouldn't be surprised. For all that I love her, I still know very little about her. We had that one month . . ."

Tuke shook his head. "I would give my best horse's left ball to have seen that fight. Hell, I'd give both balls."

"I'd have given much to *be* there," sighed Kagen. "To have fought beside her."

"It sounds like she did not need you or anyone," observed Filia.

"Even so."

"Tell me, brother," said Filia, "how sure are you that she was not killed? I mean, legend has it that the oldest vampires turn to dust when they're slain, and Maralina has to be nearly as old as Sárkány."

Kagen managed a small smile. "She left me a note."

As he began digging in his pouch, Filia said, "Do you think that Duke Sárkány was among those she killed? Not that there would be aught but dust, as I said."

"He was there. Here, read this," he said, producing one of the two pieces of parchment left for him by Maralina. "Read it aloud."

Filia took it, angled it to the lantern light, and read the note aloud.

> *Kagen, my love, I wish I could still be here when you come, and I know that you will come. I saw it in my mirror.*
>
> *Duke Sárkány came last night with his knights. They wanted to use me first and then destroy me, for Sárkány knows that I am a threat to his master and his god. They broke into the tower by means of magic, and this was their undoing, for that magic broke the spell my mother cast many years ago.*
>
> *I am free now, and woe to those I hate.*
>
> *The duke is dust now and he can never return. His evil is ended. I pray that when he descends to hell that the souls of all those whose lives he destroyed are waiting.*

I have left you gifts to help you in this war. A cask and tapestries. I believe you will know how best to use them. You are a general now and do not need instruction from me.

There is a great war coming, my love. When it has raged and passed, the world will not be the same. I may not survive the war. I pray that you will, but so much rests on chance. Even I cannot see the future for it has been stirred with great vigor and all is in motion.

Beware the Witch-king. He is kin to none who love peace. Let not sentimentality or mercy stay your hand. The Witch-king has become the enemy of nature itself and the magicks he works are unmatched. The world you know is in great peril. But the larger world hangs by a slender thread, and the flame of life is so very fragile. His ascension is coming—it will be on the night of the first new moon of winter. A great storm will rage, and if he is unchecked, that storm will consume this world.

The forces aligned against you are dreadful. He has armies you know about and those you do not. Beware and be wary.

You have been touched by elvinkind and by faerie folk, both in response to your kindness and grace. May that offer comfort and be a shield.

My time is short for this tower is doomed. Know this and take whatever comfort you may—there are others who hate the Witch-king and fear his wrath. When things are the very darkest help may come, unknown and unlooked for.

One last thing, sweet Kagen, I know that your brothers have ventured to the Winterwilds to find great books of magic and to decide the fate of Fabeldyr. Those magic books are not there. The Hakkians already have them. The Hsan scrolls are of little use now, for they warn of the Witch-king's ascension, but that is now known.

But Fabeldyr is in the north, with her tears and her blood. Jheklan and Faulker Vale are in the gravest danger, for even I—even those with such vision as I have—cannot know what will happen if her chains are broken. I fear that in her despair she will call out to her god, and that Vathnya the god of fire and tears may answer. Then woe to us all. There are forces at play in this universe far greater than anything you can imagine. One wrong move up in the frozen north may doom us all.

I love you, my hero, my champion. I love you, my friend. I do not know if one such as me—cursed and unloved by my own kind—will survive this war. I do not know if I should, for I am as much monster as faerie. Perhaps any world beyond the smoke of war will prosper in my absence.

Should you survive this war, Kagen, find a mortal woman who is good and strong. Perhaps, on summer nights when you are alone and allow yourself to dream, then dream of me and know that I will always love you. Think kindly of the princess in the tower whose heart you saved.

—Maralina, daughter of Titania à-Mab, queen of the Baobhan sith

CHAPTER ONE HUNDRED ELEVEN

It was a long note and Filia had begun reading it in a normal tone, but toward the end her voice broke in places. When she was done, she handed it back to Kagen, who folded it, kissed it, and tucked it safely away. Tuke looked away into the lantern light, and its golden glow glimmered on the tears that ran down his cheeks.

The three of them sat in silence for a long time.

It was Filia who broke the silence. "She said that you were

touched by elvinkind and faerie folk. I can guess that the latter was when you offered her your blood to save her life when you first met . . ."

Kagen nodded.

"But elvinkind?"

"I skipped that part," said Kagen, and he told them about the strange encounter in the deep forest. When they asked to see the wound, he unlaced his shirt and showed them.

"It looks like something from ten or twenty years ago," said Tuke. "Not weeks. Can you feel it?"

"Mostly no, unless I'm actually thinking about it," Kagen said. "And now and then it tingles, but only a little. It did that as I approached Maralina's tower, and again when I saw that old crow that follows me about."

Filia nodded. "There are old stories about people being marked by the elvinkind," she said.

"Sure," said Tuke, "the 'Ballad of Tehmor-linn' is one. That sensation you mentioned saved him from a witch in one stanza and from a werewolf in another."

Kagen retied his shirt. "Yeah, well, don't start composing the 'Ballad of Kagen the Damned' anytime soon."

"Ha! You joke, but I've heard three different versions of that so far."

"Gods help me," groaned Kagen.

"Kagen, we've heard your tale," said Filia, "but we have one of our own."

Kagen caught something in her expression. "What's happened?"

Tuke refilled their cups. "Do you want the good news first, or the bad news?"

"Is the good news actually good?"

"Mostly," said the Therian. "As you've seen, our army has grown, and they love the new flag."

"How many are here?"

"In this camp?" said Filia. "Just shy of forty thousand. A bit more than half are Unbladed, and that means most of the Brotherhood are with us. Good fighters, as you can imagine. The rest are a mixed bag of volunteers, ex-soldiers, farmers who we're training as pikemen, poachers good with bows."

"That's hardly good news, damn it," Kagen said, thumping his cup down. "I'd hoped for more by now. The war is already—"

But Filia shushed him. "You asked how many were *here*, and I told you. But this is not the only camp. We have eleven rally points throughout northern Argon, Nehemite, eastern Theria, and southern Vahlycor. Big camps, I mean."

"Are they as big as this?"

"Oh, this one is far from our largest camp," laughed Tuke.

"What?"

"There's one in Theria with *three times* our number."

"Samud is close to that," said Filia. "And that doesn't count the navies. Theria, Samud, and Vahlycor have ordered all their ships to sea."

Kagen grunted. "Since when? When I spoke to Clementius, I got the impression that none of the sub-monarchs had committed to war with Hakkia."

"And that," said Tuke with sadness in his eyes, "is the bad news."

They told him about the attacks by Duke Sárkány's knights on the royal families of every single one of the nations that used to form the Silver Empire.

"Vulpion of Zehria, King Horogillin of Nelfydia, and Queen Egnes of Vahlycor are confirmed dead. Crown Prince Ifduril of Ghenrey is badly wounded and may not last the week, and King Thespo of Sunderland lost an arm, an eye, and most of his family. Prince Regent Mondas Huvan of Zaare is injured but we have no word of his condition. Beyond that . . . there are deaths aplenty. King al-Huk of Samud lost his own son and heir, and Queen

Lliaorna's consort was slain. And there was the close call with Queen Theka at sea."

"Gods of the Pit," swore Kagen, pounding his fist onto the table hard enough to spill everyone's beer. The news hit him very hard and he had them go over it again so he could make sure he understood. "And these were vampires?"

"Without a doubt," said Filia. "Except for the attack on Theka's ship, I mean. In all other cases the assassins were vampire knights of Sárkány's order. They were seen and, in some cases, fought. None were taken alive, alas. Some of the smaller nations are in turmoil, of course, but al-Huk immediately called for war."

"My queen, Theka," said Tuke, "rounded up all the Ravens and Hakkian diplomats in her court and had them beheaded. She sent the heads by ship to Argentium with a formal declaration of war and a clear refutation of the Witch-king's legal claims to the throne. It's war now, my brother."

They sat with that for a few moments.

"There's more," said Filia.

Kagen gave her a bleak look. "Tell me."

"They went for Mother Frey, too," said Filia. "Thank the gods she survived, but Lady Frost was badly hurt and many of her people killed."

"Frey lives?" he asked.

"She does." Filia's face was haunted as she added, "She was bitten, though."

"Bitten? By a vampire?" cried Kagen. "What does that mean? Do we know if the bastard made her drink his blood, too?"

"She says not. Nor was Frost made to drink. The vampire was killed before that could happen. The vampire killed one of Frey's bodyguards, too. The Samudian, Brace, not the little hairy Therian."

Kagen got up, took his beer and walked with it to the far side of the tent and stood for a while, sipping it and looking inward at his own thoughts. "Brace was a bit of an ass, but he deserved better than that."

"He died to save Frey and Frost," said Tuke. "That'll earn him a song at least."

"I think he'd like that," Kagen said distantly.

"What matters most," added Filia, "is now most of the other nations are going to war against the Witch-king."

When Kagen turned, there was conflict etched onto his face. "I suppose I should not examine a gift horse's teeth," he said.

"The expression is that you shouldn't fondle a gift horse's balls," said Tuke.

"No, it's not," countered Filia. She got up and crossed to Kagen. "I get it. They waited and waited while the kings and queens sat safe behind their walls and watched as the Ravens burned the Gardens and did all manner of evil. But, even so, have some compassion for them. They are all rightly afraid of the Witch-king's magic. They feared the vampires and the Hollow Monks and the Red Plague."

"And only acted when their *own* lives were on the line," said Kagen bitterly. "On one hand, I'm happy they're finally getting off their asses, but had they acted sooner we might have caught the Witch-king before he rebuilt his personal power."

Filia punched his arm. A knuckle punch into a spot that hurt rather a lot.

"What the hell was that for?" he demanded.

"For being a horse's ass."

"Or balls," suggested Tuke, but they ignored him.

"What matters is that we now have an army fifty times bigger than the one we thought we'd have. The entire west is rising. And the monarchs of the most powerful nations are ready to march to any piece of ground *you* pick, and to do it under *your* banner."

He stared at her. "*What?* Why? If anything, I should step back to stand in my own place. Captain of the Bloody Bastards, going to war without affiliation."

"So help me Father Ar, I will punch you again."

"She will, too," warned Tuke.

Kagen drank the rest of his beer and stalked back to the table for more. Tuke poured it for him.

"I don't get this. I was leading the army *we* built, but only because I couldn't talk either of you into doing it."

"Nor can you now," observed Tuke. "Though, I take your point. The thing is, my friend, you have become the face of this war. Ever since the sub-monarchs saw you perform your own magic trick on the night of the coronation, they've viewed you as the leader of the rebellion."

"That's bullshit. I just wanted to kill the son of a bitch."

"So did they, but all they did was follow the law and tradition and sat on their royal asses while you damn near killed the single most dangerous sorcerer in the world." Tuke grinned. "They are very likely ashamed of themselves for not acting sooner."

"And they're seeing the consequences of that hesitation," said Filia. "Al-Huk has to bury his only heir. Nelfydia and Vahlycor have vacant thrones. This shows everyone that the Witch-king was never going to be the benevolent ruler he bragged he was that night. He isn't here to right the wrongs—inarguable wrongs, mind you—committed by the Silver Empire. He's here to conquer the west and very probably the rest of the world. Only one person—as far as everyone sees it—stood up to the Witch-king right from the beginning, and that was you."

"It was *us*, damn it," swore Kagen as he rubbed his sore arm. "You were there with me."

"And I'm sure we'll have statues in museums and maybe a town square named for us," said Tuke with a sigh. "History isn't fair. Besides, you're a Vale, and more to the point, you're the son of the Poison Rose."

"He's right," said Filia. "If your mother hadn't died, everyone would be looking to her to be the general in this war."

"I'm *not* a fucking general."

They both smiled at him. "Like it or not, laddie," said Filia, "yes you are."

CHAPTER ONE HUNDRED TWELVE

Mad Mari Heklan knelt before her king, and he placed his hands on her head and blessed her to Hastur and Azozeth.

"Rise, cousin," he said.

She got to her feet. Mari's face was red from the bitter weather, but bright with good humor.

They were in a small meeting room off of the grand hall. Only them and no one else, except guards on the other side of a stout, locked door.

"Tell me of our enemies," said the king as he walked to a pair of leather chairs by the fire and indicated she join him. "And of your plans for them."

"Our spy network has earned their gold pieces, Majesty," she said in her blunt, gruff tone. "As you predicted, the great houses of Argon rose as soon as word reached them of the deaths of their royal cousins. Gallopers have burned up the roads between the palaces in Samud, Theria, Nehemite, Vahlycor, Zehria, and the rest. I believe Nespar told about the fleets."

"Yes," said the Witch-king, "and I had an audience with the admirals. Our fleets dominate Haddon Bay and squadrons are patrolling the entire western coastline. The rebels may put everything that floats a-sail, but I do not much care. This war will be won on the ground."

"By Hastur's staff, my king, yes it will," agreed Mari, her face growing redder and hotter at the thought.

"But we need to win that ground war, Mari. Where do we stand?"

"In terms of simple numbers, sire, we are well-matched. Perhaps we have a slight edge because Bulconia has sent twice as many troops as they promised."

"In exchange for . . . ?"

"Zaare. They covet the vineyards. And they would like to negotiate parts of Nehemite so that when this is done the Bulconian nation is the same size as it was before the Silver Empire pushed them back."

"If I agree to that, when can additional troops be sent?"

"At once. They are already massing in camps hidden in valleys all along the western range of the Cathedral Mountains. If you send a message promising those territories, they will send fifty thousand light cavalry. They're the ones who ride those squatty steppes horses, the ones that can run all day long. Those raiders are every bit as good as the Samudian archers."

"Did you tell them where they would have to ride *to*?" asked the yellow king.

"I did, Majesty."

"Then draft a note and bring it to me to sign." He sat for a moment, watching the fire dance and leap. "Where and when will you meet Kagen on the battlefield?"

"I have allowed the rebels to name their own ground," she said.

"The Field of Uthelian?"

"Exactly so, lord."

"Tell me why," said the king. "The obvious reasons and the real reason."

Mad Mari smiled at that. "The obvious reason is that it is as convenient for us as for them. It's in Argon, which allows everyone to use the trade roads to get there. Their army is now so big that they cannot get enough of their forces into place by any other routes. Not with all of the baggage trains and followers. There is high ground on both sides of that field, which allows for us to have as defensible a spot as theirs, and I have already sent two legions of the Ravens to claim our side of the field."

"Have they done that as well?"

"They have. And there has even been some communication between both sides."

"To what end?"

"A discussion of the rules of war. The issue of quarter, truces to remove the wounded from the field, rules for treatment of prisoners, and grants of protections for the civilians in the baggage and ambulance trains."

"Will they honor that?" asked the Witch-king. "Kagen slew the commander of the Firedrakes under a flag of truce."

"That has been discussed, and we have accepted—for convenience's sake—that it was a misunderstanding. Nonsense, of course, but it allowed us some leverage in terms of our negotiation."

"Tell me, Mari, will *we* honor that agreement?"

"That is up to Your Majesty's pleasure."

"No, high marshal, I leave it to you."

She nodded, expecting this. "I think I will," she said. "For as long as it serves our ends. And it has a useful effect."

"Which is?"

"It keeps them thinking that this is a straight fight. My strategy is to keep them focused on a battle fought according to the old way of thinking. Soldiers and knights, archers and pikemen, perhaps a siege engine or two. With the necessary truces at sundown and bugles to start the new day. All orderly. All according to the time-honored rules of *civilized* warfare."

The Witch-king chuckled softly. "Civilized warfare. Such an absurd concept."

"I've always found it both amusing and useful, sire."

He looked at her. "Now tell me the *other* reasons why you have agreed to fight the battle there."

"One reason is that it encourages them to think that this is a war like others they have known. Your own restraint in using magic since the Night of the Ravens helps sell this. And there is a comfort to believing there will be a stand-up battle with no *obvious* involvement of magic. At your request, sire, we've done little to prevent them from amassing their armies, and I agree that it serves our ends. The more of them on the field, and—more usefully—the more nations and resistance groups who participate, the greater will be the effect of an ultimate defeat on their part. We want to establish that we can defeat them in even combat, and that we have the greater reserve of Hastur's blessing and your magic to enforce our victory."

The king nodded.

"And," continued the lord high marshal, "a great field battle like this draws the eyes of the entire empire, my king. Their spies will be reporting the movements of our troops and the arrival of the various mercenary armies. That last part helps us because it suggests we are desperate and do not believe in our *own* ability to win in any contest of armies. The eyes of every nation, every person, will look toward the Field of Uthelian and expect the future to be decided on that frozen patch of land. In their comfort, they will reveal all of the ways in which they are soft. And you will be there to watch what happens when we change the rules of the game."

"Ah, my dear cousin," said the Witch-king, "that pleasure will belong to you. The field and that fighting are for you to shine. Jakob Ravensmere and his assistant historians are poised to write your chapter into the great story of this world."

Mari frowned. "You will *not* be there, sire?"

"No," said the Witch-king, and he told her why. Some, at least, of why.

It made her smile.

Beneath his veil, unseen by her, his smile was wider, richer, and filled with the delight that comes from knowing his own truth.

"The Witch-king has made his move," said Mother Frey. She was so thoroughly wrapped in blankets that she looked tiny and oddly like a child. "Reports are coming in from across the empire."

"The Hakkians tried to break us," said Frost. She sat in a large armchair. She wore a dressing gown of blue silk embroidered with summer flowers, and her maids had fixed her hair and deftly applied makeup, but it was artifice. Nearly every part of Lady Frost that was visible was wrapped in bandages. Her arm, which she had broken on the Night of the Ravens, was once more in a sling, though this time to keep her from tearing the forty-nine stitches that closed wounds from the vampire's nails. The ragged bite mark on her shoulder was heavily dressed and it gave her a somewhat hunchbacked appearance.

"They tried," echoed Frey. "But they did not succeed. Rather the reverse."

The house had been fortified since the attack. Three times per day every window and doorway was smeared with a paste made from garlic and wild rose. A group of fifty Unbladed had been engaged by Hop at Frey's direction, and they patrolled inside and out. The guards were also daubed with the paste, and if they did not like it, none of them complained. Not after hearing what a single vampire had done. They each carried spears made from dogwood and arrows of hawthorn.

"And what now?" asked Frost in a weak and timid voice. Her aura of personal power had been torn to pieces that night and rebuilding it was a slow process. Frey feared for her, and hoped the horrors of that night had not taken the heart from her friend and patron.

"The Witch-king forced us into open rebellion," observed Frey. "He has demanded war and now he will have it."

"It makes no sense," said Frost. "He doesn't have the troops to fight the entire empire."

"He has tens of thousands of mercenaries."

"Yet they will be fighting on foreign soil, on lands unknown to them, and with every hand raised against them. They will be ambushed at every crossroad and hedgerow."

"We are fighting a sorcerer, my dear," Frey reminded her. "He did not conquer the empire with swords alone."

"But he has not used magic since," countered Frost. "It's well-known that he spent a dangerous amount of his powers on the Night of the Ravens."

"To be sure, and it unsettled everyone," said the old nun. "But the Witch-king is subtle. I doubt there is anything he does without careful planning."

"What are you saying? That he will win?"

"I have no idea," said Frey wearily. She reached for a cup of water, moving by reflex, then hissed as pain shot through her. Frey closed her eyes for a moment, then tried it again, this time being slow and careful. She sipped, paused for breath, and sipped again. "We have done what we could, Helleda," she said after a while. "You and I and our friends in the cabal—we have done much. Perhaps our time in this game of kings and castles is over. Now it is up to the nobles and the surviving monarchs to wage war the best way they can. With armies and navies and force of arms."

"And what if the Witch-king takes to the field to fight them with magic? What hope will we have?"

"Then I think we must look to the Vales," said Mother Frey. "Kagen should be in Arras now and, gods willing, be sharing the Books of Hsan with Lady Maralina. And his brothers, Jheklan and Faulker, will have reached the Winterwilds, too. No, my dear friend, we are not without hope."

Hop Garkain sat in a chair outside of Mother Frey's bedroom. He could hear the conversation between the two women, but paid it little mind.

His own thoughts were elsewhere.

That morning he had buried his best friend. Although Brace could be a pedantic and officious bastard at times, Hop knew that a lot of it was artifice. Brace had once been part of a noble house in Samud, but his personal excesses in the forms of gambling, dueling, and womanizing had gotten him exiled. Not from the nation but from his family. They had refused to let him use the family name and the rebuke was so thorough that Brace had even changed his first name, adopting one that sounded more Nelfydian than Samudian. A wanderer's name. An Unbladed name. Once he had been sent away, his parents buried a stone in the family graveyard.

Now Brace was in an actual grave. Hop had considered having his birth name carved into the marble monument, but anger and resentment led him to cast that idea away. His blood kin rejected him. Hop knew him, not as Bracenghan ah-Fahr, but as Brace the Unbladed, and that was what the stonemason had carved.

> Here lies Brace the Unbladed
> Friend and Hero

Let anyone deny those words, he thought. *Let anyone say he did not die saving those two fine ladies and I will cleave them in twain and piss on their corpses.*

He had been injured in that fight, but it was Brace who saved Mother Frey. Helleda Frost, too. Brace had fought like a demon, even when he was mortally wounded and knew he must die. Brace never stopped fighting.

While he sat there, Hop used a small whetstone to slowly,

methodically, thoroughly sharpen the blade of his war axe. Other soldiers were detailed to guard the room, but they stood well back. If any of them thought ill of the burly mercenary for weeping as he worked, none of them dared speak it. And by keeping their silence they saved their own necks.

CHAPTER ONE HUNDRED FIFTEEN

When Kagen was alone, he removed the parchment from his shirt and set it on a small table. He wanted to read it again, but not yet.

Instead he dug into one of his saddlebags and retrieved the second note from Maralina. The one that was clearly much older. The one that had stabbed him through the heart. The one he had not shared with Filia and Tuke.

He read it again.

"Gods damn it," he breathed.

The contents of that note changed the shape of the world. It called so much into question while at the same time forcibly altering his insights into his family and into the Silver Empire itself.

"Damn you," he said to the names written on that page. "Damn you to everlasting hell."

CHAPTER ONE HUNDRED SIXTEEN

King al-Huk stood on the quarterdeck of the *Falcon's Claw,* hands clasped tightly behind his broad back. The ship plowed through the frigid waters of the Western Reach, heading for Tull Belain.

His spies had reported that a hundred Hakkian troop transports were being outfitted there, ready to load mercenary armies waiting on that island and several others. Other ships were being prepared to transport thousands of warhorses, and the pieces of siege engines which had been built away from the mainland, using rare hardwoods that grew on Belain. Whole forests had been cut down to make those weapons, as well as to reinforce the ships in case they needed to ram pursuing craft. In all, there were thirty-eight thousand foot and ten thousand light cavalry waiting to be taken to the coastal towns in Samud and Theria. All set for a counterattack once those nations marched their armies into Argon for the battle that would take place on the Field of Uthelian.

"Deck there!" cried the lookout up in the crow's nest. "Land ho!"

"Where away?" called back the sailing master.

"Three points on the starboard bow," came the reply. "I can just make out the old volcano."

The master looked up at the darkening sky.

"We won't make it before nightfall, Highness," he said.

The smile that curled al-Huk's lips was not a pleasant one.

"Night is fine," said the king. "They killed my son at night. It should be night when I kill their invasion fleet. Send the word— all ships prepare for battle."

"As your Majesty commands," said the master, and he turned to the signalman to hoist the command.

Strung out behind the *Falcon's Claw* was fully one third of the Samudian fleet. Three hundred warships, each of them crammed with archers and seasoned soldiers. And on the prow and poop of each were catapults, with shot garlands piled high with hollow balls filled with spiked caltrops. Barrels of pitch and burning torches suspended over water buckets were ready by each.

"What is your desire, sire?" asked the master. "What do we do if they surrender?"

The king gave him a fierce and terrible look. The glare of a father who had just buried his only child.

"There is no surrender," he said quietly. "There is no quarter.

They offered no mercy to my son and by the gods they will get none from me."

The master, who had been at sea for forty years and who had lost two brothers and a nephew on the Night of the Ravens, returned his king's smile with one of his own.

The *Falcon's Claw* sailed on into the dwindling sunlight as clouds tightened into dark fists above the island of Tull Belain.

━━━━━▶ **CHAPTER ONE HUNDRED SEVENTEEN**

The brothers Vale and their small party hurried through the dark corridors of frigid ice, following the last echoes of that awful scream.

As they hurried along through the cold darkness, Jheklan said, "Mother Frey said we were supposed to look for books of magic. Does anything we found qualify?"

"Oh it's far too early to tell that," said Alibaxter, puffing as he struggled to keep pace. "I would need days, if not weeks, of going through what we found to determine that."

"Which we don't have," said Faulker.

"Or," said Alibaxter, "we could skip that part and do what we're actually doing now—going to find the actual source of *all* magic."

No one replied to that.

As if to punctuate his comment, there was another animal sound that found them from one of the tunnels. Not a roar this time, or even a cry of pain. It was more like a sigh of weariness.

"Where did that come from?" cried Alibaxter as they slowed to a stop. Directly ahead was a small circle chamber with corridors leading off into six separate tunnels. "Which one do we take?"

They all pointed to five different tunnels, but there was one that no one indicated.

One by one, each of them lowered their arms. They looked first at Alibaxter, then each other, and then—with very great reluctance—they walked over to the sixth tunnel, the one no one picked, for that was where the animal stink was coming from.

"Damn," breathed Faulker.

Alibaxter nodded soberly. "It's this one for sure," he said. And with that he stepped into the tunnel, holding his torch high and forward as if that could shield him from every possible kind of harm.

Jheklan loosened his sword in its sheath for perhaps the dozenth time. "I'm no coward," he said. "No one could ever call me that. But . . . I don't want to go in there."

"Neither do I," said Faulker. He patted his brother's shoulder and walked past him, following Alibaxter.

The others followed, but they did not like it. Not at all.

CHAPTER ONE HUNDRED EIGHTEEN

The Witch-king stood alone amid a horde of monsters.

They dwarfed him and reared above him, with eyes that blazed with unholy fire and claws that tore the air. Tails whipped back and forth, their spikes sometimes striking the ground and gouging out chunks of stone. Their growls were deep-chested and mean-spirited, for there was no trace of compassion or mercy in them.

The king raised a hand and the largest of the monsters lunged forward, snapping its massive jaws inches from his yellow-gloved fingers. Each fang was as long as a child's forearm, and the saliva that dripped onto the paving stones sizzled, sending up curls of steam that stank of sulfur.

Then the great beast sniffed his hand. Its eyes sought those of the king, and he reached up with his other hand and removed his lace veil.

"See me," said the king. "*Know* me."

The beast dropped down onto all fours. And, though its tail

still whipped and thrashed and its eyes continued to blaze, it lowered its head until it touched the ground.

The Witch-king touched the creature's head, his fingers wandering through the network of horns and spikes and armored ridges. "I see you and I know you, my child," he said. "Soon you will be taken from my sight but not my seeing, nor my heart. You will go and do what the right hand of Hastur requires of you, and so earn your place of glory."

The other monsters seemed momentarily confused, but then the largest one uttered a sharp snarl of warning. Chastised, they lowered their heads to the ground as well. The Witch-king smiled and turned, walking among them. These were each different but alike in their alien natures. They were all three full generations away from the things they had been. Pure, in his eyes, for if they survived the war to breed, they would bring forth more of *their* kind. New species that had never troubled this world before. The Witch-king had made their forebears and imposed these breeds—and dozens of others—onto the fabric of this reality. He brutalized the natural world into accepting their reality. The tremors of violation rippled throughout the natural world and sent echoes into the larger world.

Which was what the Witch-king wanted.

And with his children, he was very well-pleased.

━━━━━━━▶ **CHAPTER ONE HUNDRED NINETEEN**

The Prince of Games was waiting for the Witch-king outside of the zoo. He had his arms folded and leaned against a wall, and he was once more wearing the brightly colored jester's clothes.

"Enjoying your pets?" he said, his smile as thin as a razor.

The king barely paused. "Are you incapable of making yourself useful?"

"I can be very useful," said the prince, pushing off the wall and falling into step. "In fact, I have been looking over Mad Mari's battle plans."

"Who said you could?" snapped the king.

"No one said I could not."

"You test me, prince."

"I hope to advise you how best to *win* this war, my lord. But I have some concerns. Would you like to hear them?"

They had reached a pair of doors. One led to a private stairway up to the king's library; the other gave access to a busy corridor that ran beside the great hall. Guards snapped to rigid attention outside of the king's door.

Pausing and only half turning, the Witch-king said, "If you have genuine concerns about the way in which my lord high marshal wages war on my behalf, then I suggest you share them with her."

"Ah, but Mad Mari is not in the palace at the moment."

"Yes," said the king. "I am aware of that."

At his nod, the guards opened the private door and closed it once the monarch in yellow had passed through.

The prince stood there in his jester's clothes, feeling very much like the joke was on him. And for once, he did not understand the punch line.

He turned and walked away, hands behind his back. Head lowered in thought.

CHAPTER ONE HUNDRED TWENTY

Ryssa watched as the army marched away.

They were not Hakkians—neither Ravens nor regulars—nor were they soldiers of the old Silver Empire. In truth she did not know for sure who they were, except that the flag they carried looked oddly like that of the banner of Ashghulan she had seen once in a book.

But that made no sense because Ashghulan was on the far side of the Cathedral Mountains and the Widow stood in a remote stretch of forest in southeastern Nehemite.

While they passed, she tried to count them. They walked five abreast and were in groups, each with twenty rows—what she thought was called a century. She had lost count of how many centuries there were, though. Too many. An astounding number. There had to be tens of thousands of soldiers, for it had taken hours for them to pass, and behind them scores of wagons and assorted camp followers on foot. The dust cloud sent up by all those feet and hooves and wheels turned the sky a dirty brown. She had needed to cover her mouth with her cloak to keep from coughing.

She lingered in the shadows of the hedge until they were well out of sight.

"You are going to war," she said in a voice that was half hers and half Miri's, though—oddly—not quite the Widow's. "But on whose side?"

Then Ryssa turned and walked back into the woods.

Before the soldiers had appeared, she had been scouring this part of the forest, looking for something, but she had no idea what. It was like that lately—she would turn this way or that, or go into a cave or along a gully, following a call that was not actually there. She was sure no one else could hear it even if someone had been right there with her. A call in her mind, yet without words and with few clues as to meaning, yet compelling.

This part of Nehemite reminded her of the large deer parks south of Argentium, where the nuns would sometimes take her and the other orphans to learn about nature firsthand rather than from books. Even before her thirteenth birthday, Ryssa could name every plant and flower, tree and mushroom. Sometimes her ability to do that surprised the nuns of the Garden, for it was clear that she knew things that none of the orphans had yet been taught. It was that inexplicable knowledge of the natural world that had drawn Miri and her together. The youngest of the nuns was like her—able to look at things in nature and know them without having been told. Some of the older nuns, and the Gardener who oversaw the orphanage, did not like that. No, not a bit. But what could they say? It wasn't like Ryssa and Miri were conjuring demons.

One of the oldest nuns said that it was proof that the Harvest Gods smiled with special favor on the two girls, and after that the rest of the Garden staff said nothing. There were odd and cautious looks, though.

Now all of those nuns, and the Gardener, too, were dead. And all the Gardens had been destroyed or desecrated.

Nature remained despite all that.

Nature endured.

The fact that it continued on while the Silver Empire died around it seemed to prove to Ryssa that it would always endure.

Or so she thought. When she met that mother hippopotamus and her dying calf, Ryssa's faith in that endurance had been very badly shaken.

The Witch-king was bending nature's rules, twisting them the way a torturer twists arms and legs to crack the bones. Not to kill, but to disfigure. With torture, of course, it was to punish and frighten and weaken. What the yellow king was doing had a different and equally ugly purpose—he was making monsters. Taking the innocent, corrupting it through some means—sorcery, alchemy, forced mixed breeding—and creating beasts of war. Like the hippo calf.

And like others.

Three times since finding that calf she had found animals that did not belong to nature's sacred plan. An eagle with a serpent's poisoned fangs instead of talons. In its despair it had slashed itself and lay dying, calling out with heart and mind for someone to come and witness its death, someone to see and know and understand that it did not want to be this new thing.

Then there was a yearling colt whose hide was covered in plates like an armadillo, but the armor was too thick and heavy, and its leg bones had grown badly, warped and twisted. She found it limping along, frequently dropping to its knees.

And last night there had been a bobcat whose body hair had grown into a nest of stinging fireworms. It huddled in the crotch of a tree, crying in the voice of a lost child.

In all three cases, Ryssa had found them and sat with them, holding them gently. The poison did not kill her, the scaly armor's spiky plates drew no blood from her skin, and the fireworms could not set her blood to burn.

When each of these tortured creatures realized that they were no threat to her, and that she brought no harm to them, they settled into stillness, their heads on her lap. She blessed them and sang to them and kissed them.

When they died, she wept and her tears fell on their ungainly bodies.

Even Ryssa was unaware that as she walked away from each, their bodies slowly—very slowly—changed, transforming back into what nature had meant for them to be. Had she known, there might have been more peace and less hatred in her broken heart.

Now she followed another silent call.

Down hills and through a meadow of tall winter-gray grass, and to a copse of pine trees. When she saw it, she stopped walking. Stopped breathing.

It was a man.

Had *been* a man.

Now it was less than half of one. From the heart upward it was a man. Below that its body was all wrong. It moved on four legs, and its body had the big barrel chest and muscular haunches of an elk. The legs were larger and thicker than they should be, and Ryssa understood the reason. The Witch-king had wanted it to bear the weight of the human torso as well as armor and weapons. A new kind of light cavalry—centaurs.

It sensed her and turned and she looked into its eyes. They were brown and large and filled with so many awful emotions. Shock and terror, but worse than that—a cruel self-awareness, a humiliation, embarrassment, utter defeat. And despair. Such bottomless despair.

It hated what it was, and more than that, it was horrified at a level no words could ever articulate. It was not animal or man, nor any sacred combination of the two. If centaurs existed in all the history of magic or in the larger world, they would have been carefully crafted by nature, blessed into life instead of dragged screaming into a nightmare aspect.

The centaur turned to her, took a single step, and then bowed his head, covering his face with human hands that trembled.

Ryssa walked over to him and stood inches away.

"I see you," she said.

The man's face looked up in suspicious shock.

"I," said Ryssa. "See. *You.*"

It took a while for it to understand, but then the truth of her words reached head and heart. The tears changed in meaning. There was relief beyond expressing, yet a deepening self-loathing. It simply could *not* endure being what it was.

"Help . . . me . . ." it said, forcing words out from a torso that lacked a human diaphragm.

Ryssa raised her hands, but it was the Widow who took that face in hers. It was the Widow who kissed his tear-streaked face. It was the Widow who whispered secrets in his ears. Telling him of the war, and how she was going to fight it.

Then the centaur lay down on the grass, and she sat with him. Stroking his face. Using her fingers to close his eyes, then kissing those eyes.

"You are beautiful," she said. "And you are true."

When the centaur died, his face was unmarked by grief and there was a smile upon his lips that was innocence in its purest form.

━━━━━━━━▶ **CHAPTER ONE HUNDRED TWENTY-ONE**

The Field of Uthelian.

"Kagen," said Filia, leaning head and shoulders into his tent. "Throw some proper clothes on. Nice ones. There's something you have to see."

Kagen was dressed in wool trousers, half boots, and a travel-worn leather jacket lined with fur. The weather had turned fiercely bitter and there had been snow for two days. He was drinking a mug of hot tea and studying the various tapestries he had brought back from the Tower of Sarsis.

"Who is it?" he asked.

She grinned. "Just come."

He sighed, looked around at his scant choices of clothing, saw nothing that would greatly improve his appearance, and opted for a simple turquoise wool cloak that he draped over his shoulders. He strapped on his knife belts, too.

Outside the cold was like a punch in the face, and he hissed, narrowed his eyes against the wind, leaned into it, and followed Filia, who was approaching a group of riders on horseback. All of them wore heavy traveling cloaks with their hoods up.

As he approached, the riders all dismounted and threw back the wings of their cloaks. He nearly missed a step as he saw the formal crests of eight of the most powerful families in Argon emblazoned on their doublets. These were men and women who owned vast tracts of land and who were the most important advisors to the late empress. People his father, Lord Khendrick, had held in the highest esteem and to whom even his mother had shown deference.

And yet they all lowered themselves to one knee and bowed their heads.

Kagen actually looked behind himself to see who they were bowing to. And Tuke, who was standing next to Filia, covertly smacked him on the back of the head.

"For the love of the gods," said Kagen, "please, get up. I should be kneeling to you."

The most powerful of these nobles, Lord Gowry, stood slowly. "My Lord Kagen Vale, captain-general of the free armies of the west," he said gravely. "We represent the one hundred oldest families of Argon, and we pledge to you our fealty, our support, and our hearts."

Kagen stood there in a stunned silence, absolutely unsure of what to say.

CHAPTER ONE HUNDRED TWENTY-TWO

"My lord," said Nespar, "it is confirmed. Theria, Samud, and Vahlycor have launched their fleets. Samud has attacked our shipyard on Tull Belain and it is a total loss. We lost all of our troop transports. Theria did the same on Tull Varen and Tull Seklos. And Vahlycorian coastal raiders are attacking our patrol ships. Although there is no formal declaration of war from any of them, their actions clearly demonstrate that they are at war with us."

The Witch-king stood looking out of a high window in a room of the palace. The various tables were covered with maps of the Silver Empire, each subordinate state, and various key locations where troops of all sides were gathering.

"I dare they are," mused the king. "It would be strange if they had not done these things."

The chamberlain came and stood near the king. That window looked out onto a courtyard where hooded wranglers were leading strange animals into a covered walkway that let out in a paved park where more than fifty covered wagons stood waiting. Several of the strange Hollow Monks stood down there watching this, their gray robes fluttering in a breeze that seemed to touch no one and nothing else.

As each animal passed, one of the monks would sprinkle it with liquid from an aspergillum and the others would speak prayers in a language that, to Nespar, sounded like it was designed to cause pain when any normal human spoke it. His friend, Jakob, said it was a variant of the language of R'lyeh. And when he had recited two lines of it, he had a nosebleed that lasted a whole day and left him spent and sick.

"If I may ask, sire," said Nespar tentatively, "will it please you to speak with the admirals of our fleets? They are gathered downstairs."

The Witch-king considered. "Have them wait in the map room. I will be with them soon. First, though . . ." He dug into a pocket of his robes and produced a sheet of paper, handing it to the chamberlain. "Have these people gather in the great hall in one hour. Arrange wagons and escort for them. They will be leaving soon."

"As you command, sire."

"First of all things, Nespar, summon the lord high marshal and have her wait on me alone in the hall in a quarter of an hour. Do all these things for me."

Nespar bowed and left.

The Witch-king lingered there, watching his beloved animals—his new beasts, as he called them—continue toward the wagons. The first conveyances had already left, heading under guard to key places throughout the central part of the empire.

Far beyond the realms of men.

Far beyond their world.

Deep into the endless dark of space, something stirred.

Unlike false gods, it never slept. It did not need to flee into the infinite worlds of unending dreams. Instead it paused now and then. Sometimes to witness the birth of a new star. Sometimes to fly from one ancient star to another, drinking in the warmth.

At other times it might perch on a rock on a nameless world and spend years watching the first living thing being born from the boiling mix of chemicals in a muddy pool.

Sometimes others of its kind were with the thing, and they sang songs as old as time itself. Or it flew alone in the absolute cold of the void between galaxies.

On that day, in that moment, it stirred because it heard a cry of pain. Distant. So distant. And very weak.

The thing turned its head and listened for more.

CHAPTER ONE HUNDRED TWENTY-FOUR

They met in a large tent in the heart of the camp at the far edge of the great Field of Uthelian.

When Kagen entered, everyone else shot to their feet and cheered him, crying out, *"Hail, Captain-General Kagen! Hail!"*

He very nearly turned and walked out.

Filia, anticipating this, placed a firm palm flat against his back. "Don't even think about it," she warned.

The cheering went on and on until Filia herded Kagen over to a chair placed at the head of a square made of a dozen tables. A huge version of the flag, with its daggers, the sword, the rose, and the dragon, hung from the tent's ceiling, falling behind Kagen's chair. Smaller versions of it lined the inside of the tent. And another was spread out across the center of the great table.

At a signal from Filia, the cheering stopped.

"Please, my lords and ladies," said Kagen awkwardly. "Sit. Please, sit."

Yet none did. Tuke, standing behind Kagen's chair, nudged it forward so hard that the seat struck the back of his knees, causing him to sit down very hard. Only then did the others sit.

Kagen turned and looked up at the big Therian, whose expression was that of total innocence.

"I hate you," whispered Kagen.

Tuke stifled a laugh.

Kagen looked around the room. There were faces he knew—lords of noble houses, some of whom he had visited; there were generals from Argon and others from across the west. There were chiefs among the Unbladed, including Redharn and Gi-Elless, who now wore badges of captaincy.

Filia introduced the strangers, many of whom represented the various nations. Most of these wore black sashes edged in green—marks of mourning for the murdered members of the royal houses.

Kagen felt intimidated by this gathering. There were old soldiers here who had fought in many wars on behalf of the Silver Empire. Seasoned soldiers who knew much more about practical warfare than he could ever know. And yet they looked to him.

The scar on Kagen's chest tingled and he wondered if someone here, or something near, had a connection to the larger world. But he saw nothing that spoke to this truth.

Finally, Kagen raised a hand of welcome. "My lords and ladies, generals and admirals, war chiefs and friends, thank you for coming here. Thank you for joining me in this, our first—and perhaps only—formal council of war."

The crowd broke into thunderous applause.

When it ebbed, Kagen said, "You call me 'captain-general,' and I will admit that I am uncomfortable with that. My experience in combat has never once taken me onto a true field of combat."

"And, if I may," said a weather-beaten general from Vahlycor, "none of us have walked through magic's doorway to fight the Witch-king in his own throne room."

Others called out different moments of Kagen's adventures over the last months. He felt himself flushing with embarrassment.

"None of us have been blessed by the faerie folk and the el-vinkind," said a woman's voice, and he turned and saw Selvath standing with a group of others a few feet behind the table. The seer was dressed in green velvet and had winter berries in her dark hair.

"Be that as it may," said Kagen gruffly. "I will accept the rank of captain-general until this war is over and not an hour longer. It is not who I am."

This earned him some chuckles, which he found strange.

"But if this is how it must be for us to proceed, then so be it."

"Hear him," cried Redharn. "Hear him."

The officers all rapped their knuckles on the tabletop.

Kagen took a moment to collect his thoughts. The truth was that after meeting with Frey, the nobles on his journey, and Filia at the roadside tavern, he had given quite a lot of thought to how the battle might be fought. And then more so since visiting the ruins of the Tower of Sarsis.

"It's clear that you know some of what I have experienced beginning with the Night of the Ravens. Tuke and Filia have no doubt explained what I saw, what I *believe* I saw, and what they encountered with me. You know that I believe the Witch-king is my brother, Herepath. He was a Gardener and mystic of great knowledge. But there is more to the story than his going to the

Winterwilds, becoming somehow corrupted by what he found there, and returning to take up the mantle of the Hakkian king of sorcery."

He looked around.

"There is more to that story, and I will tell you all of it now, for it speaks to the motivations for Herepath's descent into madness. He was betrayed by Empress Gessalyn. They were lovers and he got her with child. Once she admitted her pregnancy to Herepath, I think he wanted her to file for official divorce and marry him. I do not know this for certain, but I believe it. Instead, the empress rebuked him and then, to keep her secret, she sent him to the Winterwilds to die."

There were sharp gasps from the nobles, but no one interrupted him.

"Something happened to Herepath up there. He went mad. Perhaps in grief for her rebuke. Perhaps in outrage for what he perceived as a death sentence. Who knows? And, frankly, I don't much care. Herepath underwent a process of change. He knew full well that dragon blood and tears were the basis of magic, and so he embraced that. He took—perhaps stole—magical power from Fabeldyr."

"Fabeldyr . . . ?" queried a general. "I do not know that name."

Kagen explained about the last dragon. "It is my belief that the Silver Empire was born, in part, to keep secret the nature of dragons. There are many old stories about how the early knights of the empire hunted the dragons and slew them. We who grew up in the shadow of the Green Religion were taught that this was to protect humanity from the threat of these magical monsters. We were told that extinguishing magic was how best to serve our gods. Much of that was a lie. I did not know it before, but I believe it now."

"If I may ask, my lord," began one of the nobles, "what do you mean by that? And how came you to change your certain belief?"

Kagen nodded and reached into a pouch on his belt for a folded sheet of parchment.

"When I went to the Tower of Sarsis, among the things left for me by Lady Maralina were two notes."

Behind him, Tuke murmured, "Two . . . ?"

"I have shared the second note with no one but I will read it now," said Kagen. "It speaks of hidden things and there are hard truths in it. Some of you may not choose to believe the things written here. That is up to you. *I* believe them, however, because I do not believe that Lady Maralina would lie about such matters. She left me this note—a page from her diary—because she wanted to keep me from making war for the wrong reasons."

He looked around.

"Will you hear me?" he asked.

It took a while before everyone nodded their assent. There was fear in their eyes, as well there should be. He knew that fear would grow.

He read it anyway.

There is a new empire to trouble the world.

They call it the Silver Empire. Quaint. The last one was blue.

It was founded by one of the families in Mithlindel. One of that secret cult from which so many of the highborn families sprang. They are a plague on this world for they both love and fear magic. Proof that they understand too little of what magic is.

What I fear is their desire to contain magic, to reduce its potency and then steal that strength for their use alone.

The High Lady of Silver Hall chased sweet Fabeldyr from the west. The dragon found refuge in the Winterwilds, but the High Lady discovered this. She sent her chief sorcerers up there with many men-at-arms, all of them with weapons of iron. I

fear for Fabeldyr. I can hear her cries. What a shame that there
are none of her kind left on earth who can save her.

A darkness is falling across the world. Magic is going away.
In my mirror I see Fabeldyr in chains. The veils between the
worlds are closing. Magic itself is fading. I know that it cannot
truly vanish while Fabeldyr lives.

The new empire has banned magic. At the bidding of the
first empress they have hunted down sorcerers and witches
and mages. She has broken from Hakkia and forced them into
spiritual poverty by slaughtering the Witch-kings.

Woe to the world if the High Lady of Silver Hall learns
how to preserve enough of Fabeldyr's secrets—her blood, her
tears—and then kill the source of magic. When that day comes,
hell itself will be born anew on earth.

And yet, the people celebrate the rise of this new empire.
They think they have been saved. They have accepted the lies
that magic is evil. As if magic could be evil, or good for that
matter. Magic is magic.

In my tower I can do nothing but watch what unfolds
in my mirror and weave my tapestries and wait for the end
of days when magic will die except for the descendants of
Mithlindel.

I fear that Theselyanna, the first Silver Empress, may have
doomed us all. Only time will tell, and alas—immortal—I will
live to see the grace of magic die. Then I, too, will perish.

Kagen set the note down and looked around.

Not everyone understood the meaning of all this. Not at first.
But then he saw the horror, the sickness, the devastation blossom
like poisoned flowers on each face.

"I believe that *this* is what drove my brother mad," he said into
the crushing silence.

Hastur the Shepherd God slept his endless sleep.

He and his half brother, Cthulhu, had once strode across the beautiful blue world that was earth. They and their slaves, the shoggoths, played with the elements of life, shaping and reshaping them, then throwing their creations into conflict with one another.

They hunted the greatest of the dinosaurs and feasted on their flesh and on their marrow.

When man rose up from the animals, puny and hunched, barely able to stand upright, the Great Old Ones coaxed them, played with their nature and their form. It was a wonderful game. They made their toys play in the bloodiest way with one another. With the animals that hunted and those that fed.

Then the earliest, least articulate aspects of man learned to make war, and these half gods who had come to earth from the far side of the galaxy encouraged them. But, to their peril.

Man overthrew the Great Old Ones.

No one remembered that war, nor how the battle was won. Even Hastur and Cthulhu and their kin had long forgotten the cause of their doom. They fled. Not from that world, not in physical terms, but into the realms of dream. Those endless places where possibility and infinity were the same thing.

Cthulhu still slept in sunken R'lyeh, far beneath the waters off Tull Yammoth, and he did not want to wake. He had been half roused through prayer and sacrifice, but that was but a moment in a longer and more complex dream.

Hastur, though, he wanted to awaken.

He wanted to rise.

He wanted to live again.

Hastur, the yellow god.

Hastur, who was well-pleased with his avatar and priest on earth.

"Well," said Tuke under his breath, "by the unquestioned balls of the gods of certainty, that's done it."

Filia, standing beside him behind Kagen's chair, had her fists balled at her side and a lump of ice in her gut.

"He didn't tell us," she said, intending it for Tuke's ears alone. However, Kagen reached back a hand and patted her leg.

As the nobles all raged and roared and tried to talk over each other, he half turned and said, "I needed to think it through first."

"Damn you to hell, Kagen," she snarled. "You are a complete and utter bastard."

"I am already damned, Filia. You know that. You both do."

Then, rising to his feet, Kagen slammed the side of one fist down on the table and roared, *"Enough!"*

The room fell into a wretched silence.

"Some of you probably think I'm lying, or that Maralina was," he said tersely. "Some of you—maybe *most* of you think I'm mad—and maybe I am—but this is the truth as I know it. Hate me if you will, but either trust me to be the captain-general in truth, or shout me down and I'll gladly walk. But whatever you choose, damn well do it right now."

He stood there, his anger filling every part of the tent.

Clementius got slowly, shakily, to his feet. He looked around at his peers. "We are all in shock and, I daresay, in pain. But you, Tumnil, and you, Lady Quorth, you've heard some of these rumors, just as I have."

The two nobles looked everywhere but at him or Kagen.

Clementius looked much older than he had five minutes ago, and his face was beaded with sweat.

"All of us knew that there were ugly truths behind the façade of the Silver Empire. The treatment of the Hakkians, the cruel repression of their magic-based religion. The inquisitors who answered rumors about even small incidents of magic with arrest and brutal interrogations, and who made certain people disappear. As Empress Gessalyn made Herepath disappear. In public and in the Garden, we toed the line and shouted our loving support of the Silver Empire, but tell me now—and speak only from your hearts—when this war is over and if we win, do you want the Silver Empire rebuilt? Do you want to live once more in the shadow of lies?"

That was met with a heavy silence.

The old noble looked at the envoys from the various nations.

"And what of your rulers? My friend, Hannibus Greel—a man respected everywhere in the empire—told me that King al-Huk and the other monarchs voted to ally themselves with one another with an aim toward a *free* west. Independent nations. Actual freedom. Do you deny this?"

One of the envoys, a gray-eyed Samudian woman, stood up. "I was told not to discuss this until after a formal alliance was made." She tapped the table. "That alliance will be made here or it will never be made. My king looks into the future, beyond the war, and has told me that never again will he bend his knee to another."

A Therian man rose. He drew a dirk and laid it on the table. "I speak as the voice of Queen Theka," he said in a deep baritone. "Theria is a free nation, now and forever. She has charged me with saying so to Captain-General Kagen Vale. If he fights for freedom in the West, then we fight with him. If he does not, Theria will fight alone."

The other envoys stood, one at a time, some with great reluctance, and said the same. And each drew a dagger or dirk or sword and laid it on the table with the hilt facing Kagen's chair.

For a long while they and Kagen were the only ones at the table who stood.

Then Jorst Ulgin, one of the richest noblemen in all of Vahlycor, stood. "I have loved Empress Gessalyn as I love my own life. I am oath-bound to her and to the Silver Empire." He paused and Kagen could see that his words cost him dearly. "But both are dead and my oath is ended. I swear now, in the hearing of all, that I cast my fortune, my vassals, my estates, and all that I have for a free west. For a free Vahlycor. This I swear."

He turned to the head of the table.

"Your words—and those of Lady Maralina—have broken my heart and I feel that it will never mend. And that is just, for I, too, heard the rumors and the old stories and chose not to believe them." He paused and wiped tears from his eyes. Then he drew his longsword and considered the fine edge of the steel, a weapon that had served nine generations of his family. "There is blood on the ground between us, Kagen Vale. I will follow you to the gates of hell if it means my country's freedom."

He reversed the sword so that the jeweled handle pointed to Kagen, then placed it carefully on the table.

So, too, did every other person in that room.

Tuke and Filia were last of all to do this. And when Filia had made her oath, she bent and kissed Kagen on the cheek.

"You're still a bastard," she whispered.

CHAPTER ONE HUNDRED TWENTY-SEVEN

The Vale twins and Alibaxter knew they were close before they saw anything. It was not merely the stronger smell, but something *else*. Something indefinable.

It slowed their steps and then Jace leaned against a wall, shaking his head slowly.

"I feel sick," he said, his lips loose and rubbery.

Faulker ran a hand over his face and looked at the glistening sweat. "So do I."

"I think we all do," said a green-faced Alibaxter. He stopped and stood for a moment, head bowed in thought. Then he nodded to himself.

"What?" asked Faulker.

"At the risk of sounding metaphysical—"

"You're a wizard, metaphysics go with the beard and pointy hat," said Jheklan.

Alibaxter smiled at that. "I suppose it does. My point is that I do not believe we are sick. None of us. Not physically. But everyone, to one degree or another, has some degree of either sympathy or empathy. What I'm feeling is less in the way of illness and more of a spiritual disgust on a profound level. And, moreover, mixed with sadness."

They looked at him but no one spoke.

"We have spent months coming here, and all that time—whether we've spoken openly about it or not—we've thought about the dragon. Not just the wonder and astonishment of knowing there *is* one, but of her condition. Of what we have been told is being done to her. The chains and torture. Now we've also heard her screams and we can smell her. That stale and sickly stink of rot, of infection. Of imprisonment trapped in filth."

He glanced around at them.

"You are all experienced fighters, and are well-used to the brutality, pain, and horrors of that life. But this is different. It is not unlike what we might feel if we were to liberate a prison camp or dungeon where people have been penned and abused. Tell me, my friends, do any of you think that Fabeldyr is merely an animal? That she is without personality or wisdom or dignity?"

No one spoke, but some shook their heads.

"There it is, then. We are aware, on many levels, of her torment, and therefore the closer we are to witnessing, the more horror and disgust we feel. We have seen what the Hakkians have done to others—here and out in the world. That paints a picture in our mind of their depravity, of their *deliberate* lack of empathy. They are acting against their own humanity in their service to the Witchking." He paused. "But there's more. We are now all aware that the Silver Empresses are Heklans, or at least were before they broke from that legacy. All of us served the empire with our whole hearts, but now we need to weigh that against what the Hakkians have done. Yes, of course there is a thousand years since the empresses broke from Hakkia, but it's in the blood. And there is a very good—even irrefutable—chance that it was the Gardeners who first imprisoned Fabeldyr. The Hakkians haven't been coming up here long enough for them to carry all the blame."

He walked over to the tunnel where the scream had come from.

"I know for my own part that I am as sick about that as I am about what the Hakkians are doing right now. I feel the weight of that guilt. I feel the outrage of it."

Alibaxter turned back to face them.

"What remains for all of us now is to decide if we stand by the Silver Empire, right or wrong . . . or if we step outside of the shadow of old oaths and do what is right."

Faulker and Jheklan glanced at each other.

"You are a total pain in the ass," said Faulker. "You know that, right?"

"He knows," said Jheklan. "Just as he knows what it is we're all going to do."

They listened to the icy air and heard a lower, less strident—or perhaps much weaker—moan of agony.

They checked their weapons and gathered at the mouth of that tunnel.

Before they started, Alibaxter touched them each over the heart and spoke a blessing. Then they entered the tunnel.

CHAPTER ONE HUNDRED TWENTY-EIGHT

He looked out over the small sea of faces and was well-pleased.

"My friends," said the Witch-king, "war is upon us. We have all felt its winds blow across the whole of the west. This will be the great war of our time, and it will decide the course of the future for everyone living west of the Cathedral Mountains. It will decide whether the great god Hastur will bestow his blessings on us, or if paganism and heresy pollute the very air we breathe."

There was a wave of discontented and angry grumbling rippling through the group, and the Witch-king both allowed it and enjoyed it.

"I know where you stand, my brothers and sisters," he said. "I see into your hearts and know that you—yes, each of you—are true. I know that your worship of Hastur is built on more than faith . . . it is built on *knowing*. And as the avatar of the Shepherd God here on earth, I rejoice at this constancy and saintly dedication."

They bowed in their humility.

"Now I set a task for you. Those who are gathered in my hall—each and every one of you—will set forth this very day and journey north to the Field of Uthelian, there to meet with Lord High Marshal Mari Heklan, my cousin and the general of all our armies. She awaits you with great joy."

He let them digest this for a few moments.

"Our enemies gather like storm clouds. Armies from every nation of what was once the Silver Empire rally together to try and erase the belief of Hastur from this earth. It is their sworn desire to destroy Hakkia, slaughter its priests, tear down its churches, and enslave its people. Mari Heklan needs you to stand with her. She needs your insights, your counsel, your wisdom and—most important of all—your *power*. For you are all mighty, and the Shepherd God will stand with you in this, our hour of greatest need. Tell me, my children, my brothers and sisters, my friends, will you fight for the freedom of Hakkia? Will you show the infidels what real magic is? Will you prove once and for all what true *power* is? Will you do this for me? Will you do this for our God?"

Their response shook the great hall and their glad and ecstatic cries went on and on.

Jheklan went first.

He crept along the corridor, crouched low to stay in the shadows, avoiding the reflected light that glimmered from some unseen source. The color and movement suggested torchlight and soon he heard sounds. The clink of metal. Voices speaking though too far away to be heard.

When he wanted to, he could move like a professional thief. Both brothers could. It was something they had learned from friends who were in that trade, and it had served them well many times over the years—in endeavors both noble and less so.

At the bend in the corridor he peered around and saw that the passage ended only five yards farther. He flattened out and wormed his way to the opening and looked into a massive chamber. Massive stalactites and stalagmites combined to form pillars that upheld a ceiling so high it was little more than a shadowy rumor. The landscape was ice in uncountable shapes and sizes, from rough mounds of cracked ice that had fallen from the roof to hills and valleys of blue-white coldness.

The presence of humans was everywhere—there were platforms built of whalebone and wood, though Jheklan could not begin to imagine where all the wood had come from. At least a hundred torches were socketed into the walls, though only a handful currently burned. Stacks of wooden crates created alleys and even small rooms, and many of these rooms were filled with casks and stacks of objects as obscure and arcane as those littered all through the glacier's cave system.

And everywhere he looked he saw Hakkians. At least fifty; mostly men and a handful of women. They wore leather and furs and were busy filling one set of crates with bottled blood and the other with a clear liquid that he guessed were the dragon's tears. The Hakkians spoke amongst themselves, laughing and joking. As if this was normal. As if this was any other day in some kinder place.

The tunnel mouth in which he lay was at the top of a long set of stairs carved from the ice, and the position gave him a clear view of everything. Those stairs were broken, however, which explained why there was no recent activity in the tunnels through which his party had come. All that was left of the top part of the stairs was a narrow ledge of ice that vanished out of sight on either side of the tunnel mouth.

He saw a table on which was a series of deep tubs. One was filled with water, or something like it. The others had different items, but he was too far away to guess at what they were, though even from that distance Jheklan could smell an odor emanating from there. It was a strong, sulfurous stink that had the methane odor of pig shit. He realized that it was probably dragon dung.

On other tables were small iron braziers over which pots were suspended, their contents boiling steadily and issuing steam of the most disturbing kinds. Every once in a while, a Hakkian would scoop some out with a wooden ladle and pour it into the third trough. He worked with two other Hakkians as they prepared the various liquids and then poured them into canisters that were about a foot tall. They moved with extreme caution and very great delicacy. Once filled, those canisters were carried over and set into holes cut into the ice. Every part of that process was done with almost absurd care. It made no sense to him.

But he could not see the dragon herself.

Then the wall near where he lay shuddered as if something hugely heavy struck it.

With horror, Jheklan realized that the dragon was right there, right around the corner. It took more courage in that moment than in the whole of his life for Jheklan to inch forward and look around the edge and there it was.

There *she* was.

Fabeldyr.

He had expected something ten times the mass of an elephant, and set about with gleaming scales of green and yellow, and wings like the god of all bats. And, to a degree, those things were there. Not the scale, though, for the monster was perhaps the size of only two elephants. It was obvious her scales had once been a lustrous green—for there were still hints of that—but they were faded, coated with a sickly rime of yellow and pink frost. It stood on legs that seemed too frail to support its mass, and then he saw that it was held upright by chains with links as thick as his fore-arm. Manacles of rusted iron were locked around its limbs, and its leathery wings—torn and ragged—were spread wide and pinned to the ice wall by heavy metal spikes. A thick band of steel encircled the great beast's snout, trapping its massive jaws shut. All of the dragon's claws were gone, leaving only raw and festering sockets in the pads of its feet. And everywhere, covering nearly every inch of the creature's body, limbs, and face, were scars. Old and new. Marks—*proof*—of comprehensive and generational torture.

Her head drooped and her eyes were closed in sleep that looked as deep as death itself.

Then he saw something that changed this view.

A group of three Hakkians were climbing up onto a pipe-and-board scaffold. One held a wooden bucket, the second held an iron rod whose end glowed bright yellow from having sat in a brazier of hot coals; and the third a kind of oddly shaped funnel. As they approached the dragon suddenly woke and recoiled from them as far as the chains and wall allowed. But the man with the glowing brand tapped her mouth with it. The dragon groaned in pain—the same kind of weary sound he'd heard before—and opened her mouth. Saliva dripped from her fangs and the roof of her mouth, and the man with the funnel placed it to catch the liquid, directing it into the bucket held by the third.

The process had the unhurried pace of something done a thousand times. And there were many overlapping burns all around the dragon's mouth. Jheklan watched this until the men were done and the bucket three-quarters full. Then they turned away, climbed down, and took the bucket to the table with the troughs. With great care, the man poured the spittle into the first trough.

So, thought Jheklan, *the stories were wrong. The Hakkians have use for blood, tears, and saliva. Shit, too. But why?*

The dragon wheezed slowly, weakly, slumped against the resistance of the chains, and it struck Jheklan to the center of his heart that immortality had its darkest and most sickening qualities. For Fabeldyr had to witness all of that murder and live on and on knowing that one day her bones, too, would be tossed upon that pile.

Jheklan had never hated anyone as much as he hated these Hakkians, and worse still the madman who had sent them here. Biting down on that rage lest he shout it out, Jheklan crawled backward from the edge, rose to his feet, and ran back to the others.

With each step his mind burned with the image of that huge, magnificent, ancient creature reduced to a wretched hulk that knew only the abuse that filled every moment of her life.

CHAPTER ONE HUNDRED THIRTY

"You may fire when ready," said King al-Huk.

The sailing master nodded to one of his mates, who ran forward to where a crew of sailors waited. The catapult was cranked back and the ropes tightened so that they creaked and groaned, as if they yearned to be let loose. Two men hoisted a ball into the iron cup. They wore gloves up to the biceps to keep the pitch off their skin. Each round weighed fifty pounds, and they rattled with the many-spiked caltrops within. There was more pitch inside, and the ball was soaked in it.

As soon as it was seated, they backed well out of range. The captain of the catapult team waved on the torchman, who lit his brand, approached the side of the device, and touched the flame to the heavy metal ball. It blazed with hellish orange light. Then the captain kicked the lever release. The ropes twanged and the hurling arm whipped up and forward, sending the fiery ball high into the night sky. It scratched across the ceiling of the sky and arced down to the row of transports snugged into finger piers. They all had their yards crossed and sails tied up.

The ball struck the fore-topgallant mast of the third ship and burst apart. The flames ignited the pitch within and the impact scattered the burning caltrops. Like a swarm of blazing wasps, they struck, the spikes digging into masts and spars, reefed sails and the hulls of the ships on either side. And many of the spikes struck Hakkian sailors.

Everything caught fire.

It was winter and everything was dry. The tar on the rigging and the paint on the hulls ignited. Within seconds the transport was fully engulfed. The crew screamed and ran, many jumping over the rails onto the dock or into the water. Both ships that flanked it caught fire as spikes struck their yardarms.

The captains of the other ships—many of whom were on land, in taverns, or brothels, or their own homes—came running, screaming for their sailors to cut their cables and fend off.

But the sky above them was filled with more of the flaming balls hurled by King al-Huk's hundreds of warships.

It was as if hell itself had risen from the ocean to spew death to the fleet.

Aboard the *Falcon's Claw*, the grieving king watched his enemies burn.

"There they go," said the miller's wife.

She and her particular friend, the town healer, stood at a second-floor window, the sash down and shutters half-open. They both wore woolen shawls embroidered with patterns of forest scenes. The miller's wife wore one with the bright greens of spring; the healer wore one with the rich golds and reds and yellows of autumn. Neither wore them much in public because they were too obviously inspired by the Green Religion. But the upstairs room faced north and the sun was in the southeast.

"Aye," said the healer. "All the young men and women marching to war."

"My nephew's down there. See him? Hard to miss with all that red hair."

The healer nodded. "And may the blessings of Father Ar and Mother Sah go with him."

All along the street men and women were coming out of their houses and falling into line with the others. The procession was led by Lord Quillin, whose family had become fabulously wealthy as fabric merchants and now owned a mansion on the hill outside of town. Behind the lord were his knights—sixty of them in full armor and riding magnificent horses. These were followed by fully a thousand men and women from lesser houses riding farm horses and cart horses and anything with two pairs of legs. One ambitious lad rode to war on the back of a donkey.

Once they had all trotted past, then came the volunteers, most in ordinary clothes with scant armor and often as many farm tools as formal weapons. But they marched proudly, heads held high.

"And not a Hakkian in sight," observed the healer.

"Nor will you find a one," replied the miller's wife. "I heard from the poulterer's lass that they arrested the Hakkians stationed in the town hall. Bagged all twenty of them, though one or two may have been knocked on the head. The rest are in jail, and I doubt they'll like what's served to them for their supper. Spit and dung, if they're lucky. Ground glass if they're not."

The healer glanced at her friend and felt her heart sink. The miller's wife had been her closest friend these forty years and more, and had always been a gentle soul. But with the coming of the Ravens and what they did to the Gardeners, she had watched her friend grow colder and hard. So hard.

Aloud, the healer said, "I pray to the gods for the safe return of those brave young men and women."

"And death to the Witch-king and all Hakkian scum," added the miller's wife with real venom.

"Yes," said the healer absently. "Yes, that, too . . ."

CHAPTER ONE HUNDRED THIRTY-TWO

They huddled together in the shadows. Jheklan used the tip of a small knife to etch a rough map of what he could see of the cave.

"There are a lot of those pricks down there, though," said Jheklan. "We need to distract the Hakkians so we can free the dragon."

Jace glanced at him. "So, we've decided that freeing the dragon is our plan? Not killing it?"

Jheklan turned a reptilian glare on him. "Why? Do you want to kill it?"

But Jace shook his head. "No I do not. Even before you described what they did to the thing, I was thinking that we should set it free. I just wanted to make sure we're all thinking the same thing."

"Yes, we damn well are," said Faulker between clenched teeth.

The others nodded. None even hesitated.

"Good," said Jheklan.

"What happens when we do that?" asked il-Vul. "I mean, if we can. If we're not cut to pieces by all those Hakkians?"

"The one advantage we have," said Jheklan, "is that most of the Hakkians weren't armed. I saw a place in one corner where they have their swords, spears, axes, and bows stacked. There was only one fellow standing guard over them. And three other soldiers with spears keeping watch overall, though not what I'd call *attentively*. Bored sentries are poor sentries, as my mother used to say."

"Okay, but then what?" pursued the Samudian. "Will the dragon try to eat us if we set her free? Or, worse, what if setting her free doesn't work?"

"How could it not work?" asked Lehrman.

"Think about it," said il-Vul. "What I'm saying is that the thing has been chained up for a long time. If it's really the last dragon, like Mother Frey told you, then it's been in chains for something like a thousand years. It won't even be able to walk. Once the chains are off, its own weight might crush its bones. We could kill it by freeing it."

It was a very real concern and the full weight of it landed heavily on their shoulders.

Then they all noticed Jheklan was smiling.

Faulker narrowed his eyes. "Oh, brother-mine, you have that look you have when you have a plan."

"I think I do."

"Let's hope it's better than the Kelters Wells debacle."

"Will you stop with that, damn it?" said Jheklan testily. "That was your fault, brother. You showed up drunk and with no trousers."

"Well I'm sober as a saint now."

"Good, because you're going to sneak down there and destroy their weapons."

"I am? *How?*"

"They're using oil lanterns instead of fire," said Jheklan. "I saw a barrel of oil, clearly marked so even you should find it. Get down there, secure some oil, douse the weapons, and on my signal set them alight."

"Just like that? Easy as kiss my hand?"

Jheklan studied him. "How many times have I heard you brag that you're the stealthiest of us? You bragged to the eldest daughter of that Nehemitian diamond merchant that had you not been so devout a son of the Harvest Gods that you would have made a master thief."

"I was saying that because I was trying to get laid."

"Are you saying you *aren't* skillful and sly?"

Faulker grinned. "You're such a prick sometimes."

"Oh it's just the deep faith I have in you, dear brother."

"And a devious prick, at that."

Jheklan said, "Now listen close, lads, for this is what I have in mind."

━━━━━▶ **CHAPTER ONE HUNDRED THIRTY-THREE**

They met at a crossroads in northern Argon.

The warlords of three mercenary armies, riding with aides and guards well ahead of their forces, met with Lord High Marshal Mari Heklan. Four folding chairs—all richly appointed—were placed in the precise center of the crossroads. Beside each was a table for hot mulled wine on the right and a small brazier of burning coals to their left. At Mari's nod they all sat at the same time, doing it precisely to allow no deference.

"We are well met, my friends," said the marshal.

To her right was Unka the Spider, war chief of the Free Wanderers, a storied private army whose forces came from lands directly east of the Cathedral Mountains, though Unka was from Gefhelm. To Mari's left was Elslee, known as the WarBride of Alya-ta, a blocky woman with a flat face and a terrible scar that ran from one side of her face to the other, bisecting her nose. She had one milky eye but the other was as black and bright as polished obsidian. Seated directly across from Mari was a giant of a man dressed in the fur of snow leopards and with a heavy red-gold beard. He was Lord Morn from far Skayan.

"You have traveled far to fight alongside the warriors of Hakkia," said Mari. "And to raise swords in the service of the Witch-king and his god, Hastur the Shepherd."

"We have come to fight for gold," said Unka flatly.

"And land," added Lord Morn, "for we were promised that."

"We fight for our own gods," sneered WarBride. "We pray to no others."

Mad Mari nodded. "We do not ask you to worship Hastur," she said. "But the lands west of the Cathedrals are his domain. Respect is owed."

"Respect you have," said Lord Morn. "But I, for one, bend my knee to no one. Not god, man, or witch."

The others grunted agreement.

The marshal's smile did not falter. "We have enough people willing to bend the knee, my friends. Had I wanted to meet with more of them I could walk into any town in the west and demand it. No, what I need are swords and spears and fighters who do not fear to swim in oceans of blood. And for that, gold will be yours, and more than ten wagons could pull. Land will be given that is rich with fertile soil. And on those lands you may build any church you choose, so long as you do not spit on Hastur's shadow."

The three mercenary warlords looked at each other. They nodded.

"Tell us," said Unka, "where they are whom you want us to kill."

"Close, my friends," said the marshal. "The Field of Uthelian is less than a day's march. My own troops are massing there now. The enemy has begun setting up their camp across the field. All neat and tidy, all according to the rules of *civilized* warfare."

WarBride and Unka both spat on the ground. Mari, smiling, spat, too.

"War is not civilized," growled Lord Morn.

"We are not civilized," she said. "And we will show them the true meaning of war."

CHAPTER ONE HUNDRED THIRTY-FOUR

The line of covered wagons moved along the roads of Argon with hundreds of soldiers to guard them. Uthelian was close, and signs were posted assuring all that safe travel was granted to the place of battle. The signs carried both the eclipse of Hakkia and the new symbol of Kagen Vale's army.

The drivers of the wagons laughed at the signs, which was fair enough. When Argonian nobles and their legions passed the same spot ten hours before, they, too, had laughed.

Each wagon was heavily draped, and the drawings covered with sigils and symbols from the language of Hastur and the Great Old Ones. The guards had each been tattooed on face and body so that they did not grow sick or go mad from seeing those symbols. They wore talismans soaked in blood and sulfur and asphodel to protect them when they had to feed the beasts.

The few peasants who chanced to be near the road when the wagons passed were not protected in any way. One, a bean farmer who had been a deacon in the local Garden before the Ravens came, reeled away and vomited lice and ticks onto the grass when he beheld those symbols. When his friends found him later that day, his body was a husk, devoured from the inside out.

A girl of nine was in a tree with her dolls when the wagons rolled past. She watched them, counting their number because she had recently learned to count. Before she reached twenty her eyes went blind, and she lost her grip on the branch. Her body aged into corruption within an hour, and she was never found.

All along that road, the last flowers of winter, the hardiest ones that could endure the cold—pansies and daffodils and hellebores—withered, too. Their petals fell like tears as the carts rolled past.

Even the birds of the air felt the wrongness of the wagon train. Those flying ahead of any flock died and fell from the air, while the others veered off in alarm and sought the safety of pine trees where they could not see the wagons, nor be seen by what crouched within.

Only one single bird watched them and endured it.

He was an old crow—ancient beyond the counting of his days— and he sat upon the limb of a winter-bare oak tree as the wagons passed. His black eyes missed nothing and witnessed every horror, every appalling twist of the natural world that moved along the road.

When the wagon train had vanished into the confusion of a snow squall in the north, he fell like a dead thing from the limb, but flapped his wings inches from the road. Then he flew low and fast toward a crossroads and when he reached it, the crow took the path less often traveled.

CHAPTER ONE HUNDRED THIRTY-FIVE

Ghelluger Vilx was a comprehensively disappointed man.

When he had enlisted with the Hakkian army, having grown up on a farm near the border of Ghenrey, he was bored and poor and wanted adventure and fortune. The recruiting sergeant had promised exactly that, and Vilx made his mark, received his five silver dimes laid out on a drumhead, and broke the news to his family. They smiled through their pain, hugged him, and watched him walk off toward the other recruits waiting in a patient line on the road.

That had been six years ago.

After training, he had been assigned to guard a grain warehouse in Chively, then he guarded an officers' barracks at a fort way over by Ghul. After that he spent a whole year walking the perimeter of an outpost down south on the border of the Waste, where absolutely nothing of interest happened at all. And a year ago Lord Nespar had sent him as part of a detachment all the way to the Winterwilds where, in the unending cold, he stood guard over a pile of weapons and food stores, in a cavern of ice, near an ancient fucking dragon whose shit smelled like sulfur.

Vilx hated his life. Even the dragon had only been interesting for a few days. It did naught except roar, moan, groan, sigh, and shit. The only good part of all that was that, as a guard, he was not required to shovel dragon shit. That task was assigned to one of the two prisoners left over from the group of Gardeners. They shoveled shit, they washed clothes, they served food, they were made to kneel and recite prayers and praises to the Witch-king, and every now and then the big sergeant, Bullor, dragged one of them into a tent and had his way with them. Bullor did not care that the last prisoners were male because he had already used the last of the women, and when she cut her own throat rather than allow herself to be violated one more time, Bullor pissed on her corpse and had her friends drag her body outside to let the snow apes feast on her.

It was an awful place to be, but even with Bullor's foulness and the atrocities inflicted on the Gardeners—something that Vilx himself played no part in—he became bored. He had long since catalogued all of the different flavors and varieties of boredom. The only thing that gave him even a flicker of hope was that this operation up here was coming to an end. Or that's what the rumors contended.

The crates of blood and tears were nearly all packed, and they would soon be moved out of the glacier and onto ice-schooners that were on their way to what used to be the Silver Empire. He did not know what would happen to the old bitch dragon. He wondered if they would kill her, reckoning that the blood and tears they'd harvested would last for centuries. Or, maybe they'd let her rest so that they could start it all up again once she was healed.

That's what the Gardeners had done. When they first found the dragon, she was deep in some kind of sleep. The first party of scholars had sent for chains to be fashioned and brought up, and the dragon was still asleep when she was shackled. Vilx wondered if she had slept through the process of having her wings pinned. He didn't know, and there weren't many more details of all that. It had happened more than a thousand years ago.

Now it was just a job. The dragon was asleep most of the time, except when they cut her for blood and burned her to make her weep. Vilx did not particularly enjoy that. He was not a cruel man. But because it broke up the monotony, he looked forward to it in a strange, distracted way he chose not to examine too closely.

He paced for a while by the stacked weapons. Ten paces one way and ten the other for an hour, then stood for an hour. That was his rhythm. No one bothered to check. The other soldiers— more important than he ever was or would be—ignored him as thoroughly as they ignored the ice walls.

Vilx finished another round of pacing and walked around behind one of the stands of spears that were arranged like corn sheaves, loosened his codpiece, and pissed into a hole his urine had been tunneling for weeks now.

He never heard the footfalls of the man who came up behind him.

His first awareness of trouble was when a hand clamped over his mouth, but before he could even react to that, a blade slipped between his ribs and found his heart. He died right there and then. No real pain. Only a momentary surprise and vague disappointment. Then nothing at all.

Faulker lowered the guard's body to the ice floor, stripped off his fur-lined cloak, and handed it to Jace, who put it on. He handed the helmet and spear, too, and Jace took up his station by the weapons. He even began pacing very slowly, the same way the guard did, affecting the regularity of the bored sentry.

Faulker, il-Vul, and Lehrman began to quickly and quietly remove the weapons from the crate. But then Faulker signaled them to stop and pointed to a long row of small canisters against a nearby wall. Each canister was set into round holes that had been carefully cut into the ice just as Jheklan had described. But what his brother hadn't been able to see from his vantage point was the Hakkian word for *caution* hand-painted on each. There were at least five hundred of the canisters in the ice near at hand.

He looked at the tables where the three Hakkians were carefully—very carefully, indeed—filling more. And suddenly Faulker's eyes widened slowly as he realized what he was seeing.

It was a secret hidden from the world for many centuries. A mystery that scholars of war endlessly debated. Something that everyone had thought was lost to time.

Until the Night of the Ravens.

And now he understood what it was and the fiercely guarded secret for its creation.

"Gods of the fiery Pit," he breathed.

It was *banefire*.

CHAPTER ONE HUNDRED THIRTY-SIX

Tuke and Filia walked into Kagen's tent and found him seated at a table upon which maps were spread.

"Oh, good," said Kagen. "I know you're both busy, but I wanted to go over some things."

Filia took a bottle of wine from atop a chest, considered the label, nodded, and uncorked it.

"The first legions are ready to march," said Tuke. "Do you want to watch them go?"

"In a minute," said Kagen. He accepted a glass from Filia and waved his friends to chairs. "Listen, I did not want to say this in front of all the nobles and generals. Not after that bit of theater at the end."

Filia cocked an eyebrow. "Theater? They swore their lives and fortunes to you."

"And I appreciate it, but let's face it, it could have been done with far less drama."

Tuke laughed. "You are the worst politician in history."

Kagen shook his head. "I'm not a politician."

"Yes, yes, and you're not a general, either."

"In name only."

"My point, brother," said Tuke, "is that it matters to *them* that they make their oaths in public. The first ones to have done it will be in the better songs. But their declarations will be recorded in the history books waiting to be written."

Kagen merely grunted.

"And it will matter to the people who follow them," added Filia.

"And I appreciate the symbolism of all of that. Don't think me ungrateful."

"Even though you *sound* ungrateful?" mused Tuke.

"As you pointed out, I am a lousy politician," Kagen said. "I'm sure the historians who write their books will ascribe some glorious and inspiring speech to me. And I suspect the two of you will have some hand in writing it."

Tuke spread his hands. "Anything is possible."

"Well, I've been thinking about the best way to use the gifts

Maralina left for me, and I have a plan that none of those nobles or generals will like."

"Will *we* like it?" asked Filia.

Kagen smiled. "Oh, I doubt it very much."

"To clarify," said Tuke suspiciously, "will we like it more than when you talked us into going through a magic tapestry into the great palace?"

"There is a very good chance," said Kagen, "you'll like it a lot less."

And he told them.

He was completely correct in his assessment. They hated his idea.

━━━━▶ CHAPTER ONE HUNDRED THIRTY-SEVEN

Faulker huddled with Lehrman and il-Vul and told them about the banefire.

"It's made from dragon spit?" gasped Lehrman.

"And dragon shit?" said il-Vul.

"And other stuff," said Faulker, "but yes. Come on, think it through. You have to remember when the sewers under Povelia blew up five or so years ago? It was gas released from all that human and animal shit. Something about it burns. Well, they've got plenty of dragon shit, and even a man with no nose could smell the sulfur and other gasses in it."

"But the spit . . . ?"

Faulker shrugged. "Fabeldyr is a fire-breathing dragon, after all. So, there has to be something in her to *cause* that fire. Look, it doesn't much matter right now. Ask Alibaxter if we can get out of this. We need to destroy those weapons and help Jheklan and Jace with what they have planned. And we need to find a fast way out of here."

"Wait," said il-Vul, pointing. "Looks to me like they are nearly done packing things up. See there? They are bringing in sleds."

The presence of the sleds was interesting to Faulker. It was clear no such conveyances had been brought in the same way he and his companions had. There had to be a way directly out of the chamber, one the Hakkians used regularly.

"Keep watching the sleds, boys," he said quietly. "We need to find that exit before we start making things interesting."

The answer to that came more quickly than they expected. One Hakkian, clearly an officer, began shouting for men to take two fully loaded sleds outside. Faulker and the others edged around the tables of weapons to see where he was pointing. What had at first appeared to be nothing more than a cluster of stalagmites in what Faulker judged was the southeast corner, proved to have a path running between the pillars of ice. He crabbed sideways, keeping well-hidden behind stacks of crates and barrels, until he had a better view. The corridor was poorly lit, but there was definitely a glimmer of light that proved it was a path.

"Perfect," murmured Faulker.

He glanced at the open mouth of the corridor where his crew had come, but there was no sign of anyone. That was fine, though. Jheklan was very cautious and crafty, and besides, his brother was waiting for a signal.

Faulker had an excellent idea as to what kind of signal he could send. Something unmistakable. He took a light hold of il-Vul's jacket and pulled him close.

"Are you as good a shot as everyone thinks?"

"I'm Samudian," was il-Vul's answer, and Faulker nodded.

To Lehrman he said, "I'm a pretty good shot, too. So you be ready to throw."

"Throw what?"

Faulker told him, adding, "And both of you stay well clear of the table of weapons."

They nodded and moved off to take their positions.

As Faulker unslung his bow, he felt eyes on him and spun.

There was no one behind him, however. The feeling of being seen persisted and he scanned the huge chamber looking for a sentry. No cry of alarm had been raised, though. He frowned, wondering if it was an unseen Jheklan trying their familiar telepathy of sustained stares to draw his attention.

No Jheklan.

Then, with a shock and a shiver that turned every drop of blood in his veins to ice water he heard a soft growl and he realized that the dragon's eyes were open and looking directly at him.

He could *feel* the raw power of that gaze. There was no mistake. She was totally aware of him, and—he thought—she knew he was equally aware of her scrutiny.

The connection was a thousand times more potent than when he beheld the newborn creature who broke free from the ice. It was the strongest single moment of shared awareness in all his life. Even stronger than what the family called the "telepathy" he and Jheklan seemed to possess. Far stronger. It was so potent a thing that he felt humbled by it, but not dwindled as he had been on the Frozen Sea. This was different than anything in his life experience.

The dragon was *seeing* him. Knowing him on a level that laid him bare, and it stripped away his humor and artifice, his affectation and all of his natural defenses. It was a knowing that ran far deeper than the shared understanding he had with Jheklan.

It made him want to weep, but not for fear.

When she looked at him there was a mutual knowing. And also a sharing. Images and knowledge seemed to flood into him, filling his mind with things he could not have otherwise known. It hit him like an avalanche and all he could do was accept it. See it. Understand it as best he could.

Faulker saw this dragon as she had been ages ago. Immensely powerful. Filled with vitality and unmarked by generations of deliberate cruelty. In those few seconds he saw her grace and nobility, her empathy and her understanding.

It also spoke to her trust, which had been as innocent as that of the newborn creature in the ice. When she had met travelers and mystics from history's yesterdays, she had been willing to share her gifts. With them and with the world. She, and the others of her kind, had brought magic to the earth as a gift. They seeded this and many worlds with infinite potential and whispered secrets to them for how to build bridges between the world of humans and the infinite realms of the larger world. And with worlds beyond those that circled the only sun Faulker knew. Hers was a star-spanning race that had come into this universe at the moment of its birth. Born of fire, they were the first life.

The first life in the universe.

Her kin traveled through star systems and galaxies and structures that humans had no name for. Billions upon billions of years of life. There elvinkind and faerie folk and merpeople and other races knew of them and honored them.

The first humans had worshipped them as gods, but they were not that. They existed long before the concept of godhood was first imagined. They were the family of possibilities, and they touched all living things with the gift of intention, of co-creative thought so that the birds of the trees and the fish of the seas and the creatures of the forest could impose their desires on the evolving world.

But the dragons had flaws, they had limitations.

They did not understand the concept of covetousness. They had no concept of treachery and malice and greed.

It was humans who taught it to them.

Humans, who embraced fear and lived according to its precepts, discovered that there was one thing that even the mighty dragons were powerless against.

Iron.

The echo of this fear was present in hundreds of legends Faulker had learned. Iron was used against evil witches and the older vampires of legend. It was used against demons and sprites.

Iron was the bane of magic itself.

And it was men with iron weapons who began slaughtering the dragons. Many—*many*—of Fabeldyr's kinfolk were killed easily because of their simple trust. They did not tremble when men approached with swords and spears and iron chains, for they did not understand that men could possess malevolence in their hearts. It was not even a thought, a theory, a concept in the minds of the dragons. Perhaps those dragons who went to live on other worlds in the infinity of the universe, but not on earth, and Fabeldyr only knew what the earth-dwelling dragons knew.

So the dragons died.

Those who were forced to learn such horrible truths tried to hide, to flee, to reason. They did not even fight back, for they were not warlike. Only Vathnya, god-king of all dragons held such understanding, but he had only touched the face of earth once, when he brought his children to settle on this world. But Vathnya was so very far away and the dying dragons of earth had not called out to him in time. Now they were all gone, save one. Fabeldyr tried to utter that plea, to scream that cry for her god, but by then it was far too late. By then she was in chains, and the iron weakened her powers and stifled her voice. Now she was too weak. Now she was dying.

Faulker understood that the Hakkians, having robbed her of everything, were going to kill her and keep all of the secrets of magic for themselves. For the Witch-king. That insight further chilled him, for it brought understanding. The thousands of bottles of Fabeldyr's tears and the gallons upon gallons of her blood would give the King in Yellow limitless power. And once the dragon herself was dead, all of the wild magic that existed because her heart still beat, would fade. The innocent beasts, like the one in the ice, would die. The veils between worlds would seal themselves shut forever.

The only magic that would survive her death would reside with he who had her blood and tears.

That was how the world would end. That was how the Witch-king would conquer all. If he wanted to, he could use those treasures to wage war on the realms of the larger world, denying them their magicks, and enslaving them all.

All of this filled Faulker's mind in the space of seconds. It beat him down to the ground and nearly killed him. The weight of this knowledge, of these crimes, was crushing. Fabeldyr had looked into his heart and mind and shared unbearable truths with him.

Unbearable.

Horrible.

Truths.

Worse still was a simple phrase, a plea whispered into his mind.

Do not let me die in chains.

He lay on the ice floor and wept silent tears. The sobs that wracked him hurt his muscles and bones and, a thousand times more acutely, his heart and soul.

Do not let me die in chains.

"No," he said very softly. "I damn well will not."

CHAPTER ONE HUNDRED THIRTY-EIGHT

"By the ironclad balls of the god of audacity," breathed Tuke. "You are completely out of your gods-damned mind."

"You're a suicidal idiot," growled Filia.

Kagen sipped his wine and let them yell. They did so, for quite a while. When a sentry stepped halfway through the tent's opening to ask if there was a problem, Tuke and Filia yelled at him, too.

Kagen said, "It's okay, Durss. Flee now while you can still save yourself."

The guard retreated.

Filia stomped over and got in Kagen's face. "We are on the eve of war. Half of our people are already setting up camp on the Field of Uthelian. The Hakkians are marching there as we speak. And you want to *leave*?"

"Leave for a while," said Kagen. "And I need you to help me."

"Be damned to that," swore Tuke. "I think I'll call Durss back in here and have him help me wrestle you to the ground so we can bind you until you come to your senses."

"Listen to me, both of you," said Kagen, his patience wearing thin. "My plan is a sound one. You don't like it because you're not going and because it's—"

"Stupid?" suggested Filia. "Suicidally unsound?"

"Weird," said Kagen.

Tuke pointed an accusing finger at him. "Twice now you've gone to the Tower of Sarsis and both times you came back weird. Weird-*er*, I mean."

"Times are weird. Magic has—"

"Mother Sah help me," snapped Filia, "but if you say 'magic has returned to the world' I will cut your throat and let Horse chew your bones."

"It's true, though, whether you like it or not. And we would be fools not to try and use it to our benefit. Or do you forget how close magic got us to killing the Witch-king? Had it not been for magic, we would now be citizens of the Yellow Empire. Our entire mission to Vespia was to find weapons of magic." He paused and managed a small smile. "I know that you both want me to play the role of general, but I keep telling you that it's not who I am. I'm a fighter. A knife fighter, to be precise. I am at my best when it's me, my blades, and room to move. We *have* generals who understand the best way to position and move our troops. Gods, you saw what a cock-up I made with the Firedrakes."

"We won that fight," Filia pointed out.

"That's hardly the point. The plan I just explained to you two is one that plays to my strengths. It plays to what I have learned from Frey, from Maralina, and from my mother. I am best when I am free to move where I want, and to attack without any formalities. That's who I am."

"But . . ." began Tuke.

"I know you'll each have a dozen good reasons why I shouldn't go. And I trust your wisdom, but my mind is made up. Hell, I would have already gone except that I was waiting for something."

"For what?" Filia demanded.

"To say goodbye, my friends," said Kagen. "Not to be poetic, but we are flotsam in the river of time."

"Not poetic at all," said Tuke.

"True, though I am committed to doing this. You two have to run the war," Kagen said.

"The hell you say," protested Tuke.

Kagen held up a hand. "Hear me out. With all that is about to happen, there is little chance we three will ever meet again. It breaks my heart to say it, but I am a realist. War is upon us. It will sweep through our lives, and the lives of everyone. When its waters recede, the world that is left will be different from anything we've known. All of us have already buried people we know and love. It may be that each of us falls, and if—in doing so—we can preserve the best of the old world and help the world to come to be a better one, then we'll have lived good lives. I have made peace with my own death, and I will go about my mission with a clear heart and no fear of the grave. I am damned already, and I do not care for redemption. Every part of who I am is committed to killing the Witch-king. I will likely die trying. Nor do I care what history books will say of me except this—I was rich in my family and in my friends. I love you both and if there is a world beyond this one, I will look for you there. If not, then let us part as friends."

Filia looked like she wanted to hit him. Instead, she pulled him into a ferocious hug. Tuke wrapped his arms around them both.

"You bastard," he said. "You beautiful, mad bastard."

Kagen disentangled himself. "Now . . . will you help me?"

"How can we help?" asked Filia quietly.

"Can you spare Redharn and Gi-Elless and six others? Biter, Borz, Giffer, Pergun, Hoth, and Urri."

"That's everyone who came out of Vespia with us," said Tuke. "Why them?"

"Three reasons," said Kagen. He ticked them off on his fingers. "They've stared magic in the face and held their ground. They're among the toughest sons of bitches I've ever met. And . . . the real truth is, the war can't spare you two. General Filia and General Tuke, hereby and irrevocably appointed."

Despite the tears in her eyes, Filia burst out laughing. Tuke tried to keep a straight face, but then the laughs bubbled out of him, too, deep and booming. And Kagen laughed, too.

Outside the tent, Durss smiled and shook his head. If the captain-general and his two top aides could laugh like that, then either the world itself was mad, or—just maybe—there was some small hope.

―――――――――► **CHAPTER ONE HUNDRED THIRTY-NINE**

"I thought that razor-knight thing would have come to help us by now," said Desalyn. She was not pouting, as she often would while pretending to be Foscor.

Her brother merely nodded. He was too depressed and frightened to say much.

They were in Lady Kestral's room, having taken the secret way. They checked to make sure the door was securely locked, then they sat on the floor near the circle of protection. Before there had been a swirling pillar of wind in which a demon had been trapped. Now the mingled sand and salt surrounded what appeared to be an empty few square yards of bare stone floor.

"Maybe it died," said Alleyn after a while.

"It can't *be* killed," insisted his sister.

"Captain Kagen killed one."

"Oh. Right."

They sat and looked at the empty circle.

And all the while a pair of eyes watched them from a crack in the wall. A spy hole they sometimes used and thought no one else knew anything about.

The eyes that watched them swirled with colors—greens and browns and flashes of red.

CHAPTER ONE HUNDRED FORTY

Faulker Vale rose slowly from the floor.

Every part of him exploded with pain. He felt an impossible weariness. His skin shrieked from cuts and burns. His muscles ached with atrophy and deadly weakness. His heart labored in his chest. Then, with shocking clarity, he realized that he was feeling what *Fabeldyr* felt. Her burns, her scars old and new. Her dying body.

That pain tried to own him but rage had already conquered him and it would not yield its place to any kind of weakness.

He turned to where il-Vul and Lehrman waited for him. There was confusion on their faces and Faulker realized that he had been on the ground for far too long. Five of the sleds were already gone, and a sixth was being pushed toward the exit.

With a sneer of hate on his face, he drew a line across his throat. It was not the agreed signal but it was eloquent enough.

The two Bloody Bastards nodded. They even grinned before ducking out of sight.

A moment later an object flew high over the stacks of crates. It was a good throw and a graceful arc. Faulker had his bow up, an arrow on the string, his hands as steady as they had ever been. One Hakkian—the officer—looked up as the thing passed directly overhead.

And Faulker shot it.

His arrow struck the canister square in the center.

And the banefire exploded.

The Hakkian officer simply ceased to exist. The two men nearby who were pushing an empty sled in place to be loaded vanished in a ball of incredible red-gold flame. The sled flew to pieces, sending splinters of wood and shards of metal in a thousand directions. The sound of the explosion was louder than summer thunder.

The Hakkians stared at the scorched space where three men and a sled had been, and there was nothing left of them but burning chunks that fell in a slow rain to the icy floor.

Then one of them saw Lehrman running away from the weapons table.

"Ware! Ware!" yelled the soldier. *"We are attacked!"*

All of the Hakkians stopped what they were doing and ran to fetch their weapons.

Maybe those running fastest did not see the canister sitting atop the table. Or maybe they were too deeply committed to their rush that they did not have time to fully understand what it was. What it *meant*.

Then il-Vul's arrow whistled past them and struck the banefire when the leading Hakkians were less than one step away from their swords and spears.

Faulker dove for the ground as the cavern shook as if a giant's fist had punched downward. Stacks of crates toppled, spilling blood and tears onto the ice, but no one paid attention to this as the force of the blast turned the Hakkian weapons into a hornet's swarm of death. The whole front rank of the enemy crumpled, their bodies slashed to red rags even as they burned.

High above him, Jheklan crawled along a narrow ledge that separated the corridor and the dragon. He had a cold chisel thrust through his belt and a heavy mallet in hand.

With each blast he was shoved against the wall, but he forced himself to relax so that his own muscular tension did not make him rebound and fall. Alibaxter, who was climbing out when the banefire blew, was knocked back into the corridor.

Jheklan balanced himself on that precious ledge, fitted the chisel into the cuff on Fabeldyr's left arm, and swung the mallet. The iron was thick and the chisel bounced off the bolt and he nearly dropped both his tools.

He took a breath and tried again. This time he anticipated the shock and could feel the sharp steel bite into the iron.

He hit again and again.

Hitting the head of the chisel with precise blows.

Below him, Jace crept out of hiding with a second mallet and his own chisel. He set to work on the manacles on the dragon's feet. Jheklan saw him pause, frowning at something, and when he leaned out to look, Jheklan saw that there was a second set of shackles attached to the wall beside the dragon, however, they were scaled for human wrists and ankles and currently empty. He felt a small twinge at the sight of them, but could not grasp why, or what they meant. So he returned to the urgent work at hand.

He and Jace worked with the fury of demons.

Faulker shuffled sideways as he fired arrow after arrow, this time at a Hakkian who was snatching up torches and lighting them from a lantern he smashed onto the ground. The torch and some knives were the only weapons the Hakkians had, but that was still too much for Faulker. Even unarmed, the enemy had a great advantage in numbers.

His arrow took the man in the throat, and he fell. The torch rolled away against another stack of crates.

The rest of the Hakkians were caught in that bubble of fatal confusion. Lehrman was hurling banefire canisters and il-Vul was blowing them apart, which made the Hakkians want to flee—but to where? The exit was the best option, but they were dressed for manual labor in an ice cave, not for survival out in the bitter cold. They also needed to protect the tears, blood, and banefire for their king, and failure was certain death.

Their only possible option was to fight.

They scattered and snatched up any tools they could find—axes, shovels, crowbars, even iron bar stock and slats of wood. Many hid behind the precious bottles, believing that would save them. Surely the enemy would not want to destroy such precious things. Surely the enemy had come to steal those things for their war against the Witch-king.

Faulker and il-Vul disabused them of this belief by striking canisters wherever Lehrman threw them fast and with terrifying accuracy. He aimed for any place where two or more Hakkians took refuge.

Jheklan and Jace worked like madmen.

No one was looking at them because no one had seen them. Faulker and the other lads were keeping the fight to the far side of the cavern.

Alibaxter knelt at the open mouth of the corridor, his clothes in disarray and his beard singed from flying bits of flaming debris. Nevertheless, he had a crowbar in his hands. He used it as a brace to stand, and then took a daring first step onto the ledge.

Jheklan saw him and understood at once what the young wizard was up to. He shifted himself closer to Fabeldyr, allowing Alibaxter room. The wizard reached the first of the iron spikes that pinned the dragon's left wing to the wall.

"I hope this does not cause you more pain," he said, his words clear in a brief gap between explosions. Then he dug the split-claw of the bar around the pin, braced his feet, and with a great grunt of effort threw his weight against it.

The spike groaned in protest . . . but it moved.

Faulker fired two arrows at the approaching Hakkians, hitting a man in the stomach and a woman in the eye socket, dropping both so that the soldiers behind them tripped. Then Lehrman tossed another canister and il-Vul shot it as it dropped to about head height.

The blast scattered the enemy and splashed blood onto all the crates and the sleds of bottles.

Suddenly there were new shouts and Faulker wheeled to see the Hakkians who had taken the first batch of sleds outside come pouring into the cavern. They had ice-axes and snow shovels, and they swarmed toward il-Vul. The Samudian retreated, firing constantly, but he was running out of room, and there was no clear space for Lehrman to toss another canister.

The archer took three of them before the others dragged il-Vul to the cold floor and cut him to pieces.

Enraged, Lehrman hurled canister after canister at them, and Faulker fired as fast as he could. The angle was bad, and he only struck the third, but that was enough. Il-Vul, master archer of Samud, went to the realm of Father Dagon and Mother Hydra with the men who had killed him.

Lehrman had no choice but to run, though in the confusion he lost sight of where Faulker was. He snatched up several canisters, tucking them under one arm while trying to scare the Hakkians back with one he held over his head.

Faulker kept trying to get a shot, but had no good angle. There were stacks of crates in the way and Lehrman kept moving. He had an idea, but without Lehrman it was useless. The other option was one that felt exceptionally—suicidally—dangerous, which was to shoot the canisters where they were, slotted into the holes cut in the ice. But they were so close to one another. To destroy one would almost certainly mean blowing the whole glacier half-way to the moon.

If Faulker had been alone, he would have chosen that option. But Jheklan was there, fighting to free the tortured dragon. Leh-rman and Alibaxter and Jace were there, each of them fighting with courage despite the certainty that they could not win this fight. The moment of surprise had passed and now only numbers would win out. The desperate gambit cracked under its own weight, leaving all of them at the mercy of the Hakkians.

And so, he cupped his hands around his mouth and yelled to Lehrman.

"To me!" he cried. "To me."

Lehrman, his arm back to throw another canister, looked mo-mentarily puzzled.

"To me, damn your eyes. To *me!*"

Lehrman threw the canister, but he pivoted as he did so. It sailed over the knot of Hakkians, all of whom scattered. Faulker rose up and snatched the jar of banefire from the air. In a move as smooth as if he had practiced it ten thousand times, he tossed the canister underhand, brought up his bow, drew an ar-row with the hand that had just released the banefire, nocked, pulled, and fired. And then he leapt backward against a stack of crates that immediately toppled and crashed down around him and on him.

He did not see the blast.

He felt it for one second, and then the force of the blast knocked even more crates down on him. Squashing him, driving the air from his lungs, pinning him, and snuffing out all light.

Desalyn said, "Do you remember how we helped Lady Kestral create the razor-knight?"

Alleyn turned and looked at her. "Of course I do. Why?"

They both sat on the floor now, each on opposite sides of the circle of protection.

"It's just that—if that one died somehow, or somebody killed it . . ." She trailed off, her meaning clear enough. Alleyn's eyes went wide.

"You want us to try and summon a *new* one?" He gasped.

"Maybe."

"You're crazy."

"Everything's crazy," countered Desalyn.

"No, I mean we'd get it wrong and then where would we be? Maybe we'd accidentally make one that would just kill us or eat us all up or something bad like that."

Desalyn gave him a look that made her look a lot older than her six years. It scared Alleyn.

"We're probably going to die anyway," she said.

"No! Captain Kagen will come back to save us."

"No," she said. "He won't. I think maybe he's already dead."

"What? Why would you say something like that?"

"Because it's been so long and he hasn't come back. He's either dead or he hates us. I mean . . . after what we did."

They both remembered everything Gavran and Foscor ever did, including the awful rebuke of Kagen's claims that they were the children of the empress. Even spitting in his face.

They sat there, burdened by the weight of it. Neither wept, though. They had cried themselves out too many times. And, besides, eyes that looked red from crying would betray that they weren't the Witch-king's children after all.

"Then what *can* we do?" pleaded Desalyn in a wretched little voice.

Jheklan heard the blast but did not look. He was too busy swinging the mallet.

He and Jace worked like madmen. Alibaxter, too.

The tough steel blades of the chisels bit deeper and deeper still into the ancient iron. The pins and shackles had been well made, forged by a master of that art, designed to restrain the mass and physical power of a dragon.

Jheklan cursed as he hammered.

He prayed to his gods, naming each member of the Harvest pantheon with each blow. One strike was for Father Ar, the sower of seeds and the bringer of life. Another was for Mother Sah, the bearer of life and the angel of death that returned each thing to the soil to participate in regrowth and new life. Another was for Geth, the prince of pestilence and famine, and another was for Lady Siya, goddess of learning, scholarship, and skepticism. He struck for Vunis, demon of the forge who crafted the farming tools for the gods, and for Puyinsol, god of rain. He struck for Bewyn, goddess of the sun and her sister Luryssa of the moon.

His muscles ached from the heavy blows. Lances of pain shot through his wrists and up his arms. His back hurt abominably for having to maintain his balance there on the ledge while striking such powerful blows. Despite the relentless cold, sweat ran into his eyes and mingled with his tears, stinging him with salt, blinding him.

Yet he labored.

When the first bolt parted, he lost balance and fell against the arm of the dragon. How he managed to keep hold of the chisel and mallet was beyond knowing. The dragon's scales were cold, almost dead, and that made him feel death's icy breath on the back of his neck.

He realized with a shock that he could not reach the beast's other arm. And so he shoved his tools through his belt, braced himself, and whispered an apology to the dragon as if what he was about to do was a transgression, a violation. Then he reached out and caught a scale on her chest, stepped out with a foot onto the ridge of another scale, and pulled himself away from the ledge.

The huge creature was breathing shallowly, and it pushed him outward as she inhaled. He clung to her for balance, and as he waited for her exhale, he heard something. In truth he *felt* it more than heard it. A deep *thump-thump*.

The heartbeat of a dragon.

It made him want to weep like a child.

For wonder that this was all real. For horror that the heartbeat was faint and irregular. The pulse of something very near death.

"Please," he begged. "No. By all that is holy, no."

She inhaled, drawing him close again and Jheklan reached for another scale. And another. Clinging to the chest of the dragon as he made his slow and agonizing way over to the other arm.

Pain ignited in his chest and stomach and he looked down to see that the edges of those scales were razor sharp, and they sliced through leather and wool and flesh. Deep as sword slashes, erupting blood that ran down inside his clothes and left a red smear across the dragon's body.

Jheklan bit down on his pain. If the dragon could endure pain for centuries, then he could bear it for moments. Even if what he was doing would kill him.

"*No,*" he sobbed.

Below him, Jace was still hammering away, the blows ringing like cracked bells. Somewhere else—Jheklan could not tell—Alibaxter was groaning and gasping as he fought with the spikes driven so deeply into the wall.

By the time Jheklan reached the far side of Fabeldyr and stepped onto another section of ledge, he was bleeding heavily. His whole body trembled with fatigue and blood loss and shock.

And yet he took his tools from his belt, fumbled the chisel into place on the thick pin between the arms of the shackles, raised the hammer, and struck.

He struck again and again, losing more of what little strength he had left with each blow.

If this is my end, he thought, making it a challenge and a prayer, *then by all the gods and graces I will see this beautiful monster free. On my life and on my soul, I swear this, and let this be my oath. As a man of this world, I accept the guilt for what has been done to you, Fabeldyr. There is blood on the ground between us.*

The cavern—lit by the weak flames of lanterns and sudden starbursts as the banefire exploded behind him—was growing strangely dark.

Jheklan knew he was dying.

That should have filled him with despair.

Instead, he began to laugh as he swung the mallet over and over and over again.

When the pin broke and the shackle fell away, Jheklan was only dimly aware of it.

The chisel dropped from fingers that were swollen and numb from the incessant shocks. His mallet dropped heavily to the ice, bounced once, and skittered away.

He fell, too.

He leaned outward, backward, downward.

And Jheklan Vale dropped from the high ledge down and down . . .

CHAPTER ONE HUNDRED FORTY-THREE

"Well, damn me twice," said Kagen as he looked at the seven Unbladed who stood before him. "You are a right bunch of bloody bastards, aren't you?"

"In point of fact," said Redharn.

She and the others were dressed for winter, and their fur coats were crisscrossed with leather belts from which hung an improbable number of weapons. Axes, knives, spears, swords, bows, and quivers crammed with arrows. Each of them had a rolled tapestry wrapped in cloth and slung slantwise across their backs.

"I've explained it all," said Kagen. He smiled. "Do I even have to ask if you're ready for this?"

"Are we going to stand here like we're on parade," asked Red-harn, "or are we going to be about it?"

Kagen took his bottle of *eitr* from a table and slid it into a leather pouch.

"Let's go have some fun, shall we?"

Durss, the sentry outside, heard laughter but then it stopped abruptly. He leaned sideways and peeked in through the slit in the tent flap, blinked, leaned head and shoulders in, then finally stepped into the tent.

It was completely empty.

CHAPTER ONE HUNDRED FORTY-FOUR

It was a long journey, but Ryssa did not mind.

Walking was good. It gave her time to think. It gave her time to go inside her head and heart and speak with Miri.

And it gave her time to meet the animals in the forest.

Before Queen Theka set her down on the mainland, Ryssa thought that this strange connection she had with the natural world was confined to the creatures who swam beneath the waves. That seemed to be in keeping, given that those abilities were born during the ceremony to rouse the dreaming god, Cthulhu.

Yet it was not the case. Every animal she met—beast or bird or bug—seemed to understand her. They knew that she meant them no harm, and—much more importantly—that it was her wish to stand between them *and* harm.

As she walked through fields and forests, she heard the birds gossiping about her, and it was a delight—a rare pleasure these days—that she could understand them. It was not like translating a language in her head. Not at all. They did not speak in that kind of language. However, meaning was conveyed and understood, and that understanding was in her mind, too.

It was beautiful.

By the time she reached the Field of Uthelian, there were animals following her. She had not asked them to, but they did anyway. Many of them, large and small. They came by secret ways, staying away from people. They spoke to one another in the way that animals can. But there was more to it now, for the lion and the rhinoceros and the hummingbird and the recluse spider could understand the language of the others.

Ryssa did not question this. It was magic.

She was magic now, too. Or, at least, its vessel. For the real magic was the Widow. Even Miri was only a ghost.

The Widow was magic.

The Widow had traveled all this way to see what a war in a world where magic flourished would be like. And what her role, if any, would be in that war.

CHAPTER ONE HUNDRED FORTY-FIVE

Alibaxter saw Jheklan fall.

Jace did not. He was on his knees beside the shattered remains of the last ankle cuff. His hands, blistered and bleeding, lay palm-upward on his thighs. His head was bowed and he wept with weariness and the enormity of what they were all doing.

Across the cavern, Lehrman lay dead, his body smashed by shovels and pierced by axes. Faulker was in a tomb made from a dozen heavy crates, and a small river of blood ran out along the sloping floor, finding other streams of red until they emptied into the lake of gore that covered much of the cavern floor.

A score of Hakkians stood, their bloody tools in their hands and one by one they turned away from the men they had killed and from their own fallen comrades, to see the wizard clinging to the wall.

"There's one more of the sons of bitches," growled one of them, pointing with his bloody spade.

Beside him, one of the others saw a bow and a handful of arrows laying near the corpse of a Samudian. He snatched it up, fitted an arrow to the string, and fired. The range was less than thirty yards, and the arrow flew straight and true. The barbed point struck hard and deep into the lower back of the young wizard.

In the silence, his cry of pain was crystal clear. The crowbar dropped from Alibaxter's hands. He leaned back and, making no attempt to catch himself, fell.

Down and down.

He struck the knee of the dragon's left leg and the impact drove the arrow the rest of the way through the wizard's body so completely that as Alibaxter tumbled the rest of the way, friction tore it all the way out. The entry and exit wounds poured blood as he rolled and thudded down next to where Jace knelt.

The Argonian cried out, grabbed the young wizard, and pulled him to safety behind the titanic bulk of Fabeldyr. Several more arrows chased them. Two struck the ice, one chunked deep into the dragon's leg, right above the red and festering band where the shackle had eroded the scales down to raw meat.

Jace tore Alibaxter's cloak off and wound it around the young man's waist to stanch the wounds.

"Am I dead . . . ?" asked Alibaxter dazedly.

"Hold on, mate," soothed Jace. "Just hold on."

Alibaxter looked up at the dragon. "I . . . I'm sorry . . ." he whispered. Then his eyelids fluttered and closed.

Fabeldyr stirred feebly. She looked at her wrists as if she did not understand what they were. Her left wing was free but hung slack, pinned to the wall by her shoulder. There was one more spike through her right wing, and for the moment that was all that held her up.

"Hurry, lads," yelled the senior-most of the surviving Hakkians. "That big bitch is nearly free. Grab fresh pins. Someone fetch some hot iron. Move, damn you, *move.*"

They ran for the chest of supplies that had been kept at hand since the ancients first chained this creature. They pulled out new pins and hammers and ran toward the dragon. As they rounded her bulk, they saw Jace, once more on his knees, holding an utterly slack Alibaxter against him.

"Here's for you, you bastard," snarled a Hakkian as he grabbed Jace by the hair, yanked his head back and cut his throat with a small knife. Then he spit into the Argonian's upturned face and kicked him away. Jace landed on Fabeldyr's foot, his dying heart pumping blood on her mangled toes.

Alibaxter sprawled onto the ice floor.

"What about him?" asked another Hakkian.

"Look at the poor sod," said the man with the knife. "He's already dead."

The men with the shackles moved into place and began clamping the cuff around Fabeldyr's legs.

"Hold her," cried the leader. "She's moving. Damn it, I said watch! She's—"

Fabeldyr's right arm swung down, heavy, nearly limp, but still powerful and swatted the leader. The blow picked him off the ground and hurled him halfway across the chamber. He struck a wall and his body burst apart, spraying blood and splinters of bone.

Immediately, two men with hot irons jabbed her in the stomach. The stink of burning meat rose sharply and it tore a howl of pain from the dragon.

"Pin the shackles," yelled one man. "Pin them or we're dead."

They tried. They were fast and efficient. They were trained for this. The dragon was in unbearable pain, some of it from those raw and ragged spots where the iron cuffs had been. Some from the fresh burns. Hakkians hammered at her with shovels and poles, beating her back against the wall.

But Fabeldyr was awake now.

With the iron gone from her limbs, she was more awake than she had been in more than a thousand years. Her mind pulled itself from the dream state into which she had retreated. Her yellow-green eyes, though milky with disease, cleared. She inhaled, taking the scent of blood and death. And fear.

She tried to move, but her limbs were so weak, the muscles atrophied. Fresh pain exploded within her and it tore cries from her. The men beat her and stabbed her and burned her. Her right shoulder would not move and when she turned her head, Fabeldyr saw that one remaining spike. It was driven through tendon and cartilage and leather, pinning the wing solidly to the ice, as it had for ages.

"Burn the bitch," cried the Hakkians who were fumbling with the shackles. "For the love of Hastur, *burn her!*"

With a savage wrench, the dragon threw all her bulk against it, summoning what little power she had left. There was a screech of metal and the sharper crack of breaking ice, and then the wing tore free. Blood sprayed the wall and the pain was dreadful.

But Fabeldyr, the last dragon of earth, was free.

The Hakkians yelled in terror as they fought to restore her bondage.

An arrow whipped across the cavern and struck one of the shacklers in the back. He pitched forward, striking his head on the dragon's shin. The others turned to see a trembling, bloody man with a scraggly beard, torn clothes, and a bow in his hands.

"Leave her be, you fucking bastards," cried Faulker, as he fired again.

And again.

Killing Hakkians. Hurting some.

Then he reached for another arrow and found nothing.

Emboldened, the Hakkians regrouped. Ten of them turned back to their work with chains and shackles. The four remaining soldiers gripped their shovels and began stalking toward Faulker. They even smiled at the thought of how they would repay this fool for the damage that had been done. Their comrades lay dead, most torn apart by banefire. They yelled at Faulker, telling him the things they were going to do to him.

Faulker dropped the bow and dragged out his sword. He could barely stand, but there was no choice left but to try and take as many of them as he could before they tore him down. He looked around and saw Alibaxter and Jace.

And Jheklan.

All of them were bloody and lay in awful stillness.

Fear of death turned to hatred and he stumbled forward, needing to kill.

Needing to avenge.

Needing to . . .

Fabeldyr's eyes suddenly blazed with a furnace-bright light. Brighter than the sun at noon on any summer's day. Brighter than the heart of a bonfire.

She looked at him.

She looked down at the dead men around her feet. At the Hakkians and at Jheklan and the others. At the men who were struggling to put her back into bondage.

She looked at the rows upon rows of her own blood. And her tears.

With a monstrous bellow of pain and outrage, she crouched down and belched a torrent of fire at the Hakkians. They saw it and turned to run.

The fire caught them.

It enveloped them, a thousand times hotter than the banefire. In an instant they were nothing but twisting, withering, melting, dying, screaming grotesqueries. They lost even their imitation of humanity as the fire burned them down to blackened bones and then ash.

And then nothing at all.

None of that flame touched Faulker, though the heat of it drove him back. Not one spark fell upon Alibaxter, or Jace, or Jheklan.

She recoiled, her flame cutting off at once, and Fabeldyr crouched, trembling, staring at the place of her torment.

Then she reared up and with the last of her strength, she uttered a roar that soared upward to the ceiling. The force of it atomized the ice—miles of it—rising up and up in clouds of steam. Stalactites fell and the walls cracked and that cry punched through the night sky and into the clouds and out of the skin of gasses that covered the earth. The cry tore through the endless and eternal blackness of space. It ripped through the veils between all worlds. It went on and on until, in the inky depths of eternity, it was *heard*.

CHAPTER ONE HUNDRED FORTY-SIX

He is.

He is older than the concepts of good or evil. Older than duality.

He is time's knife, cutting without malice or remorse.

The birth and death of suns are a beautiful moment to him. His eyes see all the way to time's first breath and onward into the last cold sigh of entropy. Magic was born in his heart and it speaks with his voice.

Love was the first emotion he created. Hate was the last he learned. And he knew both in their fullest measure. He is no crueler than entropy, but he does not feel its lash.

No thing, from the most graceful and tender stem of a newborn flower to the spider who spins her web, is unaware of him. There is no creature, from those millions who swarm in a drop of rainwater to the basilisk who kills with its stare, refutes his majesty.

On wings as broad as forever, he comes.

Through the starlit forever of night, he comes.

Through the hearts of burning suns and the absolute cold beyond the edge of the universe, he comes.

In answer to the cry of Fabeldyr, the last dragon of earth, he comes.

Upon hearing her cry of despair and need, he comes.

Woe to the wielders of whip and knife and branding iron, for he comes.

He is Vathnya, firstborn of this reality. And he comes.

With his four consorts, his children, his insightful family, he comes.

With Vorth, the Worm of Nightmares, he comes.

With Scriosta, the Destroyer, he comes.

With Uktena, the Horned Terror, he comes.

With Yamraaj, Winged God of the Underworld, he comes.

For Fabeldyr, he comes.

Let this and all worlds tremble, for in his wrath, he comes.

■■■■■■■➤ CHAPTER ONE HUNDRED FORTY-SEVEN

The Prince of Games reeled.

It was as if a physical blow had struck him in the center of his chest. He staggered backward, knocking over a table and sending a wine bottle and glasses crashing to the floor. The flames in the fireplace flashed outward as if chasing him with burning fingers.

The glass in the windows exploded inward, sending swarms of shards slashing at him. He threw up his hands and instantly his palms and wrists were reduced to bloody ruin.

The prince spun, stumbled, and fell.

The sound was in his ears and in his head, and he groaned in pain and fear.

Never once in his endless life had he felt so overwhelmingly assaulted.

"Hastur . . . ?" he wheezed. His face was lacerated and there was blood in his eyes. "Hastur, have you come?"

But as the roar faded to an echo, he realized that this was not the advent of the Shepherd God.

This was something else.

The Prince of Games, son of chaos, immortal trickster, had never known real fear before. Not like this. Not this far beyond his control. He was nothing to it. A flea. Less. A grain of blowing sand on some forgotten beach.

He lay there, shivering with fear and horror.

A word slipped from between his lips.

"Vathnya . . ."

To hear his own voice speak it made it impossible for the next sound to be anything but a scream.

In his private chamber, the Witch-king lay naked on the floor before the statue of Hastur.

He was curled into a ball, bathed in sweat, shivering with terror though he did not know why.

The king crawled with the comprehensively aching slowness of the dying over to the statue, reached for it with trembling fingers, grasped it with desperate strength, and pulled himself to the marble. He coiled his limbs around it, clutching the ankles of the Shepherd God, murmuring prayers for mercy, for protection.

The roar echoed in that chamber, smashing into the walls, rebounding, finding and bruising him.

For such a long time.

Far away, on the edge of the Field of Uthelian, two women froze.

Both in different parts of the same Argonian forest. They were miles apart from one another, and yet they stopped moving at the same moment.

One was very young, but powerful.

The other was very old, but powerful.

The sound of that roar struck them like a great wave, staggering each. The sound of it—and worse, the intention within in it—made every nerve ending in their bodies shriek with pain.

The young woman opened her mouth and screamed in a voice like the shout of a thousand birds.

The older woman ground her teeth together and kept her screams inside.

They stood, leaning toward the sound as if leaning into a blowing gale.

The pain spiraled higher and higher. Unmerciful, unforgiving, unheeding of their agony.

When it passed, they both did the same thing.

Each bent one knee, then bowed their heads.

They each accepted the truth of what was coming, and the knowledge that they might not endure its passing.

Then Ryssa rose.

Lady Maralina rose.

Each turned their faces to the north, tears in their eyes. Then each turned back toward the Field of Uthelian.

The Widow bared her teeth in fury.

The daughter of the queen of faeries smiled.

Faulker picked himself up off the floor.

Fell.

Rose again.

Fell again.

His body felt strange. There was something terribly wrong inside of him.

Somewhere, far off, he heard men yelling. Angry voices with Hakkian accents. It took him a long and strangely difficult time to work out who it might be. One part of his mind was busy trying to convince him that he was home, that he was sixteen, and that he had fallen from the east tower of the palace, his rope of knotted bed sheets coming loose as he attempted to descend in rather great haste from the room of General Chull's eldest daughter. Or, perhaps, the general had cut the rope. If he had, it was fair enough. The general had found his eighteen-year-old daughter naked, holding a blanket to her breasts while she tried to block the window with her body.

That was one thought. His mind resisted making the memory a truth, though, because he remembered that fall. Breaking a leg, some ribs, and a collarbone. He remembered healing and then being bent over a barrel and receiving two dozen stinging blows on his ass delivered with a flexible rod by his very angry father.

So, if that was a memory, what, then, was this?

The world tried to tell him, but he fended it off. He did not want to be in the Winterwilds. He did not want to be cold like this. He did not want to be as badly hurt as his body kept insisting.

He did not want to be dying.

Despite his resistance, his eyes cleared and he saw the shattered ceiling and the stars above that. His mind cleared, too, though more slowly.

He turned away from that sight, but this was a mistake, for he saw bad things.

He saw pieces of dead men. He saw smears of blood and great patches of ice covered with ash. He saw the great, slumped mass of Fabeldyr.

He saw Jheklan.

His brother was sitting up with his back to the wall. Chains—most of them melted now—lay around him. Jace lay nearby, his eyes and his throat wide open. He saw Alibaxter trying to get up, and falling. Again and again, much as Faulker had.

Then he heard those Hakkian voices.

A dim part of him understood why there could be voices where everyone else seemed to be dead and silent, or dying and silent.

"There were guards at the door," he said in quite a reasonable voice. "There were men who took the sleds out."

His voice sounded too normal, and that frightened him, because nothing should be normal. Pain flared in him and for a while all he could do was try and not scream.

Don't let them know you're still alive, you fool, he told himself.

The light in the cavern dimmed like a candle in a capricious breeze.

Darkness took him, but not all the way down. Just to a spot below the surface. He could not see anymore, but he could hear. Faulker thought he was dreaming because what he heard were shouts, challenges, the twang of bowstrings, the clash of steel.

Who the hell is fighting? he wondered.

Surely not Jheklan, if he was still alive. Not Alibaxter.

Who then?

Could Cat and the others come up, wounded as they were?

That made no sense.

I'm dying and I've lost my mind. That seems unfair.

There were screams. The kind of screams men make when steel bites deep or arrows find their true mark.

Who, damn it? Who?

He summoned what little strength he had to open his eyes. It was the hardest thing he had ever attempted, for each lid weighed ten thousand tons.

His head was still turned and he saw people he did not know fighting the Hakkians. A big, red-bearded brute was swinging an axe with incredible speed and force. As Faulker watched, he sheared through a Hakkian's forearm, checked his swing, and on the return cut the man's head off. All of it in the space of two seconds. Less, maybe. It reminded Faulker of the way Hugh used to fight—that rare blend of great strength and shocking speed.

A woman moved past him. Samudian by the look of her. She had a short bow, the kind used for close fighting, and she drew and fired with astonishing speed.

Other figures milled around. Maybe twenty overall, and every few seconds a Hakkian fell. Only Hakkians.

He saw one man take a shallow slash across his face—not at all deep—but he spun, vomited, dropped to his knees, and then fell flat on his face. Dead, or as near to it.

That made little sense to Faulker. The only time he had ever seen so minor a wound end someone's life was when he had watched his mother fight.

But the person who killed the Hakkian was not a woman.

He was big, lean, strong, and . . .

Faulker suddenly cried out. A word. A name.

"Kagen!"

━━━━━━━━━▶ **CHAPTER ONE HUNDRED FORTY-NINE**

Tuke Brakson looked up into the northern sky. There was a deep crease between his brows, and his tattooed face was pulled into a frown of doubt.

"Did you hear something . . . ?"

"Hear what?" asked Filia. Then she saw Horse looking that way, too. Quite a lot of people were.

"That sound," said Tuke uncertainly. "Like a roar or . . ." He stopped and shook his head. "It's gone."

Filia laughed. "By the Gods of the Fields, are you getting pre-battle jitters? Do you need someone to hold your hand?"

For once Tuke was not in the mood for banter. "No," he said. "There *was* something."

"Well, my love, there's something right here. Look."

Turning away from the north took effort, and he shivered once as he did so. Then he immediately forgot whatever it had been and gaped at what he saw.

A line of riders was approaching. There were at least a thousand of them, and at the head rode a bannerman with a long pole socketed into a cup by his right heel. The flag that flapped in the cold wind was turquoise and it showed the emblem of daggers, sword, rose, and dragon.

Tuke noted that absently, but what made him stare in frank astonishment was the woman who rode at the head of the column beside the bannerman.

"By Dagon's balls," he breathed. "She dares come here?"

"Clearly she dares," said Filia. She drew the longsword she had taken to wearing now that she was a general of the rebel army. It was a gift from Mother Frey, sent with Clementius. Filia walked ten paces forward, stopped, and used the tip of the blade to draw a line along the frozen ground in front of her. Then she took one step back, though she did not sheathe her sword.

The woman slowed her horse and stopped on the far side of that line, holding a fist high so that the entire line of riders rippled to a stop behind her.

"Hail, General Filia alden-Bok," said Ghuraka, war chief of the Unbladed of Nelfydia. "Hail, General Tuke Brakson."

Filia pointed her sword at Ghuraka's chest.

"What the fuck do you want here?" she demanded.

Instead of immediately answering, Ghuraka reached down into

a saddle bag and brought forth an urn made from the horn of a mountain goat. She removed a wax stopper, took a breath, and upended the urn. Dust and ashes fell out and were caught by the wind and blown away.

"Branks, whom I loved, died of the wounds inflicted upon him by Kagen Vale."

Tuke stepped up to stand beside Filia. He had his heavy-bladed machetes in his hands. "So what?"

"He died because of my weakness," said Ghuraka. "He died because of my treachery."

"Too fucking bad," said Filia. "Why are you here?"

"What I did goes against all that the Brotherhood of Steel stands for. I am ashamed. You may not believe it, but it is true. I have disgraced myself before Kagen, before the Unbladed, and before the gods."

"There's a war about to start," said Tuke. "Perhaps you could gallop in the general direction of a point . . . ?"

Ghuraka looped a leg over the horse's head and slipped down to the ground. She drew her own weapon—a bola that was as blade-heavy as a butcher's cleaver—and held it in both hands.

"With this steel I have killed more enemies than I can count," she said. "It has tasted a river of blood."

She knelt and placed it carefully on her side of the line.

"There is blood on the ground between me and Kagen. And there is blood on the ground between me and each of you," she said in a voice that shook with emotion. "I renounce my leadership of the Unbladed. If you will have me, I am yours to command. For my sins, I only ask that you put me in the front line. I do not ask for mercy or pardon. I ask that I may kill as many of the enemy as I can before I die."

She bowed her head and waited.

Behind her, the thousand mercenaries dismounted, knelt beside their horses, laid their weapons on the ground, and bowed.

Filia and Tuke exchanged a long look. Then Filia stepped closer, bent, picked up Ghuraka's cleaver, and said, "Get up."

The lady of the Unbladed got slowly to her feet. She looked old, worn, ugly, and naked without her arrogance and her weapon.

Speaking quietly so only Tuke and Ghuraka could hear, Filia said, "If we met anywhere but here, I'd slit you from cunt to chin and leave you for the rats. But even a piece of shit like you can be useful."

She shoved the handle of the weapon hard against Ghuraka's stomach.

"Take it. Lead the charge. Be useful right up until they cut you to pieces."

Ghuraka took the weapon, holding it as if it were as brittle as glass.

Filia turned, waving to a lieutenant to have the newcomers positioned in the vanguard. Then she walked away.

Tuke smiled as he turned to follow her.

CHAPTER ONE HUNDRED FIFTY

Kagen and the Bloody Bastards fought the last of the Hakkians in the ice cavern.

It was a brutal fight, short and mean, and even when the last two Hakkians turned to run, Gi-Elless chased them with two arrows. Neither arrow found a mortal spot—not spine or heart or lungs—yet both fleeing men toppled forward and lay dead on the ice.

Into the silence, the Samudian archer said, "Now I can see why you like having this *eitr* stuff on your knives."

"Helps even the odds," said Redharn.

The others laughed. All of them had coated their weapons with *eitr*, the god-killer poison.

Kagen, though, barely heard them. He ran over to where Faulker lay and dropped to his knees.

"Do you live, brother?" he cried.

Faulker's eyelids kept wanting to close. "There's . . . room for . . . debate . . ." he wheezed. Then he caught Kagen's sleeve with a weak hand. "Jheklan . . . see to . . ."

His lids closed and he fell into silence. Kagen pawed open Faulker's coat and pressed his ear to his brother's chest. "He yet lives," he gasped. "Hoth, do what you can."

Hoth, the most skilled of the Bloody Bastards in terms of battlefield medicine, hurried over. He unslung his pack and began examining Faulker.

"Will he survive?" pleaded Kagen.

"Let me work. Go see about the others."

Kagen got up and wheeled, then staggered over to where Jheklan sat against the wall. His brother's eyes were open, and Kagen began to smile, to rejoice.

But his steps slowed and as he reached Jheklan he knew that those eyes looked beyond this one and into another world. He collapsed onto his knees, and fumbled for Jheklan's hand. It was utterly slack. Kagen pressed it to his lips.

"I'm sorry, Jheklan," he whispered. "I'm so sorry."

He heard gasps and small cries. Then someone pulled heavily on him, trying to take him away from the body. Kagen slapped it away.

Tried to.

But his hand hit something immovable.

Something heavy. And scaly.

He turned and looked into the milky, red-rimmed eyes of the dragon. Fabeldyr's paw pulled at his shoulder. It was sluggish and yet irresistible, and Kagen fell back. Fabeldyr lay on her side, breathing slowly and badly, yet she reached past Kagen and wrapped that massive paw around Jheklan.

And pulled him across the ice. Against her. Against her own breast.

Where he would be safe.

Kagen Vale bowed his forehead against the dragon's deeply scarred body and wept.

As did the dragon.

CHAPTER ONE HUNDRED FIFTY-ONE

"Everything is going wrong," cried Dessalyn. "Can't you feel it?"

Alleyn shivered and clutched his sister's hand. "Yes," he said in a small, fractured voice. "But what can we do?"

"Oh," said a voice behind them, "I can think of all sorts of fun games we can play."

They screeched and spun and saw him standing there. Slim and small and wearing the clothes of a court jester. The Prince of Games stood fifteen feet behind them, smiling in all the wrong ways.

The Prince of Games held his hands up, palms out.

"Don't be afraid, little seedlings," he said in a pleasant voice. "I am not here to hurt you."

They scrambled away from the circle of protection and instead sought shelter in each other's arms. Foscor pulled out her dirk and held it in a tight fist at the end of a straight arm.

The prince came over to a point just out of her reach, crossed his ankles and sat down cross-legged on the floor in front of them. He drew his own knife—a long, slender blade that was as wavy as a slithering snake. The blade was four times longer than hers.

He glanced down at his knife, then with nimble fingers reversed it in his hand so that the hilt was toward Desalyn.

"If you want to defend yourself, little girl," he said, "always use the better weapon."

She did not move.

"Go on, take it. It won't bite you and nor will I, tasty as you both look."

Finally Alleyn reached out a tentative hand and took the handle. He closed his small fist around it and then, with a sudden and vicious movement, jerked it out of the prince's hand. The blade lacerated the prince's palm and fingers, and blood splashed on the floor.

Grinning, the prince held up that hand, showing the deep wounds. He flicked his wrist, spattering them with droplets of blood. Each drop immediately turned into a beetle with a glittering opalescent shell. The children screamed and lunged farther away, swatting and slapping at the bugs.

But the beetles flew into the air, met, became a swirling column, and then turned to sparks that floated gently to the floor. The children stared at the sparks as they burned out, leaving only faint dark smudges on the stone. When they glanced back at the prince, there were no cuts or blood or any mark at all on his palm.

"If I came here to do you harm, sweet ones," murmured the prince, "you would already be screaming to join your brothers and sisters in the grave."

An expression that—had the children been older and wiser— would have looked like self-disgust flickered across the prince's face. Then his usual oily smile grew once more.

"How . . . how did you get in here?" stammered Desalyn. "The door's locked."

"Oh, I think we all know how I got here. The same way you two scoundrels did." The prince affected to look surprised. "Dear me, did you think only you knew about the secret passages? Silly, silly. Of course I know. I daresay I know many things that might surprise you. Things you would like to know. Things that the Witch-king would absolutely *hate* that you knew. Oh my, yes."

The twins exchanged a guarded look.

Alleyn, still holding the knife, said, "Like what . . . ?"

"Like some circles of protection are designed to keep bad things *in*," said the prince softly. "While others . . . well, they're more like prisons, aren't they?"

"Prisons?" asked Desalyn.

"Yes, sweet morsel . . . you've seen one such. Don't pretend you haven't."

Again the children exchanged a look. The prince's smile brightened perceptibly.

"Attend, children," he said, "and learn."

He stuck his index finger into his mouth and with spit drew a square on the floor.

"If someone wanted to keep something of great value inside one—a person, I mean—no demon need be summoned to guard it. A cage of almost any kind will do—steel bars, say, or . . . even a block of ice. Then all that's needed to lock the prison is a circle of salt and sand and a few simple herbs. Herbs that are available in any of the palace's eleven kitchens. But I suspect it would be more interesting and so much more fun if you were to unlock that cage."

Alleyn frowned and pointed to Kestral's circle with the dagger. "This one?"

"No, no, no, my boy," said the prince. "That one is best left as it is. Trust me on this. What I meant is the *other* cage . . . it just begs to be unlocked."

"We don't have that kind of key," said Desalyn.

The Prince of Games put his forefinger deep into his mouth and moved it around in an ugly way. Then he pulled it out and placed the tip of the finger on the floor outside of the spit circle he'd drawn. He looked from Desalyn to Alleyn as he moved his finger in a straight line, leaving a glistening smear behind him.

His line bisected the circle.

"Now," he said happily, "isn't that easy? Isn't it fun?"

Desalyn said, "He'll be mad if we do that."

"My sweet little sucklings . . . he is already mad. He has been quite mad for a very long time. Even before he went to the Winterwilds. He is as mad as the moon. So, one little irritant more won't—*can't*—make him madder."

"He'll *know*," insisted Alleyn.

"Oh, he may guess, but if you do this sooner than later, then . . . why . . . he will have many other things to worry about. This least of all."

Then he rose to his feet and stood above them.

"Oh, you can keep the knife," he said casually. "You never know who you might need to stab someday."

Then he turned and left. He paused at the entrance to the secret passage, gave them a sly little wink, then vanished into the walls.

They never saw him again.

CHAPTER ONE HUNDRED FIFTY-TWO

Tuke and Filia sat on their horses. Filia's great hound and a pack of others, all dressed in spiked armor, sat to one side of her. Trumpeters stood beside Tuke's horse.

The Field of Uthelian stretched before them.

The field was vast, stretching a mile across and two wide.

On the far side of it, partly hidden in a thick grove of pine trees, was the army of Hakkia. It was a sea of armor, of spears, of mounted cavalry, of siege engines, and of foot soldiers standing in battalions of one thousand each. The companies of archers stood apart and slightly behind the wings of the army, their quivers full and yew bows ready.

There were tens of thousands of conscripted and enlisted pikemen forming a huge arc in front of the Hakkian force. They knew that they were the first to attack and would be the first to die, but stood with heads high, knowing that their god was very much on their side. They all wore sashes of Hakkian yellow to honor the King in Yellow and his god. Their god.

The Hakkian flag, in all its variations, flew boldly in the cold air, and with them countless banners of each smaller army, each battalion, each company, each platoon.

There were other groups behind the army, but their numbers were hidden by the trees. Far too many to count, and Tuke felt ice forming around his heart.

"By Dagon's balls," he breathed.

"Well," said Filia, "you wanted to be a general."

"When did I ever say that? Tell me—when?"

She laughed. And if that laugh was a bit forced, Tuke could not blame her. There was not one person on the whole of the field who did not feel fear, of that he was sure. Even that Hakkian woman, Mad Mari, probably felt it. Or, at least, he hoped so.

He resisted the urge to turn and view his own troops. He and Filia had already watched them take up their positions. They knew the numbers, the weapons. All of it. To look again could be construed as doubt—which, in fact, he felt.

At the last tally, taken as the two armies formed up, General Lyss said that the numbers seemed about even. Tuke should have taken heart from that, since his side had some companies in reserve, hidden in the forest on their side of the field. He hoped and prayed that his reserves outnumbered Mari Heklan's.

But he doubted it.

He turned to Filia.

"Tonight is the dark of the moon," he said. "The Witch-king will be casting that spell of ascension. Do you think Kagen will be able to stop him?"

"He stopped the coronation," said Filia. "He may have started out as a soft city boy, but he's changed over the last few months. He is not the Kagen I once knew. So . . . to answer your question,

I *hope* he can. Or, at very least, stall it long enough for the war to wash up against the walls of the palace."

The sky above them was clear, but only directly overhead. In the north, storm clouds were gathering, and they were dark with fell promise.

"Maralina told Kagen there would be a storm," said Filia.

"Yes," agreed Tuke. He sighed heavily. "What do you think is our best strategy right here and now? Shall we attack those bastards? Or wait until they make the first move?"

"I don't think we have a choice," said Filia with an uptick of her chin.

He looked and saw that the Hakkian foot soldiers were beginning their advance. A heartbeat later he heard the enemy trumpets.

"We are no more generals than Kagen, my love," he said as he drew one of his machetes.

"We're all pretending to be heroes, dear heart," she observed. "Everyone is looking to us now, so we had better play the parts assigned to us."

She, too, drew steel.

They raised their blades into the winter sunlight.

On either flank, ten thousand archers raised their bows.

"Death to the Witch-king," roared Tuke, his deep-chested voice booming out and carrying across the expanse of the Field of Uthelian. He and Filia swept their swords down at the same time and the sky was darkened by a storm of arrows.

CHAPTER ONE HUNDRED FIFTY-THREE

Hoth came over and knelt beside Kagen, placing one hand on his shoulder.

"Faulker will live," he said. Then, after a moment he added, "May the gods accept Jheklan into their arms and guide him into the green fields of heaven."

Kagen rose and walked over to Jheklan, squatted down and kissed his brother's cold cheek. Then he placed his palms against Fabeldyr's laboring sides.

"I fear she is dying," said Gi-Elless.

"I know," said Kagen.

"There's nothing I can do for her," said Hoth.

Kagen nodded and walked slowly up to the dragon's head. It was the size of a large wagon. He ran his fingers over her spikes and then along her cheek. Her eyelids were closed and except for the slight movement of her sides as she labored for breath, she was utterly limp.

"I am sorry this was done to you," he said. "You are beautiful, Fabeldyr. Do you know me? I have met you so many times in dreams. You *are* magic to me. You are the most wonderful, glorious creature in all of creation. I know the words of a man—let alone one who is damned—mean nothing to you. But please know that not all people are like those who hurt you."

The dragon opened its eye and looked at him.

"I don't know if my brother Herepath is one of those who hurt you. I suspect he was, and that fills me with shame and horror and sadness. My brothers Jheklan and Faulker are not like him. They are good men. Foolish and brash at times, but men of heart. Jheklan died trying to save you." He glanced back at her claw, which still pressed Jheklan's body to her scaly side. "Thank you for sheltering him now. He deserves grace. So does Faulker." He paused. "I do not."

Suddenly the scar on his chest flared. It was not a tingle this time but a sharper sting, as raw as when he was first cut by the elvinkind's knife. He clapped a hand to it, but did not cry out. Instead he accepted the pain as his due. He would have accepted a thousand times greater pain if it could have helped his family atone for Herepath's crimes. And, maybe for the crimes of others of his family line. Had his mother known of this? Had her fore-bears helped the Silver Empresses—those secret Heklans—drive the dragons to the edge of extinction? Had any of his mother's side of the family participated in the capture and torture of this creature?

It hurt his heart to think so, and as much as he wanted to shout denial that anything so appalling, so heinous, so cruel could have been done by someone with whom he shared blood, there was Herepath to consider. His crimes were as bad, and worse.

He stroked Fabeldyr's cheek slowly, tenderly.

"If I could trade my life for yours, I would do it."

The big eye blinked. Once. Very slowly.

"But not yet," said Kagen. "There is still work to be done. There is so much to be done. My friends—everyone I know and care about—are in this fight. At sea, on the Field of Uthelian, and here in this terrible place with me. And we have much work to do. Herepath remains free, unchallenged and unchecked, and I cannot allow that."

A tear, as clear as crystal, formed in the corner of the dragon's eye and rolled down over his fingers.

"When that is done, and if I am still alive, I will come back here. I will find a way to build a tomb for you. First, though, I will destroy that." He stabbed a finger at the remaining jars of blood and tears. "I hope I am doing the right thing. I know your kind—your family—brought magic into this world. I understand now, finally, what a gift that was. Yet I cannot allow what's in those jars to be used by people like Herepath and his Hakkian sorcerers. I cannot. Will not."

Kagen bent and kissed the dragon's cheek, and his tears fell onto her tortured skin.

"Farewell, Fabeldyr. I will pray to whatever gods will listen to take your soul into the green lands."

Her eye closed. She breathed still, but there was a longer pause between each new breath.

Kagen rose, bowed low, and backed away. Then he turned to see all of his people standing behind him. Faulker was seated on a crate, his face and body swaddled with bandages. A small man sat next to him, also bandaged. He was young, dumpy, disheveled, but alive. Kagen had never met him before but knew who he was from Mother Frey's description.

"Alibaxter?" said Kagen. "Do you live?"

"I do, Lord Kagen," said the wizard. "For now, at least."

Kagen licked his lips. "You understand these things. What counsel do you have?"

The young man looked around. At all the death, and at the jars.

"If Fabeldyr dies," he said weakly, "magic lives on because of that." He coughed and dabbed blood from his lips. "I heard what you told her."

"And . . . ?"

Alibaxter reached for Jheklan's fallen mallet, which lay near his foot. It hurt him badly to pick it up. He considered it for a moment and then held it out to Kagen.

"Better a world without magic than one ruled by its darkest aspect."

Kagen took the mallet.

"We have work to do," he said to the Bloody Bastards. "Giffer, you and Pergun go outside. If there are any Hakkians still there, yell and we'll come. If not, there are sleds out there with more of these jars. Smash them all. Every last one."

"W—wait . . ." croaked Faulker. "Kagen . . . please, listen to me . . ."

Kagen bent close. "What is it, brother?"

"Yes, smash the bottles of tears . . . and blood . . . but not the clay canisters."

"Canisters?" Kagen frowned and then followed Faulker's weak

gesture. He went over and lifted one of the canisters, hefted it. And grinned. "Well . . . damn . . ."

CHAPTER ONE HUNDRED FIFTY-FOUR

The terror and the pain passed.

It took time, for it hit the Witch-king hardest of all. Yet it passed.

He released his iron hold on the statue of Hastur, rolled over onto his hands and knees, panting like a dog, dripping sweat onto the stone floor.

Getting to his feet took time, but with each passing moment he felt more of his strength return. Much more. By the time he was standing upright, all traces of the weakness had vanished, leaving in its place a feeling of immense power.

A brilliant yellow light rippled along his limbs, crackling like lightning. It engulfed him, penetrated his flesh, digging deep into the tissue all the way to his marrow. It hurt—Gods of the Pit how it hurt—but he did not care. He knew what this was.

Hastur's blessing was upon him.

In him.

Of him.

Restoring everything that the scream had taken from him and then giving more. Much more. He looked at his arms and saw them swell, the muscles swelling as their fibers became denser. When he closed his fists, the knuckle tendons creaked and popped. As he drew in a deep breath, he felt his chest expand and, with white-hot pain, his back broadened.

"For your glory, o' god of the fields!" he cried, and his voice was deeper, stranger. "Fill me with your power, great Hastur! Let me truly become the King in Yellow. More than your avatar in spirit, make of me your vessel in the flesh here on earth. All that I am and have ever been is for you."

The yellow lightning crackled, burning the air, filling it with ozone, remaking the Witch-king in the forge of the Shepherd God's will.

The Witch-king dressed quickly, pulling on his layers of garments. The undergarments were tighter than they were, as was the cotton tunic he wore beneath his robes. He put on the cowl and tied the lace veil in place and stood there, feeling the power swelling within.

It was the most wonderful feeling. Uplifting, enlarging, transformative.

He unlocked the door and pulled it open, and there was such strength in his arm that the heavy metal door flew open and slammed into the wall. The startled guards spun, their weapons half-drawn.

"Tell Lord Nespar I want all of the court magicians in the great hall at once. The new moon is rising and the storm is already growing. I can *feel* it. Hastur calls me to ascend. It is time to begin."

The sergeant slapped his sword back into its scabbard and ran to do his master's will.

CHAPTER ONE HUNDRED FIFTY-FIVE

The archers did terrible work. Dreadful. The front ranks of the Hakkians crumpled, even with raised shields. It was an unrelenting rain that deluged the approaching army, ferreting out each little chink in armor, each gap between shields, each opening in leather.

The Hakkian officers called no retreat, though. Their sergeants cracked whips and beat men with knotted rope's ends, driving the pikemen into the storm. Their own archers lined the edge of the woods and fired back, but they were no match for the Samudians.

For the thousands of Samudians who drew and fired, their aim made true by such a deep and profound hatred for those who killed their king's only child.

The humidity of that cold afternoon clung greedily to the mass deaths. As blood burst from arrow wounds, the air pulled at it, coveted it, allowed it to turn the very air an ugly pink. Breezes walked the bloody mist across the field, swaggering in delight at its gaudy dress.

The thick air also carried the smell of blood everywhere. That coppery tang, the heavier odor of iron. It brought those tastes as well, seasoned with salt from all that gore, and mingled grotesquely with the faintest memory of dead grass and new pine into the perfume of slaughter.

Ryssa hid in her tree, staring in horror at the slaughter on the field.

Inside her head, Miri's reaction was different. She loved seeing so many Hakkians fall. The difference between them was something Ryssa had noticed before, but never spoke of while Miri was alive. The intensity of it frightened her, and the glee with which Miri's ghost celebrated all those deaths was appalling. Disgusting.

And yet she felt like a hypocrite. When Hakkians had attacked her on that island, and again at sea aboard the Therian ship, Ryssa felt no compassion for the enemy sailors.

Why now, then?

It was a question that tore at her.

CHAPTER ONE HUNDRED FIFTY-SIX

"Are you still alive?" asked Faulker.

"More or less," replied Alibaxter weakly.

Even with their wounds dressed and hot food in their bellies, the two of them were in bad shape. Faulker had never been seriously injured before, and it made him feel old and nearly useless. He had to force himself not to think about Jheklan, because that made him cry, and sobs threatened to undo Cat's careful stitchery.

Instead, using what little strength he had, he spent his time cleaning Fabeldyr's wounds and talking to her. Cat tried to explain that the creature was in a coma and unable to hear him, but he fended her off.

He had a bucket of soapy water and a rag and had to lean against her bulk to sponge away crusted blood and old feces. At first her body trembled at the merest touch, and it tore into Faulker's heart to think that this magnificent creature had become so habituated to torture that she recoiled by reflex at *any* contact. He hoped that, if she was dying, then at least her last memories of humans would be kindness. The more he worked, the more regular her breathing became. He told this to Alibaxter.

"Yes," said the wizard. "It's calming her."

Faulker looked at the young man. The arrow wound had been cleaned and sutured, but every time he moved a wince of agony shot across his features.

"Tell me," said Faulker as he washed the slumbering dragon's face, "are you able to make some of that soup or stew? It did us all a power of good. Maybe it'll help this old girl."

Alibaxter got up and stood swaying dangerously for a moment. "I can try," he said. "It might help all of us, come to think of it."

Faulker looked at him. "You're a good lad," he said. "You have more courage than many warriors I've known."

The look of surprise on the young wizard's face was genuine and profound. His eyes were wet, and Faulker wondered if anyone else had ever complimented him on courage. Or on anything.

"Do what you can," he said gently.

While Alibaxter tottered away, Cat came over. She was stiff

from her own wounds and sat down with great care on a small block of ice.

She spoke quietly. "That was good of you. What you said to Alibaxter. And . . . what you're doing for the beast."

"Her name is Fabeldyr."

"Fabeldyr, yes." Cat shook her head. "All the way up here, I was never sure I believed she was real. Even after what we saw in the ice the other day."

"I know," he said as he used the rag to catch soap before it reached the dragon's eye.

Cat stood and watched him for a long time, saying nothing. Then, she murmured, "She's beautiful."

"She is."

Cat walked away and came back with another pail of hot water and a rag. Without comment she began washing the other side of Fabeldyr's face as the smell of Alibaxter's soup filled the frozen chamber.

CHAPTER ONE HUNDRED FIFTY-SEVEN

Strange eyes watched from the woods and from high above the Field of Uthelian.

Vultures swirled in slow circles hundreds of feet above the dead and dying. Nightbirds cried from the pine trees. Cold-drowsy snakes watched from the shelter of fallen logs, and rats from small gullies on the edges of the field that were cut by centuries of rain, but which now filled with water thick with blood.

But other eyes watched as well. Some of them were as old as the field itself. Some older. Others had been born into the world with the return of magic.

None of these cared for the life or death of the humans, but on some level—deep within their race consciousness—they knew that much depended on this war. Whoever won would possess the right to bend magic to their will, and that bred hate in their hearts.

The imps and sprites and dryads and elvinkind—never in numbers great enough to challenge the dominance of upstart man—watched and waited. Hoping and fearing in equal measures when this war would reach its icy hand for them.

On her armored horse Mad Mari, flanked by two generals, watched.

"Surely, Lord High Marshal," cried Mingus, commander of the 5th Hakkian Foot, "we must pull the men back."

"Must we?" mused Mari Heklan. "Say you so?"

"We're losing too many on a direct assault," pleaded Plower, commander of the 3rd Hakkian Light Horse. "We should withdraw and let them make their charge. Our strength is in our cavalry."

"Keep your horsemen ready," she said to him. And to Mingus, she added, "Every eye is on those arrows and their effect."

"Yes, that's what I—"

"And while they are all looking this way, they are looking nowhere else."

It was then that a new chorus of screams—faint, distant, but torn from many voices—rolled over the dead and dying to reach their ears.

The archers faltered. The whole line of the rebel army turned to look behind.

The screams rose in intensity.

Mad Mari looked delighted.

"*Tuke*," yelled Filia, staring in horror as she twisted around in the saddle. "Gods save our souls—*look!*"

He turned, too, and his eyes went wide as he saw what she saw. Others saw it. Thousands turned away from the massacre on the field. They cried out in chorus with the screams that reached them from behind their lines.

The forest behind them—a vast density of pines and firs—was burning.

Burning.

And within that forest men and women burned, too.

CHAPTER ONE HUNDRED FIFTY-EIGHT

Two small figures moved through shadows and along secret ways.

Desalyn led the way, reaching back to clasp Alleyn's hand very tightly. They had a small oil lantern to light their way, though they now knew these corridors so well that they could almost manage in total darkness.

Madame Lucibel had put them down for the night, and all that day they had done their very best acting as cruel, mean-spirited Foscor and Gavran. That performance was always exhausting, and they hated it. Though fooling the wicked Lucibel was, in its way, fun.

"This is crazy," whispered Alleyn.

"Everything's crazy."

"But we're *trusting* the Prince of Games now?"

Desalyn shot him a quick look over her shoulder. "Not trusting, exactly."

"Then what?"

She went on several more steps before she said, "Hoping, I guess."

Alleyn shook his head. "Hope."

He said it with such a lack of optimism and belief that they did not speak again until they reached the right hidden door. And there they stopped, both of them panting as if they had climbed five flights of stairs.

"Are we sure we want to do this?" asked Alleyn.

"No," Desalyn said at once. "But . . ."

He nodded. "Yeah."

She stood on tiptoes and looked through the peephole.

"It's empty."

"Are you sure?" he said.

"Yes. Look for yourself."

He did and agreed that the room was empty. There were no candles or lanterns lit, though a big fire blazed in the fireplace.

"There's a fire," said Alleyn. "Looks new."

She looked again, up and down, and shook her head. "He's not there. I'm sure of it."

Even so, they paused, both feeling the enormous weight of what they were about to do. The costs, the dangers, and the uncertainty of what it all meant.

Alleyn drew the big knife that the prince had given them. The blade had been thrust through his belt, and it was so sharp that it nearly severed the leather band. The lamplight turned the silver steel to gold.

"Let's do it," he said with far more confidence than he felt.

Desalyn pressed the latch and the door opened inward a few inches and they were bathed with sudden warmth. The secret hall was chilly, but the room was almost hot from the big stack of burning logs. Alleyn, who had the knife in both small hands, stepped in first, but Desalyn was right behind him, her small dirk glinting like a needle.

The alchemy laboratory was completely empty except for the bottles and vials, pots of ingredients, and all of the strange stuffed monsters. As they moved into the room, they could feel the glass eyes in the many taxidermized faces glaring at them with stern disapproval.

They crept across the floor to the far corner where the block of ice stood. Even with the heat it was still frosted. The shape of a tall man was still there—a smudge of darkness with no visible details. The circle of salt and sand was unbroken, with not even a grain out of place.

Desalyn looked from it to the fireplace. "I wonder who made that fire."

"You know who did," said Alleyn.

They stood and stared at each other.

"Either we do it or we run away," said Desalyn.

Alleyn abruptly hugged his sister with one arm, careful to keep the dagger out to the side for safety.

"I guess we have to do something," he said into her ear. "We need to be brave like Captain Kagen. I think *he'd* do this."

She nodded, sniffed, and stepped back.

They went over to the corner and knelt down in front of the block of ice, sitting on their heels.

"What do you think will happen?" she asked.

Alleyn glanced at the fireplace but said nothing.

Then he raised the knife in preparation for defending them both as Desalyn sucked the tip of her finger and reached out. She placed it on the floor an inch from the outer edge of the circle. They both repeated a little prayer to Mother Sah and Father Ar. Almost a nursery rhyme. It was all they had.

Then she pushed her finger along the stone floor, paused ever so briefly before making contact, and then broke the circle. The sand and salt parted as easily as if it had just been placed.

There was a sudden rush of cold air that knocked them both backward. It was as if the circle somehow collected and contained the frigid air around the ice. When they looked down at their clothes, there was a rime of ice crystals.

They scuttled backward and got to their feet, Alleyn brandishing the dagger.

The cold faded and was gone, leaving only a wet sheen on their clothes.

Alleyn and Desalyn stood there, trembling, uncertain. Watchful.

The block of ice stood there. The shadowy figure within remained as he had always been. There was no visible change at all.

"It didn't work," moaned Alleyn.

Desalyn said nothing at first. She took a single tentative step toward the ice.

"*Look,*" she said, pointing with the same finger with which she had cut the circle. "See?"

He looked. And saw.

On the side of the ice block that faced the fireplace, a bead of condensation was forming. As they watched it grew heavy and then rolled crookedly down to the floor. Another chased it.

And another.

They turned and fled, suddenly terrified at the thought of being there when the ice melted completely. They vanished through the secret door and crouched there in the dark, their lantern forgotten.

The shadows seemed to gather too closely around them. Fingers of cold trailed down their spines. Desalyn and Alleyn made not a sound as they took turns looking through the spy hole, watching the ice melt. They saw a pool of water move outward from it, washing over the now useless salt and sand.

They saw the frost vanish by slow degrees from the surface of the block, and a face slowly begin to emerge. The man inside looked dead.

Until his eyes opened.

CHAPTER ONE HUNDRED FIFTY-NINE

"Get out of the forest," bellowed Tuke. "For the love of the gods, *get them out of the forest.*"

The span of forest behind their side of the field was half a mile deep but stretched for hundreds of miles in either direction. There was a break about halfway through in which a deep stream ran. So far, the blaze was on the other side of it, but those woods were packed with the rebel army's heavy cavalry and two companies of foot soldiers. The plan had been to signal the charge as soon as the Hakkians sent their horsemen out to protect their pikemen from the archers.

But now the tightly packed crowds of rebel forces were trapped by their own numbers. The trees and withered grasses caught fire with astonishing rapidity, and the blaze shot left and right from each burning tree as if the whole of the forest was made of sun-dried kindling.

"Tuke," cried Filia, as they raced back through their own lines, "they must have soaked the ground and trees with oil before we got here."

"Oil stinks, damn it. How could we have missed it?"

"Oil infused with pine sap," she said. "It's an old trick and I'm a bloody fool for not having thought of it."

By the time they reached the near side of the stream, the forest on the far side was fully involved. Angry yellow and orange flames raced up the skin of each tree, withering the pine needles, igniting the sleeping oaks and maples, turning the dense bushes and shrubs into walls of death.

They saw soldiers staggering as they burned. They saw horses, mad with pain, running with their manes ablaze and empty saddles—and their fallen riders in that heavy armor roasting in the oven heat. The smell of roasting flesh mingled with the scent of burning pine, polluting the air with horror.

Lord Gowry, dressed in his family's coat of arms, staggered toward the edge of the bank. All that could be seen of him was his blistered, scorched face. He screamed and screamed as he tried to make it to the water, but he suddenly spasmed, clawed at the hot armor over his heart, and fell face-forward into the water. Steam rose up around his corpse.

"General Filia!" someone yelled, and she turned to see a young galloper racing toward her.

"What is it?" she snapped.

"The enemy are on the field. Their cavalry!"

"Shit!" Filia wheeled, leaving Tuke to do what he could for the disaster in the woods.

She raced back to the front line in time to see the surviving pikemen split neatly apart as ten thousand Hakkian knights came racing over the corpses of the fallen. The rebel army's archers were in disarray because of the fire, and her troops at the front were scattered.

"Re-form the line," she screamed. *"Gods damn you all, re-form the lines!"*

CHAPTER ONE HUNDRED SIXTY

The razor-knight stood in the pit in central Vahlycor.

The world seemed to have moved on and forgotten it, but it stood there in its silent rage as the first drops of the coming storm fell lightly on him.

The trap had been built well. The sides were tapered in and soaked with oil so that he could not climb out. The floor was a maze of sharpened stakes and iron spikes. And the pit was very deep. He had spent weeks punching the walls, trying to beat a slope that might allow his escape, but the ground here was thick with dense rock. His fists, though incapable of taking injury, had only managed nine feet of slope. At that depth, it would take a year to fight his way out.

It was a trap conceived by someone who understood well the powers—and limitations—of a razor-knight. The fact that it was inevitable that he would eventually escape puzzled the monster. It suggested that by the time it gained its freedom, it would no longer be a threat.

And so it stopped its labors and thought about that.

All the while the image of the Witch-king burned in its furnace of a mind.

Then something struck the back of its helmet.

The razor-knight whirled, spreading its many-bladed cloak like batwings. A small stone lay on the ground. The monster looked up and saw a figure standing at the very edge of his pit. A man dressed in leather and wearing a fur-lined cloak. He had dark curly hair, pale eyes, and there were ghosts in his eyes.

"It is a strange thing to see so mighty a creature be so helpless," said the man.

The razor-knight flexed its powerful hands. "Have you come to torment me? To mock me?"

"Actually, I have not," said the man. "I've come a very long way to give you a choice."

"A . . . choice?"

The man unslung a heavy pack and from it drew two items, handling each with the utmost care. In his right hand he held a slender canister marked with the seal of the Hakkian eclipse. In his left was a rolled tapestry tied with turquoise ribbons.

"You know what these are?" he asked.

The razor-knight's eyes burned red. He said, "I do."

"Pick one," said the man. "But choose wisely."

The razor-knight considered and then slowly raised one arm and pointed.

The man nodded, weighed the item in his hand and then tossed the rolled tapestry down into the pit. The razor-knight snatched it out of the air.

"I hope to all the gods that I am doing the right thing," said Kagen Vale.

Then he turned and was gone.

Ryssa stood on a tree limb and tried to see what was burning.

The smell of live trees dying was everywhere.

She heard the cries of people caught in the conflagration.

She heard other cries, too. Things that lived there. Birds of a hundred kinds. Gophers and deer and rabbits and bears. Screaming as they burned, or running to find some spot of safety in a world gone mad.

Within the cacophony of shrieks, Ryssa heard her name. It found her on the hot wind, exhaled from the doomed forest. It was not any human version of her name, nor was it an animal calling out to her in strange imitation. Yet it was her name all the same. The essential version of her name, of who she was.

Calling to her.

She leapt down from the tree and ran into the woods, running as fast she could toward the wall of fire. Smoke, gray and thick, curled upward from dying trees. Animals ran toward her. They saw her and she them in ways that no other person could understand.

Tell me, she cried. *Tell me where. Tell me how.*

Coyotes told her. And badgers. A doe running with her one surviving fawn told her. And a bear, burned and weeping blood, told her.

So Ryssa ran.

In her heart she could feel Miri's anger rising, and now she welcomed it. Demanding it. Needed it.

She broke through one section of the forest where a brook created a natural firebreak. Ryssa plunged down the bank and into the water, calling the trapped and confused animals to her in thought and strange words that formed on her tongue, though she had no idea where they came from.

Animals broke from the other side, staggering and coughing from the smoke.

To the creek. To the water.

They came. Dazed and terrified, they came. Tripping and staggering, falling down the slope, splashing into the water. Ryssa sent them upstream and down. The birds of the forest swirled around her in panic, but the black birds—the crow and starling, grackles and even black vultures—the nightbirds, dove at the animals, nipping them, goading them, tricking them out of panic and into a flight to safety.

Some people came out of the woods, too, and many fell into the stream to douse flames on their clothing and hair. Ryssa left them to it. They were not her concern.

The exodus of animals was slowing as the woods emptied or the stragglers were consumed. Through gaps in the smoke she saw Hakkians—scores of them—stalking forward with torches. Looking for more things they could infect with their angry yellow fire.

In her soul, Ryssa and Miri became one. They became the Widow.

The Widow raised her voice to the sky and cried out in a voice no human being other than the girl and the ghost inside her had ever heard before. The roar of the fire tried to mask that voice, but the Widow threw all her power into it.

And far away, in another part of the forest, voices answered.

Not deer or bear or woodchuck.

Much stranger voices.

Angry.

Filled with hate and mourning, which are dreadful companions.

Coming to join the war.

CHAPTER ONE HUNDRED SIXTY-TWO

The mages and sorcerers gathered in the great hall in the palace of the Silver Empresses. They wore their robes, each marked by the sigils of different spiritual orders and secret clans. Each had a staff or crystal or wand—something that they used to focus their considerable power. One enchantress from the Ishka Sisterhood had jewels—rubies and emeralds—sewn into the skin of her face. A spellcaster from the Cellesine Church was covered in tattoos of sacred geometry over every inch of his skin.

Beside each was a small wooden table made from alder—that sacred wood that is white when freshly cut but which soon turns to a rusty red like old blood. Upon these tables the items of their craft were set, ready to hand.

When the Witch-king entered the hall, they all bowed very low, for they knew that this was a holy moment. A statue of the great god Hastur had been brought in and set upon the dais so that the head of the Shepherd God was above that of the mortal king.

The Witch-king bowed to his court sorcerers and then turned to the statue. When he bowed, he did it all the way down, abasing himself on the floor. As did everyone else.

"Great Hastur, god of mercy and life, protector of the faithful and punisher of the unjust, we pray to you in our humility," he said. "Grant us your blessings on this sacred day. Strengthen the arms of those far from here who lift swords in your name. Weaken the hearts and cripple the arms of our enemies, those who would see your statues torn down, your banners trampled, your likenesses desecrated, your name erased from history."

"So we all pray," chanted the others.

"Come to us in the hour of our greatest need, o' great one."

"So we all pray."

"We beseech you to end your long dreaming sleep and awaken to our love and our prayers."

"So we all pray."

"And, sweet god of power and love, we beg you to manifest with us here, in spirit and in the flesh."

"So we all pray." If there was a slight hesitation before this last response in the litany it was because this part had not been spoken before. Yet the Witch-king was more than the head of state, he was the high priest of the Hakkian faith. His word was never to be questioned. Even so, the response was more scattered.

"This we pray," concluded the Witch-king.

"So we all pray."

The King in Yellow got to his feet without hurry. Turned and exchanged another bow with the sorcerers, then mounted the dais and sat upon his throne. There, in the shadow of the huge golden statue, he spread his arms wide to include everyone in the room.

"My sisters and brothers," he said in a ringing voice, "shall we change the world, now and forever?"

There was no hesitation this time. Every sorcerer and mage and witch roared out a thunderous cheer.

CHAPTER ONE HUNDRED SIXTY-THREE

Rain was falling as Filia galloped through the mass of the army, yelling at them, beating some with the flat of her sword. Horse growled and snapped, scaring many with an immediate threat that tore their focus away from the looming one.

The Hakkians were galloping across the field.

"Cavalry," cried Filia. "To me. Form the line."

Despite the panic, there were enough soldiers and knights among them to begin relaying her orders, to be extensions of her will. And the line re-formed. Not as straight and with fewer riders, but Filia saw that there was enough.

Hoped and prayed that there was enough.

She had no speeches and would not have given one if she had. Instead she stood in the stirrups and pointed with her sword.

"Kill the bastards!" she roared.

Then she kicked Dog's flanks and the horse surged forward.

The line of Hakkians was like a tidal surge, moving with great speed, lances lowered. Filia pulled her line into a curve and they rode like madmen toward the center of the enemy. If she could punch through, then it would blunt the impact of Mad Mari's charge before it hit the forest behind Filia. That would allow the archers to rally and re-form and attack the separate flanks. She just hoped Tuke was back there organizing that.

The distance melted away and with a sound like the collision of enemy thunderstorms. Thousands of horses slammed into one another, or scraped past, or died and tumbled. Spears sought horseflesh or man flesh and the force of the charge buried these deep. Many in the two leading edges, even as they killed their enemies, were jerked out of the saddle by the force and tilt of their own spear thrusts, the leverage snapping them over their horses' heads and down into the meat grinder of countless hooves. Some spearpoints skittered off of shields and twisted those holding the weapons sideways in their saddles with such force that arms broke and spines were wrenched. They screamed as their horses plowed on, bearing crippled and dying riders.

Filia had rarely been in a cavalry charge of any size, but as a caravan guard she had faced enemies on horseback. She had lived this long because she was devious and supple. She had no spear, and instead met the spear of the enemy directly in front of her with a savage downward parry that stuck the spear into the ground as surely as a planted flag. Her backswing cut the rider across the lower back.

The mass of riders stalled because of the friction of impact, and it became sword to sword. Filia had a spiked buckler on her left hand and she used that and her blade, guiding Dog with heels and knees. Everywhere she looked there was a Hakkian, and her sword moved like silver fire. Within seconds her arm was red to the elbow.

There was a moment of weariness as the first flush of strength lagged, and then the joy—the sheer lust—of combat took hold of her. The pain, the weariness, the fear all fell backward as the killer that she was emerged. As she pushed forward, she left a trail of murder and mayhem behind.

The knights on either side of her followed in her wake, and, as some fell, others spurred forward to ride beside her.

Arrows whipped through the rainy sky and fell in the center of the melee, but she could not care if they were Hakkian or rebel shafts. Horse and his pack of spike-armored hounds raced among the legs of the horses, leaping to tear at legs and throats—not caring if they were human or equine. Their spikes were coated with *eitr*, and everything they brushed against died.

Twice, though, Filia saw a horse belonging to one of her side scrape against one of the dogs and fall. She had warned her people, but even so she hated to see it happen.

She fought on. Soon she found herself in that moment of confusion where it was impossible to tell whose side was winning. All around her people were killing, dying, screaming.

Then she heard a trumpet blast. Immediately the Hakkians peeled off, wheeled their horses and raced back to their side of the field. Filia looked up as a shadow crossed the sun, but it wasn't a shadow—it was the biggest flight of arrows she had ever seen.

The Samudian archers had regrouped and, backed by archers from every other company, they were counterattacking. They shot high to arch their arrows far above and beyond the center of the melee. The Hakkian cavalry should not have retreated but instead pressed on, forcing more of the confused mingling of the armies. Filia did not know who blew the retreat, but it was the first mistake Mad Mari had made.

It did not make up for the rebels milling in hysteria when the woods were set alight, but it was a moment for breath.

Across the field, Mari Heklan was watching things with an amusement born of great complacency.

She was not the kind of commander who cared much for the

common soldier. Her one-of-us demeanor when inspecting her troops was all affectation. The Witch-king knew it, but few others did. And her game was to keep even her generals in the dark about her strategies because it lent her an air of mystery. That was something Hakkians appreciated.

Now, as she watched the enemy deal with one kind of problem after another, she ignored the cost in terms of Hakkian lives. With every response to one of her stratagems, she learned more about the rebels. It allowed her to spot weaknesses, assess strengths. It allowed her to make fresh choices rather than be a slave to a formal battle plan.

What made it so much more fun was that the Witch-king—whom she adored—had given her so many wonderful toys to play with. These were hidden in the forest behind her, or in the hills on the far side of the rebel army.

She was, arguably, the happiest person on the Field of Uthelian.

CHAPTER ONE HUNDRED SIXTY-FOUR

There was no one at all in the damp room in the third subbasement of the palace. There was only a palace cat resting atop a barrel whose presence and contents had been forgotten years ago. The cat had a belly full of meat and had licked all the best bits from the rat bones scattered about, and was busy with the fastidious chore of cleaning herself. She was gravid and would drop her babies in a few days, and yet she was still quick enough to catch plenty of food. Especially lately, since the rats had fled the upper floors, having no taste for it.

And there was a pack of hounds the Witch-king let roam the top two basement floors, and one of them had killed and eaten the calico Tom who had gotten the cat pregnant. So the expectant mother had sought the safety of the deeper levels.

One floor above her was noisy because it was where prisoners languished behind barred doors. Scores of them. Once in a while some would toss pieces of meat to her. It was usually rancid, but the cat didn't mind. Not with kittens on the way. She would eat her treats while the prisoners talked to one another. Some even recited poetry or sang. The cat liked the sound of singing voices, and often lingered there, listening, until guards came and banged their clubs on the cell bars. Or dragged a singer out and beat him bloody on the stone floor.

Mostly, though, the cat enjoyed the quiet down here, and a nest of old cloth and straw was waiting in a corner behind crates. She also liked the complete darkness. The cat was on the edge of a nap when suddenly a man was in the room.

He did not come in through the door. There was no warning at all. One moment the room was empty and the next he was there. Tall, dressed in furs, with a lantern in one hand and a knife.

The cat leapt to her feet, arching her back to look bigger as she hissed sharply, baring yellow teeth. The man looked at her but that was all. He did not swipe at her or kick her or yell.

He turned, though, and spoke to the empty air.

"Come ahead," he said in a whisper. "It's clear."

The cat recoiled, crowding herself back into a corner as another person was there. Suddenly, abruptly there, and she had a drawn bow in her hands.

"Biter, Borz, come on," she called over her shoulder.

There was another man—huge, with wild red hair and an axe. Then another. Soon there were nine people in the room. Each of them dressed for the bitterest winter. Each of them with rolled bundles strapped across their bodies. Each with satchels crammed with canisters hanging from their shoulders.

The cat ran behind the crates and hid, trembling with fear, peering out cautiously from the shadows.

"Kagen," said Redharn, "is this the right place? Doesn't look like a palace basement to me."

"How many palace basements have you seen?" asked Gi-Elless.

"You know what I mean."

Kagen walked over to the door and bent close to peer at the wall. Then he laughed. "By the Gods of the deepest Pit, I know this room. Be damned if I don't." He pointed to the wall and the others leaned close to see a few very crude drawings of women with improbably ample bosoms and men so endowed they could never have walked. Initials were used as signatures. Kagen traced two sets of these—JV and FV.

His smile was bittersweet.

"Jheklan and Faulker brought me here several times when I was a lad. That's their art."

"How old were they when they carved those?" inquired Gi-Elless. "Ten?"

"Fifteen or sixteen," said Kagen. "Neither was much of an artist."

"Nor an anatomist," mused the Ghenreyan poet, Hoth.

Kagen explained where the subbasement was located. "We have a lot of stairs to climb, and some narrow passageways to follow. It'll take time and we need to be absolutely silent."

As he reached for the handle, Redharn asked, "What about Faulker and the others. Alibaxter and that woman, Cat, and the others? Shouldn't we bring them through the . . . um . . . tapestry?"

Kagen considered. After the cavern had been secured, the exit checked, and all of the blood and tears destroyed, he sent Urri back the way Alibaxter said they'd come. The Nehemitian had competed in mountain-pass runs with others from his village. Alibaxter warned him about the corpses, the evidence of the Red Plague, and the spell that inhibited the Twins. Urri ran off, making a lot better time along the flat ice floors than he used to in the steep and rocky mountains of his homeland. By the time Kagen returned from his trip to where the razor-knight was trapped, Urri had returned.

"No," he said. "Leave them be. They're all too badly hurt to be of help, and there's food and fresh water back there. Besides . . . someone should be there with Fabeldyr."

Not a one of them refuted this.

"I'll leave a tapestry for them to use," added Kagen. "It will take them to Argon, but suggest they wait until someone comes to tell them the battle is over. Or, if they can't bear being here anymore. Their choice."

He spoke distractedly, though, and Urri understood. The weight of grief Kagen felt for his brother was shared by his friends, even though none of them had ever met the Vale twins. And all of them shared Kagen's horror and regret for what had been done to the noble beast, Fabeldyr.

Kagen unslung the tapestry he carried and set his satchel of banefire down very gingerly.

"We don't need these furs," he said. "They'll only slow us down. Shuck everything you don't need. Food, water, all of it. We need to move light and fast and if we can't do this in a single day, then we never will."

Pergun glanced at him. "How do you know that?"

Kagen rubbed the scar on his chest, but did not answer.

When they were disencumbered, Kagen opened the door and crept out. He snapped his fingers lightly, enough to signal the rest of the Bloody Bastards to follow him.

Like a file of ghosts, they drifted through the many rooms and hallways of the third subbasement. Nine of the deadliest fighters alive, hunting for the most dangerous sorcerer on earth.

CHAPTER ONE HUNDRED SIXTY-FIVE

Filia reined in and signaled her own troops to re-form the line. Chasing the Hakkians was tempting, but she was more than half-certain the retreat was itself a ploy.

"Fall back and regroup," she ordered as she wiped rainwater

from her eyes. It was still a light drizzle, but the clouds were thickening and there was nearly continual lightning in the north.

Saying it was one thing, but getting the battle-maddened knights—many of whom had never been in a serious battle before—to disengage was another matter. She had to enforce her order with yells and kicks and even the flat of her sword.

I spent more time beating my own people than I did the gods-damned enemy, she thought.

But soon cooler and wiser heads prevailed and the entire cavalry fell back and re-formed near the forest. Runners came hurrying out with water or wineskins. Armorers ran everywhere with replacement weapons. A few even carried out portable grinding wheels and within minutes sparks flew in a score of places as new edges were put on battle-blunt swords, or nicks honed down to keep swords and axes from splitting.

Tuke emerged from the smoke, his face ashy and his eyes running red. He and Filia touched hands, though neither dismounted.

Filia gestured to the burning woods on the far side of the stream.

"How bad?"

"Bad enough," he said, accepting a waterskin from a runner. He drank deep then splashed more over his head and face. "Best estimate is eight hundred dead. Twice that number wounded. Burns, of course, but also broken bones from mad flight through the smoke. And they burned most of the baggage train. We lost nearly all of the bundles of extra arrows. Maybe the *eitr,* too. I have people looking for it."

"Gods of the Garden . . ."

"How did your lot do?" asked Tuke, nodding to the field, which was littered with bodies. Dozens of people from both sides were on the field under truce flags, pulling the wounded to safety.

"I have no idea. We stopped their advance, but at a cost."

Tuke rose in his stirrups, shading his eyes with a hand. "What are they doing? Are those ambulances?"

She looked, too, and it was evident that the Hakkians were pushing a whole line of covered wagons onto the field. Not pulling them with horses, but actually pushing them. Unlike the ambulances agreed to by both sides, these did not show the white flag.

Filia whirled. *"Archers!"*

Her order was relayed and soon sergeants of the Samudian archers ran up to her for instructions. She pointed.

One of the sergeants was a grizzled old woman with piercing blue eyes. She peered across the field. "Those wagons are all chained in the back," she said. "And look, they're rocking back and forth as if something inside is trying to get out."

"Damn, you have eyes like a hawk," said Filia. Then, to Tuke, "Chains on ambulances?"

"It's some damned trick."

Filia told the sergeants to bring their squads forward. But even as the Samudian ran to obey, the handlers of those wagons unlocked the chains, let them fall, spun, and ran back to their lines.

The doors of each wagon burst open and animals burst forth.

Huge creatures. Ugly, massive, bizarre. Some were similar, but none were the same. One looked like a rhinoceros, but instead of one or two horns, it had a crest of them—all of them long and sharp, like a nest of spears. Two more were some kind of gorillas whose bodies were covered in chitinous armor, and their fists were sheathed in more spikes. There were things like lions, but with two snapping heads; and a brute like a hedgehog but with a scorpion tail arching over its back.

Hideous deformities. Unholy and unnatural.

At least a hundred of them.

They raced forward, pouncing on the civilians seeing to the wounded, goring them, hooking them with horns and tossing them into the air so they fell with bone-shattering force. Others trampled the wounded, roaring with dark delight at the screams. Within seconds the field was an abattoir, with screaming wounded unable to defend themselves.

Filia saw the enemy commander, a lumpy and brutish woman reports said was Mad Mari Heklan. She raised a yellow horn to her lips and blew a long note that rose high into the air. Immediately the deformed monsters raised their heads and looked past the remaining wounded at the wall of rebels.

The creatures each responded to Mad Mari's call with a roar of their own. Some were deep bellows, simian screeches, strange trumpeting, and something like the shrieks of mountain cats. Their chorus spoke of hate and hunger, and nothing of what filled the air sounded like it had any origin in the natural world. The sounds filled the listeners with terror and dread.

Then Mad Mari blew another note, and the legions of unnatural beasts charged.

Straight toward Tuke and Filia.

CHAPTER ONE HUNDRED SIXTY-SIX

Kagen led the Bloody Bastards along the corridor of the third sub-basement. They found nothing of use in any of the rooms, nor did they find any Hakkians.

"Here's where we get sneaky," he told them as he pressed on one of four boltheads that held a cobweb-draped sconce to a mossy wall. A section of wall shifted inward, exhaling stale air that smelled of rat droppings and dead insects. Awful as that was, it was a stale smell that suggested disuse, and that was comforting.

They entered the passage and closed the door behind them. There was a flight of stone stairs with extremely shallow but steep steps. Redharn, who was the largest of the group, had to climb very carefully because only his toes would fit the stairs. He wound up bending forward and climbing like a dog.

At the top of the stairs was a T-junction with three passages heading off in different directions. Kagen took a moment to orient himself, then picked the left-hand way. They followed him in silence, going only as fast as absolute quiet allowed.

At the next turning, Kagen held a finger to his lips and pointed to another of the nearly invisible hidden doors. He knelt, spat on his fingers, and on the dirty floor drew a rough, quick sketch of four guards sitting at a table. Then he hung his lantern on a peg and drew both of his knives.

Biter, the brutal fighter from the Weskian crocodile clan, looked at the blades and raised his eyes in silent enquiry. Kagen's reply was a grim nod. They were not taking prisoners. It made the Bloody Bastards smile.

The four guards were seated around a wooden box, all of them intent on a game of marbles and straws, but they were directly around the corner.

Kagen considered and sent Gi-Elless, the best archer among them, and Borz, to the left. He led everyone else to the right. When they were all in position, Kagen nodded to Gi-Elless. She and Borz had bows ready and stepped silently around the corner and loosed their shifts at the same time. There were no screams and only a mild *thump-thump* as bodies collapsed to the ground. Then Kagen, Redharn, Hoth, and Urri stepped quickly around the corner. Their poisoned blades flashed and drank deep. One of the four guards made a strangled noise, but Pergun was there to clamp a hand over the dying man's mouth.

It was all the work of a few seconds.

"Find me some keys," he ordered and Hoth ran off to search.

They looked at the rows of closed cell doors. Kagen held a finger to his lips and waved everyone back, then approached the first cell. He peered inside. The light was bad, with only what lamp-light angled in through the grill in the ironbound wooden door.

"There's no one there," he said.

There were no prisoners in any of the cells.

It explained why the guards were so distracted—they had noth-ing to do and maybe the dungeons were where they went to gam-ble, relax, and dodge work. That had been their mistake.

Kagen stepped over a corpse and led the way toward the first set of stairs.

CHAPTER ONE HUNDRED SIXTY-SEVEN

Filia was filled with horror at the sight of the army of monsters the Hakkians had released. Beside her, Tuke was struck mute. There were cries and even screams from the knights that formed their line. Fighting cavalry and armies on foot was one thing, and all of them were prepared for that. Even the fires were natural.

But this.

This.

None of them had ever seen such creatures. The sight of them triggered primal dread. That atavistic fear of monsters from nightmares and old stories stabbed them deeply, trying to take the hearts of even the most seasoned fighters.

Then a dog changed things.

Horse ran onto the Field of Uthelian and stood between his mistress and the monsters which were now halfway across the withered grassland. He stood with the wide-legged, bullish stance of the war hound, his spikes glistening with poison and spilled blood. He lifted his scarred and ugly head and uttered a long, baleful howl of pure malicious challenge.

Then the rest of his pack ran out and stood with him. All of them howling, and then the howls turned into growls. Every sin-gle one of the oncoming monsters was as big as Horse, and some many times bigger, but the hounds stood their ground, muscles rippling beneath their hides, drool flying from their lips.

"By the savage balls of the god of dogs," said Tuke, his voice creaking with stress. "I'll be thrice double-damned if I will let a pack of mutts fight while I sit here shitting my pants."

He raised one machete high above his head.

"Kill the buggers!" he roared, and then kicked his horse into a canter. Thunder boomed overhead and all around the field there were bright flashes of lightning.

Filia twisted in her saddle and glared at the knights around her. "Did you come here to watch or to fight, damn your eyes?"

She kicked Dog's flanks and charged forward.

That was enough to break the spell. By ones and twos, and then suddenly by hundreds, the cavalry surged forward like a tide. They tilted lances down and raised axes high as they rode toward madness and death.

Tuke and Filia outpaced the others, with Horse and his pack all around them.

The closest of the creatures was a gigantic black goat with boar tusks as well as unnaturally large horns, and Tuke steered his mount toward it. The thing turned and tried to disembowel his horse, but Tuke chopped down with a powerful cut of his weapon, hacking the side of the monster's neck. It was not a killing blow— not at first. But the *eitr* burned through the wound and into the bloodstream of the monster, and even as it tried to turn to bite at Tuke's leg, its own legs buckled and the thing went down.

Tuke spun and shouted, "They're not immortal. They can die. So by the gods let's kill the bastards."

The knights came on faster and faster, screaming challenges or just yelling at the top of their voices. The wave of cavalry hit the oncoming monsters.

It was immediate and mutual carnage.

The rhinoceros slammed into the horse of Sen Fermok, the

colonel of the 3rd Vahlycorian Mounted, and a man with more medals than could fit onto even his broad breast. The huge horns punched through his mount's belly and up into his right thigh and stomach, lifting horse and rider into the air and tossing them into two other riders, sending them down in screams and sprays of hot blood.

The thing immediately turned and trampled two of the armored dogs. Their spikes could do nothing against its thick armor, but the pads of its feet were ordinary flesh. As it crushed the life out of the dogs, the god-killer poison on their spikes pierced that flesh, and it fell atop them, ending their dying screams.

A knight drove a spear through the throat of a giant boar, but its whipping scorpion tail killed his horse, and the dying horse fell badly and that killed its rider.

Samudian archers ran onto the field, trying to get clean shots at the monsters, but there were too many of the cavalry in the way.

A thing like a hippogriff launched itself into the air and flew toward the archers. They shot at it and hit it, but it killed a dozen of them before the poison and the arrows ended its unholy life.

The monsters were able to be killed, but they quickly learned to avoid the spears and swords. Their mass stalled the riders as they smashed into the cavalry, tearing the throats out of horses and then rending the riders. A swarm of things like centipedes but eight feet long, fiery red, with heavy chitinous shells, did terrible damage as they ran beneath horses and then bucked upward, knocking the animals over and into the paths of other riders. These gigantic insects were covered with poisonous spines and soon they were killing dozens for each of them that was stabbed to death with spears.

Dog, Filia's horse, was attacked by them and it cried out in great pain and then staggered. Filia managed to leap off Dog's back as it died and fell. But that left her on foot with a centipede rushing toward her. She slashed at it as she backed away, but her sword merely bounced off the armor, doing no harm. The big hound, Horse, was nowhere to be seen, and Filia was in a clearing littered with corpses as the tide of battle raged around her.

Suddenly a sound broke through the din of battle.

It was a huge trumpeting noise, but not made by any instrument. Everyone turned, even the mutant creatures, as a line of massive forms—each of them bigger than even the hippopotamuses and rhinoceroses ill-bred by the Witch-king. Gray shapes that ran forward, trumpeting with fury.

Elephants.

Dozens of them.

And all around them, moving like a riptide, were tigers and gorillas and wolves and panthers. Scores of animals. None of them strange. None of them deformed. Above them, the sky was filled with eagles and falcons and condors and other birds.

There were no riders on any of these animals, they wore no armor.

And yet there was a figure running with them. A woman. Young and small and dressed in mourning clothes.

The Widow, coming to war with the beasts of the natural world.

For a moment the knights were held in check by surprise and doubt. Many thought this was yet another Hakkian trick, and their hearts sank.

Then the first of the elephants reached the closest of the Witch-king's creatures—a false basilisk who leaped at the pachyderm with fangs and claws. The elephant crashed into it and trampled it beneath thirteen thousand pounds of mass and fury.

A tiger rushed past it and tackled one of the scorpion-boars, hitting it with such shocking speed that the creature died before it could sting the cat.

Despite the rain, swarms of wasps and bees and hornets flew

past the Widow and descended in clouds onto the Hakkian animal handlers. The muddy ground writhed with cobras and mambas and vipers and rattlesnakes.

Filia stood beside her dead horse, sword in hand, staring in frank astonishment. The world had clearly lost all of its power to make sense, but she did not know whether to feel optimistic or let herself simply go mad.

CHAPTER ONE HUNDRED SIXTY-EIGHT

The sorcerers of the Hakkian court had each been assigned their place in the open floor of the great hall. The precise placement was designated by the Witch-king, but Nespar oversaw the actual arrangements. Jakob Ravensmere was helping, but often stopped to sketch the patterns of crystals and salt-sand mixtures and candle placement for the book on the history of contemporary magic.

The pattern created was essentially a large representation of the eclipse, with the corona picked out in colored sand and ground yellow crystals. Candles of various thicknesses were placed to represent stars in their correct degree of brightness, and also key constellations whose position in the sky that evening was considered to be greatly propitious. Bowls of incense of twenty-three different kinds were lit from flames the Witch-king himself conjured into being. That ball of fire hovered in the air between the throne and the diagram and as soon as the last stick of incense was lit—a blend of sandalwood and ground bark from the upas trees—the fireball winked out.

A small group of musicians were let into the room, each of them an apprentice from the School of Holy Sound, one of the most ancient secret societies in Hakkia. They unrolled rugs intricately embroidered with musical symbols that, collectively, equated the Great Note that they believed was the first sound heard at the dawn of creation. It was a note no one ever played, for it was very dangerous, but it was allowed to be included in different kinds of visual art.

The musicians positioned themselves on cushions and tuned their lyres and tested the reeds of their flutes and the tautness of hand drums. These ascetic musicians had begun training for this day since the ascension of the Witch-king was announced within the circles of those sworn to secrecy.

And it was to be an ascension. If the ceremony went according to the old rituals, the Witch-king would call the god Hastur to wakefulness and invite him to stand—fully physical—in the center of the hall. During the ensuing reading of sacred texts and casting of spells, the Shepherd God would imbue the King in Yellow with great power, elevating him to the status of demigod. Once that happened, the Witch-king's power would increase tenfold, and, as the *true* living embodiment of Hastur and with the god himself walking beside him, he would crush the rebellion and conquer the west.

Several times Nespar and Jakob met each other's glances. They were excited by what was happening, though each also felt excluded. One was a facilitator and the other a historian. They would, at least, be witnesses to a glorious event.

This had been planned for the week after the coronation that would have made Gethon Heklan the Emperor in Yellow, but Kagen Vale had spoiled that. Now the coronation would follow the ascension. Proof that the will of Hakkia and its god could not be denied.

The Witch-king sat on his throne and watched. With each second his destiny drew closer.

━━━━━━━━━━▶ **CHAPTER ONE HUNDRED SIXTY-NINE**

Kagen and his team reached the first level of the palace.

He led them along a complex series of halls and peered into a number of rooms before finding one that was empty. It was a general storage room in which was stored mundane items like candles, cleaning supplies, rolls of cloth, and other things. He eased the door open, checked more carefully, and then entered. The others followed. The fact that there were nine of them, including himself, pleased Kagen. He was superstitious and nine was always a lucky number for him. He just hoped that luck would serve him in what was to come.

"I wonder how Tuke and Filia are doing," mused Gi-Elless. "I wish I could be there."

"They'll be fine," lied Kagen, who did not truly believe that. At best he *hoped* they would survive the battle on the Field of Uthelian. It was likely to be very bloody, and even if the rebel army won, that victory would not ultimately matter if the Witch-king was still alive. This war needed to be won on both fronts. On three fronts, he thought, mentally correcting himself, because the combined navies of the former empire were likely already engaged with the Hakkians.

Borz opened the door and checked the hallway and reported it empty. "What's the plan, captain?" he asked.

Kagen spoke quickly and quietly. "The great hall is four corridors from here. There's no hidden door there, alas. But there's a room just along this passage that was always used to store extra guard uniforms. I'm hoping the Hakkians use it for the same purpose. With even a little luck we'll be able to transform ourselves into guards." He eyed Redharn, who was nearly as tall and broad as Tuke. "Most of us, anyway. But we'll figure something out for you."

"And then . . . ?"

"I want to look for some very important people," he answered.

Tuke and Filia rallied their knights, pulling them back to allow the swarm of animals to attack the mutants.

"Where in the total fuck did *they* come from?" demanded Tuke.

"Hell if I know," said Filia.

"And who's that woman in black?"

Filia shook her head. "Don't know that either, but if I had a brother, I'd let her marry him."

The battle raged. In most cases the Witch-king's creatures were more powerful and larger, but the elephants were like avalanches. And there were far more of the woodland animals.

Tuke tapped Filia's arm and pointed. "Did you see that?"

She had, and they both stared. Several of the Hakkian monsters were retreating from the onslaught. A few even stopped fighting and crouched down in what appeared to be submission.

"It's a trick," warned Filia, but as they watched it became apparent it was not a ploy. Those animals seemed unwilling to fight natural creatures of their original kind. The cougars among the mutations would not attack or even counterattack the lions and tigers and panthers. The deformed rhinoceroses backed away from those who accompanied the woman. All across the field the battle was slowing.

Then one of the hippopotamuses—a dreadful beast with armor and spikes—lay down and rolled over, offering its stomach and throat to a huge female. The normal hippo stalked toward it and stood for a moment, suspicious and angry. The mutation offered no surprises, no attempt at further combat. Not even when the normal hippo lunged forward and caught its throat between immensely powerful jaws. Blood sprayed upward in a red geyser and the mutation thrashed, cried out . . . and died.

A cougar did the same, allowing a panther to savage its throat. Then a rhino. A boar.

"What the hell is going on?" breathed Filia.

"I . . ." began Tuke, then he shook his head. "It's like they're giving up. Like they know they are—and this may sound stupid— *wrong.*"

"Wrong? What do you mean."

"Wrong," Tuke repeated. "Not natural. Not normal. It's like they hate what they've become."

It was an absurd assumption, and yet it played out like that all across the field. A silence fell among the humans watching as the animals of the natural world systematically slaughtered those bred so long and carefully by the Witch-king.

Only a few unnatural beasts stayed on their feet and they glared at the woman in black. One of the scorpion boars suddenly charged at her.

And another of its kind wheeled on it and stung it a dozen times before the monster could reach the woman. Not a normal boar, but a monster. It killed one of its own to protect the woman who had brought her army from the natural world.

Across the field, Mad Mari stared in utter shock at the slaughter.

It was wrong. The Witch-king had spent so much of his time, invested so much of his magic, in creating these creatures. He promised that they would massacre much of the enemy. This should have decimated the rebel cavalry, leaving them open to a fresh assault of her own.

For the first time since coming to the Field of Uthelian, Mari Heklan felt a twinge of fear.

Even so, she had more—much more—to use in the Witch-king's name. She spun in her saddle and glared down at a line of small figures dressed in gray robes.

"You lot . . . if you came here to fight, then now is the time."

The Hollow Monks bowed. Every inch of their skin was covered with the smoke-colored cloth. There was no way to read anything about them. But they walked forward with unhurried confidence.

A troop of archers followed obediently, and all along the front of the forest wall small catapults were pushed into place. None of them had the range to reach the rebels across the meadow, but that was not their purpose.

The Hollow Monks walked twenty paces out onto the field and the archers fanned out to form a line in front of them. They knelt, drew arrows, fitted them to the strings, and waited.

The catapult teams brought a cart of small red cloth bags out from the trees and runners took one each and placed them in the bucket of the catapults. The archers raised their bows.

The lead monk knelt, picked up a handful of loose dirt, and tossed it into the wind, watching which way the breeze took it. He nodded to Mad Mari.

"Do it," she said.

"By your command," said the monk. To the catapult teams he said, "In succession. *Now.*"

The catapults snapped forward in a line, hurling the red bags high into the air. As each reached its zenith and began to fall, an archer fired at it. The range was not great and the bag easy to spot against the clouds. The arrows punched through the cloth and red powder puffed onto the breeze, which wafted it away from the Hakkians. Nor did the breeze carry it to the rebels. In fact the breeze was so light that the dust began to settle down onto the field where so many soldiers from both sides lay dead.

The animals looked up, sniffing the air, and suddenly they bolted, running off the field as quickly as they could. The Widow retreated, too, though she looked confused and uncertain about what was happening. The distress of her animal army frightened her, so she simply fled.

Tuke laughed as he watched the dust settle.

"Well, as a response to what just happened," he said, "that was anticlimactic. What were they hoping? To make us sneeze to death?"

Filia was less amused and leaned forward over the horse's withers to study the field. "No . . . that was too elaborate to be nothing."

A rider came galloping up from behind them.

"General Filia, General Tuke," he cried.

"What is it?"

The young man pointed backward. "There are reports of troops heading this way from the far ends of the forest. They're close. Their approach was hidden by the fires and smoke."

"How many?" asked Tuke.

"What kind?" asked Filia.

"Colonel Srendal says that the ones on the left flank look like light cavalry. They have Hakkian and Gelhemian flags."

"Mercenaries," spat Filia. "It's probably that prick Unka. He's been working deals with Bulconia and tribes throughout the Cathedral Mountains."

Tuke said, "Who's on the right flank?"

"The colonel said he recognizes their flag. It's WarBride from Alya-ta."

"Gods above and below," Tuke breathed. "The cannibal queen."

Filia frowned. "Who?"

"Another mercenary. A madwoman from the east. My father told me about her. She's fierce as hell and tends to feast on the bodies of any officer she kills in battle."

Filia grinned at him. "Even dark meat?"

He laughed. "You don't mind the taste."

"I rather like it," said Filia. "But I'm not willing to share."

The rider looked enormously uncomfortable but then his expression changed to one of abject horror as he looked past the generals. They turned to see what alarmed him, and both immediately felt their hearts freeze.

Now they understood about the red bags and the gentle fall of dust.

On the field, the Hakkians and the rebels who had been killed were stirring. One by one they rose to their feet despite dreadful wounds. Some had entrails trailing, others had missing limbs. None carried weapons but that did not matter. They stared with dead eyes toward the thousands of the rebel army. Their mouths opened and closed, broken teeth snapping. Everything about their expressions and postures spoke of mindless hate and bottomless hunger.

The clouds opened and heavier rain fell as the living dead from both armies sent up a demonic howl and began limping, staggering, shambling, and then running toward the waiting rebels. Toward the smell of fresh, living meat.

CHAPTER ONE HUNDRED SEVENTY-ONE

Two figures watched from a hole in the ground that was invisible behind tall stalks of green grass. Each wore a hooded cloak camouflaged in shades of green and brown and gray. The rain fell on them as they watched.

They were patient. Their kind had learned patience over many ages of the world. Cold of blood and of mind.

"They will slaughter each other," said the younger of the two. Younger, and yet very old, for they were both from a long-lived race.

"Yes," said the elder. His face was far more crocodilian than his companion. Patterns of rigid, glistening scales swept back from his blunt snout. He had fewer teeth than the youngling beside him, but the remaining ones were curved like daggers and wickedly sharp. "It will be beautiful to watch."

The younger reptile leaned on his spear, eyes bright with the thought of slaughter. "Who will win?"

The elder laughed. It was a faint, creaking, hissing, ugly laugh. "What does that matter? When this war is over, there will be far fewer of them."

The younger one nodded. "And there are so many of us."

"Oh yes."

They watched, barely moving, their eyes rarely blinking.

The older one touched his companion. "This is their war," he said. "Our time will come, but now is not that day. Let us go."

They watched a moment longer and then they turned and vanished into the earth, going deep into the endless darkness there.

CHAPTER ONE HUNDRED SEVENTY-TWO

The rebel army was caught between the hammer and the anvil. The dead rising on the field and mercenary armies approaching from behind.

Tuke felt as if the world was collapsing around them, and yet he hoisted a fool's smile on his face as he turned to Filia, who sat on a horse whose rider had died.

"Take your pick, my sweet," he said with an affectation of gallantry. "Shall it be the living or the dead?"

"Is neither an option?" she asked.

"Alas, no."

"The dead, then."

He brought his horse close to hers and leaned far over to kiss her lips.

"I love you," he said.

"You're a romantic idiot," she said, but then she grabbed him and kissed him very hard and very deep. Then Filia pushed him—gasping—away. "Go fight. But you come back to me, you hear?" She pointed a finger at him. "And don't you dare swear by your balls or anyone else's."

He laughed, then placed his hand on his heart. "On my sacred honor."

Then he wheeled his horse and galloped off through the rain.

She watched him for as long as she could, and was disturbed to see the smoke of the burning forest swallow him whole, making him vanish as if he had never existed at all.

Then she turned to the problem at hand.

The dead were rising and staggering toward her. Rebels and Hakkians. It did not matter how badly mangled they were, they rose anyway. Those with broken limbs crawled along the ground, climbing over the corpses of dead animals which—thank the gods—had not resurrected. Those whose bodies were more or less whole stumbled for a while and then began to run. Not well, not with grace or balance, but also without fatigue or hindrance from the wounds that had killed them.

Filia looked up and down her line. The knights were staring in mute horror as friends, sons, daughters, brothers, and sisters came loping toward them, teeth snapping in anticipation of fresh meat. They were the most powerful part of her army and yet many of the knights made warding signs as they backed their horses away from the oncoming swarm.

"Shit," growled Filia, then she cupped her hands around her mouth and yelled, "*Archers!*"

"General," called a voice and she turned to al-Agha, the master archer sent to the rebel army by King al-Huk. The archer was an old man, but he had that kind of obvious toughness that made him look as dangerous as he was. "This is the Red Plague. The dead can only be killed by a mortal wound to the head or decapitation. Nothing else will stop them."

Even as he spoke, his sergeants were running forward with squad upon squad of Samudian archers.

"Then *go*," snapped Filia.

The archers' quivers were only half-filled, the rest already having been used, and most of the reserves burned along with the baggage train.

"Stagger lines," roared al-Agha in his leather-throated voice. "Straight shots only. No arching fire. Pick your targets and conserve your arrows. One shot one kill or by Mother Sah you will answer to me."

The sergeants echoed the order up and down the line. They formed a set of lines, with every other archer a pace back from the front, but filling a gap. This allowed them to fire in sequence—front line, back line—as fast as they could draw and aim.

The dead came on in their thousands, crying aloud in moans that spoke of unassuageable hunger, dead fingers clawing at the air.

"Fire by lines," ordered the master archer, and his disciples proved why Samud was second to none when it came to the bow.

The arrows thrummed in the air, striking the front wave of the dead. At that range, three out of every four fell. Al-Agha bellowed support and mockery of the kind that made soldiers try harder. "If-Tull, who taught you how to shoot? The family dog? Yo-Tigrin, don't you know the arrow goes in the eye socket not the damned shoulder? Uf-Nara, why in the many hells did you shoot that one in the balls? Did he roger your wife?"

The archers laughed at the abuse even as they fired.

Yet the dead came.

With a start she realized that those dead who had been merely wounded had not fallen. Was the *eitr* not effective against these things? She wheeled on the master archer and asked him, and she saw him go pale.

"General, the runners who brought up the last of the arrows may not have had time to season them with the poison," he cried, aghast.

"Then by the gods, we better hope they have *enough* arrows."

They both knew they did not. Filia knew that the archers were going to run out of arrows before they ran out of monsters to kill. And the whole of the Hakkian army was marching slowly across the field behind the living dead.

As Tuke galloped toward the rear, he yelled to different groups— axmen from the forests of Nehemite, spear-hunters from Zaare, burly farmhands from Vahlycor with their pitchforks and scythes, and masons from Sunderland carrying battle hammers. And many hundreds of Unbladed from throughout the west. Some had been there for the battle with the Firedrakes, others were newcomers Tuke did not know.

"Unbladed to me!" he bellowed as he galloped. "All of you bastards with me. The mercenaries are coming."

"We *are* mercenaries, big man," growled one broad-shouldered man with a pair of chain maces.

"From the east," Tuke shouted back. "They came here to try and prove they're better at it than the Brotherhood of Steel."

"Well," said the man, spinning the spiked balls on the ends of the chains, "fuck that."

He and the others began running to follow Tuke. Some of them had burns from the fire, others were black with ash. Many of their friends had died in the blaze. Many of their friends were lost and probably dead in that dying forest. All of them were ready for red revenge.

Tuke reached the rear of the line and saw how bad things were since he left not twenty minutes before. Nearly all of the baggage train was burning. A few people were pulling the unturned wagons away. Several dozen Hakkians dressed in cloaks painted to look like forest shrubs lay dead, most with their torches still in hand. Their deaths mattered little for the forest arson was damage done.

He rode out onto a smaller field known as the Downland,

which was really a shallow valley between sections of the huge forest. Unka's riders were approaching at a cantor, conserving their horses' energies for the battle. WarBride led a massive force of foot soldiers, though skirmishers on ponies ranged along the fringes of their company. Both armies would combine and then attack within minutes.

Before the battle, in the last council of war last night, several plans had been drawn for dealing with attacks of all kinds. Tuke, who was not a true general any more than was Kagen or Filia, waved to every officer and sergeant he could spot. He rapped out a series of orders, phrasing them badly, but was greatly encouraged when the officers took what he said, rephrased it into the kinds of orders his subordinates were used to, and suddenly his own army began to take shape.

Tuke had ordered the burning wagons to be pulled away from the edge of the forest and pushed into some semblance of defensive walls.

"What about the gaps?" asked a sergeant. "We don't have enough for a full wall."

"I know. I want to force the enemy to come at us in straight lines rather than as a wave. If they come through the gaps, then we can fight them from three sides at once."

A colonel gave him an appreciative smile. "A slaughterhouse kill box," he said. "I like it. Are you sure you were never in the army?"

"No, but I've laid a trap or two in my time."

With a laugh the colonel and sergeant rode off to organize this.

Time was short, but there were a lot of eager hands to set the trap. The enemy would see the gap-toothed line form, and maybe they had plans for dealing with it, but at least the fight would start on his terms, and that thought steadied Tuke.

He wondered how Filia was doing, then realized the danger

of such thoughts. He needed to stay focused and so chased all thoughts of her—and of Kagen—out of his head.

Filia watched in horror as the last of the Samudian arrows struck their targets. The archers had brought more than three thousand of the monsters down, and the dead were heaped in mounds that formed berms three-quarters of the way across the field. That left thousands more on the far side of the corpses.

She broke her cavalry into halves and sent them to the ends of the berms to intercept the Hakkians, who—seeing this impediment—were galloping hard to attack around the ends.

Then she called up the foot soldiers, having the sergeants reorder the ranks so that spearmen worked in partnership with those who had blades. Axmen and those with maces were called to the front.

As the living dead climbed over the mounds of corpses, the spearmen stabbed their weapons into stomachs or chests, not trying for the kill but to stall them so the fighters with axes or maces could cut heads or smash skulls.

Some of the spear thrusts actually killed the dead, and those, Filia knew, had been seasoned with the god-killer poison. She tapped a runner and told him to bring more of the poison to the front.

"I think we're nearly out, general," the young man stammered.

"You think? Damn your eyes, find out."

He tore away.

The spear-axe teams were fighting with incredible ferocity. It was demanding, brutal work, and it slowed the attack. But Filia knew the horrible truth—the dead would never tire, nor could they be dissuaded from their purpose.

She dismounted and drew her sword, sending her mount to the rear. Horses were too vulnerable for this kind of combat. But she whistled for Horse, whose spikes had been newly coated with *eitr* before this attack.

"Hunt," she told the hound. "Scratch and run. No bites. Heed me, Horse, *no bites.*"

The dog's tail wagged and he took off with his pack behind him. They scaled the mountain of the dead and vanished down the other side.

We're all going to die here, she thought. Nothing she saw around her offered any proof to the contrary.

CHAPTER ONE HUNDRED SEVENTY-THREE

They found the guardroom easily enough, and were clustered around the door. Kagen nodded to Redharn, who turned the handle very gently until the lock clicked, then he pulled it open fast.

Kagen rushed inside, startling a handful of guards who were in various stages of undress. Fresh uniforms were laid out and they were obviously preparing to don formal armor for their shift.

Borz was the last of the Bastards to enter the room and he closed the door quickly but quietly while Kagen lunged at the man closest to him. Kagen had both daggers in hand and the blades darted out, nicking that man and the one near him. Gi-Elless lunged for another, with Urri taking a fourth. A fifth man was a few yards apart and he lunged for a glaive standing against the wall, grabbed it, and spun toward the intruders. Redharn did not use his axes but instead batted the weapon aside with one hand and punched the guard full in the throat. The man clutched his throat, eyes bulging as he looked around for help. The other four guards were already down, victims of the god-killer poison. The choking soldier puddled down, eyes bulging with shock as he died.

"There's one more," called Borz, and he jerked open the door to a privy. A man crouched there, his drawers halfway pulled up, eyes wide with terror. "Shall I . . . ?"

"No," said Kagen. "I'd like to ask this poor son of a bitch some questions. And I'll bet he will answer every single one."

CHAPTER ONE HUNDRED SEVENTY-FOUR

Alleyn wanted to run away and hide.

Desalyn did, too, but her curiosity was a stronger anchor than her fear. She kept her eye pressed to the spy hole, watching.

Watching.

The heat from the fireplace was intense, but even so the ice seemed to be melting unusually fast. The floor was awash and there was a danger that it might reach the door and spread out into the hall. If so, the guards would have to do something. Maybe run for the chamberlain. Maybe come in.

Alleyn pointed this out, being—in his fear—perfectly reasonable.

"Not yet," said Desalyn.

"What are you waiting for? We'll get caught."

"I want to see."

"See what?" cried Alleyn. "It's a demon or something like that."

"How do you know? It could be someone else."

"Like whom? Everyone's dead."

Desalyn shook her head. "No. *He* came for us once."

Alleyn pulled her from the spy hole and stared at her. "Are you serious? Do you think that's *Captain Kagen* in there? All froze?"

"Maybe . . ." she said weakly.

"You heard Nespar and Jakob talk about him. Kagen's a general. He's making an army and he's going to come here. How could he already be here?"

She took a long time answering.

"I just think it is," she said. Then went back to the spy hole. After a few moments she added, "Besides, it kind of looks like him."

"What? Let me see."

She stepped aside as her brother looked.

The block of ice was half melted now, and the right shoulder and side of the man's face were nearly exposed. The eyes that had opened before were shut again, and once more he looked more dead than alive. Alleyn studied the features. They did look a little like Captain Kagen, but . . .

"It's not him," he said, stepping back.

"You don't know that," Desalyn snapped.

"It's not. Go look. Tell me that's Captain Kagen. Tell me that you know for sure."

She did look, but as more and more of the figure became visible doubt began to chew at her.

"Maybe it's one of the funny ones," she suggested. "Faulker, maybe. Or Jheklan."

They took turns looking and guessing. All the time the ice melted with unnatural rapidity.

"I'm going back in," Desalyn announced.

"*What?* No," yelped Alleyn. "You're nuts. Don't—"

The door clicked open and Desalyn stepped into the alchemy laboratory.

"Stop," hissed her brother, but she just flapped a dismissive hand at him. She went to the edge of the broad pool of meltwater, then took a very tentative step into it. There was so much that it lapped around the soles of her slippers, soaking into the brocade. She tensed against the frigid water, but it was warm. Pleasant. That was both a comfort and another strangeness. Even with the fire roaring like that the liquid shouldn't be as warm as bathwater, yet it was.

She moved forward, stepping deliberately so as not to make noisy splashes. Alleyn stood at the edge of the little lake, fists balled tight. Desalyn looked over her shoulder a few times, and on the third, Alleyn gave a small nod of encouragement.

When she reached the foot of the ice block, she stopped and looked up into the face of the man. There was no movement of his chest, no twitch of eyelid or lip. His skin was blue-white. Some of his chest was visible, and she saw several small scars. One was a crescent or half-moon—a thin arc with the bow upward and the ends pointing down. The scar was nearly white and looked old.

She considered the shape of him. He was thin, with wiry muscles, but they were not like Captain Kagen's. Up close she could see that now. The captain's muscles were bigger and harder.

And although the face looked familiar, it was because it looked *like* Kagen. Just as it looked like Jheklan and Faulker, and even a bit like poor Hugh.

But the mouth was different. There was a hardness to it. A cruelty or maybe sadness . . . sometimes they looked the same to her.

On impulse she raised her arm and reached toward the stranger, one finger extended to poke that cold flesh. If he was dead and this wasn't Kagen, then the mystery wouldn't even matter. That was her thought. But if he was alive, then—

"Don't," said the dead man in the ice. "Do not touch me."

She shrieked, snatched her hand back, and stumbled away. Her feet slipped in the water, and she fell on her bottom, which knocked another cry from her.

"Desalyn, no," gasped Alleyn, running and splashing toward her.

The door swung open, and two guards came in fast, naked blades in their hands. They rushed at the children.

▶ CHAPTER ONE HUNDRED SEVENTY-FIVE

The chanting filled the air of the great hall.

Scores of voices rose together, speaking in one of the oldest tongues from Hakkia's distant past. A dead language spoken only in ceremony; a language forbidden to anyone outside of the brotherhood of magic users.

It was an ugly language, filled with strange clicks and pauses, with intonations that hit the listener like blows, and whispers that filled the guards in the room with sickness. Two of them had to stagger out of position in order to vomit in the privacy of an adjoining cloakroom. This was not noticed and even if it had been, no one would have cared.

The entirety of the focus of every magician in the room was the ascension. The chanting conspired with the rising incense and the glow from the candles to create an atmosphere of power. On his throne, the Witch-king sat with closed eyes, looking inward at who and what he was, feeling who and what he would become. The change was already beginning. He could feel it building on top of the first transformative wave that had happened in his private prayer chamber. That had hurt but in an ecstatic way, like the self-flagellation of a true penitent—a glorious act of prayer and praise for the watchful Shepherd God. Every metamorphosis of tissue and bone, each reshaping of organs and glands, was at once a torment and an act of worship.

He needed to scream, but knew that such a reaction might weaken the spell, or even break it, and too much time, sweat, blood, energy, and planning had gone into this moment. It was a dream begun long before he had gone to the Winterwilds. It was a destiny that had been waiting for him his whole life, and through hardships and sacrifice and even acts of brutal cruelty, he had brought himself here. To this perfect moment.

It required so much of him to remain silent, to sit in stillness. Sweat boiled from his pores and ran down his limbs. His heart galloped in his chest. The exquisite pain soaked into every part of him. Nearly from the beginning his phallus had become engorged. Twice he had ejaculated as the pain spiked inside of him, yet both times he ground his jaws together to suppress all sounds.

A mage stepped from the pattern of changing sorcerers and approached the dais with a bowl from which smoke arose from the burning of a blend of organic elements that included poppies, peyote, salvia, cannabis, ayahuasca, betel nut, jimsonweed, tobacco, coca, kava, nutmeg, nightshade, mimosa, morning glory, the skin of certain frogs and toads, and five different kinds of fungi. He bowed and held it up. The Witch-king leaned forward, using one hand to raise his veil and the other to waft the smoke toward his nose. It was bitter, pungent in awful ways, and it struck his mind with the force of a hammer.

He reeled back, his body instantly contorted by muscle spasms. He could feel rips opening in his biceps and abdomen and all along his spine. Screaming would have helped him bear the pain, but the Witch-king would not—absolutely would not—utter a sound.

Even if it drove him mad.

Even if it killed him.

CHAPTER ONE HUNDRED SEVENTY-SIX

The palace guards grabbed the twins and pulled them savagely back from the melting ice block.

They screamed and kicked at the guards. Alleyn tried to pull the big dagger, but the guard holding him slapped it out of his hand. Desalyn pulled her dirk, but the other guard slapped her across the face. It knocked the light from her eyes and the whole right side of her face bloomed with an angry red.

"What in the nine hells are you doing?" gasped the first guard. "That's *his* daughter. Gods above and below, we're going to be in real trouble."

And a voice said, "Oh, you're in much worse trouble than you think."

The guards and the twins turned to see a big man standing behind them. His face was a mask of deadly anger, eyes hotter than the blazing fire.

It was Alleyn who shouted his name.

"Captain Kagen!"

Kagen did not even bother to draw his daggers as he strode forward toward the guards holding the Imperial Seedlings.

The one with Alleyn tossed the boy aside with such force that he slid through the water and struck the foot of the ice block. Then the guard rushed Kagen with a raised sword.

Kagen stepped into the swing, checking the guard's wrist with his left forearm and striking him four times with incredible speed—nose, right eye, temple, and throat. The blows were powered with rage and hate and fear. And love, for here were the children he had been oath-bound to protect. It did not matter to him in that moment that they were corrupted by their adoptive father. It did not matter that they were Herepath's bastards, born out of an illegal tryst with the empress.

They were children he loved.

They were children upon whom his oath, his soul, his honor, his worth as a man were based. Each of those four blows carried that force of need, that power of will. Each did dreadful damage, and the last was fatal, and all of it in a single moment.

Then Kagen stepped toward the other guard, but this one—the one who had hit Desalyn—now clutched her in front of his own body and laid his sword blade across her throat.

"I'll kill her," he warned.

"And then what?" said Kagen. "If you harm her, your life will mean nothing. The Witch-king will flay you alive and do the same to everyone you know and love. Though, let's face it, I'll kill you first. Hurting her and being skinned by your king would be a mercy compared to what I will do."

The man's eyes flicked left and right as if looking for more than the door out of the room. He seemed to be looking for some way to step back into a point before he had made the two worst decisions of his life.

Desalyn stood stock still, frozen by the cold steel against her windpipe. Her eyes were full of pleading as she looked up at Kagen. And then her lips formed a word.

Her name.

Not Foscor.

Desalyn.

Kagen felt the floor tilt under his feet as the truth of that hit him.

He did not let it show on his face. He relaxed his posture, affecting an almost casual stance.

"Listen to me," he said conversationally. "We're both in a bind here. We both know that you can't hurt the girl."

"I will, I swear it."

"No," said Kagen. "You won't, and here's why. Right now the Witch-king doesn't know anything's happened. The only person who could tell him is that asshole over there." He ticked his head toward the second guard. "He's dead. He won't be ratting you out and I sure as hell won't tell the Witch-king. The only person who knows you made a bad choice is me, and if you give me the girl—alive and unharmed—I'll let you go. You can run, gather up anyone who matters to you, and get the hell out of Argon. I hear Bulconia is a nice place to retire. Maybe one of the islands. The choice will be yours. Free the girl and go."

"How can I even trust you?"

Kagen placed his hand over his heart.

"I give you my word," he said. "I swear on my immortal soul that I will not lay a hand on you."

The man hesitated.

"Every second you waste is one less second you have to get to safety."

The hand holding the sword trembled.

Kagen waited. Desalyn's eyes bored into him, but he made himself ignore her and kept his eyes on the guard.

"You swear?" asked the guard.

"On my soul."

It took one more long moment, then the guard lowered his sword. With a sudden jerk he shoved Desalyn toward Kagen and bolted for the door.

Kagen caught Desalyn in the crook of his left arm, reached over his shoulder as he pivoted, drew his throwing knife from the sheath just below his neckline, and threw. The blade spun once and buried itself into the socket at the base of the guard's skull. The throw was lightning fast and very hard, and the knife buried itself deep into the brain. The guard fell bonelessly and slid five feet along the polished marble.

"It's your bad luck that I'm damned," mused Kagen. "No soul to swear on."

Still holding Desalyn, Kagen ran over to where Alleyn lay. The boy was awake but dazed. Kagen gathered him up with his right arm and knelt there, holding the children close.

"Kagen," wept Desalyn. "I *knew* you'd come."

Alleyn suddenly wrapped his arms around Kagen's body. "Kagen! I'm sorry I'm sorry I'm sorry . . ." The words tumbled out.

"I have you, Alleyn," said Kagen. "I have you, Desalyn. You're safe now."

Fat drops of cold water fell on Kagen's shoulder and then a voice, raw, weak, but full of anger.

"Take your hands off those children," it snarled.

Kagen looked up at the figure who was nearly free of a block of ice. Naked, pale, with eyes filled with madness and desperation and pain.

The eyes of his brother.

The eyes of *Herepath Vale.*

Fabeldyr's single cry of need and despair echoed through airless space.

It was in the nature of magic that this sound was able to flourish there, and to go on and on until it found the ears that could hear such a cry.

Hear and respond.

Closer and closer did Vathnya and his consorts come.

They, firstborn of the universe's firstborn.

Scriosta and Uktena, Yamraaj and Vorth—all of them soaring through infinite time and space in answer to one lonely, faint, dying plea.

CHAPTER ONE HUNDRED SEVENTY-EIGHT

Kagen shot to his feet and dragged the children away from the man.

"Be damned to you," growled Kagen. "This is another wizard's trick."

The ice man was free from mid-thighs up and he struggled feebly against the ice that still held his legs. Small cracks appeared in the block and water continued to flood the floor.

"Kagen," called Redharn as he charged into the room, his big axe raised. "What madness is this?"

The rest of the Bloody Bastards came in behind him, weapons drawn but each face wearing a mask of confusion and uncertainty. The twins huddled close to Kagen, and he backed up until he could set them down safely. Even then they clung to him. The ice man reached for them, but with his legs trapped he could do nothing more. Gi-Elless had her bow drawn.

"Say the word, captain, and I'll kill that thing," she said softly. "The arrow's covered with *eitr.*"

That made the ice man turn toward her, his eyes going wide and becoming less glassy.

"*Eitr?*" he said in a voice so weak it was barely audible. "How . . . came you . . . to have the god-killer poison on a Samudian arrow?"

Kagen called to Pergun and Urri to each take one of the children. They protested but he assured them it would be fine. Once free, he drew his daggers and stood in a combat crouch, the blades crossed in front of his heart.

"These blades are seasoned with *eitr*, too," he said to the ice man. "Whatever you are—demon, golem, monster—one scratch and you'll be dead."

That seemed to calm the ice man. He smiled faintly and looked down at his body, and at the ice around his legs.

"You . . . have me at a . . . disadvantage," he said. Then he looked at the weapons in Kagen's fists. "Gods of the Harvest . . . I know those blades."

"Who or what are you?" demanded Kagen. "Why do you wear my brother's face? Or is this another of your hellish Hakkian tricks?"

The ice man studied him. As he did so, a big chunk of ice fell away from one leg. He made no attempt to free his other, though. His skin was a deathly color, but there was a faint flush of pink appearing on his cheeks and upper body. He began to speak and choked on his words. He swallowed as best he could and tried again.

"Are you Kagen Vale or is this another of your enchantments, Gethon?"

Behind Kagen, he heard Redharn say, "Um . . . what . . . ?"

"Stand firm," snapped Kagen. He took a step toward the ice man. "Dare you call me by that name?"

"What should I call you, then?" answered the man. "You were always so clever at glamours. You were always so fascinated by theriomorphy."

Kagen had to fish for what Frey had told him about that. Theriomorphy—the ability to change one's shape.

"I am Kagen Vale," he said. "Former captain of the palace guard and oath-sworn servant of Empress Gessalyn. Or I was until you had her murdered."

The look of shock and horror that appeared instantly on the ice man's face was profound.

"Murdered . . . no . . . you lie, damn you. She yet lives. There are her children. Can you not see the shadow of her face on theirs? She is not dead. My Gessalyn—my love . . . she lives. Say she lives."

"Kagen . . . ?" said Gi-Elless.

"What's he mean?" demanded Alleyn.

"Please," begged the ice man, "tell me that you lie. Tell me she lives."

Kagen took another step closer. "If you were really Herepath then you would not mourn her. Not the woman who rejected and condemned you. The woman who sent you to your death in the frozen north."

The ice man stared at him. "Is that what you think happened? That she *banished* me?"

"What, then? When she found out she was pregnant with Herepath's children, she sent him to the Winterwilds so he would be forgotten. So he would die."

"Kagen—if you are truly Kagen," said the ice man, his voice firming in his anger. "You were always naive. You even thought your prophetic dreams were only dreams. Banished? No. Condemned? That's absurd. She sent me north because she suspected Gethon Heklan had found a trove of great books of magic. She believed he had found where the last dragon had gone to hide, and Gessalyn wanted that creature—the one you dreamed about—found and protected."

The last chunk of ice toppled away, but the ice man did not

move. Kagen's knives were within easy striking range, and he was naked and weak. He looked around, frowning.

"I do not know this place. These things . . . they are the tools of alchemy, of sorcery. I recognize them. They belong to Gethon Heklan, the Hakkian Gardener. The vile traitor. But he did not bring all this to the north. This isn't the Winterwilds. Is this a castle? Gods above, is this the palace?" He turned alarmed eyes to Kagen. "Where *am* I? Why do *you* have Mother's knives? Where is she? Gods of the Green World, Kagen, tell me what has happened!"

Kagen had no idea what to say.

So many things that he had accepted as truths now hung on slender threads. His hands gripped the knife handles so tightly they trembled.

When he spoke, there was no certainty at all left in his voice.

"Can it be? Are you . . . are you him?" he stammered. Then, "Herepath . . . ?"

The ice man sagged, dropping to his knees in the meltwater pool.

"Kagen," he gasped. "Kagen, my brother . . . for the love of the gods, help me . . ."

![chapter divider] **CHAPTER ONE HUNDRED SEVENTY-NINE**

At the edge of the Field of Uthelian, Lady Maralina stopped and stood in the heavy rain. She turned her face south toward Argentium and closed her eyes.

Her dead heroes and kings and princes paused in their work. For the last hours they had broken apart the wagon in which she had escaped the town of Arras. It was taking a new shape now, that of a war chariot.

They worked without comment and without pause. They never tired for they had slept in their graves long enough. They were but faint shadows, nearly invisible in the sunlight. Clouds were coming in, though, and when one passed overhead, they seemed more substantial, though the only witnesses were the lady and the two monstrous black goats that stood nearby, waiting to pull that chariot.

Maralina let the wind tell tales to her, and one breeze whispered about two brothers in a forbidden room in the palace of the dead empress.

She smiled.

"Destiny's wheel turns and turns," said Maralina. Then she looked up at the clouds. "And fire is coming, too."

She turned to her army of the dead and nodded, for they were diligent in their work.

"Fire and tears," she whispered to the winter wind. "Blood and fate. The wheel turns and turns and turns."

CHAPTER ONE HUNDRED EIGHTY

Kagen sat on the sodden floor with Alleyn and Desalyn huddled close. The Bloody Bastards formed a tight ring around him, and in the center of that ring, wrapped now in a half-soaked blanket, was Herepath Vale.

Biter, who understood healing better than the rest, had crushed some herbs into a cup he took from a shelf and then filled it with wine. With Pergun's help he poured the wine into Herepath's mouth until the swallow reflex kicked in. Herepath coughed and gagged, but he got enough of the wine down to restore him from the semi-swoon into which he'd lapsed.

Now Herepath sat there, indifferent to the water, taking small sips from the cup and staring intently at Kagen and the children.

"They are her children," he said softly. "They are Seedlings."

"Yes."

Herepath's eyes were filled with a strange mixture of love and sadness.

"Kagen . . . are they . . . I mean, do they *know?*"

Kagen shook his head.

"Know what?" asked Desalyn.

"Hush now, sweetheart," soothed Kagen. "Let us talk and then we'll explain everything to you."

The children nodded, though it was clear they were full to bursting with unasked questions.

Herepath glanced at the ice, of which little now remained.

"How long?" he asked. "What is the year?"

"What is the last year you recall?"

"It was spring of the twenty-fifth year of the reign of Empress Gessalyn."

"Ah," said Kagen, still trying to accept the reality of this. "This is the twenty-ninth year."

Tears filled Herepath's eyes. "So long . . ." he breathed. "Gods . . ."

"Much has happened," said Kagen.

"Before you tell me, brother," said Herepath, "answer me this. Does she live? I ask, because I believe this *is* the palace, and you spoke of a Witch-king. Are my worst fears now the truth of the world?"

"She is gone," said Kagen. "Much has happened, and the world is close to burning down."

Those words struck Herepath as hard as an arrow. He closed his eyes for a moment, fighting for control.

"Tell me," he said when he could trust his voice. "Tell me everything."

And so Kagen did.

"I was drugged by a whore on my night off," he began. "And I woke to the sound of my own damnation."

King al-Huk stood on the quarterdeck of the *Falcon's Claw*.

Queen Theka of Theria stood on her own ship less than a bow shot to port.

They both looked at the burning sea.

It was still afternoon, though twilight was not far off. Dense purple storm clouds covered the sky. Lightning flashed within them, and low growls of thunder in the west promised a storm. The underside of the clouds glowed with flickering orange, reflected from the ten thousand fires below.

The Hakkian fleet had come to war, slipping from ports on many small islands, and sailing from inlets in Hakkia and from captured ports in Argon. Every ship that flew the black-and-yellow eclipse flag had come to challenge the rebel fleets.

And now every single one of the Hakkian ships burned.

Every one.

A light rain was falling, but it did nothing to quench those blazes. Ships from Nehemite and Vahlycor and even Behlia and Ghenrey had come to join the battle, cracking on with every possible sail set. There were even smaller ships from Tull Yammoth, a nation not known for waging war that had never joined the Silver Empire. Their mainsail displayed the image of Cthulhu with his bulbous head and beard of tentacles and spread bat wings. Seventy-eight privateers under letters of marque from independent island nations had come in answer to calls sent out by Hannibus Greel and countersigned by al-Huk.

Never in the history of the world had so many ships of war come together with such haste and such hate.

The fighting had been calamitous, and many a rebel ship burned, too. A third of the Samudians and Therians were destroyed. Half of the Vahlycorian ships were ablaze or had already sunk.

And yet . . .

Every Hakkian ship was burning down to the waterline. The

crews, mad with fear, had swum toward the enemy vessels, begging for mercy, crying out for quarter.

There was no quarter, no mercy to be found.

The swimmers were fended off with boarding pikes or shot with arrows. Not one Hakkian was pulled from the thrashing surf.

Al-Huk turned toward Queen Theka and stood there until she saw—or perhaps sensed—him and faced him. Their last meeting had gone badly, with hard words and bitter accusations. Now the young queen nodded to him, and he returned it, placing his hand over his heart. She did the same.

Then the king called for the admiral and flag captain and bade them send a signal to all ships to turn and set course for Haddon Bay.

CHAPTER ONE HUNDRED EIGHTY-TWO

There was no time for tears, but they wept anyway.

The children disintegrated into sobs as Kagen told Herepath of the deaths of the empress and her consort, and of the murders of the Seedlings. Kagen did not go into great detail, but it was clear that Herepath was able to excavate meaning, and he wept, too.

Then Kagen gave a concise account of what had happened to him. The deaths of their parents and brother, Hugh. The razor-knight. The gods appearing and turning their backs on him. His meeting Tuke, Filia, and Frey. The ascendency of the Witch-king, the atrocities inflicted across the empire by the Ravens and their mercenary hirelings. He spoke of the Unbladed and attempted assassination at the coronation. He told of his journey to Vespia to find the Seven Cryptical Books of Hsan. He spoke about the Tower of Sarsis and Lady Maralina. And of Frey sending Jheklan and Faulker to the Winterwilds. And he spoke of Jheklan's heroic death. Then he told Herepath of the war which was blazing now.

He said all these things and then sat with the room in utter silence.

Herepath got shakily to his feet and went and stood in front of the fireplace, steam rising from his soaked blanket.

"I never much liked Jheklan," said Herepath. "He and Faulker always played foolish games. But I think it was my fault that I never bothered to know who they became as men. And now you tell me they risked their lives to save the entire empire. You tell me Jheklan has died a hero, doing what I could not. He freed Fabeldyr. Gods . . . how blind I have been."

He paused, then added:

"It is a shame the dragon is dying, too. She might have saved him. Dragons, after all, are magic. But now I think it's far too late for Jheklan to be saved and too late for beautiful Fabeldyr."

"For what it's worth," said Kagen, "the Twins went up north without being told that you were the Witch-king. Jheklan died thinking you were still, well . . . you."

"And what am I? A cold, aloof, effete snob? An ascetic who looked down my nose at the antics of brothers who I regarded as—at best—nuisances and not as family? I do not deserve to bear the same last name as them. Or as you. And I failed Gessalyn and I failed Fabeldyr. It is a danger for anyone to put their trust in me. The academic who aspired to be a sorcerer and who is, in truth, nothing much at all."

After a moment, Kagen rose, letting Gi-Elless and Biter each take one of the children. He came over and stood beside his brother.

Herepath turned to him. "How you must have hated me."

"I guess I did."

"Do you still?"

"If you are my brother in truth, and if Gethon Heklan used a glamour on me and stolen memories to make me believe he was you, then no. Of course not. But then, I don't really know your story. All I know is what Mother Frey surmised, and she is wise but not infallible."

Herepath nodded.

"From what you tell me, Kagen," said Herepath, "I know we have very little time. But let me tell you about these same events from another perspective. I will endeavor to be concise, but there are things you must know."

"Tell me, then."

In truth, Kagen was already more than half convinced this man was his brother. But then again, he had been convinced of it months ago in the throne room. He had his thumbs hooked into the belt from which his daggers hung in their leather sheaths. Close at hand, and he knew he could draw them very fast.

"Yes," he said, "Gessalyn and I were lovers. And yes, when she became pregnant, the timing was wrong because her consort was away when the conception likely happened. Some would call what we did treason, and I suppose it was. We called it love, and love is how I will always remember it." He paused and closed his eyes for a moment, looking inward. Then he glanced at Kagen. "We knew that our secret needed to remain untold. I suggested that I absent myself to Skyria for a year or two. The consort, not being the brightest lad, would probably not care much about the math. Most men find the whole science and process of conception, pregnancy, and delivery unpleasant and try not to think about it, anyway."

"That's true enough," agreed Kagen.

"However, while I was making some plans to go to Skyria, Gessalyn's spies within the political circles of the Garden began hinting of a new threat."

"Do you mean the Office of Miracles?"

"What? No. Frey was very much respected, but there are other offices, including some mostly or entirely unknown to her. The Imperial Inquisitors still exist, even though that is something most people do not know. Their office was never closed down,

and its existence was kept secret even from the Office of Miracles."
He shook his head. "Politics. Wheels within wheels."

"Go on," prompted Kagen.

Herepath nodded. "Rumors began circulating that a man named
Gethon Heklan was becoming a force within the secret cults of
Hakkia. Notably the cult of Hastur. He was a firebrand in clan-
destine meetings, but in public was skilled at playing the role of
a well-intentioned and not very bright scholar. That was a role
he played to perfection, and he fooled even the senior Gardeners. He fooled me, in fact. First in Skyria, when I was there, and
then when we were at a convocation in Hakkia. There were clues,
though, and I should have picked up on them. His knowledge
of Vespia was oddly acute, and he knew much about the history
of dragons. He held to the old belief that it was the blood and
tears of the race of dragons that brought magic to this world. He
sought me out because I also believed this. I had even written a
paper speculating that the last dragon, Fabeldyr, was likely in hiding in the Winterwilds, a place where few humans ever visited."

"All of that is true."

"So I found out. Gessalyn deputized me to go and investigate
this. It took time to organize a party of scholars to go, ostensibly
to relieve other Gardeners who had been up there for years. It is
a bitter place, but fascinating in its way. So many strange artifacts
trapped in ancient glacier ice. Evidence of a high civilization that
predates our own. Very high, in fact, for I found images of men in
strange suits of armor walking on the surface of the moon." He
paused. "That is a discussion for another time."

"Yes," agreed Kagen.

"Once the legitimacy of my expedition was set, I went to the
Winterwilds."

"Wait," said Kagen, "I had been told that you were already
there when Heklan arrived. That's what Frey thought."

"She is right so often that it is difficult to catch when she's wrong," said Herepath with a small smile. "No, Heklan was there years before me. I arrived at about the time when my children were likely born. I . . . never saw them before today."

Herepath dabbed at his eyes.

"When I got there, it was obvious that Heklan had managed to achieve a position of some dominance over the site. The Gardeners were working *for* him. Some of that was accomplished because a large detachment of Hakkians had followed Heklan's party of Gardeners, arriving a few weeks later. Over time their presence was established and Gethon Heklan was running everything. So, when I arrived, it was obvious to me that the Gardeners were in fear of him, even though Heklan still played the role of affable fool."

"Did he capture you?" asked Kagen.

"Not at first, but I was watched constantly. Heklan allowed me freedom of action to a degree because I was rather better at those kinds of excavations than he was. I say this plainly, Kagen, because it explains why he let me more or less direct the dig site. It was I who found evidence to suggest that Fabeldyr was, indeed, there. It was I who found her in a cavern. It was an incredible day. Wonderful. And, oh Kagen, she was so beautiful. Nothing at all like what you described in your dreams. Strong, and graceful. Brilliant and kind."

Kagen saw the lights in Herepath's eyes as he spoke. There was remembered joy and respect and love there. And it moved him deeply.

"I managed to communicate with Fabeldyr in a limited way. Through meditation and shared dreams. I told her about you and the dreams you had. She said that you were different. Special."

"Special how?"

"She said that you were touched by the grace of the larger world."

"Not when I was a lad."

"Which is what I said to her, but she said time is a wheel,

and the larger world does not experience time in the way we do. She said that you would offer the gift of life to a dying immortal, and that would mark you in one way. And that you would be marked by the elvinkind for an act of mercy." He turned to Kagen and parted the blanket, touching a crescent scar on his chest. "Marked like this."

Kagen stared at the scar, which was identical to his own. "How . . . ?"

"I, too, have had my adventures, brother. And my meeting with the elvinkind is a story worth telling, but it is not part of this matter, so we will leave it for another day. If we have another day."

Kagen touched his own chest, and nodded.

"Once I had discovered Fabeldyr, Gethon Heklan changed. His true nature emerged," continued Herepath. "He revealed himself as the person in direct blood lineage from two important families. On his mother's side he is descended from a younger sister of Theselyanna of Mithlindel."

"The first Silver Empress," said Kagen.

"You are not surprised?"

"We've been putting pieces together ourselves. So, let me guess, on his father's side he was descended from the last Witch-king, the one killed by *our* ancestor, Bellapher the Silver Thorn."

"My, my, brother, you impress me." There was just a hint of Herepath's old haughtiness in that, and it somehow heartened Kagen, knocking away another brick in his wall of doubt. Herepath sighed. "One night Heklan called me into Fabeldyr's chamber and demanded that I teach him how to talk with her. Demanded, take note. When I saw that he had put the great beast in shackles, I was appalled. I sought to free her, and he had his guards restrain me."

Herepath paused for a moment, his expression wry.

"By then I knew how things were. I am no fool, Kagen, and even though he played his role so well, I had begun to suspect he was more than he seemed. I had also begun to carry knives with me. Daggers, much like those." He nodded to the Poison Rose's blades. "I fought back and accounted myself well enough, but there were far too many of them. They beat me unconscious, and I woke up in chains, bound to the same wall as Fabeldyr."

"I saw those chains," said Kagen.

"Heklan tortured me," said Herepath, and he opened his blanket to show the many scars of vicious treatment. Then he wrapped the cloth more tightly around his shoulders. "He used potions and spells on me, and then he began using some very old and very dangerous magicks. Sorcery of a kind that was forbidden even before the rise of the Silver Empire. He . . . invaded my mind, Kagen. It was a kind of rape. He took whatever he wanted and in doing so left scars there, too." He touched his head. "He took memories of Gessalyn, he took secrets about the palace. He learned about our family. Then, one day I awoke to see him standing in front of me *as* me. It was terrifying. Like looking into a distorted mirror. He had once written a paper about that kind of sorcery."

Kagen said, "'On the Nature of Consciousness, with Additional Notes on Thought Transference and Psychic Theriomorphy.'"

"How—?" began Herepath, then nodded. "Ah. Mother Frey told you of it?"

"She did."

Herepath shook his head. "With my stolen memories and his spells, Heklan *became* me. I think he appeared as me to the other Gardeners up there and by that deception learned who was plotting against Heklan. Then, when he had all that he needed from me, he cast another spell. I fainted away and dreamed that I was drowning in the Frozen Sea. Then . . . I woke inside this room. Inside enchanted ice. With years of my life gone. With my love, my sweet Gessalyn, murdered. And all those beautiful Seedlings. With

Mother and Father dead. And Hugh. And now Jheklan." He suddenly turned and gripped Kagen's hands, squeezing them with desperate force. "Gods of the Harvest, Kagen, this was *not even a day ago* for me. For me the ice cave and Fabeldyr and all of it are less than an hour ago."

His knees buckled and he sank down to the floor, his face in his hands, sobbing hard enough to break the walls of the palace. Kagen knelt and gathered him close, holding him.

Holding his brother.

He kissed Herepath's head and leaned his forehead against his brother's.

"Your children live," he told Herepath. "They will understand in time. They will come to know you and love you. And they are the future for which we are fighting. The crown of Argon is theirs, even if not the Silver Empire. They are Gessalyn's gift to you."

Herepath looked up with a red and swollen face, eyes filled with tears and pain. And only the smallest flicker of hope.

"Now, listen to me, Herepath," said Kagen. "Twilight is upon us and the new moon is rising."

"What of that?"

"The Witch-king is going to perform some kind of spell that will allow him to become a—"

"Gods of life and death," cried Herepath. "Do you speak of his *ascension*?"

"I do."

"And yet you let me prattle on about the past when our future is about to be stolen. Gods, you're a fool, Kagen. We need to act now. Tell me that you have an army ready at your call? Tell me that you have a plan, at least."

"I have the soldiers you see," said Kagen, "and we had a plan. Now, though, I think that plan is about to change."

In central Vahlycor there is a pit filled with spikes.

It is empty of life, but something moves deep within it. Pinned to the wall by the broken pieces of metal is a heavy tapestry. The bottom of it flutters as the vagaries of wind occasionally swirl down into the pit.

Embroidered onto the tapestry is an image of people fighting and dying. Of fires burning and blood flowing. The stitchery gives it all a strange sense of reality.

It hangs there in that empty space.

The rain falls and slowly begins filling the hole with puddles and shadows.

CHAPTER ONE HUNDRED EIGHTY-FOUR

General Filia led her fighters over the mounds of the dead and into hell itself.

She had her spiked buckler and longsword, and prayed that there was still enough *eitr* on each. As one monster lunged at her—a black-bearded knight in the livery of her own country, Vahlycor—she smashed its reaching hands away and slashed it across the thigh. The cold hands gripped her cuirass, but as it lunged forward for a bite, its knees went loose and it collapsed.

That heartened her, because too many of the living dead wore helmets over chain mail coifs or steel gorgets, preventing decapitations. Visors, too, were hindrances to sword cuts. But if *any* cut still worked, then she had a chance.

Horse found her and the huge dog fought beside and behind. Although it was an animal, Horse was a seasoned fighter who understood what did and did not work. The commands Filia had given him—to scratch rather than bite—made fighting more difficult, but as the dog's poisoned spikes brought down one after another of the creatures, Horse became excited. He slammed into the monsters, slashing and tearing with the spikes on his helmet and body armor.

Some of the other dogs in his pack fell, though. Either because their spikes hit armor rather than thin cloth or exposed flesh, or their poison was already spent. The creatures piled atop several of the hounds and tore them to pieces.

This enraged the rest of the pack, and their renewed savagery was horrible to witness.

Filia slashed right and left. She cut off hands and feet when no other targets were viable. She punched with the fist holding the sword, hitting the enemy in the face to knock their heads back and expose throats to her buckler's spikes.

Sweat poured down her face, stinging her eyes, but on she fought.

On the other side of the field, Tuke's troops were in frenzied combat with the combined forces of Unka the Spider and WarBride. The mercenary armies were tough and fresh, but they had to pass between burning wagons, and the Unbladed were the first fighters they met.

Mercenary to mercenary, with no quarter asked or offered, and no rules of fair combat observed. This was not what the mercenaries from the east were expecting. Mad Mari had said that the main rebel force were farmboys and soft offspring of the nobility, all of them weak from a thousand years of relative peace in the Silver Empire. They were not expecting the sophistication, brutality, and cunning of the Unbladed.

Even so, the combined eastern armies were bigger, and their mass—with thousands pushing from behind—began to tell. The burning wagons trembled and then fell over as Unka's men used spears to lever the vehicles off-balance. As each one crashed inward it drove the defenders back away from flaming debris. And that widened the narrow entries.

The mercenaries riding the small horses from the steppes moved with disheartening agility, rearing to kick, twisting to avoid spearmen, all while their riders steered with their legs and used their small bows to fire arrow after arrow.

Then WarBride burst through the gap and charged at Tuke. He did not know if she somehow recognized him or it was his bad luck, but the cannibal queen uttered a loud ululating howl and raced at him, whirling a whip above her head, the length of which was wrapped in spikes and barbs.

Tuke, on foot, wanted no part of that savage lash and he flung himself to one side, diving onto the dirt, skidding, then rolling sideways just in time to save his chest from being crushed by her horse's hooves. WarBride's horse responded to every subtle command, twisting, lunging, kicking, stamping as it chased the Therian.

Tuke tried to disembowel the animal, but a hoof caught him above the left elbow, breaking his arm and sending one machete whirling away like a sycamore seedpod. Agony exploded all through Tuke's body and he crawled on both knees and one hand. But the horse chased and WarBride's whip caught him across the back. His leather jerkin saved him, but the impact flipped him over onto his broken arm.

He convulsed in searing pain, yet somehow managed to hold onto his other machete. As the whip rose and came down again, Tuke cut sideways with all of his failing strength. It was not enough to sever the weapon, but it jerked it from her hand. However, the whip handle had a lanyard that looped around her wrist, and the force of the awkward blow pulled her halfway from the saddle.

Tuke rolled onto his knees and slashed again, and this time caught her across the side of her calf. WarBride screamed in pain and the horse, nicked by the end of Tuke's cut, reared and leapt forward. WarBride fell.

But she was cat-quick and threw herself at Tuke. She was a woman of considerable size and bulk—very fit and wearing a mix of chain mail and plate. The impact knocked the air out of Tuke and sent him crashing back to the ground, and this time he lost that second machete.

WarBride straddled him and began raining down blows with her mail-covered fists. Tuke could only use one hand to defend himself, and with every third punch WarBride struck his broken arm. The pain was unbearable, clouding his eyes with sparks.

His strength was failing, and he was taking terrible damage. So he bent his knees, braced his feet on the ground, and with a cry of rage he bucked his hips up and twisted his waist, sending her falling sideways. Tuke did not try to get up. Instead he pivoted on his hip and began to kick. He was a very big and very powerful man, and he had long legs and heavy boots. He kicked her in the wounded leg, in the crotch, in her stomach, but she kept swinging, using her pain to build her intensity to a point where nothing mattered except murder. Then Tuke rocked back onto his shoulders, brought both knees to his chest and kicked out with every bit of power he possessed.

He heard two sounds in a microsecond—the impact of his heels under her jaw and the wet *snap* of her neck.

WarBride fell backward, utterly slack.

Tuke lay on the ground, bleeding, aware that he had a broken nose, badly cracked ribs, and a broken arm. Pain tried to own him entirely.

He was never quite sure how he got to his feet. Everywhere around him was chaos. There were bodies everywhere, and the air was filled with screams. He wanted to scream, too.

Tuke saw one of his machetes and limped over to fetch it. His broken ribs shrieked as he bent over. But he got it and closed his hand around it, trying to draw strength from the weapon that had seen him through many battles.

There was no longer a gap between the wagons. The fight was everywhere. He saw Unka the Spider, the other enemy general, and began heading in that direction. In his semi-dazed mind he thought that if he could stop that man—kill or wound him badly enough—it would help his people win the battle. What swirled around him looked like a nightmare, with no side appearing to hold the advantage.

Once he was outside of the broken wagon barrier, however, things looked different.

The two mercenary armies, many on horseback, were crushing his forces. Not in one-to-one combat, but through sheer force of numbers. Their archery was a key factor, and almost all of the rebel archers were with Filia three hundred yards in the wrong direction.

Unka was yelling to his riders to rally behind him as he prepared to make a direct attack into the heart of the rebel camp. Realizing this, Tuke began to call for his Unbladed to form a line.

"We can't let them divide us," he roared. "They'll blindside Filia and the front line."

The Unbladed came, but not in great numbers, for they were still engaged in brutal close combat with the mercenaries. And many of their number lay dead on the ground. Though the fight had not been raging long, the rate of attrition was shockingly high.

"Hold fast, lads," Tuke said weakly. "Hold on . . ."

He staggered forward, raising his machete as two of Unka's riders galloped toward him with spears raised to kill him.

On the field with the living dead, Filia and her hounds had carved a deep path through the monsters. One of the undead creatures came at her and surprise nearly froze her.

It was Ghuraka. The leader of the Unbladed.

Dead, with half of her face cut away. One eye glared its unnatural hate at Filia. The other hung down on the ruin of her chin. Her teeth were broken but they snapped as Ghuraka charged.

Filia sidestepped, parrying with the buckler and then slashing with the sword.

And Ghuraka did not pause. She did not fall.

The last of the god-killer poison had been spent.

Filia cried out as the Unbladed ghoul clawed at her with bloody and broken fingers. She parried, kicking hard at Ghuraka's thigh. The shock knocked the woman to her knees and Filia leaped up, twisted, and brought the sword down in a heavy butcher's cut. The monster's head went rolling away, but came to rest facing Filia. The mouth worked for another two seconds, and then the eye glazed over and her expression settled into one of profound shock.

Filia crouched there where she had landed, gasping for air. The fight raged on, but beyond the undead she could see the Hakkian army coming. They were slow about it, and it occurred to her that they did not want to attract the dead to turn on them. Mad Mari rode at the front of her army, and as the main force of Hakkians emerged from the trees, Filia realized that her spies had grossly underestimated their numbers.

It was a tide of bodies. Tens of thousands of them, fresh, uninjured, marching in precise squares. She turned to look behind her and saw in the distance, the fight with the mercenaries.

This was Mad Mari's plan all along—to use monsters and magic and the Red Plague to force the rebels to reveal their strength, but also to wear them out, to separate them.

It was at that moment that Filia alden-Bok knew her army was going to lose.

There was no other possible outcome.

The dead were all around her and the living were marching in unstoppable numbers. Her heart sank in her chest.

Fabeldyr moaned in her sleep.

Faulker jerked his hand back, afraid he had caused her some unintentional injury, or touched too sore a place. Suds dripped from the bunched cloth he held.

The dragon's eyelids fluttered for a moment and she seemed to be looking at him.

"I'm sorry," he said immediately. "I didn't mean to . . ."

His words failed him as fat drops of water fell splatting on his face and hers. Faulker looked in surprise to see what looked like rain falling from the far shadows of the lofty ceiling. The drops were cold but not frigid, and as he stood there, the rain grew strangely warm.

"What in the hells . . . ?"

Alibaxter came tottering over, his face as confused as Faulker felt.

"Is this your doing?" demanded Faulker. "Did you try some damned spell?"

"No, no," cried Alibaxter. "I was making more soup and reciting a prayer for our dead friends. No spells."

"Then tell me why it's raining in a gods-damned ice cave."

"I . . . don't . . . know." The young wizard stared up at the falling rain.

Suddenly one of the huge stalactites cracked off and plummeted down. Alibaxter dove out of the way, and Faulker faded back, spreading his arms as if they and his body could shield Fabeldyr from further harm. The tons of ice struck the floor and exploded, sending pieces flying everywhere. Some struck Faulker, battering him down to his knees.

The rain fell harder, and there were other ominous cracks above.

Faulker lunged out, grabbed Jheklan and pulled his dead brother away as another spike of ice dropped. He pushed Jheklan's stiff form against Fabeldyr's belly. He was trembling with cold, with grief, with fear, and with doubt. The world was falling apart around him and there was nowhere to run, nothing he could do to stop it.

The ice ceiling was cracking apart as it melted, and now the falling water was a downpour of such intensity that he could barely breathe.

"Wait for me, brother," he whispered to Jheklan. "I'll be with you soon. You won't have to be alone."

Ice and rain fell with relentless intensity.

CHAPTER ONE HUNDRED EIGHTY-SIX

Herepath stripped the tallest guard and put on his clothes. Then went over to the couch on which the imperial twins sat between Redharn and Gi-Elless.

"This must be so strange and frightening for you," he said in the kindest, gentlest voice Kagen had ever heard him use. Alleyn and Desalyn pressed against the Unbladed.

"You're not our father," hissed Desalyn.

"You're some kind of monster," Alleyn snarled.

Herepath bowed his head. "A monster? Maybe. But I *am* your father. I loved your mother more than anyone on earth. I know that's too much for you to hear right now. Maybe you will always think me a madman and a liar. If so, I will understand. But know this—I will always love you and I will do everything that is within my power to protect you. Everything. No matter what the cost. Even if it means I lose you again."

A huge boom of lightning shook the palace. Herepath rose and glanced at the window, against which hard rain was hammering. Then back at his children.

"You do not deserve any of the harm that has come to you," he said. "You do not deserve to have witnessed the horrors that you have. Life has been unfair to you. It has been cruel to you. If you want to hate anyone, do not waste it on me. Hate the man who tore your world—and my world—apart. Gethon Heklan. Sorcerer. Murderer. Usurper. My brother, Kagen, and I are going to try and stop him. To . . . *kill* him. That is a hard thing for any adult to tell children. But these are dreadful times. Please believe that there will be life beyond these days. Life for you both. Happiness. Even hope."

With that he turned from them and took a sword and a dagger from the dead guard he had stripped. He walked over and stood with Kagen.

"If we are to do this, let us be about it."

Kagen looked him up and down. Herepath was thinner than he remembered, and despite having been frozen in ice for years, he seemed far older than he should have been.

"Tell me, brother," he said quietly, "have you been a Gardener so long that you've forgotten how to fight?"

Herepath gave him a look as cold as all the ice in the Winter-wilds.

"I am also a son of the Poison Rose," he said. "Now let's go show the Witch-king what that means."

Kagen had Pergun take the imperial twins to one of the secret ways that would lead out of the palace. Then gave him the address of one of Frey's allies, where the children could wait in safety. They vanished, with Desalyn and Alleyn pausing briefly to look at the two Vale brothers. Their expressions were unreadable, and then they were gone.

"Tell me," said Herepath when that hidden door was closed, "what weapons have you brought?"

Kagen explained about the tapestries and then unslung his pack and very carefully handed a canister of banefire to Herepath.

"So, the Hakkians manufactured it after all. I'm not surprised," said the Gardener. "I knew the secret of how it was made—from the saliva of dragons and certain chemicals from her dung. I told no one about it, though, because it is too dangerous a thing to be allowed to have on hand. I don't trust the wisdom or restraint of the common man to use it with any care." There was a hint of his aloof asperity that Kagen found oddly touching.

"He stole everything from your mind," said Kagen.

"And for that I will make him pay." Herepath nodded to the pack. "Do you have any of that *eitr* left?"

Kagen dug into his bag and produced a small vial. "Nearly forgot I had it."

Herepath took it and began seasoning his weapons. "It may not work on the Witch-king if he is well into his ascension, but I expect I'll find a good use for it."

"Let's be about it then," said Kagen after more thunder crashed outside.

"Wait," said Herepath, glancing around at the alchemy laboratory. "Kagen, have you noticed how closely Heklan modeled this room after the one I used to have? He must have stolen this from my memories, too, the fiend."

"If we had more time," said Kagen, "maybe you could whip up a potion or two, but we have to go now."

"Give me but a moment." Herepath shook his head as he went over to a table crammed with jars of chemicals and potions, made a few thoughtful choices, found a canvas sack, and placed the items inside. Then he nodded. "Now I am ready."

Redharn looked at him. "You really know how to use that stuff?"

"Yes," said Herepath smoothly, "and I daresay better than Gethon does."

They entered the secret ways and turned in a different direction from where Pergun had taken the children. Redharn and a few of the others made warding signs, but Herepath looked the other way and did something Kagen had not seen in many months. He raised his hand in a Gardener's blessing.

As the Gardener turned, he became a Vale, a son of the Poison Rose, a hunter and a killer, and they all ran through the darkness with hate in their hearts.

CHAPTER ONE HUNDRED EIGHTY-SEVEN

The mercenaries brought their arms back to throw their spears, and Tuke stood on trembling legs, hunched over with pain, with only one machete. He knew that he looked at his death, and in that moment, time seemed to slow down.

He saw each rise and fall of the horses' hooves. He saw rain falling slantwise, striking Unka's men, the impacts bursting with small droplets. He saw muddy dirt kick up behind the animals. And he saw the slow-motion grace of the muscular arms, and the elegant beauty of the spearpoints—finely formed steel etched with filigree.

He saw all of this in a moment that was stretched to forever.

In his periphery he saw his soldiers fighting with all of their skill and bravery. The Bloody Bastards—those that still lived— and the rebels. All of them splashed with blood that now ran in pink lines of rainwater. He saw arrows fly with slow elegance through the troubled sky.

Tuke wished he could see Filia, just to know that she yet lived even if this was his end. He grieved for the loving heart that would break in her chest, and he prayed to Mother Hydra to give her strength and healing.

He raised his weapon as high as his broken body would allow.

And then darkness seemed to obscure his vision. It was not the shadow of a cloud. It was not his own death. Not yet.

It was something else. Intensely dark. Huge.

Something that stepped into the path of the galloping horses.

Then the world went mad, for what happened next made no sense.

The horses and their riders seemed to fly apart in a bursting cloud of brilliant red. Shockingly bright red painted on the canvas of the moment. The two spears spun away, their shafts snapped in multiple places. The meat of men and animals thudded to the ground.

All around him the fighting stopped.

Everyone and everything simply stopped.

Tuke stood, machete raised, as the dark thing that had just killed the mercenaries turned slowly to face him.

It was something he had seen before. Faced before.

But it could not be here.

They had left it in the dense forests of cannibal-infested Vespia. It was a monster out of a nightmare.

It was a razor-knight.

The thing towered over Tuke, looking down at him with eyes made of living fire. The blood that had splashed on it melted into the stygian armor as if consumed by it.

Tuke held his machete, ready to go down fighting.

But the razor-knight turned away again. It walked toward a knot of WarBride's pikemen. They pressed together in their terror, but as it stalked toward them, they summoned their courage and attacked, stabbing with a score of pikes and spears.

Unka's cavalry charged the monster.

Archers fired at it.

Swordsmen surrounded the thing, chopping with their bright steel.

And it did them no damned good at all.

Filia and Horse fought the dead while the living marched toward her.

She yelled orders to her officers, and they to their sergeants, but Filia could not get to high ground to see if the rebel troops were responding. Perhaps they had lost heart when their friends and family members rose from death as monsters. As she cut and slashed and hacked, Filia tried to imagine what she would do if it was an undead Tuke facing her.

I would die, she thought, meaning it two ways. Her heart would die at the certainty of his death, and then her body would die because she did not think she could fight him. Not Tuke.

Tuke was love to her. He was joy and hope. He was the future, beyond the borders of war and death.

But still she fought. Killing Hakkians and rebels with the same flagging energy. Killing the dead.

How Mad Mari must be laughing at the army of resistance spending its resources in fighting those they had already killed. And fighting their own. Fighting those who, moments before, had been beside them but who the dead killed and the Red Plague brought back.

By the gods, how she wanted to be within arm's reach of Mari Heklan. It would be so satisfying to kill that beast of a woman even if it was Filia's last act.

Then a sound tore through the air and she stepped back from the creature she'd just decapitated. The hollow but piercing call of a horn soared over the field, and all of the living who were not locked in combat with a monster turned to look. Filia saw the Hakkians turn, too. All of them looking north.

"Gods below," she gasped. "Now what?"

In the small gap of both time and space, she saw past the undead to a patch of clear ground. A chariot had ridden onto the field, and the sight of it tore a cry from her, as from many others.

It was made of black-painted wood and unadorned and was pulled by creatures every bit as strange and unnatural as those that had attacked an hour ago. They looked like goats but were larger—larger by far—than even the most massive warhorses. Their coats were as dark as midnight and their horns were exaggerated and grotesque, curling out over nightmare versions of goat faces. The animals cried aloud, but louder still was a horn blown by the rider of the chariot.

It was a woman with long hair that whipped out behind her.

She wore an elaborate headdress that was bizarre and monstrous. The centerpiece of it was a human skull with one empty eye socket and one glass one painted to look like that of a dragon, with a black slit of a pupil and radiating blue flames. Atop the skull was an ornate golden crown set with teardrop crystals set in a ring around a disk that could represent the sun or moon. Large teardrop crystals formed a pyramid above the skull's brow, with the topmost pointing its tapered spike upward while the others were pointed down. From either side of the skull stretched massive impala antelope horns, while ram's horns curled out and down from the back, nearly to her shoulders. And the skulls of nightbirds rose up behind in a bold fan-shape framed by feathers dusted with gold.

Around her, obscured by falling rain and gathering mist, were vague shapes that ran without a sound. Men with armor of a kind that Filia had only ever seen in very old paintings. Nearly a hundred men with sigils on their chests unknown anywhere in the present world. They carried axes and two-handed swords, some of which looked rust-eaten and brittle. They uttered no war cry or challenge. Their feet splashed in puddles but without noise. Even their chain mail was silent.

As they approached, something happened that Filia could not understand. The dead, who still swarmed in great numbers, *also* turned to face these newcomers. Despite the lack of sound, they appeared to all become suddenly aware of the silent army.

And those hushed warriors ran directly toward the dead.

With a unified snarl, the living dead staggered forward, forgetting in that moment the living they had been fighting and devouring. They growled and snapped, but Filia thought she heard a different note in their cries.

Was it fear?

Could it be fear? How could the dead fear anything?

As the tall woman in the strange headdress drew her chariot to a stop, the ghostly soldiers ran to form a curved line between her and the hungry dead. For a moment silence fell across the Field of Uthelian.

Then the woman raised a horn and blew another note.

And the ghosts of pale kings and princes, of heroes and champions, attacked the risen dead.

Filia stared, her sword forgotten in her hand. Horse cowered beside her, whimpering in fear. The Hakkians stood silently, eyes wide in confusion, their officers paused in the act of ordering them to attack.

The ghosts did not pause—they moved with incredible speed but without sound as they met the onrushing ghouls. Their blades flashed and maces crashed and the dead began to fall. Some of the undead cannibals leapt upon the ghosts and bit them, but as soon as their teeth sunk into the gray flesh of these warriors, the dead withered, their flesh drying in a flash as if the process of decomposition was sped up many hundreds of times. Their muscles shrank and tendons contracted and their teeth fell out. The cartilage and sinew holding their bones together became dust and the rain washed it away as they collapsed to the ground.

Filia heard her name called and she turned toward the woman

in the chariot. Instinctively she understood that this woman had said nothing aloud, for the sound was only in Filia's head.

Filia alden-Bok, companion of Kagen Vale. You were once his lover and now you fight as his trusted ally and friend, said the voice. *For his love of you and of Tuke Brakson, I have come to fight beside you.*

"Who are you?" Filia asked aloud.

You know who I am.

"Gods of the Fields . . . Are you *her*? You're Lady Maralina . . . ?"

The enemy is poised to strike, said Maralina. *You have but seconds to rally. Come, let us draw blood together.*

"This is madness," breathed Filia. "Shouldn't you be with Kagen?"

He has other allies. Let us show the enemy what madness means.

With that, Maralina snapped the reins and the two monstrous goats reared up, crying out in horrifying voices. Their hooves struck down and the shock of it seemed to punch upward into the sky, which split apart with red lightning and a deafening crash of thunder.

Filia whirled toward her stunned and motionless army. She raised her sword and yelled as loud as she could.

"Death to the Witch-king!"

They stared at her. Then, one soldier, a common pikeman from some rural farm, raised his weapon. "Death to the Witch-king," he cried.

And then the shock and stillness shattered as thousands upon thousands of rebels from every city and town from Sunderland to Nelfydia screamed out the same words. The same shout. The same promise.

Filia yelled with them as she turned and ran across the field with her entire army behind her. The storm raged overhead. The kings and heroes fought the living dead. Maralina laughed louder than the thunder as Chernobog and Baphomet pulled her chariot toward where Mad Mari was staring in abject horror.

Faulker knew it was his end.

He could bear it only because Jheklan had already gone on ahead. Even though they were not true twins—born, as they were, a year apart—he felt as if Jheklan were his other half. In every wild scheme, dangerous adventure, and fierce battle they had been side by side. Never apart. Not until now.

So, Faulker was willing to die if there was nothing else he could do. Living without Jheklan felt small, hollow. Not worth the effort.

He hunkered down over Jheklan's body and gathered him up. His brother's flesh was cold and still, but Faulker didn't care. He leaned his shoulder against the dragon's great bulk and tried not to be afraid of the dying.

Massive chunks of the ceiling collapsed. He had seen Cat and the rest of the expedition scramble up and into the corridor that led to escape. Alibaxter lingered there, too, calling for him.

"Leave him," the wizard shouted above the din of falling water. "Come on, there's still time."

But Faulker just shook his head.

"*Please,*" begged the wizard.

Faulker gave him a small, sad smile and shook his head again. He held Jheklan with one arm and reached out to place the open palm of his other hand against the rows of scales over Fabeldyr's struggling heart.

It took a moment for the truth of it to sink in for Alibaxter. The young man sagged a bit, his face falling into grief but also understanding. He nodded.

And yet Alibaxter did not run. He stayed there in the mouth of the corridor as meltwater fell in torrents. Already the cavern floor was awash. Small waves lapped against the dragon and the brothers.

"Hey," Faulker murmured to Jheklan, "at least there will be

people to tell the tale. We might finally get that song we always wanted."

His voice broke as he said this.

Suddenly a massive chunk of ceiling fell, shattering into thousands of fragments. Light poured down, and Faulker looked up, confused. Was it the sun? This far down?

He did not understand how the glacier was melting at all, or why the meltwater was warm rather than cold. Steam rose from it in clouds, and the light turned it into a golden haze that seemed to flicker.

Faulker stared at it.

The steam was rising quickly but then it seemed to vanish as if the sunlight was drying the droplets of water. The cavern was warmer now, and getting warmer moment by moment. How was that even possible?

Then another huge section of the ceiling vanished, but it did not fall. Instead it was simply gone, as if pulled off from above. Which, of course, was impossible.

The heat kept rising, and now all of the ice around him was melting. The walls. The floor. The steam was hot, too. He cringed back from it, clawing Jheklan's corpse closer.

That golden light was everywhere above, so bright he could not look at it.

Too bright to be sunlight.

Far too bright, but what else could it be?

Fear wrapped itself around his heart, and Faulker stared in terrified wonder as something seemed to block the light. Just for a moment.

Something big.

Huge.

There was a huge sound like a house burning out of control. That kind of roar. And he realized that it was not sunlight melting the cavern.

It was fire.

Above the fire, the dark shape reappeared, and it was as if—impossibly—the shape was *causing* the fire. Sending it downward in long sprays. The heat was oppressive and he felt faint. His vision was simultaneously blurred by steam and dried by heat as the dark mass descended into the cavern.

Faulker hovered on the edge of darkness as he suffocated from that infernal heat.

Then the fire abated and something crouched there in the center of the cavern.

It was so massive. Bigger than any living thing he could imagine. Its body was black and veined with red that glowed like lava. It stood there on two titanic rear legs, its body upright, claws flexing as steam whirled around them. Gigantic wings stretched out and these were so vast the leathery tips touched the near and far wall. And above it, looking down from a hundred feet above where Faulker, Jheklan, and Fabeldyr lay, was a head that was at once hideous and beautiful. Huge jaws opened to show rows of teeth as tall as a man, and a forked tongue that snapped and twisted. A nest of horns fanned back from the mouth and brow, forming a kind of crown, and its eyes—Gods of the Pit, those eyes—were not the eyes of a simple animal, but were filled with ancient wisdom, immeasurable understanding, and bottomless rage.

The thing was fifty times more massive than Fabeldyr.

It was a dragon. It was one of the dragons Alibaxter had told him about. How Faulker knew *which* one was something Faulker could not comprehend. He just knew.

Scriosta the Destroyer had come to earth and had found his sister. Found her marked by chains and torture. Burned and scarred. Dying.

The creature glared its hatred down at Faulker Vale, and opened its mouth to punish this man with fire and hate.

And fire filled the cavern.

CHAPTER ONE HUNDRED NINETY

The room was filled with energy.

Anyone could feel it. Even the stones of the floor vibrated with it, the mosaics in the wall trembled at its caress. In places it was even visible, with strange shimmering shapes—cones and stars and pyramids and orbs—appearing like translucent mirages. Sometimes it was a single three-dimensional geometric structure and then the entire great hall seemed to be painted over with an entire city of those forms. There were ruins in Skyria and Vespia of the same bizarre architecture. These were buildings and ramps and courtyards and long sets of stairs that were clearly never meant for human beings. They were too big, and even in the reduced scale of illusions that was obvious to any insightful mind. And everyone in that hall was a sorcerer of great subtlety and deep knowledge.

These cities came and went—some wrapped in vegetation of unnamable kinds, others shrouded in ice or drowned beneath blue waves. Then the shimmering images changed to show clusters of stars and planets. One was where two suns hung in an alien sky, and swirling between them was an improbable number of planets, uncountable moons, and rivers of shattered rocks that floated through the void. This faded to be replaced by an even greater system where seven suns dominated a complexity of a hundred worlds—some rocky, others bloated gas giants.

Voids opened, revealing within them other universes, one inside another inside another into true infinity. Through these voids strange shapes flew across the face of forever. Vast monsters in the shape of dragons but as large as planets.

The hall was plunged into sudden darkness so intense even the hundreds of candles burned black and lightless.

"O', Hastur, Shepherd God who stands above all," chanted the priests and magicians. "Fill your vessel with your holy presence that he may unite all the warring tribes of earth and bring them to the true faith. This we pray, Hastur, chief of the Great Old Ones, superior godhead of all creation."

The Witch-king stood at the top of the dais, arms stretched above him. His yellow robes swirled as if he stood in a windstorm as wild as the hurricane raging outside.

Since the ceremony began, the Witch-king had visibly changed. He was taller and broader of shoulders and chest. His loose robes were growing tight and slits had opened in the fingers of his silk gloves. He was breathing heavily as the exertion of *becoming* drew on the resources of the human parts of his body.

He turned toward the statue of Hastur, and it, too, seemed larger. The empathetic and loving smile carved into the statue's handsome face seemed to be sterner than before, the eyes more amused but without their gentle benignity. The smile taking on qualities of mockery.

The Witch-king lowered his arms and then pointed one long finger at a magician near the foot of the dais who was using the smoking end of a joss stick to trace sacred symbols in the air.

"You, my child, loyal son of Hakkia, servant of the Yellow God," said the Witch-king in a voice as deep as the thunder without. "Come and give your love and your heart to our god."

The magician began weeping with joy and he rose from where he had been kneeling, bowed low to the king, and then walked like a man entranced to the golden statue. He knelt again and wrapped his arms around one of Hastur's legs.

"I give my love willingly and completely," he cried. "My heart, my life, my soul is yours."

His body suddenly stiffened and then began to shake with spasms so intense that his kneecaps drummed a tattoo on the marble floor. His eyes lost all color, turning white as eggshells and, as the others in the hall watched, the brown of the man's hair faded to a snowy whiteness and then to a translucency. His flesh paled, as did the sacred tattoos on his face and hands. Every bit of color on him, even his clothes, was leeched away, and there were lines of every hue flowing toward and into the statue, there to vanish.

When the process was done, the man still knelt there, but all earthly colors were gone from him and instead he had taken on a new hue. A color that had no corollary on that plane of existence. A color from beyond the stars, one that no human eye could behold without risking madness.

Then the man's body collapsed. Not merely down to the floor, but in on itself, as if he had become a hollow thing, defined only by paper as thin as tissue. And that, too, dwindled down to scraps that were caught in the strange winds around the Witch-king, torn to dust, and then vanishing entirely.

Some of the sorcerers in the room cried out in exultant joy at the sight of this miracle. Others shouted praise for the sorcerer who had demonstrated a faith beyond anything they had witnessed before.

Some, however, screamed in horror.

They looked wildly around as the lines of guards against the wall turned and marched to the big doors in the back of the room and to the smaller doors behind the throne platform. The guards pounded on the doors, six beats then four then six. At once there were sounds from the other side of every door—that of hammering. Not of fists, but of mallets and nails. The great hall was being sealed from without.

The hammering went on and on, telling the story that this was no small blockade but a total encapsulation of the hall. Then the last pounding noises ended. The guards inside turned toward the magicians, all of whom were staring now—even the most devout looking uncertain. At a word from the sergeant, the guards drew their swords and took up combat postures. They said nothing nor did they move, but the message was clear even to the meanest intelligence—no one was to leave that room.

Faulker did not even turn away.

This was certain death, and he clung to Jheklan as Scriosta the Destroyer leaned forward to exhale that fiery blast.

Then the world went dark, lightless.

Faulker screamed, thinking he was falling into the pit. The heat was unbearable and yet . . .

He did not burn.

Jheklan did not burn.

Then he realized that the darkness he saw had a shape. He raised his head and looked up and to either side. The blackness was edged with fiery light, but it was not death's cloak falling over him. It was leathery and huge, with a curve at the top from which three crooked fingers extended; and it tapered to a point twenty feet to his right. Below, brushing the melting floor, were serrations like those on a bat's wing.

Wing.

"Gods of the Pit!" he cried as he understood. At the moment when the gigantic black dragon had spat its fire, the dying dragon had covered him and Jheklan with her wing, saving them from incineration.

Sheltering them.

The fire slowed and stopped. More meltwater rained down and ran in rivers all around them. Steam hissed in the air.

The wing trembled weakly and then folded back against Fabeldyr's side to once more reveal the immense mass of Scriosta.

In the tunnel's mouth, Alibaxter stood, eyes wide and mouth hanging open in pure shock.

Fabeldyr's weight shifted and Faulker fell away from her, pulling Jheklan with him. He would never let go, no matter what happened. Faulker had to kick backward as the tortured dragon struggled to get to her feet. It took terrific effort and twice she fell, then Scriosta reached out and—with surprising gentleness—wrapped one massive foot over her back and helped her up.

Faulker looked into the Destroyer's eyes as he looked at Fabeldyr. There was awareness and understanding and pity.

And there was love.

Scriosta uttered a series of hisses and clicks and growls. A language of sorts, Faulker guessed. After a while, and with a hoarse voice, Fabeldyr replied.

He lay there, shocked, half-scalded, and felt his absolute terror melt and change into a kind of fascination.

I'm listening to dragons talk.

That thought walked slowly through his mind. As he considered the insanity of that, as well as its absolute truth, he hugged the cold body of Jheklan as tightly as he could.

I wish you could see this. Gods of the Harvest, how I wish you were here with me to see this.

Then the bizarre conversation between the two dragons ended and they both turned their monstrous heads and fiery eyes toward him. And then Scriosta suddenly reached out a massive claw and it closed around him and Jheklan, extinguishing all light.

CHAPTER ONE HUNDRED NINETY-TWO

As Maralina drove toward the front line of the Hakkian army, Mad Mari waved frantically for her sorcerers. They clustered around her, both human mages and the deadly Hollow Monks.

"Whatever that thing is," cried Mari Heklan, "*kill it.*"

Some of the sorcerers looked uncertain, a few were openly afraid, but most grinned with a malicious delight. They were brimming with unspent power. They hurried forward and the soldiers stepped hurriedly out of their path.

The chariot was tearing across the field.

One of the most powerful of the wizards, Prythor of Vendelos, pointed to the two giant black goats. "Those are the Witch-king's children. How dare she suborn them to her will. For that I will break her and as she lies dying, I will watch as a hundred soldiers use every hole of her. She is a faerie slut who deserves even worse than that."

Prythor stepped forward, raising his hands to the raging storm and shouted a long-forbidden spell.

"Y' uln mgn'ghftor l' h' fm'latgh bthnkor ng h' ah'r'luh orr'e ph'nglui li!"

The very air seemed to recoil from those awful words, and above them lightning ripped downward at his command, trying to burn the flesh from Maralina's frame and send her soul to everlasting torment.

Maralina raised her hand and as she did so, Nightsong materialized in her pale fist. Her action began at the moment of his spell and as the shadow-sword rose into the air, so the lightning struck.

The blast was immediate and enormous, and it sent a shockwave out in all directions. Any Hakkian or undead corpse in its path erupted into blue-white flames that burned them to ashes. The fading edge of that shockwave knocked most of the sorcerers down and tumbled Mad Mari from her horse. She landed hard in the mud.

Of Prythor there was nothing left except mud charred to cracked crystals.

And before the gathered magicians could recover, she was among them.

Maralina waved her hand and the harnesses around Baphomet and Chernobog fell away, freeing them. The goats jumped forward and crashed into the massed pikemen. Maralina alit from the rolling wagon as lightly as a dancer, leaving the chariot to slam into two Hakkian generals who were trying to flee.

The lady of the tower walked forward, Nightsong in her right hand.

The Hollow Monks formed a barrier between her and Mad Mari. They dug into pockets within their voluminous gray robes and produced small blue spheres and hurled them. One burst in the air directly in front of Maralina and burned with sapphire flame.

And she waved it aside with her left hand.

The others threw their globes, filling the air with intense explosions. Only when six detonated at the same moment did she pause, but that pause was the length of a heartbeat. Then she was among them.

Nightsong was a blur of shadows that slashed through the Hollow Monks. Their robes collapsed emptily to the mud or were whipped away by the storm winds. Two of the monks pulled off their gloves, revealing mottled hands ripe with lesions and tipped with poisoned claws. They grabbed her, tore at her.

She allowed it, amused as their triumphant cries changed to shrieks of pain. Their robes turned into twisting tangles of gray snakes that crushed the demons within the cloth.

A hundred yards behind her, Filia and the hounds were running to join the battle, and behind her were the remnants of the rebel army.

Filia saw what Maralina was doing, and her mind tried to resist, to make her want to stop and turn aside. This whole war was polluted with magic and who was she but a human woman? This was not her fight.

But it was her war, and that kept her running. Despite the deep weariness in her body, despite the pain and terror, she ran.

And before she knew it, she was among them. The Hakkians outnumbered her forces, but they were distracted, watching their powerful sorcerers fall one after another to a woman. One woman.

The rebels hit them hard, taking the moment offered to them.

Filia and Horse struck at the same moment, she with her sword and he with his spikes and fangs—for he was fighting the living now. His pack swarmed behind him, and screams challenged the thunder.

Maralina saw Filia alden-Bok as the young woman fought. Her reaction surprised her, for she had never thought much of the mortal world. Her ghosts were also her victims—men she had drained dry to feed the blood hunger inflicted upon her by Duke Sárkány and enchanted by faerie magic. The first human she had ever cared about was Kagen the Damned—a mortal touched by many kinds of magic. Dragon magic in his boyhood dreams, prophecy by Selvath the Seer, her own magic, and more recently the grace of the elvinkind.

But Filia was nothing but a woman of barely thirty summers.

Who was she that deserved consideration? She was not Kagen's lover. In a blink of time's eye she would be dust and bones. So who *was* she that Maralina should even care?

And yet she did care.

Maralina cared about her. She cared about the laughing giant, Tuke. She cared about Herepath, who was damned in his own way. She cared about Jheklan and Faulker, who had gone to the ends of the earth to free Fabeldyr and were dying because of that act off foolhardy bravery. All of them had wandered through her magic mirror. Each had told his or her story to Maralina in the mirror's polished face.

She paused in the slaughter of the sorcerers and spoke to the storm winds.

"*Éan oíche,*" she murmured.

And at once the nightbirds rose from their shelters in the trees and hurled themselves into the storm, coming to their mistress's call. For weeks now they had been gathering, waiting for that summons. Tens of thousands of crows and grackles, starlings and blackbirds, cormorants and black vultures. Other birds had come with them, too. Falcons and eagles and hawks, cassowaries and great horned owls, magpies and lammergeiers. Even seagulls and pelicans had come from the coast. They pushed through the heavy rain and fought the winds as they sought out the enemies of the Lady Maralina.

The birds flew into the forest through which the Hakkian army was rushing to reach the Field of Uthelian. The first ranks of soldiers staggered out from among the trees, their weapons lying where they had dropped, desperate hands clawing at eyes that were no longer there. The birds savaged them, ripping noses and ears, lips and eyes, and the bigger ones slashing throats.

Chernobog was crying aloud in its deep, creaking voice as it stomped on soldiers and ground them into the mud or struck mounted soldiers and sent them hurtling through the air to smash into trees or other Hakkians.

A few dozen yards away, Baphomet was busy kicking in the last of the wagons in which the Witch-king's mutated animals had been carried. The smell of their wrongness made it intensely and acutely aware of its own. That infuriated the monster goat and it smashed the wagons to splinters and then vented more of its rage on the pikemen who tried to bring it down with spears.

The creature passed directly in front of Filia and there it paused, glowering at her. Then, it bent its forelegs and bowed to her. Filia stopped dead in her tracks and stared. Some of the Hakkians even stared—first at the kneeling creature and then the muddy, blood-stained woman to whom it showed such unexpected but reverent deference. Those soldiers flung down their weapons and ran screaming. The goat straightened and vanished into the darkness of the forest, creating shrieks of pain wherever it went.

Filia saw this all around her and, despite everything, she laughed out loud. For the world was indeed mad.

"More!" roared the Witch-king and he pointed at another wizard. And another.

As each approached the statue of Hastur, they bowed to the King in Yellow and then flung themselves upon the floor in an ecstasy of sacrifice and self-destruction. The space in front of the dais was heaped with empty clothes.

Arcs of static electricity leaped from metal fittings on the abandoned garments and to the golden statue, which was now glowing as if lit from within. One of the mages tried to kiss Hastur's feet and his body was engulfed in sparks and fire. He lay there, burning until the enchantment drew off his life energy, leaving only ash.

The Witch-king staggered as his body continued to change. He was not weak, but as his muscles and bones expanded, his balance became awkward, requiring time to master this new form.

The storm outside was nearing its peak and soon the world was going to change, and he was changing to suit the world to come.

The thought of it brought him close to tears. All of his life, Gethon Heklan yearned to be someone of importance. At first, he chose the path of a Gardener, despite how the Green Religion was privately despised in Hakkia. But it was a pathway to learning. More books, more fields of research, more opportunities for knowledge were made available to the Gardeners than to anyone else in the empire. That knowledge *filled* him and *fed* him, though he was always careful to affect the appearance of a well-intentioned, well-educated buffoon. Tolerated with amusement by those who considered themselves his betters.

Gethon could bear that, because there were deep secrets hidden in the libraries of the Garden. It did not even require much guile. Diligence and patience were his greatest powers, and he used them day after day and year after year. He went to the ancient excavations in Skyria, learning the subtleties of the researcher's trade. With those tools he dug deep into Hakkia's own history. The arcane languages he learned allowed him to read texts that might otherwise have been meaningless to him. History taught him, and his own repressed culture kept him going even after quiet insults, prejudice because of his heritage, and other slights.

He had learned and grown wiser, and with each new thing he discovered, each new technique he mastered, each new experience he went through he became the man he wanted to be. He became the rightful heir to the mantle of the Witch-king.

At times it felt as if the stolen memories of Herepath Vale tried to impose themselves on his mind, as if the Gardener was attempting his own sorcery. There were moments when the Witch-king had spoken to the skull of the empress, as if she were his own lover. And moments when he felt grief for having killed the Poison Rose. But over time, Heklan had mastered himself completely, growing in power with each victory over the lingering personality of Herepath. He was many times more powerful than he had been back in the Winterwilds.

And now he would become a demigod.

He looked out over the sea of faces. Even with so many sacrifices, there were scores of magicians and sorcerers working to bring about this new age of the world. *His* world. The world of Hastur and his beloved son, Gethon Heklan.

Something caught his eye and he turned to see another shape begin to shimmer into existence. It surprised him, though, because that part of the ritual—the Rite of Remembering—had been accomplished an hour ago. Why would something new materialize now?

Then something seemed to fly out of the shimmer. A small clay jar or . . .

Canister.

In the sliver of a moment between when he realized what this was and opening his mouth to shout a warning, the canister landed on the hard marble floor.

And exploded.

CHAPTER ONE HUNDRED NINETY-FOUR

Tuke Brakson watched a nightmare unfold before his eyes. It was not *his* nightmare, but it was nonetheless terrifying.

The razor-knight, who had come so close to slaughtering all the Bloody Bastards in Vespia, was now moving like a plague through the combined forces of Unka the Spider and the late WarBride.

The enemy had nothing that could stop it. A dozen men with axes surrounded the thing, and now all of them lay dead. None whole. Riders had charged it, firing arrow after arrow, and now riderless horses wandered in confusion across the battlefield. Swordsmen by the score did their best to find chinks in its armor, looking for vulnerable flesh; but the razor-knight was not a living thing. All those swords lay shattered near the bodies of the men who wielded them.

At first Tuke's army—the remaining Bloody Bastards and several thousand rebels—had stood there dumbstruck, immobile and afraid that this was some doom come to take everyone in that place of swords and fire. But then Tuke staggered among them, kicking some, swatting others with his machete, yelling at the top of his voice.

"Fight, you whore-begotten sons of bitches! Fight, or by Dagon's balls I'll kill you myself."

And so they found their courage and remembered their steel and rushed forward, flanking the razor-knight, giving him a wide berth, as they attacked the confused mercenaries.

Tuke limped after them, clutching his broken arm to his body, unaware of the blood that leaked from his nostrils and ears, and from the corners of his mouth.

━━━━━━━━━━━━━━▶ **CHAPTER ONE HUNDRED NINETY-FIVE**

It was a flower of destruction that bloomed in the center of the great hall of Argentium.

Beautiful in its violent purity, a puff of gray and red that expanded outward faster than sight or thought. A ball of fire swelled out from it, pushed as if by a hurricane wind. The wizards closest to the blast vanished entirely, ripped to pieces so small and ragged that they did not look like they had ever been human.

Those behind them were flash-burned, impaled by flying splinters of bone, deafened, blinded, and concussed. More than a third of the candles in the room were snuffed out, and the complex arrangements of salt, sand, flower petals, precious stones, and bowls of incense were scattered, their sacred geometric connections snuffed out.

On the dais, the Witch-king threw an arm up to cover his face and burning debris lacerated it, cutting him to the bone. Blood poured from the wounds, and he was driven back and down onto his throne, sitting with such force that the blood from his wounds splashed the statue of Hastur.

Lord Nespar, Chamberlain to the King of Hakkia, was not as lucky as that. He had been standing near a brazier when the banefire exploded. The force of the blast blew the brazier into a whirling storm of ragged pieces of copper that shredded the old man, and the coals set him alight. Dying, screaming in the most terrible pain imaginable, he staggered toward the throne, begging the greatest sorcerer in the world to help him. To save him.

Instead, the Witch-king ignored him as he looked wildly across the room to see who had thrown the banefire. Nespar collapsed, his mind horrifically aware as he felt himself burn to death.

Jakob Ravensmere saw his best friend and most trusted ally die and it snapped something inside his mind. A moment ago he was rehearsing in his thoughts the way he would describe this ceremony in the history book he planned to write. The adjectives and verbs, the balance of accuracy and hyperbole that would excite the imagination. And now he saw destruction and death and ruination.

Gethon Heklan saw a group of men and one woman, all dressed in the livery of palace guards, stepping through the shimmering wall. He only recognized two of them, and shock jerked him upright from his throne.

Kagen Vale.

And worse . . . *Herepath.*

"Guards!" he shouted, his voice deep as a bull roar. He pointed. "The enemies of god! In Hastur's name, stop them. For Hastur's glory, *kill* them."

The guards, dazed and shocked by the explosion, recovered enough to remember their duty. Some had seen the effects of banefire firsthand, and they were the first to react, rushing toward the intruders.

They shouted challenges as they rushed forward, tripping over or sidestepping sorcerers who crawled around, screaming in pain, dazed, vomiting, cursing, and praying.

One of the mages climbed to his feet, read the situation, and shouted to his brethren.

"*Assassins!* Protect the Witch-king! Do you hear? Assassins . . . blasphemers!"

There were at least thirty guards and twice that many wizards, despite the number killed by the banefire. Kagen had a handful of fighters and his brother.

He did not wait to be overwhelmed.

"At them," he bellowed and hurled a second canister of banefire. It flew toward the dais, but the Witch-king was already shaking off his initial shock. He waved his hand in front of him and spoke a word of power, and the banefire veered sharply away and struck a wall. The blast tore a huge and ragged hole, sending a ton of burning debris down into the courtyard below. Wind-driven rain immediately blew into the hall, and Kagen could see the massive storm beyond. Lightning flashed and flashed.

He drew his daggers and stepped toward the dais, but a magician grabbed his right arm.

"Kill me instead," the man cried. "I give my life for my king."

"Fine by me," said Kagen, and slit his throat. The man fell back, eyes bulging but a beatific smile on his dying lips.

Kagen immediately lost sight of Herepath as he continued toward the dais. All he wanted or needed to see was the Witching-king. He heard the battle begin in earnest, though. There were two more banefire blasts and as the deafening echoes faded all he could hear was the clash of steel and the grunts of skilled fighters locked in deadly combat.

A guard tore across the room to intercept him, and Kagen saw two more coming fast. The guard swung a sword at his middle, and Kagen skittered to a stop, sucking back his stomach and using one gloved fist to punch down on the flat of the sword as it made its lateral move. The blade dipped and Kagen licked out with a dagger, nicking the man's sword arm. The guard actually started to laugh at so feeble a wound.

The laugh died as he died, the *eitr* wrapping his mind in blackness.

The other guards closed in, trying to brace him, one to each side. Now Kagen almost laughed because the Poison Rose had taught all of her sons and daughters better than that. He slid quickly to one side, closing in on the left-hand attacker, checking a sword thrust with an X-block of his daggers, then kept the pressure with one and with the other slashed the guard across the eyes. As the man screamed and reeled back, Kagen swept the foot that was about to step, and that tilted the guard into the path of a spear thrust. Then Kagen jumped in and past the remaining guard with a fast cut across his windpipe.

He landed inches from the dais as the two guards collapsed into death behind him.

The Witch-king was right there, just beyond reach.

"You have no sword this time, you piece of shit," growled Kagen, his heart lifting with the thought that all of this could be over in seconds.

The Witch-king's response was to grab the arm of his throne and throw it—all five hundred pounds of it—at Kagen as easily as if the chair were made of straw. Kagen tried to dodge, but one arm of the throne struck his hip and sent him spinning.

Redharn waded into the oncoming guards, his war axe striking a sergeant hard enough to cut the man's head and right arm from his body. As he checked his swing for another blow, Gi-Elless fired two arrows. One-two, fast as lightning, striking a soldier and a sorcerer.

The other Bloody Bastards fanned out, forcing the guards to separate and come at each of them with less overwhelming support. They were all skilled, all veterans of the Vespia campaign and the battle with the Firedrakes. The *eitr* on their weapons was diluted through use, but it was still there. Whoever was cut reeled back and if they did not die, they fell thrashing to the floor in unbearable agony.

The magicians of the court were slower to recover, even with the call to protect their holy king. A few, though, snatched ceremonial daggers from their sashes or picked up sacred crystals to throw.

It was Herepath who met their advance.

He was not a true sorcerer, though he understood much of the magical arts and knew a few dozen minor spells. His genius was in alchemy, and he drew one of the jars of powder he had taken from Heklan's alchemy table. He retreated a few steps to give himself time to mutter a few words of power over them, then as a knot of sorcerers rushed him, he hurled the jar at the floor. It exploded—though not with the flame or force of banefire—and clouds of white smoke swirled upward, the tendrils entangling the magicians. The smoke writhed like snakes, coiling around their waists and arms and throats, constricting so sharply it dropped them to the ground.

Then Herepath walked among the three and his poisoned blade dealt death even as the illusion melted away.

The wizards closest to him paused in doubt, not knowing who or what they faced. That hesitation was something the Poison Rose had taught him to exploit, and so he moved into them, cutting and killing.

Kagen slammed into a sorceress, and her body cushioned his fall at the cost of her own ribs, which splintered. They landed on the floor and Kagen rolled off of her, gasping in pain, blinking in surprise.

The throne lay nearby, and he spent a moment staring at it, trying to understand how any ordinary man could have done what Heklan just did.

Because he is no longer ordinary.

The truth burned through his practical mind, insisting that its truth be accepted.

With sinking horror, Kagen realized that they had been too slow, had made too many pauses before confronting the Witchking. He looked up to see the yellow king walking toward him without hurry or care that there were deadly fights all around him. The lightning and thunder were his processional march, and his smile was that of certain knowledge in his victory. He even looked bigger—half again as massive as he had been the last time they fought.

"No . . ." breathed Kagen.

The ascension was already too far underway.

CHAPTER ONE HUNDRED NINETY-SIX

The battle on all parts of the Field of Uthelian and the forest in front and behind it had ceased to look like any form of organized warfare. It was a massacre, an orgy of murder. There was no pattern, no orders called and received, no lines.

All there was in that moment, was the war.

All there was to be seen or felt was carnage.

Lady Maralina walked through the Hakkian lines with no shield or attempts to protect herself. She had Nightsong and she had the speed and power of both a faerie of royal blood and a vampire of the elder world. She cried aloud for the sheer joy of being free from her castle, and the longer she lingered in the mortal world the more powerful she became.

It was as she glutted herself that two dreadful thoughts occurred to her.

The first was that she could never allow herself to be seen by Kagen. He had loved the tragic, captive woman in the tower, but that version of Maralina was less than a ghost. It was her last pretense at humanity, her last glamour. Now, she was ten feet tall and her face had resumed the beautiful and terrible aspect of the *Baobhan sith*. She was not human and never would appear so again. Nor did she want to see sweet Kagen grow old and die in what, to her, would be a heartbeat.

The second thing she thought filled her with an intensely dark joy. When her mother had rejected her as unclean after Sárkány's seduction and infection and then locked her away, Maralina had been crushed with guilt and shame. She had accepted her condemnation as just by the laws of the faerie realms. But no more. Now she was greater than Sárkány ever could be and that power was melded with the power of the faeries that she had earned over sixty thousand years. Once this battle was over, she would take her army of beloved ghosts and lay siege to the hidden realm of the *Baobhan sith*. To conquer or to destroy—either outcome would bring her joy.

So she fought on with crimson joy singing in her heart.

Her ghosts, having killed the last of the living dead, moved like smoke on the storm winds to find her. These spectral champions and kings could not be hurt—they were more than dead, they were spirits. Arrows and blades passed through them and left no mark nor encountered substance. Yet when the pale warriors struck, their blades took real hardness at the moment of contact.

It was nightmarish to behold, and many ran screaming. Even some of the rebels staggered away, covering their eyes with their arms.

The two gigantic goats lay dead in the woods, finally brought down by the last of the Hakkian sorcerers, and these mages now stood around Mad Mari.

Filia saw them and then saw the lord high marshal of the Hakkian armies. She had her magicians with her, a bannerman, and five knights. Far too many for Filia to tackle alone.

So she tried anyway.

With her pack of hounds and her bloody sword, she charged.

━━━━━▶ **CHAPTER ONE HUNDRED NINETY-SEVEN**

The winter sky was full of dragons.

Uktena the Horned Terror and Yamraaj, Winged God of the Underworld flew in rhythm, and between them, dangling limply from their massive, clawed feet, was Fabeldyr. Her head lolled and her tongue lolled, and her tail swayed in the cold wind as the sister dragons bore her away.

Above them all, hovering in the air and defying impudent gravity to dare impose its will, was Scriosta. His wings beat once every now and then. He was a black mass against the purple clouds, his substance defined by the glowing orange and red lines cut deep into his skin.

The front of the glacier was mostly melted, but only for a quarter mile in either direction. Billions of tons of meltwater had washed from the destruction and some of it nearly reached the Frozen Sea before it slowed and turned back to ice.

So much more remained, though. The camps of a dozen old expeditions, the miles of corridors, the countless workrooms, artifacts of ancient cultures, and millions of frozen bodies—gray, aware, eternally hungry—left over from the cataclysm that had ended the world that was. The deep footprint of man on an otherwise pristine cap of ice over the small blue world.

Scriosta's lips curled in disgust. This was a beautiful world, and everywhere he could see the marks of man's interference, his cruel indifference, his greed for resources. That story had been there to read in the walls of ice, but had the scholars learned anything from it? Fabeldyr had said that yes, some had. But her scars told a bigger, uglier, and less forgivable story.

The dragon who, like Uktena, Yamraaj, Vorth, and the great Vathnya, had been born with the universe itself, hated the sight of that glacier and its secrets. He inhaled long and slow, his body expanding, becoming larger and larger until Scriosta filled the whole of the sky. He held it in, setting that air alight, infusing it with his hate, and then he exhaled.

The blast of fire was hotter than the surface of the sun, and it lasted a very long time.

When it was done and Scriosta sagged away, the whole of that glacier was gone. Instead it was a surge of water that fell down the face of the world. Much of it emptied into the seas, lifting every craft that sailed upon it, and flooding islands and coastlines. The rest swept down through the shadowlands and the unexplored wastes, into the infinite channels of the Cathedral Mountains, into drought-dried rivers and withered lakes, and farther down into Nelfydia, Zaare, and everywhere else. The height of the water lessened as it went, nor did the wave destroy everything in its path. Some, in later years, would swear that it flowed around certain cities and towns and villages, and who was to say they were lying?

It raced southward under a stormy sky, heading toward Argon.

The dragons flew on ahead of it, with Scriosta ranging ahead to take the lead.

CHAPTER ONE HUNDRED NINETY-EIGHT

Kagen got to his feet. His daggers lay close by and he dove for them, rolling and coming up with one in each hand.

The Witch-king paused, eyeing the blades. Perhaps wondering if the poison could harm him. Kagen knew that there was no way for the man to know that it was not the ordinary venom used by the Poison Rose but the true god-killer.

"Come kill me if you can," he taunted.

Kagen brought his blades up, taking refuge behind them. He faked left and dodged right, slashing the Witch-king across the thigh. But all he felt was the softness of cloth and no resistance of flesh and bone. A clean miss. As he recovered from his lunge, he caught a slash of yellow as the Witch-king's fist drove into him. The blow was awkward in angle but devastating in effect. Kagen was once more sent flying and this time there was no one to catch him. He hit the wall near the hole torn by banefire.

Cold rainwater struck him like a flight of tiny arrows.

Kagen dropped one knife and fumbled in his pack for his last canister of banefire. He got it out as the Witch-king rushed toward him, fist raised for another murderous blow. Kagen threw the canister at the floor between them and hurled himself sideways.

The Witch-king once more waved a hand and sent the canister flying away. He did it contemptuously, not looking or caring where it landed.

In fact the banefire flew thirty feet and struck the golden statue of the Shepherd God, and it blew the statue into a thousand shining fragments.

Only then did the Witch-king turn to see, and for a moment his face was filled with horror.

"No!" he roared and thrust a fist in the direction of the storm and jerked it back and toward the shattered statue. Lightning, torn from the sky, shot into the hall and split into many crackling fingers of burning energy, each striking a piece of gold.

Kagen took that moment to rush the Witch-king. He drove his shoulder into Heklan's stomach, catching him unaware and driving him back. But only so far. It was like hitting a sack of rocks. The Witch-king grunted and swatted at his attacker, but Kagen ducked and slashed at his legs, this time going deep enough to rip through flesh. Blood splashed through rents in the yellow robes.

And yet the Witch-king did not fall.

Instead he reached back to the throne and tore a leg from it, then raised it like a club to smash Kagen.

Herepath saw the lightning strike the pieces of Hastur's statue and static discharge buffeted him against one of the magicians. The man tried to grab him, but Herepath crouched and turned and punched his dagger into the wizard's crotch. The blade caught in the pelvis and was torn from his hand as the dying magic user collapsed.

That left Herepath with a sword. Unlike Kagen, this was his

preferred weapon and it was a good blade with decent balance. He turned and met the rush of a guard, parried, blocked, feinted, and lunged for a killing thrust.

"You never forget some things," he murmured to himself, pleased that years of scholarly life had not completely blunted his fighting skills.

He was in one of those brief oases of calm that happen in combat, when—for a moment—there was no threat immediately directed at him. He saw the Bloody Bastards fighting with savage force, though now there were only four left. Redharn and Gi-Elless, and two whose names he did not know. The rest had fallen, though none without recruiting a retinue of servants for the afterlife.

Most of the wizards were down, victims of banefire, poisoned steel, some practical alchemy of his own, or killed by flying pieces of Hastur's statue.

Then Herepath saw something that made him frown.

Those chunks of lightning-struck metal were not where they had fallen. He turned and looked around. *None* of them were anywhere to be seen.

"What in . . . ?" he began and then he saw something that tore an inarticulate cry from him.

The statue of the Shepherd God was *whole* again. There was not a crack or seam to show where the pieces had been rejoined. The golden skin shined with a polished luster. He stared at the statue, confused by more than its reassembly. Was it . . . *larger?*

He looked up and even this question melted from his mind, for the haughty face of the statue was looking at him. There was consciousness and awareness in those eyes.

And there was a pure and pernicious delight in the smile that formed on the great god's mouth.

Kagen rolled away, his speed born of terror. He came up and slashed again, once more drawing blood and once more the *eitr* failing to kill the demigod Heklan was becoming. Kagen did not know if the poison was simply spent, or if Maralina had been wrong that it *was* able to kill a god.

He ducked another swing and tried to cut the Witch-king across the face, but succeeded only in tearing aside the lace veil. It revealed the face of a man he had never seen before.

Gethon Heklan sneered at him.

"Who did you expect, *little brother?*" he mocked. "By Hastur's staff you are as feeble of mind as of body."

"If you think so little of me, you piece of shit," snarled Kagen, "then why did you try so hard to have me killed or captured?"

"Oh dear, did you think it was because I was afraid of you? Of *you?*" The Witch-king laughed. "I had Herepath's memories and that means I have his memories of your dreams of Fabeldyr. I wanted you in chains or in pieces because I did not want that knowledge shared. You, as a person, are less than nothing to me. And now, even that knowledge of the last dragon doesn't matter. We have moved on and now . . . now I have become a god."

Kagen scooped up a bowl of fuming incense and pitched it at the Witch-king's face and charged again. He drove the knife into Heklan's thigh, driving it to the hilt. Blood sprayed from the point as it tore through the back of the man's leg.

Roaring with pain, the Witch-king stepped forward, swinging another huge punch. Kagen dodged back, but miscalculated how close to the wall he was and his shoulders smacked against the torn edge. The punch struck an inch from his right ear, cracking the wall and tumbling more bricks out. Kagen fought for balance as the rushing wind tried to suck him up out of the building and into the storm.

He ducked into a crouch to catch his balance and scuttled sideways under another punch, and rose up, slashing again at the Witch-king, catching his face this time. He used his free hand to deliver as hard a punch as he had ever used. It staggered even the Hakkian giant, driving him back. Kagen did not pause but rushed forward, slashing, punching, kicking. He could feel the weirdly dense muscles rupture, the abnormally thick bones crack. He kept hitting and hitting, clinging to the belief that the process of turning Gethon Heklan into a demigod was not *yet* completed. He was still more man than god, and Kagen could not let him complete his transformation.

He lost himself in the savagery of his attack. He drove the dagger into Heklan's chest, gave it a single vicious turn and left it there, and as the sorcerer reeled, gasping with the shock of the pain, Kagen hit him over and over again. Kagen felt his own hands crack, his skin rip and tear as he hit, but he would not pause. Even as his breath burned in his lungs and his body wanted to collapse from the exertion, he kept hitting, driving the mad king backward across the hall floor. They stumbled over corpses as the battered living fled from their path. Kagen jumped and kicked the Witch-king in the stomach, landed and pivoted to hit him in the face with five brutal elbow strikes. The Hakkian's teeth shattered and his nose collapsed and he fell against the dais steps.

Even then Kagen did not stop. He grabbed a fistful of yellow robes, straddled the weeping, battered king, and kept hitting him with a brutality that rose even above what he had done to Branks in Nelfydia. Rage was not even what defined him in that moment. No, a hotter flame fueled him.

The Seedlings who had been butchered.

The empress, killed in her bed.

Thousands of Gardeners who had been brutalized and crucified.

All of the people across the face of the empire who had awakened to invasion and slaughter on the Night of the Ravens. Whole families executed. Countless women and children raped. Babies murdered in their cribs.

And his parents. His father, his brothers, Degas and Hugh,

who died defending this palace. Jheklan, dead in the frozen north. And his mother, the Poison Rose, torn to pieces by a razor-knight.

It was not fury or even hate that drove him. It was love. It was grief. And it was the horror of what other atrocities the Witch-king would commit if he was allowed to become a demigod.

He hit and hit, ruining the face of his enemy so that it looked like no one. Not Herepath, not even Gethon. It was a mask of torn meat and blood. Kagen hit and hit and screamed all the while. And then, distantly, weirdly, he became acutely aware that the entire chamber had gone silent. There was no more fighting, no shouts or cries.

He paused for a moment to see if it meant his small band had won.

Kagen saw only Redharn and Gi-Elles still standing, though neither of them were unbloodied. Around them were many dead Hakkian soldiers and sorcerers. But . . . strangely . . . a few of the guards and wizards still stood. They, and the remaining Bloody Bastards, seemed to have forgotten the weapons in their hands. They stared upward in a mute, shared, awed silence.

Herepath, who was much closer and surrounded by the last of the sorcerers, had also stopped his combat, as did those he fought. They, too, looked upward.

Not at Kagen and the dying king he held in one hand, but past them. Above them.

And so Kagen turned, too.

For on the other end of the dais—looming far above it—stood a golden giant. At least fifty feet tall and growing in size and mass with each second.

Hastur, the Shepherd God, *was alive.*

Even dying, the Witch-king laughed.

Kagen felt his heart go cold in his chest.

Faulker Vale believed he was dead and that this was some strange version of the hereafter.

He *felt* alive, but nothing that was happening to him was possible. That was obvious.

He could not be clutched in the claws of a gigantic dragon. There was nothing in his life that made that make sense.

This was the end of all things, and he knew it.

Jheklan, cold and stiff, lay against him, both of them in utter darkness.

There was a sound of wings, but they were too big, the beats too slow and heavy, to be real. Faulker fumbled for Jheklan's hand, found it, wrapped his fingers around his brother's icy ones. If this was not yet death, it was at least *dying*.

It seemed to go on and on. Time lost meaning for him. As he lay there on tightly closed scaly fingers, Faulker fished inside himself for those few prayers he still remembered. Neither of the Twins were deeply religious. They had grown up in the Harvest Faith, but had mostly left it behind.

Now his need for faith, the need for there to be someone in the heavens willing to at least listen to a prayer, was overwhelming. He leaned his forehead against Jheklan's and, weeping in grief and fear, prayed for a quick and painless end.

Then the movement changed and the sound of beating wings changed. Light appeared, blinding him despite it being filtered through heavy storm clouds. Cold rain hammered down on him as Scriosta opened his taloned paw and tumbled the two brothers— the living and the dead—onto a rooftop.

Faulker, still holding his brother's hand, looked wildly around. This was not the Winterwilds. Impossibly, the buildings he saw around him, misty with the rain, were familiar to him. They were the towers of Argentium, near Haddon Bay, and directly across from the palace.

How could it be?

How could any animal, even a dragon, have borne them the whole length of the continent, from the glacier to here so quickly? It was impossible.

It was magic.

He lay on the slates of a roof and stared.

Above the palace he saw the shapes of other dragons and they held Fabeldyr—now completely limp—between them. Another dragon perched atop another tall building—the imperial treasury—across the square.

The sight of Fabeldyr's utter slackness tore Faulker's heart. It hurt him nearly as much as Jheklan's death, and he knew with utter certainty that far more than magic was going out of the world. A kind of grace, innocent and beautiful, was dying, too. As it faded, Faulker knew the world would become substantially less. A place with none of the possibilities of the unexpected left. What a dull and dreary place it would become, he thought, even though he had long believed that magic itself was a myth. Now he understood, though that insight had come far too late.

If this is the end, he thought, squeezing Jheklan's hand, *then let it be so.*

Then he realized that the dragons were all looking at the palace. At the corner of it where the great hall was located. Part of one wall was broken already and the whole structure seemed to tremble as if it was ready to collapse.

But that was not it at all.

No, not at all.

He saw the roof of that part of the palace explode upward and for a moment he thought that maybe Kagen had set off all of the canisters of banefire at once. Yet there was no fire. Instead there was a huge cloud of brick dust and debris rising into the stormy air, and inside of that some kind of golden glow.

Faulker watched, astonished.

And then his eyes grew wider.

The gold was not a glow at all.

It was a figure.

It was a giant, rising, growing even as he watched. Fifty feet tall. A hundred. Larger and larger. Naked, muscular, with a face that was both handsome and haughty. Faulker stared at it and screamed.

CHAPTER TWO HUNDRED

Kagen staggered away from the dais, leaving the dying Witch-king there, unremembered in that moment of monumental shock.

The Shepherd God had come into being. Real. Massive beyond understanding and still growing. The entire ceiling and five floors of the palace were gone, smashed upward and away as the giant grew. Huge chunks of stone and splintered beams rained down and Kagen had to scramble to keep from being crushed. He saw Herepath there, frozen in abject shock, and Kagen looped an arm around his waist and bore him away. The wizards who had been clustered around his brother did not move fast enough, and they vanished under that crushing weight.

Kagen and Herepath stumbled and collapsed against the far wall, pulled to relative safety by Redharn and Gi-Elless. None of the other Bloody Bastards were left.

"Who has banefire?" demanded Kagen, and Gi-Elless handed over her bag, her hands shaking, her eyes staring upward. Defeat was written on her face. On all their faces.

The Witch-king lay bleeding to death, but that victory seemed pointless now that the Hakkian god had manifested.

Kagen dug a canister out and hurled it with all his strength.

"Die, you evil son of a—"

The rest of his words were wiped away as the banefire struck one golden leg. The blast was enormous. The Witch-king threw up one arm as if that could protect him, but the explosion obliterated him utterly. One moment he was there, and then there was nothing of him except blood and burning meat. His yellow robes were shredded and only his lace veil, bloody and torn, floated in the air, pushed by the bloom of heat.

Storm winds pulled the smoke outside to reveal the damage done.

The dais was destroyed. Jakob Ravensmere, who had crawled to safety into a niche nearby, was torn to rags. The wall behind where the throne had been was cracked and pock-marked.

But the golden leg was undamaged. There was not even a smear of ash on it.

There was a huge cracking sound and the marble floor beneath those titanic feet cracked and collapsed, dropping the incalculable weight down through each basement and subbasement, exposing the bowels of the palace.

Hastur laughed at this.

He was not hurt in any way, merely amused.

The living god stepped up and out of the pit, growing still as he moved out of the ruins of the palace and into the huge cobblestoned event space in front. Each of his footsteps created earth tremors. Buildings around the square shivered. Some of the older ones collapsed, spilling their guts out onto the parade grounds.

Kagen and the others stood on a narrow shelf of what had been the floor of the great hall. Everything else was gone, taking with it the last of the guards, the sorcerers, and the blood-spattered dais. Below them was a smoking pit, and above them was the sky. Rain fell on them and they blinked it away as they watched the golden giant stand exultant.

Then Herepath raised one arm and pointed.

"Kagen . . . look . . ."

There were shapes out in the rain. Gigantic ones. Alien ones.

Dragons.

Two of them held a body that Kagen recognized with heartbreak was Fabeldyr, though how she was here when he had seen her thousands of miles away in the Winterwilds less than an hour ago made no sense. And what did that mean for Faulker and the others?

Grief kept wanting to stab him.

Faulker, too? Another brother lost even as one lost sibling had been found? It was so cruel, so unfair.

And yet, what did it matter? The world was ending.

Hastur turned to look at the dragons. The two holding Fabeldyr, another squatting on a nearby roof. And a fourth that flew out of the storm and landed on a pile of rubble that had been a grain warehouse. Five dragons. Four alive.

And he did not care.

The dragons were immobile except for the slow wingbeats of those holding Fabeldyr. None approached the awakened and manifested Shepherd God.

He threw back his head and shouted his own name. The sound of it shattered every window in Argentium. It cracked walls and collapsed houses for miles around, and even made moored ships thrash against their pilings.

"*I am God,*" he bellowed in a voice louder than thunder. "*Look upon me and know despair. For I am come to burn this world and rebuild it from the ashes.*"

Lightning burst in the sky and struck him over and over again, heating his golden skin, infusing him with its power.

And yet the four dragons merely watched.

Hastur took another step, and as he did so, he shed the aspect of humanity that he had worn through the centuries to appease his followers. Kagen could see that it was a glamour no different than when Gethon Heklan had worn Herepath's face.

Instead, even as he grew larger and more massive, he revealed the truth of what he was. Not a god of shepherds, not the patron of Hakkia, but one of the Great Old Ones, half brother to Cthulhu. A monster from beyond the stars. His body twisted into something more apelike than human, but with a massive bulbous head with gigantic lidless eyes and tentacles writhing on his scalp and all around his mouth. Huge wings burst from his back and he rose into the air, now a thousand feet tall and still growing.

He hung there, silhouetted by the lightning, roaring out in the language of his kind, repeating his claim of godhood for all of humanity and the gathered dragons to hear.

"Y' ah r'luhhor!"

I am God.

Kagen stood on the edge of the abyss and stared.

Herepath sank to his knees in despair.

There were screams rising from the people of Argentium as this monster reigned over all.

The lightning flashed and flashed.

And Kagen saw something in the clouds.

A shadow.

It, too, had outstretched wings, but those wings were a thousand times more vast than those of Hastur. Was it a shadow? Was it some trick of the lightning? Or, worse, was it another of Hastur's kind come to help him conquer the earth?

Kagen reached down and gripped Herepath's shoulder.

"Brother," he said in a wretched whisper, "are we doomed?"

Herepath raised his face to the storm and the winds. His eyes were filled with so much pain, and as he sobbed the rain stole his tears.

Then Herepath gasped as he saw what Kagen saw.

He got to his feet.

"God of fire and tears," he breathed.

It took Kagen a moment to realize this was not an oath, nor even a prayer. Herepath was naming the thing that loomed above and behind Hastur. The God of Fire and Tears.

Vathnya.

Firstborn of the universe.

Hastur sensed his peril and turned, seeing the god of all dragons. The largest and most powerful being who ever lived. Filling the sky, wings stretched miles wide. Eyes burning with rage. The great dragon reached for the monster with his titanic claws.

"I am God!" roared Hastur in defiance.

And Vathnya seized the golden giant and tore him to pieces.

It happened all at once. There was no fight. The claws crushed Hastur and ripped him apart, then flung the fragments into the storm. Lightning sought them out, but Vathnya blasted the dismembered parts with a fire so intense, so hot, so powerful that it broke the storm apart.

Not a piece, not even a flake of ash was left.

The clouds were ripped apart to reveal the wise eyes of the stars in their infinite numbers watching the drama below with unblinking patience.

Kagen and Herepath stood there. Watching.

Seeing something that was so far beyond anything they had ever imagined. For Kagen, this god of dragons was a thousand times more vast and infinitely more powerful than had been the Harvest Gods he had seen in a field near this very palace so many months ago. They had turned their backs on him and there had been a moment—merely a blink of time's eye—when the forms of Mother Sah and Father Ar had changed, had momentarily appeared not as beautiful gods but as monsters so alien and so unnatural that his mind refused to accept them.

What could that mean? Were the Harvest Gods no different than

Hastur? Were they, too, Great Old Ones who pretended humanity in form and benign love in aspect? If so, what then of his damnation?

These thoughts burned in him as he saw Vathnya against the starlight.

Then another light caught his eye and he turned, along with Herepath, Redharn, Gi-Elless and every other living person in the ruined city. In the air above the square were the two dragons who held Fabeldyr.

And Fabeldyr was burning.

That's what it looked like. Her body seemed to be on fire from within, and fiery light burst from between her scales and open mouth. Not actual fire, but light that blazed with that intensity. The glow grew brighter and brighter until it was nearly impossible to look at it.

On the roof of the building across from the palace, Faulker clutched Jheklan's hand and waited for the end. For death. He had feared it before but now he understood that all that had happened since Scriosta had attacked the glacier was leading to this moment.

This very moment.

He held on and closed his eyes.

Uktena and Yamraaj held their kin in the air, and they each wept tears of real fire.

Vorth rose up from his perch on a nearby building and raised his head to send up a howl of grief. The others joined him, including mighty Scriosta.

The sound of it was the saddest, truest thing Kagen had ever heard. It was grief but it was celebration, too. He did not understand it in its fullest meaning, but he *knew* it. The scar on his chest throbbed with pain, but even that was not an attack. It was the magic within him sharing the grief.

Kagen sank to his knees and leaned back onto his heels and he, too, howled in grief for the dragon he had met in dreams. Beautiful Fabeldyr. Gone now and forever.

And then Vathnya added his voice to the great hymn of loss and death and pure magic.

The fire inside Fabeldyr grew brighter and brighter and then with a burst like an exploding star, she exploded. Not in blood or horror. Not like the Witch-king or his golden god. Her immolation was a burst of golden light that swept outward from her in all directions.

Near the Field of Uthelian, Lady Maralina stopped and looked up. The battle was long over and she was taking her leave of mankind's war. Her ghosts were around her and they, too, stopped and beheld the sweep of golden light that blew across the sky.

Maralina removed her battle headdress and let it fall. She bowed her head and said a prayer for Fabeldyr. And she blessed the dragon for the gift she was giving to the world that had used her so cruelly. Each atom of the dragon's body was a seed of magic sown onto the winds. Where they would fall and what would grow was unknown, even to Maralina.

She held her arms high and sang a hymn to the dragon that was as heavy with grief as it was alive with joy.

Tuke and Filia sat together with their backs to a tree. Battered, bloody, but alive.

They saw the sky light up with that pure light and for the first time in many months, they were not afraid. She took his uninjured hand and pressed it to her lips. They wept, though they did not know why. The tears, when they ran down to their lips, did not taste of sadness.

In a dense part of the forest, the razor-knight looked up and saw the light of Fabeldyr's passing. It reached its arms up and the light bathed it in brilliance. When that glow had gone, so too had the razor-knight.

In a large bed in a manor house far away, Lady Helleda Frost sat holding the hand of Mother Frey. The hand felt so small and delicate and fragile.

The curtains were open and the stars had appeared after the dreadful storm. The light found them and washed through the room as it passed.

When it was gone, Helleda looked at Frey. She saw the smile. And she saw that her breast no longer rose and fell.

Peace had found the old nun.

On the building by the square, Faulker waited for death.

He held Jheklan's hand.

And he did not die.

When he dared to open his eyes and look up, the palace was in ruins, but the dragons—all of them—were gone.

Then Jheklan's fingers, no longer cold, squeezed his.

He gasped and looked down at his brother's face. It was no longer blue but had a flush of color. A bloom of life.

Jheklan's eyelids fluttered, then blinked, and finally opened. At first he looked far away, but then he smiled. Slow, small, but a smile.

"What . . . happened?" he whispered. "What did I miss . . . ?"

-1-

It took months for the floodwaters to recede, but by then it was spring.

The whole of the west had been affected. Not all of it drowned, but every part of it changed. Mapmakers were already at work updating the known world.

As the meltwaters receded or washed out to the sea, the landscape came alive with new life. The flowers that bloomed that year were of extraordinary beauty and fragrance, and sometimes they sparkled strangely on the night of the full moon. Trees that had endured the floods grew hearty and lush with new leaves.

The birds returned, and with them the bees and butterflies and all of the creatures of the natural world. The crops sown that spring yielded fruits and vegetables in such abundance that hunger was forgotten.

It was said in taverns and over dinner tables that there was a spirit in the woods. A woman dressed in black who sang strange songs and was often seen speaking with trees and birds and the animals of the woods. They called her the Widow, but there was no one alive who knew her real name.

The earth healed itself. Storms and winds cut new river channels and the last of the meltwater filled lakes. It would take years for all of the flood damage to repair itself, but not as many years as anyone thought.

They buried Mother Frey on the first day of spring.

Lady Helleda Frost gave the eulogy, Alibaxter read the prayers, and Hop Garkain sang hymns in a surprisingly beautiful baritone. Hannibus Greel was there, as were all of the surviving members of the cabal. Tuke and Filia were there, too, though they were quiet and spent much of their time apart, just watching.

Just past midnight, when all of the guests were long gone and the lights in the big manor house had dwindled to only one, a lone figure came to the grave, leading his horse.

He knelt beside the grave and placed a bundle of roses on the mound, then placed his bare palm against the headstone for a very long time.

"You were a crazy, brilliant, infuriating, incredible woman," said Kagen. "I wish you could see the world you helped save."

There were dark shapes in the trees. Nightbirds, and that old familiar grandfather crow.

"Look after her," said Kagen, and the crow gave a soft caw.

As he left, Kagen turned and looked up at Lady Frost's house. There was that single light lit, and he could see a slender silhouette. He had never met her, though Tuke and Filia had spoken with kindness and respect of her. Kagen wondered how well she had recovered from the nearly fatal attack by the vampire.

He nodded toward the house, climbed onto Jinx's back and rode away.

In the house, Helleda Frost turned out the light and watched Kagen all the way down the road. She saw him clearly and watched him farther than was humanly possible.

-3-

He shed his name like the snake crawling out of its own husk.

The Prince of Games had been a useful nickname, but it was no more his true name than Elegga, Juha, Nicodemus, Anansi, Coyote, Renart the Fox, Flagg, Kappa, Mbeku, Merlin, Yaw, Păcală, Cin-an-ev, Baron Samedi, Talihsin, Nanabozho, or ten thousand others.

He left Hakkia and then left the west itself, crossing the Cathedral Mountains on a stolen horse. Heading east to see what the great flood had done to those lands. He did not feel defeated because it was not really ever his war. Just a bit of fun and games. And some delicious chaos.

With a song in his heart, he rode into the sunrise.

-4-

Kagen, Tuke and Filia stood at the foot of a dais constructed of new cut pine. It still smelled of paint. All three of them were recovered from their wounds—at least those of the body. The scars left by all they had seen needed more time. Perhaps much more.

That was a problem for another day.

Upon the dais was a pair of simple chairs, without extravagance or ornamentation. Merely seats, each with a cushion for a little extra elevation. Two figures sat upon the chairs, dressed in white gowns edged in green and embroidered with leaves and flowers.

Crowns sat upon their heads. Small ones that would be replaced with larger ones over time. Simple ones, too, for they also lacked needless ostentation. Bands of silver wrapped in ivy and set with a flat disk on which was a symbol of two daggers crossed in front of a sword that stood vertically. At the intersection of the three blades was a rose, and coiled around that . . . a dragon. It had been fashioned to look like Fabeldyr.

Even though every monarch of the former Silver Empire was present, the crowns were not imperial. That had been agreed upon from the start. They were for the twin rulers of the Kingdom of Argon.

Alleyn and Desalyn were both wide-eyed and flushed scarlet with embarrassment. That was fine. Everyone thought it was charming.

Beside the throne stood the Steward of Argon. A tall man with an ascetic face and eyes that were older and sadder than his countenance. He wore the robes of a High Gardener. Looking out over the assembled thousands who were gathered in the Field of Uthelian, the steward called out in a strong, clear voice.

"Their Majesties invite Captain-General Kagen Vale into their presence."

Under his breath, Tuke said, "By the deeply amused balls of the god of absurdity, I think they're going to give you a medal."

"Why not? They seem to have a lot of them. You two got yours."

Filia touched hers, which was a copy of the crest on the crowns of the new king and queen. "You know I'll pawn this first chance I get."

"Of course," said Kagen and he gave her a smile.

He walked up the aisle and stopped at the foot of the throne.

The twins smiled at him. Alleyn made as if to jump up and hug him, but the steward touched his shoulder lightly and gave a small shake of his head.

"Captain-General Kagen," said Desalyn with grand formality, "we—"

"Pardon me, Your Majesty," said Kagen. "As I have been telling everyone for months now, I'm not a general. And I'm pretty sure I'm not even a captain anymore. It's just Kagen, if you please."

Desalyn looked flustered and glanced questioningly at the steward. He smiled faintly and nodded.

"*Kagen*," said the queen, "I want—"

"We," corrected the steward quietly.

"—*we* want to thank you for everything you have done for our family, our nation, and . . . well . . . for us."

"Yes," said Alleyn loudly. "We love you."

The audience laughed at this and Kagen felt his cheeks grow hot. He turned to see what kind of expressions Tuke and Filia wore and glared bloody murder at them, but their faces were conspicuously blank.

"I did what anyone would have done," said Kagen. "I did what anyone who loves you both would have done."

At this Alleyn and Desalyn both burst into tears, got up, ran down the steps, and hugged him with such force they nearly knocked him down. The steward made a single lunge to stop them, missed, and gave it up as a bad job. He stood on the dais, hands folded behind his back and met Kagen's shocked and awkward stare. Kagen saw him and they nodded to one another. Kagen to Herepath.

Brother to brother.

There was more. There were speeches and music, more speeches and the awarding of medals, more speeches and gifts given by the other monarchs, and gifts given as tokens to them. Eventually Kagen wormed his way out of the press and walked over to a pavilion where two men sat in the shade.

"And how are the Sons of the Dragon doing?" he asked.

Faulker gave him a sour look. "I kind of hate that nickname."

"You earned it," said Kagen and he repeated it loudly. Then he turned and waved to passersby. "Hey, I'm here with the Sons of the Dragon, heroes of the Witch-king War."

The passersby shouted praise.

"I really hate you," said Faulker. "And I hate that damn name."

"Oh, I rather like it," said Jheklan.

Faulker wheeled on him. "You are an undead ghoul who does not deserve an opinion."

"I'm not undead. I'm completely alive."

"Stupid ass going off and getting yourself killed. I tell you here and now, brother, if you ever die again, I'm going to let you stay dead."

"It wasn't you who brought me back to life," countered Jheklan.

"How do you know what I did or didn't do? You were fucking dead."

There was more of that argument, but Kagen wandered off.

He walked to the very edge of the field and stood looking at the massive earthworks that had begun on the new palace of Argon. It would take years to build. And one of the planned areas was a stone pyramid that would be built above the mass grave where thirty-seven thousand soldiers were buried. Kagen sighed, appalled by all that death. He bowed to the mound and turned away.

"Going somewhere?"

Kagen turned at the sound of a familiar voice and saw Filia standing a few yards away. Tuke and Horse stood on either side of her.

"Somewhere," agreed Kagen.

"And where would that be, exactly?" asked Tuke.

Kagen shrugged. "East, I suppose."

"Why there?" asked Filia.

"Why not?" replied Kagen. He paused. "So . . . where will you two go now that you've officially retired from the army as decorated heroes?"

Filia smiled. "East, I suppose."

Kagen grunted. "Why?"

"Why not?" said Tuke.

They all smiled.

When night fell and the huge celebration began, there was no sign of any of them.

THE VALE FAMILY

Lord Khendrick Vale, Kagen's father; nobleman, statesman, and advisor to the empress. Murdered during the Night of the Ravens.

Lady Marissa Trewellyn-Vale, Kagen's mother; the Poison Rose, Blade Mistress of the Silver Empire. Slain by a demonic razor-knight while defending the empress.

Lady Bellapher, the Silver Thorn. Ancestor of Lady Marissa and general of the Imperial Army during the war against Hakkia centuries ago.

Lord Degas Vale, firstborn son of Lord Khendrick and Lady Marissa.

Belissa Vale, second-born child and eldest daughter of Lord Khendrick and Lady Marissa. A widowed alchemist not seen since before the invasion.

Herepath Vale, second-born son of Lord Khendrick and Lady Marissa. Gardener, scholar, and mystic.

Zora Vale, fourth-born child and youngest daughter of Lord Khendrick and Lady Marissa. Married to a poet and living in Tull Mithrain.

Jheklan Vale, one of the Vale "twins," though a year older than the other twin. Captain of the North Riders; adventurer, prankster, and rake.

Faulker Vale, the other Vale "twin." Lieutenant of the East Riders; unrepentant scoundrel, inseparable from Jheklan.

Hugh Vale, famously powerful fighter who died defending the empress.

Kagen Vale, disgraced former captain of the imperial guard, Warden of the Sacred Garden, bond-sworn and oath-bound protector of the Seedlings.

Hendross Vale, red-haired giant, affable and a bit wild, missing and presumed dead.

THE IMPERIAL FAMILY OF THE SILVER EMPIRE
Empress Gessalyn, 53rd and last empress of the Silver Empire.

The Seedlings, imperial children of Gessalyn; all but two murdered on the Night of the Ravens.

Desalyn/Foscor, one of the imperial twins, now under the spell of the Witch-king.

Alleyn/Gavran, Desalyn's twin, also under the Witch-king's spell.

THE HAKKIANS
Gethon Heklan, the Witch-king, chief priest of Hastur and king of Hakkia.

Lord Nespar, chamberlain and advisor to the Witch-king.

Lady Kestral, court necromancer and advisor to the Witch-king.

Lord Jakob Ravensmere, royal historian to the Witch-king.

Madame Lucibel, governess of the imperial twins in Hakkia.

Mad Mari Heklan, lord high marshal of the Hakkian army.

Cat, a Therian adventurer and caravan scout; lieutenant to Jheklan and Faulker.

Alibaxter, former Gardener and ceremonial magician.

Il-Vul, Samudian master archer.

Jace, an Argonian caravan guard.

Lehrman, an Unbladed from Zehria.

THE BLOODY BASTARDS

Tuke Brakson, a Therian adventurer and one of Kagen's closest friends.

Filia alden-Bok, adventurer, Kagen's trusted friend and former lover.

Redharn, a professional fighter; lieutenant of the Bloody Bastards.

Gi-Elless, Samudian archer; lieutenant of the Bloody Bastards.

Biter, a member of the Crocodile Clan from Weskia.

Borz, a caravan scout from Ghul.

Giffer, a former Gardener from Zaare.

Hoth, moody Ghenreyan poet and duelist.

Pergun, a Zehrian spear-fighter.

Urri, a former privateer from Nehemite.

THE LOVERS

The Widow (Ryssa), orphan girl from Argentium in Argon; lover of Miri, initiate into the Faith of the Dreaming God, Cthulhu.

Miri, former investigator of the Office of Miracles; priestess of Cthulhu, lover of Ryssa.

THE CABAL

Mother Frey, former chief investigator for the Office of Miracles.

Lady Helleda Frost, Argonian noblewoman and financial backer of the rebellion.

Hannibus Greel, Therian merchant, serving as diplomat for the cabal.

THE LARGER WORLD

Maralina, daughter of the Queen of the *Baobhan sith,* the faerie folk; Kagen's lover, trapped forever in the Tower of Sarsis.

Fabeldyr, the last of the dragons who brought magic to earth; chained and imprisoned in a glacier in the Winterwilds.

The Hollow Monks, a cult of demonic sorcerers.

The Prince of Games, an immortal chaos trickster.

Duke Sárkány, immortal vampire; former lover of Maralina.

Titania à-Mab, queen of the *Baobhan sith.*

Lord Oberon Erlking, king of the *Baobhan sith.*

THE ROYAL HOUSES OF THE SILVER EMPIRE

Argon, no living monarch after the murder of Empress Gessalyn.

Behlia, Queen Weska.

Ghenrey, Crown Prince Ifduril.

Hakkia, the Witch-king.

Nehemite, Queen Lliaorna.

Nelfydia, King Horogillin.

Samud, King Hariq al-Huk.

Sunderland, King Thespo, formerly known as the Pirate Prince.

Theria, Queen Theka.

Vahlycor, Queen Egnes.

The Waste, aka Tarania, various princes, princesses, and governor-general.

Zaare, Prince Regent Mondas Huvan.

Zehria, Vulpion the Gray.

GODS AND THEIR PANTHEONS

The Harvest Gods, patrons of the Silver Empire; also called the Green Faith.

- *Father Ar,* god of sowing and agriculture.

- *Mother Sah,* goddess of reaping and the cycle of life.

- *Geth,* the prince of pestilence and famine.

- *Lady Siya,* goddess of learning, scholarship, and skepticism.

Gods of Ancient and Modern Hakkia

- *Hastur the Unspeakable,* the Shepherd God, the Yellow God, one of the Great Old Ones; half brother of Cthulhu, patron of Hakkia during the reign of the Witch-kings.

The Sea Gods/The Deep Ones, patron gods of Theria and the northern Islands.

- *Father Dagon,* chief of the Deep Ones.

- *Mother Hydra,* queen of the Deep Ones.

- *Cthulhu,* the Dreaming God, patron of the people of Tull Yammoth; one of the Great Old Ones; half brother and enemy of Hastur.

THE ELDEST AND HIS FAMILY

Vathnya, the God of Fire and Tears.

Uktena, the Horned Terror.

Yamraaj, Winged God of the Underworld.

Vorth, the Worm of Nightmares.

Scriosta, the Destroyer.

ACKNOWLEDGMENTS

Many thanks to those people who have contributed information and advice along the way. Thanks to my literary agent, Sara Crowe; my stalwart editor at St. Martin's Griffin, Michael Homler; Robert Allen and the crew at Macmillan Audio; my film agent, Dana Spector of Creative Artists Agency; my audiobook reader, Ray Porter; Cat Scully, my friend and mapmaker; and many thanks to my talented and infinitely patient assistant, Dana Fredsti. Special thanks to the winners of the dragon-naming contest: SamSarah Landis, Faith Howe, Christina Seeling, and Melvinder Singh. Thanks to David Fitzgerald, Debbie Nic Cumhaill, and Diarmaid Mac Amhlaoibh for Gaelic translations.

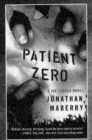

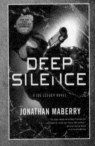

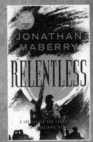

ABOUT THE AUTHOR

© Sara Jo West

Jonathan Maberry is a *New York Times* bestselling, Inkpot Award–winning, and five-time Bram Stoker Award–winning author of *Relentless, Ink, Patient Zero, Rot & Ruin, Dead of Night,* the Pine Deep Trilogy, *The Wolfman, Zombie CSU,* and *They Bite,* among others. His V-Wars series has been adapted by Netflix, and his work for Marvel Comics includes *The Punisher, Wolverine, Doomwar, Marvel Zombies Return,* and *Black Panther.* He is the editor of *Weird Tales* magazine and also edits numerous anthologies.